PENGU

Seven Years to Sin

Sylvia Day is the *Sunday Times* bestselling author of over a dozen novels written across multiple sub-genres – contemporary, fantasy, historical, futuristic, science fiction, romantic suspense, paranormal romance and urban fantasy – under multiple pen names: *three!* A wife and mother of two, she is a former Russian linguist for the US Army Military Intelligence.

She's now hard at work on *Entwined with You*, the next instalment in the Crossfire series, following on from *Bared to You* and *Reflected in You*.

Find out more about Sylvia at www.sylviaday.com.

Praise for Sylvia Day

'Several shades sexier and a hundred degrees hotter' *Woman*

'Full of emotional.angst, scorching love scenes, and a compelling storyline' *Dear Author*

'Several shades darker and a hundred degrees hotter than anything you've read before' *Reveal*

Seven Years to Sin

SYLVIA DAY

PENGUIN BOOKS

PENGUIN BOOKS

Published by the Penguin Group
Penguin Books Ltd, 80 Strand, London WC2R ORL, England
Penguin Group (USA) Inc., 375 Hudson Street, New York, New York 10014, USA
Penguin Group (Canada), 90 Eglinton Avenue East, Suite 700, Toronto, Ontario, Canada M4P 2Y3
(a division of Pearson Penguin Canada Inc.)
Penguin Ireland, 25 St Stephen's Green, Dublin 2, Ireland (a division of Penguin Books Ltd)
Penguin Group (Australia), 707 Collins Street, Melbourne, Victoria 3008, Australia
(a division of Pearson Australia Group Pty Ltd)
Penguin Books India Pvt Ltd, 11 Community Centre, Panchsheel Park, New Delhi – 110 017, India
Penguin Group (NZ), 67 Apollo Drive, Rosedale, Auckland 0632, New Zealand
(a division of Pearson New Zealand Ltd)
Penguin Books (South Africa) (Pty) Ltd, Block D, Rosebank Office Park,
181 Jan Smuts Avenue, Parktown North, Gauteng 2193, South Africa

Penguin Books Ltd, Registered Offices: 80 Strand, London WC2R ORL, England

www.penguin.com

First published in the United States of America by Brava Books,
an imprint of Kensington Publishing Corp 2011
First published in Great Britain by Penguin Books 2012

001

Set in Sabon
Printed in Great Britain by Clays Ltd, St Ives plc

ISBN: 978-1-405-91239-6

www.greenpenguin.co.uk

MIX
Paper from
responsible sources
FSC™ C018179

Penguin Books is committed to a sustainable
future for our business, our readers and our planet.
This book is made from Forest Stewardship
Council™ certified paper.

ALWAYS LEARNING   **PEARSON**

For all the readers who love *The Stranger I Married*—
I wrote this one for you.

Prologue

There was something irresistibly exciting about watching athletic males engaged in physical combat. Their base, animalistic natures were betrayed by their unmitigated aggression and ruthlessness. Through their exertions, their bodies displayed a power that stirred a woman's most primitive instincts.

Lady Jessica Sheffield was not immune, as she'd been taught a lady should be.

She could not take her eyes off the two young men wrestling exuberantly on the lawn on the opposite side of a narrow, shallow pond. One would soon be her brother-in-law; the other was his friend, a scapegrace whose wickedly handsome countenance spared him much of the censure he should rightly face.

"I would like to tumble about as they do," her sister said wistfully. Hester, too, watched from where they sat beneath the shade of an ancient oak tree. A gentle breeze swept by them, ruffling the blades of grass flowing along the parkland to the impressive Pennington manse. The home sprawled beneath the protective shield of a wooded hill, its golden stone façade and gilded window frames catching the sunlight and creating a feeling of serenity for all who visited.

Jess returned her attention to her needlework, regretting that she had to chastise her sister for staring when she was guilty of the same conduct. "Such play is lost to women after childhood. Best not to covet what is beyond our grasp."

"Why can men be boys all of their lives, but we women must grow old while we are yet young?"

"The world was made for men," Jess said softly.

Beneath the wide brim of her straw hat, she snuck another glance at the two grappling young gentlemen. A barked command stilled them midscuffle and caused her spine to stiffen. Simultaneously, all their heads turned in the same direction. She found her betrothed approaching the two younger men, and the tension left her in a slow abatement, like the receding of a tide after a crashing wave. Not for the first time, she wondered if she would ever lose the sharp apprehension she felt whenever discord was evident or if she was so well trained to fear a man's anger that she would never be free of it.

Tall and elegantly dressed, Benedict Reginald Sinclair, Viscount Tarley and future Earl of Pennington, strode across the lawn with the purpose of a man who knew well the power he wielded. She was both reassured by that inherent blue-blooded arrogance and wary of it. Some men were content with the knowledge of their own importance, while others felt the need to wield it indiscriminately.

"And what is a woman's contribution to the world?" Hester asked with an obstinate pout that made her look younger than her ten and six years. With an impatient swipe at her cheek, she brushed back a honey-hued curl the exact shade of Jessica's hair. "To serve men?"

"To create them." Jess returned Tarley's brisk wave. They would be wed in the Sinclair family chapel tomorrow before a carefully selected and elite gathering of Society. She looked forward to the occasion for a variety of reasons, not the least of which being that she would finally be free of her father's unpredictable and seemingly unprovoked rages. She did not begrudge the Marquess of Hadley his right to stress the value of social esteem and her part in securing it. It was the harsh manner in which he redressed her shortcomings that she deplored.

Hester made a sound suspiciously like a snort. "Those are our pater's words."

"And the dominant view of the world at large. Who would know that better than you and I?" Their mother's ceaseless efforts to bear the Hadley heir had cost her life. Hadley had been forced to suffer through another wife, another daughter, and five years before finally seeing the birth of his precious son.

"I do not believe Tarley looks upon you as a breed mare," Hester said. "In fact, I think he has a *tendre* for you."

"I would be fortunate if that were so. However, he would not have offered for me had I lacked a suitable bloodline." Jess watched as Benedict chastised his younger sibling for his rough play. Michael Sinclair looked sufficiently contrite, but Alistair Caulfield looked anything but. His posture, while not overtly defiant, was too proud to be remorseful. The three males made a riveting grouping—the Sinclairs with their rich chocolate-hued tresses and powerfully lean frames, and Caulfield, who was said to be favored by Mephistopheles himself with his ink-dark hair and devilishly attractive features.

"Tell me you will be happy with him," Hester entreated, leaning forward. Her irises were the same brilliant green as the lawn beneath their feet, and they were filled with concern. Her eye color was a trait inherited from their mother along with their pale tresses. Jess had taken their father's gray eyes. It was the only part of himself he'd ever given her. That was not a lamentable circumstance in her opinion.

"I intend to be." There was no way to ensure that, but what point was there in worrying Hester needlessly? Tarley was their father's choice, and Jess would have to become accustomed to it, whatever the outcome.

Hester pressed on. "I want neither of us to leave this world with the pitiful relief our mother did. Life is meant to be savored and enjoyed."

Jess twisted on the marble half-moon bench upon which she sat and placed her needlepoint carefully in the bag beside her. She prayed Hester would always retain her sweet, hopeful nature. "Tarley and I respect one another. I have always enjoyed his company and discourse. He is intelligent and patient, considerate and polite. And he is an extremely fine specimen of a man. One cannot overlook that."

Hester's smile brightened their shady location better than the sun could have. "Yes, he is. I can only pray that Father will make an equally handsome choice for me."

"Have you set your cap for a particular gentleman?"

"Not entirely, no. I am still in search of the perfect combination of traits that will suit me best." Hester looked at the three men, now talking with some seriousness. "I should like a husband of Tarley's station, but with Mr. Sinclair's more jovial personality and Mr. Caulfield's appearance. Although I do believe Alistair Caulfield is likely the handsomest man in all of England—if not farther reaches—so I will have to settle for less in that regard."

"He is too young for me to assess in that manner," Jess lied, eying the object of discussion.

"Stuff. He is mature for his age; everyone says so."

"He is jaded from lack of guidance. There is a difference." Though Jess was plagued by too much restriction, Caulfield suffered from none at all. With his three older brothers taking up the expected roles of heir, military officer, and clergyman, there had been no role for him to fill. An overly doting mother had only worsened his prospects of learning any responsibility. He was infamous for his risk taking and inability to walk away from any bet or challenge.

In the handful of years Jess had known him, he'd grown wilder with every passing season.

"Two years' gap is no gap at all," Hester argued.

"Not when comparing a score and ten to thirty-two, perhaps. But comparing ten and six to ten and eight? That is an age."

Jess caught sight of Benedict's mother hurrying toward her, a sure sign that her brief respite from the whirlwind of final-hour preparations was over. She stood. "In any case, your admiration is best directed elsewhere. Mr. Caulfield has little chance of serving a useful purpose in this life. His lamentable position as the superfluous fourth son practically ensures he will achieve little consequence. It is a shame he has chosen to cast off the benefit of his good name in favor of reckless pursuits, but that is his mistake and it should not be yours."

"I have heard it said that his father has given him a ship and a sugarcane plantation."

"It is highly likely Masterson did so in the hopes his son would take his dangerous proclivities to a distant shore."

Hester sighed. "I sometimes wish I could travel far, far away. Am I alone in such longings?"

Not at all, Jess wished to say. She thought of escape in passing, but her station was so narrowly defined. In that regard, she was at a greater disadvantage than women of common birth. Who was she if not the Marquess of Hadley's daughter and the future Viscountess Tarley? If neither of them wished to travel extensively, she would never be given the opportunity. But sharing such ruminations with her impressionable sibling would be inappropriate and unfair. "God willing," she said instead, "you will have a spouse eager to indulge you in all things. You deserve it."

Jess untied the leash of her beloved pug, Temperance, and gestured to her abigail to collect her bag. As she moved to pass her sister, she paused and bent to press a kiss to Hester's forehead. "Cast your eye upon Lord Regmont at supper this evening. He is comely, most charming, and recently returned from his Grand Tour. You will be one of the first diamonds he meets since his return."

"He would have to wait two years for my presentation," Hester retorted with more than a little disgruntlement.

"You are worth the wait. Any man of discerning taste will see that straightaway."

"As if I shall have a choice in the matter, even if he was to find me intriguing."

Winking, Jess lowered her voice and said, "Regmont is a close associate of Tarley's. I am certain Benedict would speak highly of him to our pater should that become necessary."

"Truly?" Hester's shoulders wriggled with the fevered anticipation of youth. "You must introduce us."

"For a certainty." Jess set off with a wave. "Cast your eyes away from ne'er-do-wells until then."

Hester made a show of covering her eyes, but Jess expected her sister would return to her perusal of the men as soon as the opportunity presented itself.

Jess certainly would.

"Tarley's tension is high," Michael Sinclair noted, dusting himself off and staring at his brother's retreating back.

"You expected otherwise?" Alistair Caulfield collected his jacket from the ground and shook off the few blades of grass clinging to the superfine. "He gains a leg shackle tomorrow."

"To the Diamond of the Season. Not such a bad fate. My mother says Helen of Troy could not have been more beautiful."

"Or a marble statue more cold."

Michael looked at him. "Beg your pardon?"

From across the shallow terrace pool separating them,

Alistair watched Lady Jessica Sheffield cross the lawn toward the house with her little dog in tow. Her slender figure was encased from neck to wrist to ankle in pale floral muslin that clung to her with the breeze. Her face was turned away from him and shielded from the sun by a hat, but he knew her features from memory. He was irresistibly drawn to stare at such beauty. Many men were.

Her hair was a delight of nature, the strands longer and thicker than any other blonde he had ever seen. The tresses were so pale as to be almost silver, with streaks of darker gold adding richness to the whole. She'd worn it down on occasion before her presentation, but now it was as restrained as her deportment. For someone so young, she had the cool demeanor and reserve of a more mature woman.

"That pale hair and creamy skin," Alistair murmured, "and those gray eyes . . ."

"Yes?"

Alistair noted the amusement in his friend's voice and strengthened his own. "Her coloring suits her temperament perfectly," he said briskly. "She is an ice princess, that one. Your brother had best pray she breeds quickly or risk losing his cock to frostbite."

"And you had best watch your tongue," Michael warned, repairing his dark brown hair with a quick combing with both hands, "lest I take offense. Lady Jessica is soon to be my sister-in-law."

Nodding absently, Alistair found his attention once again drawn to the graceful girl who was so perfect in both physical and social deportment. He was fascinated with watching her and waiting for some crack in the porcelain-smooth exterior. He wondered how she bore the pressure at her age, the very pressure he had grown intolerant of and now rebelled against. "Apologies."

Michael studied him. "Have you some quarrel with her? There is an edge to your tone suggesting so."

"Perhaps there is a slight sting," he admitted gruffly, "from her failure to acknowledge me the other evening. Her cut direct was a marked difference in manner from that of her sister, Lady Hester, who is quite charming."

"Yes, Hester is a delight." Michael's admiring tone was so like Alistair's when speaking of Lady Jessica that Alistair raised his brows in silent inquiry. Flushing, Michael went on, "Likely Jessica did not hear you."

Alistair shrugged into his jacket. "I was directly beside her."

"On the left side? She is deaf in that ear."

It took him a moment to absorb the information and reply. He had not imagined any imperfections in her, although he felt some relief to know there was one. It made her more mortal and less Grecian goddess. "I was not aware."

"For the most part, no one takes note. Only when the noise is high, during large gatherings, does it become a hindrance."

"Now I see why Tarley selected her. A wife who only half listens to rumormongers would be a blessing indeed."

Michael snorted and started toward the house. "She is reserved," he conceded, "but then the future Countess of Pennington should be. Tarley assures me there are hidden depths to her."

"Hmm . . ."

"You sound doubtful, but despite your excessively comely face, your experience with women is not equal to Tarley's."

Alistair's mouth curved wryly. "Are you certain?"

"Considering the irrefutable fact that he has ten years' advantage on you, I would say so." Michael threw his arm around Alistair's shoulders. "I suggest you concede that his greater maturity likely gives him a superior platform from which to note hidden qualities in his own betrothed."

"I dislike conceding anything."

"I know, my friend. However, you really should concede defeat in our recently interrupted wrestling match. You were moments away from seeing me the victor."

Alistair elbowed him in the ribs. "If Tarley had not spared you, you would be pleading for mercy now."

"Ho! Shall we determine the winner with a race to the—"

Alistair was running before the last word was out.

Within hours, she would be wed.

As the dark of night lightened into the gray of predawn, Jessica hugged her shawl tighter about her shoulders and walked Temperance deeper into the forest surrounding the Pennington manse. The pug's rapid steps crunched atop the loose gravel trail in a staccato that was soothing in its familiarity.

"Why must you be so picky?" Jess chastised. Her breath puffed visibly in the chill air, making her long for the warmth of the bed she had yet to crawl into. "Any spot should suffice."

Temperance glanced up with an expression Jess swore was akin to exasperation.

"Very well," she said reluctantly, unable to refuse that look. "We'll go a bit farther."

They rounded a corner and Temperance paused, sniffing. Apparently satisfied with the location, the pug presented her back to Jess and squatted in front of a tree.

Smiling at the bid for privacy, Jess turned away and took in her surroundings, deciding to explore the trail more thoroughly in the light of day. Unlike so many estates where the gardens and woodlands were invaded by obelisks, reproductions of Grecian statues and temples, and the occasional pagoda, the Pennington estate displayed a welcome appreciation of the natural landscape. There were places along the pathway where it felt as if civilization and all its inhabitants were miles away. She had not expected to enjoy the feeling so much but found she did, especially after hours of meaningless interactions with people who cared only for the title she was marrying into.

"I shall enjoy walking you through here," she said over her shoulder, "when the sun is up and I am properly attired for the activity."

Temperance finished her business and moved into view. The pug started back toward the house, tugging on the leash with notable impatience after taking so long to find a proper piddle spot. Jess was following when a rustling noise to the left put Temperance on alert. The dog's dark ears and tail perked up, while her tan muscular body tensed with expectation.

Jess's heart beat faster. If it was a wild boar or feral fox, the situation would be disastrous. She would be devastated if something untoward happened to Temperance, who was the only creature on earth who did not judge Jess by standards she struggled greatly to meet.

A squirrel darted across the path. Jess melted with relief and gave a breathless laugh. But Temperance did not stand down. The pug lunged, ripping her leash from Jess's slackened grip.

"Bloody hell. Temperance!"

In a flash of tiny limbs and fur, the two creatures were gone. The sounds of the chase—the rustling of leaves and the pug's low growling—quickly faded.

Tossing up her hands, Jess left the walkway and followed the path of trampled foliage. She was so focused on tracking, she failed to realize she'd come upon a large gazebo until she very nearly ran into it. She veered to the right . . .

A female's throaty laugh broke the quiet. Jess stumbled to a startled halt.

"Hurry, Lucius," the woman urged breathlessly. "Trent will note my absence."

Wilhelmina, Lady Trent. Jess stood unmoving, barely breathing.

There was a slow, drawn-out creaking of wood.

"Patience, darling." A recognizable masculine voice rejoined in a lazy, practiced drawl. "Let me give you what you paid for."

The gazebo creaked again, louder this time. Quicker and harder. Lady Trent gave a thready moan.

Alistair Lucius Caulfield. *Inflagrente delicto* with the Countess of Trent. Dear God. The woman was nearly a score of years his senior. Beautiful, yes, but of an age with his mother.

The use of his middle name was startling. And, perhaps, telling . . . ? Aside from the obvious, perhaps they were intimate in a deeper sense. Was it possible the roguish Caulfield had a *tendre* for the lovely countess, enough that she would have reason to call him by a name not used by others?

"You," the countess purred, "are worth every shilling I pay for you."

Dear God. Perhaps not an intimacy at all, but a . . . transaction. An arrangement. With a man providing the services . . .

Hoping to move on without giving herself away, Jess took a tentative step forward. A slight movement in the gazebo prompted her to still again. Her eyes narrowed, struggling to overcome the insufficient light. It was her misfortune to be bathed in the faint glow of the waning moon while the interior of the gazebo remained deeply shadowed by its roof and overhanging trees.

She saw a hand wrapped around one of the domed roof's supporting poles and another set a short ways above it. A man's hands, gripping for purchase. From their height on the beam, she knew he was standing.

"Lucius . . . For God's sake, don't stop now."

Lady Trent was pinned between Caulfield and the wood. Which meant he was facing Jess.

Twin glimmers in the darkness betrayed a blink.

He saw her. Was in fact staring at her.

Jess wished the ground would open and swallow her whole. What was she to say? How was one supposed to act when caught in such a situation?

"Lucius! Damn you." The weathered wood whined in response to its pressures. "The feel of your big cock in me is delicious, but far more so when it's moving."

Jess's hand went to her throat. Despite the cold, perspiration misted her forehead. The horror she should have felt at finding a man engaged in sexual congress was markedly absent. Because it was Caulfield, and he fascinated her. It was a terrible sort of captivation with which she viewed him—a mixture of envy for his freedom and horror at the ease with which he disregarded public opinion.

She had to get away before she was forced to acknowledge her presence to Lady Trent. She took a careful step forward . . .

"Wait." Caulfield's voice was gruffer than before.

She froze.

"I cannot!" Lady Trent protested breathlessly.

But it was not the countess Caulfield spoke to.

One of his hands was outstretched, extended toward Jess. The request stunned her into immobility.

A long moment passed in which her gaze remained fixed on the twin sparkles of his eyes. His breathing became harsh and audible.

Then, he gripped the pole again and began to move.

His thrusts began slowly at first, then became more fervent with a building tempo. The rhythmic protests of the wood battered Jess from all sides. She could see no detail beyond those two hands and glistening gaze that smoldered with a tangible heat, but the sounds she heard filled her mind with images. Caulfield never took his eyes from her, even as he rutted so furiously she wondered how the countess could take pleasure in such violence of movement. Lady Trent was nearly incoherent, coarse words of praise spilling from her lips between high-pitched squeals.

Jess was riveted by this exposure to a side of sexual congress she'd been mostly ignorant of. She knew the mechanics; her stepmother had been most thorough. *Do not cringe or cry when he enters you. Try to relax; it will decrease the discomfort. Make no sound of any kind. Never voice a complaint.* And yet Jess had seen the knowing looks of other women and heard whispers behind fans that hinted at more. Now she had the proof. Every pleasured sound Lady Trent made echoed through her, tripping over her senses like a stone skipping over water. Her body responded instinctively—her skin became sensitive and her breathing came in quick pants.

She began to quiver under the weight of Caulfield's gaze. Although she longed to run from the purloined intimacy, she was unable to move. It was impossible, but it seemed as if he looked right through her, past the façade forged by her father's hand.

The bonds holding her in place broke only when Caulfield did. His serrated groan at the moment of crisis acted like a spur to her flank. She ran then, clinging to her shawl with both arms crossed over full and aching breasts. When Temperance dashed out of a bush to greet her, Jess sobbed with relief. Scooping up the pug, she rushed toward the trail leading back to the manse.

"Lady Jessica!"

The calling of her name as Jess returned to the relative safety of the rear garden caused her to stumble. Her heart raced anew at being caught. She spun in a flurry of pale blue satin skirts, searching for the caller and mortified at the thought it might be Alistair Caulfield with a plea for discretion. Or worse, her father.

"Jessica. By God, I've been searching all over for you."

She was relieved to see Benedict approaching from the direction of the house, but relief bled into wariness. He maneuvered through the yew-lined garden paths with such a brisk, determined stride. A shiver moved through her. Was he angry?

"Is something amiss?" she queried carefully as he neared, knowing it must be to cause him to seek her out at this hour.

"You have been gone at length. Half an hour ago, your abigail said you'd left to walk Temperance, and you had already been absent for a quarter hour when I inquired."

Her gaze lowered to avoid any appearance of challenge. "I apologize for causing you concern."

"No need for apologies," he said in a clipped tone. "I simply wished to have a word with you. We are to be wed today, and I wanted to allay any nerves that might plague you before the event."

Jess blinked and looked up, startled by his consideration. "My lord—"

"Benedict," he corrected, catching up her hand. "You are chilled to the bone. Where have you been?"

The concern in his tone was unmistakable. She wasn't certain at first how to respond. His reaction was so different from the one her father would have had.

Thrown off guard by her own confusion, she began to reply almost without thinking. As she relayed the tale of Temperance leading her on a merry chase after a squirrel, Jess studied her future spouse with more care than she'd invested in a very long time. He had become a staple in her life, an obligation she accepted without need for deep contemplation. Inasmuch as she was able, she had grown comfortable with the inevitability of sharing a life with him. But she did not feel comfortable now. She remained flushed and agitated by the way Caulfield had used her to further his own pleasure.

"I would have walked with you, if you had asked," Benedict said when she finished. He gave her hand a squeeze. "In the future, I pray you do so."

Emboldened by his gentle manner and the lingering effects of the wine she'd drunk too liberally of at supper, Jess pressed on recklessly. "Temperance and I found something else in the woods."

"Oh?"

She told him about the couple in the gazebo, her voice low and faltering, her words tumbling over themselves because she lacked the vocabulary and confidence. She did not speak of the coin exchanged between the countess and Caulfield, nor did she divulge their identities.

Benedict didn't move the entirety of the short time she spoke. When she finished, he cleared his throat and said, "Damnation, I am horrified that you were exposed to such unpleasantness on the eve of our wedding."

"They did not seem to find the encounter unpleasant at all."

He flushed. "Jessica—"

"You spoke of allaying my nerves," she said quickly, before losing her courage. "I should like to be honest with you, but I fear overstepping the limits of your forbearance."

"I will advise you if that limit is reached."

"In what manner?"

"Beg your pardon?" Benedict frowned.

Jess swallowed. "In what manner will you advise me? With a word? A loss of privilege? S-something more . . . definitive?"

He stiffened. "I would never lay a hand to you or any woman; I would certainly never fault you for honesty. I expect I will be far more lenient with you than with anyone else of my acquaintance. You are a great prize to me, Jessica. I have waited impatiently for the day when you would be mine."

"Why?"

"You are a beautiful woman," he said gruffly.

Astonishment swept through her, followed by a rush of unexpected hope. "My lord, would you be displeased to know that I find myself praying for the physical aspect of our marriage to be . . . pleasurable? For both of us."

God knew she would not be able to dally as Lady Trent did. Such behavior was not in her nature.

He displayed his unease with the topic by pulling at the elegant knot of his cravat. "I have always intended to make it so. I *will* make it so, if you trust me."

"Benedict." She inhaled the scent clinging to him—spice, tobacco, and a fine port. Despite wading through a discussion he would certainly never expect to have with his lady wife, his responses were as direct as his gaze. She liked him more each moment that passed. "You are taking this conversation so well. I cannot help wondering how far I can press you."

"Please, speak freely," he urged. "I want you to come to the altar with no doubts or reservations."

Jess spoke in a rush. "I should like to retire with you to the summerhouse by the lake. This moment."

His exhale was harsh, as were his features. His grip on her hand tightened almost painfully. "Why?"

"I have angered you." Averting her gaze, she backed away. "Forgive me. And pray, do not doubt my innocence. The hour is late and I am not myself."

Benedict pulled her hand to his chest, bringing her close again. "Look at me, Jessica."

She did as he asked and was made dizzy by his regard. He no longer looked at her with discomfort or concern.

"We are mere hours away from the marriage bed," he re-

16

minded her in a voice hoarser than she'd ever heard it. "I collect that the events you witnessed in the woods stirred reactions you do not yet understand, and I cannot tell you how it affects me to learn you are fascinated by your response and not repulsed, as some women might be. But you are to be my wife and you deserve the respect of that station."

"You would not respect me in the summerhouse?"

For the length of a heartbeat, he looked taken aback. Then, he threw his head back and laughed. The rich, deep sound carried over the garden. Jess was smitten by how merriment transformed him, making him more approachable and—if possible—more handsome.

Pulling her even closer, Benedict pressed his lips to her temple. "You are a treasure."

"From what I understand," she whispered, leaning into his warmth, "duty lies in the marital bed, while pleasure exists outside of it with paramours. Do I reveal a defect in my character by confessing that I should prefer you to want me in the manner of a mistress rather than a wife, insofar as the bedroom is concerned?"

"You have no defects. You are as perfect a woman as I have ever seen or become acquainted with."

She was far from perfect, as the remembered lash of a switch to the backs of her thighs attested. Learning to disguise her shortcomings had been a necessity.

How had Caulfield sensed that she would be open to his request to watch him? How had he somehow recognized an aspect of her character of which even she was unaware?

However he'd managed it, Jess was dizzily relieved to know that Benedict did not find her sudden self-awareness threatening or undesirable. Her betrothed's acceptance gave her unusual courage. "Is it possible you might find such an interest in me?"

"More than possible." Benedict's mouth sealed over hers,

swallowing the words of relief and gratitude she meant to speak. It was a questing kiss, tender and cautious, yet assured. She caught at his lapels, her chest heaving from the effort to find the breath he was stealing from her.

His tongue slid along the seam of her lips, then teased them apart. When he entered her mouth with a quick thrust, her knees weakened. He pulled her tighter against him, exposing his need in the hard ridge of arousal pressing into her hip. His fingers kneaded her skin, betraying a growing agitation. When he broke away and pressed his temple to hers, his breathing was labored.

"God help me," he said roughly. "As innocent as you are, you have nevertheless seduced me with consummate skill."

Lifting her into his arms, he carried her swiftly to the summerhouse.

Sensitive to the highly charged situation, Temperance walked silently beside them. Then, she waited on the porch with unusual meekness and watched the sun rise.

I

Seven years later . . .

"I beg you to reconsider."

Jessica, Lady Tarley, reached over the small tea table in the Regmont family parlor and gave her sister's hand a brief squeeze. "I feel I should go."

"Why?" The corners of Hester's mouth turned downward. "I would understand if Tarley was with you, but now that he has passed . . . Is it safe for you to travel such a distance alone?"

It was a question Jess had asked herself many times, yet the answer was moot. She was determined to go. She had been given a brief window of time in which she could do something extraordinary. It was highly doubtful she would ever be presented with the opportunity again.

"Of course it's safe," she said, straightening. "Tarley's brother, Michael—I should become accustomed to referring to him as Tarley now—made the arrangements for the voyage, and I will be met at the dock by someone from the household. All will be well."

"I am not reassured." Toying with the handle of her floral-patterned teacup, Hester looked pensive and unhappy.

"You once wanted to travel to faraway places," Jess reminded, hating to see her sister so distressed. "Have you lost that wanderlust?"

Hester sighed and looked out the window beside her. Through the sheers that afforded some privacy, one could see the steady flow of Mayfair traffic in front of the town house, but Jess's attention was focused solely on her sister. Hester had matured into a beautiful young woman, lauded for her golden glamour and stunning verdant eyes framed by thick, dark lashes. She'd once been curvier than Jess and more vivacious, but the years had tempered both traits, forging a woman who was slender as a reed and serenely elegant. The Countess of Regmont had acquired a reputation for notable reserve, which surprised Jess considering how charming and outgoing Lord Regmont was. She blamed the change on their father, and his blasted pride and misogyny.

"You look pale and thin," Jess observed. "Are you unwell?"

"I grieve for your loss. And I must confess, I have not slept well since you first announced your intent to travel." Hester looked back at her. "I simply cannot comprehend your motivation."

Nearly a year had passed since Benedict had gone on to his reward, and he had been severely ill for three months prior to that. There had been time enough for Jess to reach a state of resigned acceptance to life without him. Still, bereavement clung to her like fog over water. Family and friends looked to her for the cue to leave the past behind, and she had no notion of how to give it to them. "I require distance from the past in order to grasp the future."

"Surely retiring to the country would suffice?"

"It did not suffice last winter. Now another Season is upon us, and we are all still trapped beneath this cloud hovering over me. It is necessary for me to break away from the routine into which I have fallen, so everyone can move forward with life as we now face it."

"Dear God, Jess," Hester breathed, looking pale. "You cannot mean to say that you must leave us as Tarley did for all to heal. You are still young and marriageable. Your life is far from over."

"Agreed. Pray do not worry over me." Jess refilled Hester's teacup and dropped two lumps of sugar into it. "I will be gone only long enough to make arrangements for the sale of the plantation. I shall return refreshed and revitalized, which, in turn, will reinvigorate all who love and worry over me."

"I still cannot believe he bequeathed that place to you. What was he thinking?"

Jessica smiled fondly, her gaze moving around the cheery parlor with its yellow silk drapes and blue floral accents. Hester had redesigned the space shortly after her marriage, and its style reflected the optimism so innate to her. "He wanted me to be entirely self-sufficient, and it was a sentimental gesture. Tarley knew how much I loved our trip to Calypso."

"Sentimentality is all well and good, until it sends you on a journey halfway around the world," Hester muttered.

"As I've said, I *want* to go. I will go so far as to say I *need* to go. It is somewhat of a farewell for me."

Groaning, Hester finally capitulated. "You promise to write and return as soon as you are able?"

"Of course. And you promise to write back."

Hester nodded, then picked up her cup and saucer. She downed her hot tea in one unladylike swallow. A fortifying drink.

Jess understood. She'd needed a few of those herself as the anniversary of Tarley's death loomed. "I will bring you gifts," she promised in a deliberately light tone, hoping to elicit a smile.

"Just bring yourself back," Hester admonished with a wag of her finger.

The gesture was so reminiscent of their childhood. Jess couldn't resist asking, "Will you come after me if I tarry overlong?"

"Regmont would never allow it. However, I could likely convince *someone* to go after you. Perhaps some of the matrons who are so concerned over your welfare . . . ?"

Jess gave a mock shudder. "Point taken, my ruthless sister. I shall return posthaste."

Alistair Caulfield's back was to the door of his warehouse shipping office when it opened. A salt-tinged gust blew through the space, snatching the manifest he was about to file right out of his hand.

He caught it deftly, then looked over his shoulder. Startled recognition moved through him. "Michael."

The new Lord Tarley's eyes widened with equal surprise, then a weary half-smile curved his mouth. "Alistair, you scoundrel. You didn't tell me you were in Town."

"I've only just returned." He slid the parchment into the appropriate folder and pushed the drawer closed. "How are you, my lord?"

Michael removed his hat and ran a hand through his dark brown hair. The assumption of the Tarley title appeared to weigh heavily on his broad shoulders, grounding him in a way Alistair had never seen before. He was dressed somberly in shades of brown, and he flexed his left hand, which bore the Tarley signet ring, as if he could not accustom himself to having it there. "As well as can be expected under the circumstances."

"My condolences to you and your family. Did you receive my letter?"

"I did. Thank you. I meant to reply, but time is stretched so thin. The last year has raced by so quickly; I've yet to catch my breath."

"I understand."

Michael nodded. "I'm pleased to see you again, my friend. You have been gone far too long."

"The life of a merchant." He could have delegated more, but staying in England meant crossing paths with both his father and Jessica. His father complained about Alistair's success as a tradesman with as much virulence as he'd once complained about Alistair's lack of purpose. It was a great stressor for his mother, which he was only able to alleviate by being absent as much as possible.

As for Jessica, she'd been careful to avoid him whenever they were in proximity. He had learned to reciprocate when he saw how marriage to Tarley had changed her. While she remained as cool in deportment as ever, he'd seen the blossoming of her sensual nature in the languid way she moved and the knowledge in those big, gray eyes. Other men coveted the mystery of her, but Alistair had seen behind the veil, and *that* was the woman he lusted for. Forever beyond his reach in reality, but a fixture in his mind. She was burned into his memory by the raging hungers and the impressions of youth, and the years hadn't lessened the vivid recollection one whit.

"I find myself grateful for your enterprising sensibilities," Michael said. "Your captains are the only ones I would entrust with the safe passage of my sister-in-law to Jamaica."

Alistair kept his face impassive thanks to considerable practice, but the sudden awareness gripping him tensed his frame. "Lady Tarley intends to travel to Calypso?"

"Yes. This very morning, which is why I'm here. I intend

to speak to the captain myself and see he looks after her until they arrive."

"Who travels with her?"

"Only her maid. I should like to accompany her, but I can't leave now."

"And she will not delay?"

"No." Michael's mouth curved wryly. "And I cannot dissuade her."

"You cannot say no to her," Alistair corrected, moving to the window through which he could view the West India docks. Ships entered the Northern Dock to unload their precious imports, then sailed around to the Southern Dock to reload with cargo for export. Around the perimeter, a high brick wall deterred the rampant theft plaguing the London wharves. The same wall increased his shipping company's appeal to West Indian landowners requiring secure transportation of goods.

"Neither can Hester—forgive me, *Lady Regmont*."

The last was said with difficulty. Alistair had long suspected his friend nursed deeper feelings for Jessica's younger sister and had assumed Michael would pay his addresses. Instead, Hester had been presented at court, then immediately betrothed, breaking the hearts of many hopeful would-be swains. "Why is she so determined to go?"

"Benedict bequeathed the property to her. She claims she must see to its sale personally. I fear the loss of my brother has affected her deeply and she seeks a purpose. I've attempted to anchor her, but duty has me stretched to wit's end."

Alistair's reply was carefully neutral. "I can assist her in that endeavor. I can make the necessary introductions, as well as provide information that would take her months to discover."

"A generous offer." Michael's gaze was searching. "But you've just returned. I can't ask you to depart again so soon."

Turning, Alistair said, "My plantation borders Calypso, and I should like to expand. It's my hope to position myself as the best purchaser of the property. I will pay her handsomely, of course."

Relief swept over Michael's expressive features. "That would ease my mind considerably. I'll speak to her at once."

"Perhaps you should leave that to me. If, as you say, she needs a purpose, then she'll want to maintain control of the matter in all ways. She should be allowed to set the terms and pace of our association to suit her. I have all the time in the world, but you do not. See to your most pressing affairs, and entrust Lady Tarley to me."

"You've always been a good friend," Michael said. "I pray you return to England swiftly and settle for a time. I could use your ear and head for business. In the interim, please encourage Jessica to write often and keep me abreast of the situation. I should like to see her return before we retire to the country for the winter."

"I'll do my best."

Alistair waited several minutes after Michael departed, then moved to the desk. He began a list of new provisions for the journey, determined to create the best possible environment. He also made some quick but costly adjustments to the passenger list, moving two additional travelers to another of his ships.

He, Jessica, and her maid would be the only non-crewmen aboard the *Acheron*.

She would be within close quarters for weeks—it was an extraordinary opportunity Alistair was determined not to waste.

*   *   *

From the familiar comfort of her town coach, Jessica stared at the sleek ship before her, her gaze following the proud line of its polished deck and the soaring height of its three masts. It was one of the most impressive vessels docked, which she should have expected considering how anxious Michael was about her making the journey. He would have taken great pains to secure her comfort and welfare. She suspected it helped him grieve to hover over his brother's widow, but that was one of the aftereffects of losing Tarley that made her want to flee.

The scent of the ocean drew her attention back to the industriously noisy West India docks. Excitement made her heart race, or perhaps it was apprehension. Society on the lush Caribbean island—such as it was—had fewer preconceived notions about her, and the pace and structure of social interactions were more relaxed. She looked forward to enjoying moments of solitude after the past few months of well-intentioned suffocation.

Jess watched as in quick succession her footmen carried her trunks up the gangplank to the main deck. The bright blue of Pennington livery was conspicuous among the less colorful attire of the seamen around them. Soon enough, there was no reason for her to delay in the carriage any longer.

She alighted with the help of a footman, smoothed her pale lavender silk skirts, and then set off without looking back. As she gained the deck, she felt the rolling of the ship beneath her feet and took a moment to absorb the sensation.

"Lady Tarley."

Jess turned her head and watched a portly, distinguished gentleman approach. Even before he spoke, his attire and bearing told her he was the captain.

"Captain Smith," he introduced himself, accepting the

hand she offered him with a bow "A pleasure to 'ave you aboard, milady."

"The pleasure is mine," she demurred, returning the smile he offered from the depths of a coarse white beard. "You command an impressive ship, Captain."

"Aye, that she is." He tipped up his hat to get a better look at her. "I would be 'onored to 'ave you join me for the evenin' meals."

"I would enjoy that very much, thank you."

"Excellent." Smith gestured at a young seaman. "Miller 'ere will show you to yer cabin. If you 'ave any questions or concerns, 'e can see to them."

"I'm very much obliged." As the captain went about the business of preparing to set sail, Jess turned to Miller, who she guessed was no more than ten and seven.

"Milady." He gestured ahead to an open companionway and stairs leading below deck. "This way."

She followed him across the midship, fascinated by the courage of the men climbing the rigging like industrious little crabs. But as she descended the stairs, her admiration was redirected to the vessel's impressive interior.

The paneled companion- and passageway gleamed with polish, as did the brass hardware that secured the doors and hung the flashlamps. She'd been uncertain of what to expect, but this attention to detail was a surprise and a delight. Miller paused before a door and knocked, which elicited a shouted permission to enter from Jess's abigail, Beth.

The cabin Jess entered was small but well appointed; it held a narrow bed, a modestly sized rectangular window, and a wooden table with two chairs. On the sole by one of her trunks sat a crate of her favorite claret. Although it was the smallest space she'd ever occupied as a bedchamber, she found the limits of the cabin comforting. And she was deeply appreciative that, for the next few weeks at least, she would not have to anticipate how to respond to others in a manner that made them feel better.

Reaching up, she withdrew the pin securing her hat and handed both to Beth.

Miller promised to return at six to take her to supper, then ducked back out to the passageway. After the door shut, Jess's gaze met Beth's.

The abigail bit her lower lip and spun in a quick circle. "This is a grand adventure, milady. I've missed Jamaica since we left."

Jess exhaled to ease the knot in her stomach, then smiled. "And a certain young man."

"Yes," the maid agreed. " 'Im, too."

Beth had been a blessing the past few days, keeping Jess's spirits high while everyone around her had been so disapproving of her plans.

"An adventure," Jess repeated. "I think it will be."

When the knock came at Jess's cabin door shortly before six, she set aside the book she'd been reading and stood with some reluctance. Beth was mending a stocking on the opposite side of the small table, and the quiet companionship had been most welcome.

Setting her work down, Beth went to answer the door. As the panel swung open, Miller's young face was revealed. He smiled shyly, showing slightly crooked teeth. Jess dismissed Beth to enjoy her own meal, then followed the young crewman to the captain's great cabin. As they neared the wide door marking the end of the passageway, the plaintive notes of a violin grew in volume. The instrument was consummately played, the tune sweet yet haunting. Enamored with the music, she quickened her step. Miller knocked once, then opened the door without waiting for a reply. He gestured her into the sizable cabin with a gallant sweep of his arm.

She entered with a practiced smile, her gaze locating Captain Smith as he pushed to his feet at a long dining table, along with two other gentlemen who were introduced to her as the Chief Mate and ship's surgeon. She exchanged the expected pleasantries, then turned her attention to the violin player. He stood with his back to her before the large gallery windows wrapping the stern. He was sans tailcoat, which caused her to glance hastily away. But when the captain approached to escort her to the table, she risked another furtive glance at the scandalously semi-dressed gentleman. Without tails to block her gaze, she was afforded a prime view of the man's derriere, which was quite noteworthy. It was not a part of the male anatomy she'd had cause to study before. She found she quite enjoyed the ogling when the buttocks on display were so firm and well-shaped.

As she conversed with the ship's officers, Jess glanced frequently at the dark-haired musician who coaxed such beautiful notes from the violin. The fluid, practiced movement of his arm caused his back and shoulders to flex in a manner that had always fascinated her. The male body was so much larger and more powerful than a woman's—capable of fierce aggression while also being sleek and graceful.

The tune ended. The player pivoted to return the violin and bow to their case waiting on the chair beside him. Jess caught a quick glimpse of his profile. A frisson of awareness swept over her skin. He collected his jacket from the chair where it was draped, then shrugged into it. She hadn't thought it possible that the act of putting clothes *on* could be as arousing as watching them come *off,* but this man made it so. The graceful economy of his movements was inherently sensual, which suited his air of unwavering confidence and command.

"And this," the captain said, turning slightly to gesture at the gentleman, "is Mr. Alistair Caulfield, owner of this fine vessel and brilliant violinist, as you 'eard."

Jess swore her heart ceased beating for a moment. Certainly, she stopped breathing. Caulfield faced her and sketched a perfectly executed, elegant bow. Yet his head never lowered and his gaze never left hers.

Dear God . . .

2

What were the odds that they would cross paths this way?

There was very little of the young man Jess had once known left in the man who faced her. Alistair Caulfield was no longer pretty. The planes of his face had sharpened, etching his features into a thoroughly masculine countenance. Darkly winged brows and thick lashes framed those infamous eyes of rich, deep blue. In the fading light of the setting sun and the flickering flames of the turpentine lamps, his coal-black hair gleamed with health and vitality. Previously his beauty had been striking, but now he was larger. More worldly and mature. Undeniably formidable.

Breathtakingly male.

"Lady Tarley," he greeted her, straightening. "It is a great pleasure to see you again."

His voice was lower and deeper in pitch than she remembered. It had a soft, rumbling quality. Almost a purr. He walked with equal feline grace, his step light and surefooted despite his powerful build. His gaze was focused and intense, assessing. Challenging. As before, it seemed he looked right into the very heart of her and dared her to deny that he could.

She sucked in a shaky breath and met him halfway, offering her hand. "Mr. Caulfield. It has been some time since we last met."

"Years."

His look was so intimate she couldn't help thinking of that night in the Pennington woods. A rush of heat swept up her arm from where their skin connected.

He went on. "Please accept my condolences on your recent loss. Tarley was a good man. I admired him and liked him quite well."

"Your thoughts are appreciated," she managed in spite of a suddenly dry mouth. "I offer the same to you. I was deeply sorry to hear that your brother had passed."

His jaw tightened and he released her, sliding his hand away so that his fingertips stroked over the center of her palm. "Two of them," he replied grimly.

Jess caught her hand back and rubbed it discreetly against her thigh, to no avail. The tingle left by his touch was inerasable.

"Shall we?" the captain said, tilting his head toward the table.

Caulfield took a seat on the bench directly across from her. She was discomfited at first, but he seemed to forget her the moment the food was brought in. To ensure a steady flow of conversation, she took pains to direct the discussion to topics addressing the ship and seafaring, and the men easily followed. No doubt they were relieved not to have to focus on her life of limited scope, which was of little interest to men. What followed was a rather fantastic hour of food and conversation the likes of which she'd never been exposed to before. Gentlemen did not often discuss matters of business around her.

It quickly became clear that Alistair Caulfield was enjoying laudable financial success. He didn't comment on it personally, but he participated in the discussion about the trade, making it clear he was very involved in the minutiae of his business endeavors. He was also expertly dressed. His coat was made with a gray-green velvet she thought quite lovely, and the stylishly short cut of the shoulders emphasized how fit he was.

"Do you make the trip to Jamaica often, Captain?" Jess asked.

"Not as often as some of Mr. Caulfield's other ships do." He set his elbows on the table and toyed with his beard. "London is where we berth most often. The others dock in Liverpool or Bristol."

"How many ships are there?"

The captain looked at Caulfield. " 'Ow many are there now? Five?"

"Six," Caulfield said, looking directly at Jess.

She met his gaze with difficulty. She couldn't explain why she felt as she did, but it was almost as if the intimacies she had witnessed that night in the woods had been between Caulfield and herself, not another woman. Something profound had transpired in the moment they'd first become aware of each other in the darkness. A connecting thread had been sewn between them, and she had no notion how to sever it. She knew things about the man she should not know, and there was no way for her to return to blissful ignorance.

"Congratulations on your success," she murmured.

"I can say the same to you." He set one forearm on the table. The cuff of his coat was of fashionable length, covering his hand near to the knuckle. Still, the sight of his fingers reminded her of another time . . . a night when those hands had clung to a gazebo post to leverage the thrust of his hips.

He drummed his fingertips onto the tablecloth-covered wood, breaking her reverie. "Oh?" she managed, after a fortifying swallow of wine.

"My ships also provide transport for Calypso goods."

Jess was not surprised to learn that. "I should like to discuss that arrangement with you further, Mr. Caulfield."

His brows arched, and the other men grew quiet.

"When you have time," she qualified. "There is no urgency."

"I have time now."

She recognized the hawklike precision of his gaze and understood she'd engaged his mind for business. A moment of disquiet affected her, but she prayed she hid it. By necessity, she'd come to recognize the type of men it was best not to cross, and Alistair Caulfield was certainly one of them. He flashed a bright, charming smile with ease, but it did not reach his eyes.

"I appreciate your willingness to accommodate me," she answered.

Jess watched as he stood. Rounding the table quickly but without haste, he assisted her with extracting herself from the bench.

She looked at the head of the table. "Thank you very much for a charming evening, Captain."

"I 'ope you'll join us every night."

Although she deported herself without noticeable fault, she was achingly aware of Caulfield standing very close beside her. When they left the great cabin together, that awareness increased tenfold. The door shut behind them, and she felt the click of the brass latch vibrate across overly taut nerves. Tarley had gone to great lengths to make her feel secure and without stress, while Caulfield so easily skewed her prized equanimity. He had an indefinable quality that heightened her cognizance of everything that made her feminine and, therefore, vulnerable.

"Shall we take a stroll on the deck?" he asked in a subdued tone that swirled in the enclosed space around her. He stood almost too near, his head bent to accommodate the moderate height of the deckhead.

The scent clinging to him was delicious, filling her nostrils with sandalwood, musk, and the barest hint of verbena.

"I will need to fetch a shawl." Her voice was huskier than she would have liked.

"Of course."

He escorted her to her cabin in silence, which allowed other sounds to dominate—the surefooted confidence of his steps, the accelerated rate of her breathing, the steady *whoosh* of the water against the hull.

She entered her room in a breathless rush and shut the door with indecorous haste. Sucking in a gasping breath, she drew Beth's widened eyes to her. The abigail dropped her darning on the table and stood.

"Lord, but yer flushed," Beth said in the calm, authoritative voice that made everything—including a journey to Jamaica—seem both possible and well in hand. She moved to the pitcher and basin by the bed to fetch a damp cloth. "Yer not falling ill, are you?"

"No." Jess accepted the compress and held it to her cheeks. "Perhaps I had more wine than I should have with supper. Can you fetch me a shawl?"

Beth dug into the trunk at the foot of the bed and withdrew a black silk shawl. Jess traded the cloth for the garment with a grateful smile.

But Beth's frown did not diminish. "Maybe you should rest, milady."

"Yes," Jess agreed, damning herself for opening a discussion with Caulfield. She could have waited until daylight, at least. Or better yet, she should have left the questions to her steward, who could have subsequently provided her the answers with no discomfort necessary. "I shan't be long, then you can retire to your quarters."

"Don't hurry yerself on my account. I'm too excited to sleep."

35

Jess draped the shawl over her shoulders and exited back to the passageway.

Caulfield had been leaning casually against the far bulkhead, but he straightened when Jess stepped out. Cast in the brighter light spilling out of her cabin, his face revealed a stark appreciation of her appearance that caused her to flush all over again. The smoldering in his gaze was quickly masked and replaced with an easy smile, but she remembered the feel of that stare from long ago. It had a similarly paralyzing effect on her now.

He gestured toward the stairs, and the gentle prod gave her the impetus to move. She preceded him up to the deck, grateful for the cool ocean breeze and low-hanging, yellow moon that stripped the world of color. Everything was rendered in black and shades of gray, which helped to mitigate the overwhelming vibrancy that had always distinguished Alistair Caulfield.

"What are the chances," she began, just to break the weighty silence, "that you and I would find ourselves traveling on the same ship at the same time?"

"Excellent, considering I arranged it," he said smoothly. "I hope you've been comfortable so far."

"How could anyone be uncomfortable? This is a magnificent ship."

His mouth curved, and a flutter tickled her stomach. "It pleases me to hear you say so. Should you require anything, I'm at your service. Once we've reached our destination, I have assured Michael that I'll make the necessary introductions and provide what information I can to assist you with the sale of Calypso."

"Michael," she breathed, startled to realize she had been entrusted to the care of Alistair Caulfield—a man who had always made her feel far from safe—by her very own overprotective brother-in-law. "I was unaware."

"Forgive him. I told him I would discuss the matter with you. He's overwhelmed at the moment, and I wanted to alleviate some of his burden."

"Yes, of course. That was very considerate." She started walking toward the forecastle to ease the tension gripping her. She didn't know Caulfield well enough to say he'd changed, yet the man she spoke to did not fit the image of reckless, untamed youth she had carried in her mind all these years.

"My motivation is not entirely altruistic," he qualified, falling into step beside her. His hands were clasped at the small of his back, emphasizing the strength of his shoulders and the breadth of his chest. He had always been more muscular than the Sinclairs. More so than even his own brothers.

She admired his build in ways she shouldn't. "Oh?"

He glanced aside at her. "I've been out of the country for many years, with only brief visits as necessary to prevent my mother from sending a search party after me. It's my hope that you will assist my acclimation to English society when I return, as I'll do for you in Jamaica."

"You're returning to England for a longer stay?"

"Yes." He looked forward again.

"I see." Dear God, she sounded breathless once more. "Your family and friends will be delighted, I'm certain."

Caulfield's chest expanded on a deep breath.

Recalling that the family he'd left behind was halved now, she said hastily, "Your brothers . . ."

Jess's head lowered. She regretted making him feel ill at ease, because she knew precisely how it felt to be continually reminded of what was forever lost to her.

He stopped beside the main mast. With a soft hand at her elbow, he urged her to halt as well.

She faced him. He took an unnecessary step closer. Near

enough to dance. "I'm returning to England because the reason I stayed away no longer exists, and a reason to return has unexpectedly presented itself."

Caulfield's tone was intimate. Jess couldn't help wondering if a woman was luring him back.

She nodded. "I will endeavor to be as useful to you as you'll certainly be to me."

"Thank you." He hesitated, as if he considered saying something more. In the end, he held his tongue and gestured for her to continue walking. "You wished to discuss the transport of product from Calypso?"

"Whatever obligations Calypso has are now my obligations, and I should be aware of them. That was all I wished to say. I can bring up the matter with my steward. Please, pay me no mind."

"I have the answers you seek. I want to be the one who provides them to you. Come to me with whatever you need."

Glancing at him, she found him intently focused on her. "You must be a very busy man. I don't wish to impose on your time unnecessarily."

"You could never be an imposition. I would take great pleasure in seeing to whatever you may desire."

"Very well," she said quietly.

The warmth of Caulfield's voice changed, taking on a slight edge. "Your tone suggests displeasure."

As he'd done so long ago, he somehow managed to encourage Jess to speak more bluntly than she would have thought possible. "Though I'm grateful for your attentiveness, Mr. Caulfield, I am also weary of such consideration. I'm not a woman made of glass who is prone to shattering without care. I arranged this trip, in part, to distance myself from those who insist on treating me as if I am fragile."

"I have no idea how to coddle a woman," he said wryly. "If that was my aim, I would certainly fail miserably. In truth, having met your steward on several occasions, I suspect he might have difficulty being completely forthcoming with a female. I want you to possess all the facts. The only way to be certain you have confidence in my ability to see to your interests is to be the one who shows you the contracts and terms myself, and explains whatever might be confusing."

His smile was filled with mischief. "I want to expose you. Not shield you."

Her lips curved slightly. He was charming in his own wicked way.

"The hour grows late," he said as they neared the companionway again. "Allow me to escort you back to your cabin?"

"Thank you." She was startled to realize she enjoyed his company.

Once they reached her door, he sketched an abbreviated bow in the narrow space. "I bid you good night, Lady Tarley. Sweet dreams."

He was gone before she could reply, leaving behind a rather marked emptiness in the space he'd occupied.

3

Michael Sinclair, Viscount Tarley, found himself in front of the Regmont town house in Mayfair thirty minutes into the two-hour block of time in which Lady Regmont was known to be at home to callers. He dismounted before he could change his mind and passed the reins to the waiting footman, then took the steps up to the front door two at a time. He resisted the urge to check his cravat, which he'd styled modestly with a simple barrel knot. His anxiousness was extreme, to the point that he'd dithered over which of his waistcoats was the most attractive foil for the deep blue coat he wore for her, because she had once said blue was a very attractive color on his person.

In short order, he was announced into a drawing room holding half a dozen callers. Hester sat in a butter-colored wingback in the center of the assemblage, looking as fragile and beautiful as he had ever seen her.

"Lord Tarley," she greeted, extending her hands to him without rising.

He crossed the oriental rug with swift strides and kissed the back of each pale, slender hand. "Lady Regmont. My day is brighter for having begun it in your presence."

His pleasure would be dimmed when he left, as if he

stepped out of the sunlight and into a shadow. He believed she was made for him, so much so he'd never once contemplated marrying anyone else. In his youth, he had thought it would be perfect for the Sinclair brothers to marry the Sheffield sisters and live parallel, harmonious lives. But Hadley had nursed grander plans for his daughters, and Michael's position as second son was not of sufficient consequence even to bear consideration.

He'd never had a chance to have her.

To add insult to injury, Hester was denied even a proper Season, just as her sister had been. She was betrothed almost from the moment she was presented at court.

"I thought you had forgotten me," she said to him. "It has been ages since you last called."

"I could never forget you." Although there were nights when he prayed for such to be possible.

She looked over his shoulder with a telling glance. A moment later, an efficient servant moved a damask-upholstered wooden chair to a place beside her. The other guests returned Michael's brisk nods of greeting with smiles and effusive welcomes.

"Please," Hester said, gesturing at the chair. "Sit. Tell me everything that has transpired in your life since the last time we spoke."

He settled into the seat, his gaze ravenous as it swept over her glorious features. Her golden hair was styled fashionably, with ringlets on her forehead and hanging over her ears. She wore a lovely gown of rose pink, and her neck was adorned with a cameo secured by a thick black ribbon.

"I've come to reassure you. Jessica is in good hands. Alistair Caulfield has agreed to look after her while she is away. He's lived in Jamaica for some years now and is well versed in the flow of Society and the personages in residence there."

"Mr. Caulfield, you say." A frown marred the line of her brows. "I am not certain she ever cared much for him."

"I think the feeling might be mutual. The few times I've seen them together, they both became noticeably discomfited. However, they are adults now and she requires some guidance in matters in which Caulfield has expertise. In addition, she seeks to sell the plantation, and Caulfield's property borders hers, so she has the impetus and means to conclude her affairs posthaste and return to you."

"My lord." Hester's lovely green eyes warmed. "You are deviously clever. I adore that trait in you."

Her last words caused a pang in his chest. Her adoration was only a small portion of what he wanted from her. "I cannot take all the credit. Caulfield rather fell into my lap and volunteered. I was simply in the correct place at the correct time to take advantage."

"You are a godsend." Her smile faded. "I miss her terribly already and she has been gone only one day. But listen to me go on so selfishly. She made a great attempt to hide it, but it was clear she anticipated the trip. In fact, she was quite eager. I should at least make an attempt to be excited for her."

"That is why I came by today. I know how close you are to Jessica and how her absence will pain you. I want you to know . . . I am at your disposal, for whatever you require, in the interim until she returns."

"You have always been so wonderful to me." She reached out and gently, all-too-briefly touched his forearm. An air of melancholy clung to her that disturbed him. "But you have enough new burdens without adding me to the mix."

"You will *never* be a burden to me. It is my privilege to be available to you whenever you may need me."

"You may live to regret that offer one day," she teased, brightening. "I am certain I could devise ways to torment you with it."

Although her meaning was innocent, his reaction to her

words was less so. "Do your worst," he challenged in a husky voice. "I am eager to prove myself up to the task."

A blush brought welcome color to her pale cheeks.

"Milady." The butler approached with a small, beribboned box on a silver salver. He presented the gift to her.

One of Hester's guests, the Marchioness of Grayson, began to tease her about secret admirers and how jealous Regmont would be, since his possessiveness over his wife was well known. He was unfashionably doting.

Hester opened the small accompanying card first, then set it on the chair arm beside her. Michael noted that her fingers were shaking as she opened the box, revealing a jewel-encrusted broach of obvious expense. Noting the pinched look around her eyes, he glanced at the card, which had been only partially refolded. He could make out very little of the slashing scrawl, but *"forgive me"* was legible enough. It tautened his jaw and sent a rush of questions through his mind.

"Well?" Lady Bencott asked. "Do not keep us in an agony of curiosity. What is it and who sent it?"

Hester passed the gift into the countess's waiting hand. "Regmont, of course."

As the broach made its way around the room to much approbation, Michael thought Hester's wide smile looked forced. Certainly she was too pale not to raise some concern.

He excused himself, unable to bear the feeling that something was wrong in her world, and he lacked the right to do anything about it.

It was late afternoon, and Jessica had yet to make an appearance on deck.

Alistair restrained himself from pacing by dint of will alone. If she decided to avoid him on the ship, it would make wooing her more difficult, but he was not a man who accepted defeat gracefully. He intended to build a rapport with her during the journey, and he would find a way to do it. There had to be means of establishing at least the beginnings of a deeper association. He simply had to puzzle out the key to unlocking her. Last night, he'd thought forthrightness might be the avenue of least resistance, but perhaps he had misread her.

Gripping the gunwale, he stared down at the water. It did not escape his notice that the sea was presently the same gray hue as Jessica's eyes.

By God, she was breathtaking.

He remembered her entering the great cabin for supper. She'd altered the very air around her, allowing him to *feel* her come in. The weight and heat of her regard had flowed over his spine like a physical caress. He'd arranged to be standing as he was, coatless and occupied, at the time of her arrival. He wanted her to see him as the man he was now— cultured and learned. Polished. His presentation was meant to be the first salvo in what was intended to be a slow, careful seduction.

In actuality, however, she'd struck him a blow that carried equal fierceness. She had stood there before him with guinea-blond hair piled high, her pale skin as flawless as the finest porcelain, her once slender body matured into that of a woman . . . Full, high breasts. Delicate waist. Long legs he desired to feel wrapped around his hips. There was something inherently vulnerable about her that called to every base and primitive instinct inside him.

He wanted to ravish her. Possess her.

For a taut moment, her features had betrayed her response to the realization of who he was. Seven years ago and now, she'd been drawn to him. He could use that against her, if he tread very carefully.

"Good afternoon, Mr. Caulfield."

Bloody hell. Even the sound of her voice could send lewd imaginings through his mind. It was as precise and restrained as her deportment. He wanted to turn that clipped intonation into something throatier. Softer. He wanted to hear her say his name while hoarse from pleasured cries.

With a deep breath, he faced her. "Lady Tarley. You look rested. I trust you slept well?"

"I did, thank you."

She looked more than rested; she looked stunningly beautiful. Dressed in a deep blue gown and carrying a delicate parasol, she was a vision on the deck of his ship. He did not look away from her, but knew every man within eyesight had to be equally mesmerized. She was impossibly perfect in every way.

Joining him at the gunwale, Jessica set one gloved hand atop the wood and looked out at the endless ocean around them. "I have loved sailing from the very first," she offered in a rush of words. "There is something so freeing yet calming about the lack of visual obstruction. Although I would not wish to be so isolated while alone, on a ship as fine as this, and with such a large crew, there is nothing to mar the joy. Lord and Lady Masterson must be very proud of your successes."

The sound of his father's title had the customary effect of making his hackles rise. He shook off the tension by rolling his shoulders back. "Pride is, perhaps, not the word I would use. But they are certainly aware of my endeavors."

Jessica glanced at him. The nervousness revealed by her quick speech was also evident in the way she worried her lower lip between her teeth. Though neither of them had yet to acknowledge the memory of that long-ago night in the Pennington woods, the recollection was wedged between them, more pervasive because they avoided addressing it. He wished to. God, how he wished to. There were so many questions he wanted to ask her.

45

Instead, he redirected her back to a topic they could both be comfortable with. "I agree the wide ocean is like a blank slate. The possibilities and mysteries of it are endless."

Her smile was lovely. "Yes."

"How is your family?"

"Very well. My brother is at Oxford now. Hadley is quite pleased, of course. And my sister has become a hostess of some renown. She will be most helpful to you once you return to England."

"She wed the Earl of Regmont, did she not?"

"Yes. I introduced them on the eve of my wedding, and the meeting led to a love match, as horribly unfashionable as that is."

He couldn't resist. "A night to remember."

"And your family?" A soft blush tinged her cheeks. "How do they fare?"

"As expected. My brother Albert—Lord Baybury now— has yet to produce an heir, a fact that disturbs Masterson greatly. He fears I may one day inherit the dukedom, which would be his worst nightmare realized."

She shot him a castigating look. "Nonsense. It is difficult for everyone when there is a failure to conceive. Certainly, it is distressing for Lady Baybury as well."

The sympathy in her tone clearly sprang from a deeply rooted place, which reminded Alistair that six years of marriage had not produced a child for Jessica, either.

He swiftly changed the course of discussion. "I cannot recall the time of year Tarley took you to Calypso, but the weather now is tolerably hot. On occasion, there are brief spates of afternoon rain, but sunshine swiftly follows. Most find it quite delightful, and I trust you will as well."

Her mouth curved in a way not meant to be seductive, but he found it so. "You navigate through difficult conversations with remarkable aplomb."

"A necessity in many business transactions." He glanced at her. "Are you surprised? Impressed?"

"Would you like me to be?"

"Absolutely."

One perfectly arched brow rose. "Why?"

"You exemplify the epitome of social grace. One can only think highly of those who receive your approval."

Her expression was wry. "You grant me more credit than I deserve."

Turning slightly, he faced her and leaned casually into the gunwale. "Then allow me to say that *I* would be most pleased to earn your esteem."

Jessica tipped her parasol in a way that shielded her face from him. "You are doing a fine job so far."

"Thank you. However, do not fault me for trying harder."

"You are trying quite hard enough."

Her prim tone caused his smile to turn into a grin.

This time, she was the one to change the subject. "Is the water around the island as clear as I remember?"

"Clear as glass. From the shore, one can watch the fish swim. And there are places along the coast where the depth is shallow for a great distance, far enough that one can wade out to the reefs."

"I will have to find one of those places."

"I'll take you."

The parasol lifted then. "Surely your obligation to Michael does not extend that far."

"I would enjoy nothing more." The moment the words were out, he knew he'd revealed too much in the huskiness of his voice. It couldn't be helped. Not with the image of her wet and playful in the water, with her skirts lifted high enough to bare slender ankles. Perhaps shapely calves . . .

"I believe I've had enough sun today," Jessica pronounced, stepping back. "It was lovely speaking with you, Mr. Caulfield."

Alistair straightened. "I will be here for the next several weeks," he teased, "if you should like to share the sun again."

As she glided away, she spoke over her shoulder. "I will keep that in mind."

The soft note of flirtation in her tone sent a surge of satisfaction through him. It was a small victory, but he'd long ago learned to take whatever he could.

4

As Jessica enjoyed another surprisingly delicious evening meal in the great cabin, she glanced repeatedly across the table at Alistair Caulfield. She couldn't help marveling at the man he had become. He easily held his own against the formidable, and much senior, captain. The ship's surgeon—a man who'd been introduced only as Morley—also deferred to him in a manner beyond that of employee to employer. Both men seemed to admire Alistair and respect his opinions. In return, he spoke to them as equals, which impressed Jess very much.

As she had the night before, she endeavored to ease the flow of conversation by directing it toward topics the gentlemen were most conversant with. Presently, they were discussing the slave trade, a subject she knew was a heated one in some circles. At first, Caulfield hesitated to expound upon his views and the manner in which he supplied labor to his plantation. But when Jess showed interest, he indulged her. She remembered how she'd once derided the ease with which he deviated from established mores, but now she appreciated that trait in him. Neither her father nor Tarley had ever discussed business or political matters in her presence. Caulfield's willingness to do so emboldened her, giving her the courage to broach areas she would never have otherwise.

"Do most plantations still rely on slave labor?" she asked, well aware that the abolition of the slave trade had not abolished slavery itself.

The captain tugged on his beard. "Like pirates, a law of the land won't change a trader's ways. The Preventative Squadron is too small as yet."

"Are pirates a problem for you, Captain?"

"They're a plague on all ships, but I'm proud to say no ship under my command 'as ever been boarded."

"Of course not," she said with conviction, which earned her a beaming smile from Captain Smith. She turned her attention to Alistair, steeling herself for the impact the sight of him would have. The effort was made in vain. The effect of his comeliness on the female senses did not lessen with time or exposure. "Is Calypso reliant on slave labor?"

Alistair nodded. "Most plantations remain dependent upon it."

"Including yours?"

He leaned back in his seat. His lips pursed before replying, as if he had to contemplate his answer before offering it. She appreciated his circumspection, a trait she had not attributed to him before now. "From a business perspective, slavery is cost effective. From a personal standpoint, I prefer to have individuals working for me who desire to do so."

"You are evading my question."

"I do not use slaves on *Sous la Lune*," he said, watching her in a way that indicated an interest in her reaction. "I use indentured servants. Mostly Chinese or Indians. I do have several Negroes under my employ, but they are free men."

"Under the Moon . . ." she murmured, translating the name of his plantation. "How lovely."

"Yes." His smile held a secret. "Call me sentimental."

Gooseflesh swept over Jess's arms. Once again, he seemed to reference that night in the Pennington woods. But if so, he was not going about it in the manner she would have expected. His tone was warm and intimate, not mocking or laden with indiscreet suggestion.

But why would such a lewd incident hold sentimental value for him?

Caulfield lifted his glass to his lips, his gaze lingering on her over the rim. His cool blue eyes held such appreciation, she felt it on her skin as she would the rays of the sun.

Jess reconsidered her own view of that night. The act he'd been engaged in had been obscene, and for so long she had thought only of that aspect. Yet in those moments when their gazes held, there had been ... *something else* as well. She couldn't understand it, nor could she explain it, which was part of what frightened her. If someone were to describe the incident to her, she would be appalled and find nothing positive to attach to it. But it had happened to her, and her subsequent discussion with Tarley that night had changed her life irrevocably. She'd been incited into recognizing unknown needs and given the tenacity through desire to make those needs known to the man she'd wed. The six years of her marriage had been precious to her as a result. Perhaps Alistair had gained something, too? She hoped to muster the courage to ask him one day.

"Why did Tarley continue to use slaves if there were alternate means available?" she asked, needing to find something less personal to focus on.

"Do not think ill of him," Alistair replied. "He was not directly responsible for the oversight of Calypso. There is a foreman and steward who handle such details, and they act in the best interests of their employer."

"They act in the interests of profit."

"The two are one and the same, are they not?" He leaned

forward and gave her a hard look. "I pray you appreciate that. Ideals are all well and good, but they will not feed, clothe, and keep you warm."

"*You* utilize other means," Jess argued. It did not sit well with her to think that her gowns, jewels, sprightly curricle, and a multitude of other luxuries had been purchased at the expense of the labors of enslaved men. She knew well what it felt like to be powerless and at the mercy of the whims of another.

"My other business interests afford me a bit more license."

"So I am to understand that ideals are bought with coin? Those who have enough are provided the means, while those who do not must—in effect—sell them for gain?"

"Unromantic, perhaps," he said unapologetically, "but true."

There he was. The young man who would accept any wager and take coin for stud servicing. She had wondered where he'd gone and now saw he hadn't gone anywhere at all. He had simply acquired some polish to disguise the rough edges.

"Most enlightening," she murmured, taking an overly large swallow of wine.

As soon as she was able, Jess excused herself and headed directly toward her cabin. She traversed the passageway with as much haste as decorously possible.

"Jessica."

The sound of her given name in Alistair's deep voice was enervating. She waited until she reached her door before halting and facing him. "Yes, Mr. Caulfield?"

As he had the night before, he took up all the space in the narrow hallway. "It was not my intent to upset you."

"Of course not."

Although he looked composed, the sudden rough raking of his hand through his inky dark hair suggested otherwise.

"I do not want you to think ill of Tarley for the decisions he made that helped to provide for you. He was not a fool; he took the opportunities presented to him."

"You misunderstand," she said evenly, feeling a rare exhilaration. As with Benedict, she did not fear reprisal for speaking her mind to Alistair. "I do not fault common sense, practicality, or even well-intentioned avarice. It is being underestimated that is bothersome to me. I know well enough not to weaken my interests, even for the sake of my higher sensibilities. However, I may renegotiate Calypso's contract with you to gain the funds to acquire indentured servants. Or I may find that purchasing my own ship and crew will be more profitable in the long term, thereby freeing up funds in that manner. Or perhaps increasing the production of rum is a matter I should look into. In any case, it's possible I can find the means to have ideals, if I so desire."

His eyes glittered in the dim light of the flashlamps. "I am duly chastened, my lady. I was under the impression that you meant to sell Calypso, in which case your questions pertained to the past and not the future."

"Hmm . . ." She remained skeptical.

"I once underestimated you," he admitted, clasping his hands behind his back. "But that was long ago."

Jess could not check the impulse to ask, "What altered your opinion?"

"*You* did." He flashed his infamously wicked smile. "When faced with the choice of fleeing or staying, you stay."

The sharp pang in her chest caused her shaky courage to flee. She turned to open her door, but paused to look over her shoulder before she entered her cabin. "I have never underestimated you."

Alistair bowed smartly. "I suggest you don't start now. Good night, Lady Tarley."

Once inside her cabin, Jess leaned into the closed door and willed her heart to stop racing.

Ever prepared, Beth had a damp cloth waiting. As Jess pressed the coolness against her cheeks, she saw the knowing look in the abigail's eyes. She turned and presented the row of buttons fastening her gown.

One person who could see right through her was enough for the night.

Hester had just arranged the last white plume in her upswept hair when her husband entered her boudoir in a state of partial undress. His cravat hung undone around his neck, and his waistcoat was unbuttoned. Regmont was freshly bathed and shaved, if his damp hair and shadow-free jawline were any indication. He was undeniably handsome with his honey-hued hair and robin's egg blue eyes. Together they formed a striking golden couple—he with his boundless exuberance and silken charm, and she with her mantle of reservation and faultless deportment.

Regmont jerked his head toward her abigail, Sarah, who was smoothing out minute wrinkles in the new blue gown Hester intended to wear. "I was hoping to see you in the pink with lace. It's ravishing on you, especially with my mother's pearls."

She met the maid's gaze in the mirror and nodded, ceding to her husband's wishes. The alternative was an argument best avoided.

The abigail quietly and efficiently exchanged the dresses. After the pink gown had been laid out on the bed, Regmont dismissed the servant. Sarah paled and looked miserable as she left the room in haste, no doubt fearing the worst. Although there was a pattern to the escalation of Regmont's moods, violence defied reason.

When they were alone, he cupped Hester's shoulders and nuzzled the tender spot beneath her ear. As his fingers kneaded, she flinched and he noticed. Stiffening, he looked at the spot he touched.

Hester watched him in the mirror, waiting for the remorse to cross his expressive features. In that respect, he differed from her father. Hadley never regretted his actions.

"Did you receive my gift?" he whispered, gentling his touch over the darkening bruise marring her right shoulder blade.

"Yes." She gestured to where it sat on the vanity in front of her. "Thank you. It's beautiful."

"But pales in comparison to you." The movement of his lips tickled the shell of her ear. "I don't deserve you."

She often thought they deserved each other. For all the times Jess had interceded on her behalf and taken the brunt of their father's fury, it had been her due to take it while Jess had found at least temporary peace during her happy marriage. It was the saddest sort of irony that Hester had once thought she and Regmont had a precious affinity because both of their childhood homes had been marred by paternal abuse. They understood the scars left behind and the particular traits a child acquired to survive, but she'd learned other traits seeped into the characters of those who suffered while too young. An imprint was left on the soul, manifesting itself in ways not readily evident. As was said, an apple does not fall far from the tree.

"How was your day?" she asked.

"Long. I spent the whole of it thinking of you." He urged her to turn and she did, sliding carefully around on the small vanity stool so that the mirror was to her back.

Regmont knelt before her, his hands moving to clasp the back of her calves. Laying his head in her lap, he said, "Forgive me, my darling."

"Edward." She sighed.

"You are everything to me. No one understands me the way you do. I would be lost without you."

She touched his damp hair, running her fingers through it. "You're not yourself when you drink spirits."

"I'm not," he agreed, rubbing his cheek against her bruised thigh. "I can't seem to control myself. You know I would never deliberately do anything to hurt you."

They kept no liquor in any of their homes, but he easily found it elsewhere. By all accounts he was a jovial drunk, a most entertaining and amusing fellow. Until he returned home to her, where the demons plaguing him resided.

She felt the wet of his tears soak through her chemise and pantalettes.

He lifted his head and looked at her with reddened eyes. "Can you forgive me?"

Every time he asked her the question, it became harder to answer. He was most often the perfect husband. Kind and thoughtful. He spoiled her with gifts and tokens of affection, love letters and favorite treats. He listened when she spoke and remembered anything she admired. She'd learned swiftly to be very careful with what she voiced a liking for, because he would attain it for her by whatever means necessary. But there were times when he was a monster.

There was still a part of her that was madly in love with the sweet memories they'd created in the infancy of their marriage. Yet she hated him, too.

"My dearest Hester," he murmured, his hands sliding up to the ties at her waist. "Allow me to make restitution. Let me worship you, as you deserve."

"My lord, please." She circled his wrists with her fingers. "We are expected at the Grayson ball. My hair has already been arranged."

"I will not disturb it," he promised in the low seductive tone that had once been capable of luring her into carnal depravity in carriages and alcoves and anywhere else they could find a modicum of privacy. "Let me."

Regmont looked at her with slumberous eyes. He was passion flushed and determined. When it came to his amorous inclinations, "no" was not an answer he accepted. The few times she'd attempted it, unable to bear the thought of his hands on her again even in tenderness, he had drunk himself into furies that made her regret denying him. Then he'd take her anyway, excusing himself with the orgasms he wrung from her. After all, he reasoned, she must have been willing if she'd enjoyed it so much. She almost preferred the pain of his fists to the humiliation of her own traitorous body.

Her pantalettes were wriggled out from under her, then slid over her stocking-clad calves and removed completely. His large hands cupped her knees and urged them apart. His breath caressed the flesh of her inner thigh.

"So pretty," he praised, parting her with questing fingers. "So soft and sweet and as pink as a seashell."

The Earl of Regmont had been a gazetted rake before offering for her. He'd acquired more sexual skill with his hands, mouth, and cock than any man should have a right to. When he unleashed those talents on her body, it always betrayed her. No matter how determined she was to be angry for the sake of her own survival and mental wellbeing, he was more stubborn than she. Minutes or hours, it didn't matter.

He proved his mastery over her again now, fluttering the pointed tip of his tongue over her clitoris. She vainly fought against the pleasure with closed eyes, gritted teeth, and hands clenching the edge of the upholstered stool. When the inevitable climax shuddered through her, tears sprang to her eyes.

"I love you," he said fiercely.

What did it say about her, that she could experience pleasure from the touch of a man who brought her such pain? Perhaps her father's legacy was more clearly revealed by her private life than her public one.

Regmont began his sensual assault again, urging her to lean back and open herself more fully. As he pushed his tongue inside her, her mind retreated into a darkened space separate from her body. A small blessing, that. But a welcome one.

5

"*Sail O!*"

Beth looked up at the deckhead as if she could see through it to the sudden burst of activity thundering above. "Lord, what's the meaning of that?"

Jess set her book aside with a frown. It was midafternoon, and she had remained in her cabin to contemplate her growing fascination with Alistair Caulfield. It was rather frightening, this slow careful exploration of a man she was undeniably attracted to. A man so far removed from the life she had been raised to lead that she couldn't see how he would ever fit into it beyond transient pleasure. This fascination could prove dangerous, considering her most valuable asset was her reputation.

Not that she could ever be any man's mistress, even if she possessed the reckless nature required. Her experience with flirtation and seduction was limited to nonexistent. She'd been promised to Tarley before her presentation. She had no notion of how one managed clandestine sexual liaisons. How many were conducted while standing in gazebos? How many forbidden lovers passed one another at public events without a look or smile or modicum of affection? How could such an interaction be anything but tawdry? She couldn't imagine not feeling cheapened by such careless experiences.

In the passageway, the stomping of feet and barked orders gave weight to the sense that something was amiss. The sound of a heavy object being rolled across a deck further raised her concerns.

"Cannons?" Beth asked, with eyes wide.

Jess stood. "Stay here."

Opening the door, she discovered a ship in chaos. The passageway was clogged with sailors pushing past each other as some went above deck and others came below.

She shouted in an attempt to be heard. "What's happening?"

"Pirates, milady."

"Dear God," Beth muttered while peering over Jess's shoulder.

"The captain assured me he has never commanded a ship that has been boarded by pirates."

"Then why the panic?"

"Being prepared is not a sign of defeat or fear," she pointed out. "Would you not rather have the pirates see us willing and able to fight?"

"I'd rather they not see us at all."

Jess gestured at the crate of claret. "Have a drink. I will return shortly."

Thrusting herself into the swarm of seamen in the passageway, Jess moved with the upward tide of bodies until she reached the open deck. She spun about, looking for another ship, but saw nothing but sea. However, at the helm of the *Acheron,* she discovered a sight that took her breath away— Alistair steered the vessel, looking very much like a pirate himself. Sans coat and waistcoat, he stood on the quarterdeck with legs planted wide and a cutlass strapped around his lean hips.

She was riveted by the sight of him. The wind whipped

through his dark hair and billowed through the voluminous linen of his shirtsleeves. The dangerous, reckless air about him caused her heart to race.

He saw her. Something fierce passed over his features. He shook his head, but he might as well have beckoned her to him.

Maneuvering through the roiling crush on the deck, Jess was breathless by the time she reached him. He caught her by the wrist when she came close enough, yanking her to him.

"It's too dangerous up here." Somehow, his voice carried over all the noise without his seeming to yell. "Go below and stay away from the portholes."

Looking out across the ocean again, she shouted, "I do not see any pirates. Where are they?"

Before she knew what he was about, he had pulled her in front of him. She stood between the wheel and his body. "Too close," he answered.

Yes, he was. "What are you doing?"

He spoke with his lips to her right ear. "Since you intend to converse with me under hazardous circumstances, I must shield you."

"That isn't necessary. I'll go—"

A boom caused her to jump. A moment later, a cannonball hit the water behind them, sending water splashing high into the air.

"Too late." His frame was rigid against her back, hard as stone but sun warmed. "I can't risk you."

Every breath he took gusted across her ear and sent tingles coursing down her spine. It seemed impossible that she should become aroused while on display for so many strangers, but there was no denying the tautness of her nipples, now aching from what seemed to be a sudden chill in the breeze sweeping over her muslin bodice.

Alistair's arm hitched, pressing her more tightly against

him. Her breasts spilled over his forearm. Behind her, she felt the undeniable evidence of his physical response to her.

All that stood between her and Alistair Caulfield—noted scapegrace and careless disregarder of Society's esteem—were a few layers of material. She wished there was nothing between them at all. She missed the feel of a man's larger, more powerful body over her, *in* her . . .

A year alone and a flirtatious, handsome man had made her a wanton.

Dear God . . . a year. *The date.* As the significance of the month and day struck her, her body stiffened. Only a year tomorrow since Tarley had passed. Yet here she was, pressing her derriere against a man who could have no honorable intentions toward her, and all the while she was thinking it had been seven years since she'd felt so . . . vibrant. Her desire felt like such a betrayal. She was the widow of a fine man who had given her the kind of peace and security she'd never dared to dream about. A man who had truly loved her. Why, then, did she feel so connected to the rakehell behind her? And fascinated in a way she'd never been with her darling husband.

Sensing the change in her bearing, Alistair queried, "Jessica?"

A sailor shouted directly to her right, jolting her. His coarse voice echoed through her one good ear, making her intensely aware of the chaos around them. Every yell and cry, every thud and crash reverberated through her.

Another boom followed by the splash of a too-near cannonball.

Panic welled. She struggled against Alistair's restraining grip. *"Release me."*

His grip slackened immediately.

She ran.

"Jessica!"

Her chest heaved as she darted around the industrious

crew and protruding capstans. Not since before she'd wed Tarley had she been plagued with an attack of panic of such magnitude. She was bombarded with memories of her father shouting . . . her mother's cries . . . shattered glass . . . the whistle of a switch . . . the report of a gun . . . her own whimpers of distress . . . Her recollections blended with the bustle around her into a barrage of sound and sensation she couldn't absorb. The commotion pounded against the one ear that could process sound, leaving her unbalanced. Off-kilter.

Reckless in her haste, Jess stumbled through the seamen in her way and increased her pace, desperate to return to the safety of her cabin.

Alistair slept fitfully and rose before the sun. He went on deck to work with the crew, needing an outlet for the aggravated energy that made him so restless.

Jessica had declined to take her evening meal in the great cabin the night before. And as the sun set on the new day, she had yet to appear.

What had possessed him to grab her as he had? What little progress he'd made since setting sail had been ruined in a few brash moments.

He knew the fault lay entirely at his feet. With the wind in his face and excitement all around, his blood had been hot before she appeared, and once she had, everything had coalesced into the irresistible urge to wrap himself around her and hang on.

He'd wanted to pursue her when she fled, but he couldn't leave the helm. His disappointment in not seeing her at supper had been fierce. She enlivened the table with her skilled deportment and quick wit. Her forthrightness was a delight, and he relished watching how easily she enchanted the other men at the table.

He was debating the merits of seeking her out when her

maid appeared on deck. The abigail's dark hair was covered by a frilly cap, and a sturdy woolen shawl was wrapped around her shoulders. She waved at Miller, who gawked in the manner of besotted youth, then moved to the gunwale to gaze at the sea.

Alistair crossed the distance between them and greeted her.

She gave a quick curtsy in reply. "Sir?"

"I pray your mistress is well. She was sorely missed last night. If there is anything she requires, please do not hesitate to ask."

She offered a reassuring smile. "There's no 'elp for her, I'm afraid. 'Tis a year to the day since 'is lordship 'urried on to 'is reward."

"Tarley's death is what ails her?" He frowned. Jessica had left the deck so abruptly the afternoon before . . . surely he'd had some part in that distress?

"She just needs some time alone, I think, sir. She dismissed me and means to retire early. Everything will look brighter on another day."

Giving a brief nod, he turned away. His jaw was clenched tight enough to pain him.

Bloody hell, he was jealous of a dead man. Had been envious for many years. Ever since he'd followed Jessica out of the Pennington woods and watched her seduce the very proper Viscount Tarley into satisfying the craving *he'd* roused in her. He had woken her passions, but Tarley had the right to sate them. The thought that history might have repeated itself yesterday . . .

Had the lush melting of her body against his made her hunger for Tarley?

Growling softly, he moved to the companionway and descended the stairs. He reached her door, ensured there were no witnesses, and then walked straight in.

He came to an abrupt halt. His brain processes stopped

altogether. The sight greeting him stunned him to the point that it took a long moment to remember to close the door. But when the realization came to him, he did so quickly. One last look in the passageway before the portal swung closed assured him no one else had been granted the view shredding his innards to ribbons.

"Mr. Caulfield," the object of his obsession purred. "Did no one teach you to knock?"

One long, slender, very *bare* leg stretched out over the rim of a copper slipper tub. Jessica was flushed from the heat of the bathwater and too much claret . . . if her slurred words, lack of modesty, and the bottle on the stool beside her were any indication. Her hair was piled haphazardly atop her head, giving her a disheveled, recently tumbled look embodying every carnal imagining he'd ever had about her. He was more than satisfied with the lush figure on display for him. She had lovely peaches-and-cream skin, breasts fuller than he'd pictured, and legs longer than he'd dreamed.

Bloody hell, his decision to indulge her by storing extra barrels of water for bathing had been a stroke of genius.

As his inability to speak drew out, Jessica arched one brow and asked, "Would you care for a glass?"

Alistair walked over to the stool with as much aplomb as he could muster with a raging cockstand. He collected the bottle, then drank straight from it. There was little remaining. And as excellent a vintage as it was, it failed to dull the sharp edge of his hunger, which was aggravated by his new vantage—he could see every inch of the front side of her.

Her head tilted back, and she looked up at him with slumberous eyes. "You are notably comfortable witnessing a lady's toilette."

"You are notably comfortable being witnessed."

"Do you do this sort of thing often?"

Discussing past lovers was never wise. He certainly was not going to begin now. "Do you?"

"This is a first for me."

"I'm honored." He moved to one of the chairs at the table and wondered how best to proceed. The territory was unfamiliar to him. Yesterday, he'd pushed too far too soon. He could not afford to make a similar mistake today, and yet he was presented with a naked, inebriated, uninhibited woman he had been lusting after for years. Even a saint would be sorely pressed for restraint, and God knew he was far from saintly.

As Alistair sat, he noted the case of claret by the foot of the bed. The quantity spoke of a woman who occasionally sought oblivion. It troubled him to think she'd been so attached to Tarley. How could he compete with a specter? Especially one who had so perfectly suited her in ways Alistair never could.

"Are you preparing to join us for supper?" he asked in as casual a tone as he could manage.

"I shan't be joining you." Jessica leaned her head back against the rim and closed her eyes. "And *you* should not be joining me in my cabin, Mr. Caulfield."

"Alistair," he corrected. "So ask me to leave. Although you should have someone here to assist you. Since your maid has been dismissed for the evening, I would be happy to make the substitution."

"You learned of my solitude and pounced straightaway. You are so reckless and impetuous and—"

"—apologetic about the upset you experienced yesterday."

She sighed. He waited for her to explain. Instead she said, "My reputation is very important to me."

Although it wasn't said, he understood the implication that it was not a concern they shared. "Your good name is important to me, as well."

One gray eye opened. "Why?"

"Because it matters to you."

That lone, assessing eye might have been disconcerting if he hadn't been determined to be completely honest with her. With a nod, the eye closed again.

"I enjoy the feel of your gaze on me," she said with surprising candor. "That enjoyment is quite distressing."

He hid a smile behind the rim of the bottle. She was an honest drunk. "I enjoy looking at you. I always have. I doubt I could change that. You are not alone in this attraction between us."

"It has no place in either of our lives."

Stretching out his legs in front of him, Alistair said, "But we are not in our lives now. Nor will we be for the next few months, at least."

"You and I are very different individuals. Perhaps you think my paralysis that night in the Pennington woods hints at some deeper, more intriguing aspect of my character, but I assure you, nothing of the sort exists. I was confused and mortified; there is nothing of note beyond that."

"Yet here you are. Traveling alone a great distance. Not by necessity, but by choice. I find that very intriguing. Tarley bequeathed you a source of great income. Why was he so determined to see you not merely taken care of, but exceptionally wealthy? In doing so, he provided you with the means to go in any direction you choose, while also forcing you to conduct business on a large scale. He shielded you with one hand, while pushing you into a new world with the other. I find that intriguing also."

Jessica drank the last of the wine in her glass and set it on the stool where the bottle had previously been. Sitting up, she wrapped her arms around her bent knees and looked at the door. "I cannot be your mistress."

"I would never ask you to be." He draped one arm over the tabletop, his focus narrowed to the wet curl adhering to the pale curve of her back. He was hard as a poker, throbbing and on display due to the tailored fit of his breeches. "I want no arrangement with you. I do not want to be serviced. What I desire is your willingness, your needs, and your demands."

She turned those big gray eyes on him.

"*I* want to service *you*, Jessica. I want to finish what we began seven years ago."

6

Alistair could see Jessica considering his suggestion.

"I cannot fathom how it is," she said at length, "that I am having this discussion with you, today of all days."

"Is that why Tarley settled Calypso on you? Because he wanted to preserve you as his? Because he wished to leave you with no excuse to turn to a man to look after you?"

She turned her head and rested her cheek on her bent knees. "He was too dear a man for such selfishness. He told me to be happy. To love again. To make my own choice this time around. But I am certain he was thinking of marriage, not an affair with a man who dallies about promiscuously."

Alistair's hand tightened on his glass, but he wisely held his tongue.

"Men have so much more freedom," she said on a long-suffering sigh.

"If freedom is what you seek, why marry again?"

"I have no intention of doing so. What purpose would it serve? I do not need the support, and since I am barren, I have nothing to offer men of suitable station."

"Financial considerations are valid ones, of course. But what of your needs as a woman? Will you deny yourself the pleasure of a man's touch forever?"

"Some men's hands give nothing but pain."

He knew she could not be speaking of Tarley. The rapport between them had been evident to one and all. "Of whom do you speak?"

She moved. Gripping the rim of the tub, she rose from the water like Botticelli's Venus. Dripping wet and unashamedly bare. Her hands ran over her full breasts, then across her abdomen, her gaze following her own touch. When she lifted her head to look at him, his breath seized in his lungs. It was a siren's look she gave him. One full of heat and longing and hunger.

"By God," he said gruffly, aching. "You are beautiful."

He was in a riot of lust, half mad with the need to spread her beneath him and sate the damned spurring longing that had haunted him far too long.

"You make me feel as if I am." One slender leg lifted over the edge of the tub. The sinuous invitation in her movements wasn't lost on him. It seemed drink also roused her passions.

"I can make you feel a great deal more."

Her nipples were a soft rose hue and luxuriously long. Puckered by the chill of air on wet skin, they begged for the attentions of his mouth and hands. He stroked his tongue deliberately along the curve of his bottom lip, teasing her visually with a physical enactment of the thoughts smoldering in his mind. He could please her to madness. Sex had been one of his trades, and he was damned good at it. If she but gave him the chance, he could ruin her for other men. He was determined to do so.

She did not fail to register his intent or to assess his condition; the color of her blush deepened. Looking at her towel and robe, she seemed to consider whether or not she wanted to retrieve them.

If he could, he would help her with that, if only to restore some semblance of his sanity by covering her. But he couldn't move. His body was not his own. Every muscle was tense and straining, while his cock hung heavily between his thighs.

"You see how much I want you," he said hoarsely.

"You have no shame."

"I would be ashamed if I didn't desire you. I wouldn't be a man."

A faint smile curved her lips as she reached for the folded towel. "Perhaps it was inevitable, then, that I should want you as well. Every other woman is susceptible. It would be curious if I was not."

His smile came with a host of wicked intentions. "Then the only question remaining is: what will you do about it?"

Jess paused with her fingers curled into the towel. It was madness that she should be standing before Alistair Caulfield without a stitch on. She did not recognize herself or the way she felt—uninhibited, greedy, empty.

What would she do *about it?* It was a sign of her ignorance that she hadn't considered *doing* anything at all. However, faced with the choice of taking action or not, she realized she had power. She hadn't thought of her fascination with Alistair in terms of balance of power at all. She had, in fact, felt quite powerless.

She released the towel and faced him. "If I wanted you to touch me, where would you begin?"

He set the bottle on the table and sat up with what appeared to be some discomfort. She could imagine why, considering the size of the erection so prominently tenting his smalls and breeches. "Come here," he said in the rich deep voice she was enamored with. "I'll show you."

She wavered, her first steps not quite steady. Whether that was from the wine or her own nervousness, she couldn't say.

He was impossibly handsome. Irresistibly so. He lounged

in the insubstantial chair like a sleek panther, all restrained power and suppressed violence. The muscles of his thighs were clearly defined, reminding her of his strength, which had always captivated her. It was all too easy to imagine how his body would work on a woman's . . . on *hers* . . .

A shiver moved through her as she remembered the sight of his strong hands gripping the gazebo post.

"I can warm you," he murmured, reaching out to her.

He heated her simply by looking at her. "I fear you are too much for me."

"In what way?"

With her eyes on the bulge in his breeches, she answered, "In every way."

"Allow me to prove you wrong." He beckoned her with a rather arrogant crook of his finger.

She looked at her glass, wishing it wasn't empty.

"I have the bottle here," he reminded. "Bring your glass and I will pour what remains of it."

She decided to forgo the wine but take everything else on offer. It was a conclusion hastily reached, and she rushed to him before her mind could be altered by sobriety or common sense. Knowing he could make her forget everything but him, she hurried to feel his hands on her and lost her footing on the polished wood sole. Her wet heel slipped, sending her into an ignoble tumble.

He stood so swiftly to catch her, she barely registered his movement. All she knew was one moment the sole was racing up to meet her, and the next she was flattened against Alistair's large, hard body.

"Fortunate that you left the glass behind," he teased, but his voice was whisky-rough. His blue eyes were dark as sapphires.

For a moment, Jess was at a loss for what to do. Her mind was too engaged by the feel of his body against hers and the smell of his skin.

He sat and draped her over him. "Damned if you haven't made me weak in the knees."

At eye level with him, she was riveted by the fierceness of his gaze. For lack of something wittier, she said, "I've made you all wet."

"It's my turn to perform a like service for you."

The licentiousness of his reply made her laugh.

One dark, winged brow rose. "Do that again."

"Not wise. It could have been painful had you not been so agile." Thoughts of his agility had a now predictable effect.

"Not the fall," he said wryly. "The giggle."

Her chin lifted. "I think not. I do not giggle on command."

Alistair's fingers fluttered along her rib cage. Tickled, she writhed and laughed.

He quit as quickly as he'd begun. "No more of that. Any further wriggling on your part will take this farther than I intend while you're impaired."

She realized his erection was pressing rather insistently against her thigh. The understanding that she'd been rubbing against that part of his anatomy made the blood rush to her head, which increased her intoxication.

"We are being very naughty," she pronounced.

"Not nearly naughty enough, but I intend to address that. Hold tight." He pushed to his feet and crossed to the bed. Setting her down on the edge of the mattress, he urged her to lie back, then sprawled beside her with his head propped in his hand.

The change in position affected her immediately, thickening her blood and slowing her ability to reason. She felt more naked on the bed than she had while standing. Her arms crossed her breasts.

His smile was warm and very amused. He stroked a finger across the back of her forearm, sending tingles racing through her body. "Wouldn't you rather touch me, than yourself?"

The thought was extremely tempting. "Where?"

"Anywhere you like."

Exhaling audibly, she lifted one hand to cup his cheek. His skin was whisker-coarse due to the hour. She liked it. A sweet warmth moved through her before she realized what she was doing.

His smile faded, and he grew very tense. Alarmingly so.

She pulled away abruptly. "Clearly I do not know how to conduct an affair properly."

After a sharply drawn breath, he pulled her hand back to where it had been. "Affairs are meant to be improper."

"But not romantic," she argued. "I will endeavor to touch you with only consummation in mind."

Alistair rolled to his back and laughed. He continued to laugh until she took his former position by lying on her side. His amusement was catching; she stared down at him with a smile.

"You succeeded beautifully," he said finally, his eyes still crinkled at the corners. "That is singularly the most unromantic utterance I have ever heard."

Jess felt silly, but accepted for her silliness. It was lovely being encouraged to be herself.

He reached up and cupped her cheek as she'd done to him. The tenderness behind the gesture was a surprise delight.

"Do you like that?" he asked.

"It's very sweet."

"I thought so, too, when you did the same to me. Why don't we agree to do whatever feels natural to each of us?"

Lowering her head, she licked her lips and moved to kiss him. She saw the understanding of what she was about move through his eyes. Once again, he grew very still. Expectant. Watchful. He gave her the lead in the approach, but when their lips connected, he took over. Snaring her nape with his hand, he adjusted the fit of her mouth, his lips opening under hers with barely tempered hunger.

Jess gasped as she fell into him, the lone support of her arm giving way. His lips were firm, but soft; his skill evident, but restrained. Where Tarley's kisses had been reverent, Alistair's were laced with sheer carnality. There was a wicked decadence to the way he tasted her. The approving groans, bouts of sudden fervency followed by savoring licks, and the gentle movements of his lips made her mad for a deeper connection.

Canting her head, she tried to take what she wanted. Surprisingly, he allowed her to. His touch at the back of her neck did not restrain her. It kneaded, as if he couldn't help but touch and was restraining himself to an innocuous part of her anatomy.

As if she would or could protest a roving exploration.

She turned her head to gulp down much needed air. The tender pressure of his fingertips spread outward from that one relatively innocent place, creating the phantom feel of his fingers running down her spine and between her legs. "Alistair . . ."

His given name slipped from her lips with remarkable, breathless ease. He reacted to it abruptly, rolling until she was once again on her back and he loomed over her. As he took her mouth, his hand ran down the length of her torso, stroking along her waist and coming to rest at her hip. He gripped her hip bone with a clenching of his palm, nowhere near painful but more than enough to relay his fervency. That telltale grasp excited her, made her feel powerfully feminine and seductive.

Her hands lifted to his hair, pushing into the thick tresses, gripping the strands by the root and tugging—a returning message to him that she was feeling equally passionate. The slow, deep thrusts of his tongue into her mouth so perfectly mimicked what she wished would happen between them that she grew slick and hot between her legs, the sensitive flesh of her sex swelling and throbbing.

She arched upward, pressing her aching breasts into the embroidered silk of his waistcoat. His grip on her hip tightened, pinning her down.

"Easy," he crooned, caressing her as if gentling a skittish mare. "I have you."

"Not yet," she breathed, feeling as if her body was no longer her own. "Not enough."

Alistair's mouth moved to her jaw, then to her right ear. "Let me take care of you."

"Please."

His lips slid along her throat, sucking soft enough to be felt but not enough to mark her. The sweet greediness of his mouth on her skin burned across her nerve endings in delicious torment. Her fingers spasmed in his hair, her toes pointing as he kissed across her collarbone. He made her feel more intoxicated than the wine had, while also heightening her senses. It was the best and worst sort of madness.

"Please what?" he asked, his breath gusting over the pebbled tip of her breast. He watched her as his tongue flicked lightly over her nipple. Dark satisfaction burned in his gaze when she cried out and clung to his shoulders. The velvet of his coat was soft beneath her touch, reminding her that he was completely clothed while she was completely bare.

She found the dichotomy delicious. It made her feel wanton and unabashed, two descriptors that had never been applicable to her before. "Please touch me."

"Where?"

"You know where better than I!" she cried, trying to tug his head to her breast, but unable to overcome his greater strength.

"I will," he promised in a low tone. "I will know your body better than anyone ever has, better than you. But for now I am still learning. Tell me what you like and how you like it."

Arching her shoulders back, she lifted her nipple to his mouth in flagrant offering. "There. More."

Alistair bared his teeth in a look of such feral pleasure only a fool would call it a smile. He wrapped one hand around her breast and squeezed with just enough pressure to make her want more. "With my hand?"

"With your mouth." It was the claret that gave her the courage to be so bold, and even with the added bravery, she closed her eyes against the overpowering feeling of vulnerability.

She felt the humid warmth of his exhale the second before his lips wrapped around her. The sound that left her was so raw and needy she could not believe she'd made it. Then his tongue curled around her nipple and his cheeks hollowed on a drawing pull she felt all the way to her womb, and she no longer cared what desperate sounds she made.

Lifting her leg, she wrapped it around his boot-clad calf and moved sinuously beneath him. He'd slid beneath her skin seven years ago, and he was finally relieving the itch he had left behind.

His talented mouth lifted from her, leaving her bereft.

"Lie still," he ordered gruffly. His face was flushed and his eyes bright, almost feverishly so.

Alistair was as lost to the lust as she was. Emboldened by his tenuous control, she offered a woman's knowing smile. "Make me."

7

Alistair was riveted by the woman beneath him. She burned too hot to be the same icily reserved girl he used to follow with his gaze. Whether it was the claret or her passion for him, he didn't care. He was damned grateful. Still, if she continued to writhe against him, he wouldn't have the wherewithal to stop himself from fucking her raw, a step he would prefer to take when she was fully sober and in complete possession of her mental faculties.

"Make you," he repeated finally, as her self-satisfied smile widened and she tested him again with another seductive wriggle. "And how would you suggest I go about doing that?"

The slight marring of a wrinkle between her brows ruined the image of worldly seductress. She had no idea, he suspected. He, however, had a delicious one in mind.

"You could exhaust me," she said finally, biting her lower lip. The gesture did not hide the avid manner in which she awaited his response.

Too much for her, she'd said. He had a niggling suspicion that once she'd lost all her reserve in bed, he might have a devil of a time keeping up. And God knew his appetite was ravenous when it came to her. The thought brought beads of perspiration to his forehead. How in hell was he going to walk out of this room with his cock as swollen as it was?

"Untie my cravat," he ordered.

"Umm . . ." she purred, clearly pleased with the notion of removing clothing from his person. Her hands went to the knot at his throat and began working as efficiently as her inebriated state allowed.

For his part, he was delighted that the thought of undressing him was such a pleasing one for her. He could not have chosen a better location to conduct their affair than Jamaica, where the humidity and heat lent themselves well to wearing as few clothes as possible.

When she pulled the length of linen from around his neck, he caught her wrist and grinned. Bending his head, he took her mouth, distracting her with a lush kiss. Her fervent response damn near distracted him as well, but he managed to turn her body to lie parallel on the mattress instead of perpendicular, and to secure the cravat to one of the headboard posts. Even when he caught her wrist and raised it above her head, she didn't struggle. Instead she groaned into his mouth and sucked on the tip of his tongue, jolting him so violently he felt a scorching drop of pre-ejaculate bead on the tip of his cock. She tasted of wine and lust and sin, and he wanted to drink her down. Every drop. Suspecting that even if he did, his thirst for her would go unquenched.

Only when the knot tightened around her slender wrist did reality return to her. She gasped and yanked her mouth away, her neck arching to see what he'd done. Kneeling, he caught the other wrist and secured it before she could protest.

"What have you done?" she cried, her gray eyes wide with excitement but tinged with wariness.

"Made you lie still, as you challenged. You should know how I am in regard to challenges."

She spoke in a small voice. "I am not certain I like this."

"You will." By necessity, he'd perfected the fine art of bestowing carnal pleasure. It had not been in his best interests to satisfy a woman to the extent that her interest in him was appeased; satiety alone would not have kept him afloat. No, what he'd needed was to create an addiction to his touch and the bullish stamina of his cock. He had focused single-mindedly on pursuit of that knowledge, all the while telling himself that he was honing his skills for Jessica. That he was not ruined for her, but more valuable. It was an argument he did not fully believe, but he couldn't allow himself to think of the alternative—that she might reject him for his past.

Alistair renewed his attention to her breasts. He could swear he'd never seen a more beautiful pair. They were the perfect size for her slender frame, emphasizing the petite curvature of her waist and balancing lusciously curved hips. What a travesty the latest styles were, with their high waists and straight, shapeless skirts. While he'd imagined her having a magnificent bosom, the reality was a treasure found. It would take a great deal of time to become indifferent to such charms. He would have to do his best to extend her stay on the island. When she left him, he wanted to be certain he'd had his fill of her. He could not return to having the damnable cravings that had plagued him the past several years.

He straddled her. Taking a moment to enjoy the view of her upthrust breasts and taut belly, he debated where to begin.

"Alistair," she breathed, tugging at her bindings.

Brute that he was, he found that slight show of struggle profoundly arousing. Combined with the breathless way she said his name, he was sorely pressed to hold himself back for sobriety's sake. He reached down and adjusted the fit of his breeches over his cockstand.

Jessica stilled, eyes riveted to the movement of his hands. She licked her lower lip, and he wondered if she'd ever taken a man in her mouth before. Today was not the day to progress to such bedsport, but one day . . .

Made as comfortable as he could expect to be under the circumstances, Alistair decided to continue working his way down her torso. He set one hand on either side of her head and lowered his chest to hers. He slid his knees back so he was levered over her. His thighs pinned hers down, while the spread between them allowed his aching cock to be cradled between her closed shins.

He settled in to feast, his mouth seeking and embracing the nipple he hadn't yet had the pleasure of attending to. She hissed as he suckled, the tip of her breast puckering against his tongue. She was so sensitive, and very responsive. The sounds she made as he licked the tautened peak were a bawdy delight. For all the civility she displayed in public, in bed she was unrestrained in vocalizing her pleasure. The sounds she made, the low moans and sharp pants, became aphrodisiacs.

This was the woman he'd seen in the Pennington woods. *This* was the lover he had dreamed of and hungered for until his gut ached.

Cupping her other breast in his hand, he kneaded the swollen flesh, relishing a surge of pure masculine satisfaction. Her body readily responded to his ministrations. He knew she had to be slick and hot between her legs, and he moved lower to see the evidence of her desire with his own eyes. He needed to taste it on his tongue and feel her tremble against his lips.

He licked into her navel, eliciting a shiver that racked her slender frame. She was ticklish, which he loved. He could make her laugh at will, and he was delighted. The sound was warm and throaty. Seductive. A bit rusty from lack of use, but he intended to rectify that. Her laughter came from the sensual woman inside her and not the chilly Lady Tarley who was the epitome of aristocratic hauteur.

Her belly quivered as he neared the patch of dark blond curls that shielded her sex.

Looking up, he met her gaze. "You like watching."

"And you like being watched. We have already established you are an exhibitionist."

Her prim and proper voice, tempered by panting, made him smile. "Only when you are the observer."

"I want to touch you."

"Why?"

"How will my memory linger with you, if I leave no imprint?"

Alistair responded by sliding one thigh between hers, parting her legs. If she thought they would have only this one indiscretion, she was sorely mistaken. But he thought it best not to put it in quite those terms yet. "You may have your way with me another day."

Before she could reply, he lifted and draped one sleek thigh over his shoulder. Her sudden intake of breath increased his anticipation. Her eyes were half-lidded, her kiss-swollen lips parted, her chest heaving with rapid breaths. She lifted her hips to his mouth in bold provocation. The act was not new to her. Alistair both envied Tarley and admired him. The viscount had possessed everything a man could want—he'd retained respectability and popularity, embraced an unfashionably happy marriage, and enjoyed a satisfying sexual life with a socially esteemed wife many believed was above such base needs.

Alistair could offer her so little of what Tarley had had. Aside from coin and a head for business, there was nothing to recommend him beyond his passion for her and his skill in bed. And perhaps his lack of shame and willingness to treat her as an equal.

Jessica lifted her other leg and rested it on his shoulder. She arched one brow in silent challenge.

"Temptress." He parted the plump folds of her sex and

ground his hips into the bed, attempting to relieve the nearly unbearable throbbing of his neglected cock. "You are even perfect here."

Pointing his tongue, he traced the delicate folds and crevices before circling the distended tip of her clitoris. She was as wet as he'd hoped, the silken skeins of her lust clinging to the petal-soft skin, her body's primitive plea for a hard cock to fill her.

"Yes . . ." she breathed. "*Yes.*"

Alistair fluttered his tongue over the clenching opening, groaning as her response became more frantic. Tilting his head, he licked into the tender, spasming tissues. Her thready moan enflamed him, urged him to a faster pace, until he was fucking her fiercely with his tongue. Ravenous, he ate at her, drinking in her taste and the sounds she made. She began to plea for him to finish her, then to threaten him with reprisal. He pushed farther, to the point where she began to promise him anything if only he would ease her torment.

There was a great deal he could do with such a promise.

He licked along her drenched slit, then pushed her over the edge with a lush, open-mouthed kiss to her clitoris. With parted lips and gentle suckling, he stroked over the bundle of nerves with the flat of his tongue. The first flutters of climax rippled through her, and at the height of her extremity he slid two fingers deep into the tightness of her too-long neglected body.

The headboard creaked as Jessica fought against her restraints, her delicate inner muscles tugging at his pumping fingers in time with the workings of his mouth. He tongued her mercilessly, giving no quarter, spurring her to another orgasm before the first had fully eased its grip. She screamed when she came again, her mouth pressed to her biceps to muffle the sound.

He growled as she shuddered, as hungry for her pleasure

as he'd ever been for his own. Pushing a third finger in with the others, he worked the tight flesh. The thought of how snugly she'd hold his cock increased his frenzy. Raking the edge of his teeth lightly over the hard knot of nerves, he pushed her into another climax on the heels of the second. He kept at her until she came again, driving her hard and fast. Relentless in his need to own her desire completely.

"No more . . ." she pled hoarsely, shrinking away from his avid mouth. "Please . . ."

Alistair lifted his head with reluctance, his drenched fingers pulling free of her quivering flesh. Wiping his mouth on the inside of her thigh, he slid his shoulders out from under her lax legs and then his body straight off the bed.

"Where are—" she began as he stood.

"I can't stay." He reached to free her wrists and retrieve his cravat. As the knots loosened and she pulled her arms down to her sides, he saw her wince and understood the cause. She'd pulled tight against the bonds with every wrenching orgasm, stretching muscles unused to such abuse. He reached for her shoulders and massaged them, pressing gently but firmly into the sore muscles to alleviate their discomfort.

"Don't leave," she said.

"I must."

"I want . . ." She swallowed. "I want you."

"As was my intention." Dear God, it would kill him to walk out of the room with her begging for sex. But it would be far more torturous to face regret from her on the morrow. Cupping her nape, Alistair kissed her hard and quick. "You were magnificent."

She caught his wrist before he straightened. "Why must you go?"

"I need you unimpaired. I want no self-recrimination or faulty memory between us." He began to wind his cravat around his neck. "Ask me again when you are temperate, and it will be my great pleasure to oblige you."

Jessica pushed up onto one elbow. "If you stay, I will pay you whatever you desire."

Alistair froze. A dousing with icy water could not have cooled his ardor faster. Worse, a sharp pain pierced his chest like a blade, twisting mercilessly until he staggered back from the bed to distance himself from his tormentor.

He spun away and tied his cravat with a hasty, sloppy knot. "Good evening, Jessica."

It was only by the grace of God that no one was in the hallway as he fled the cabin.

It was after midnight when Michael vaulted down from his carriage in front of the impressive three-story, columned entrance to Remington's Gentlemen's Club. He ascended the wide steps to the watered-glass double doors, which were held open by footmen liveried in black and silver. As he handed his hat and gloves to the waiting attendant, he noted the curricle-sized floral arrangement gracing a massive round table in the circular, domed foyer. Lucien Remington had long been acknowledged as a man of impeccable taste, and his establishment remained the most exclusive in England in part due to his willingness to continuously update the décor. Remington did not follow prevailing inclinations in design; he set the standard for them.

Directly ahead was the gaming area, which was the center of all business. From there, one could access the stairs to the fencing studio, as well as the many lovely courtesans and their private rooms. The lower floor accommodated boxing training and lessons. To the left was the bar and kitchen. To the right was Lucien Remington's office.

Michael crossed the black-and-white marble floor to the gaming area, then moved beyond that to the great room.

The smell of leather and fragrant tobacco helped to settle nerves kept on edge since his visit with Hester the day before.

At least that was true until the Earl of Regmont caught his eye.

Seated in one of a half dozen wingbacks surrounding a low table, Regmont laughed at something said by Lord Westfield. Also in his circle were Lord Trenton, Lord Hammond, and Lord Spencer Faulkner. Since Michael was well acquainted with all but Regmont, he felt no qualms about taking the remaining open seat.

"Good evening, Tarley," Ridgely drawled while signaling for a footman. "Seeking escape from all the debutantes eager for your new title?"

"I have an increased appreciation for the toll the Season can take on an unwed peer." Michael ordered cognac from the waiting server, as did Regmont. The rest of the men at the table had half-full libations.

"Here, here," Westfield concurred, lifting his glass in toast.

"Better you than me," Lord Spencer said. As a second son, he enjoyed a less hunted existence; the other men at the table had wives.

Studying Regmont, Michael wondered why the man was out carousing with friends when he should be home making amends to Hester. It was difficult for Michael to restrain his tongue after witnessing her unhappiness. If she had been his, he would ensure nothing marred her existence.

The footman returned with two glasses of cognac. Regmont took an immediate drink, which brought Michael's attention to the hand the earl wrapped around the bulbous glass. The knuckles were swollen and bruised.

"Engaged in fisticuffs lately, Regmont?" he asked, before taking a drink himself.

To his knowledge, the earl was a genial fellow who was well liked by one and all. Lauded by women for his golden good looks, easy smile, and ready charm, Regmont made it very difficult for Michael to like him. The man seemed too blithesome, to the point of lacking any real substance. But perhaps that was what made him suit Hester, who'd once been the merriest and most enchanting woman anywhere. She was still the latter and would always be to Michael's mind.

"Pugilism," Regmont replied. "An excellent sport."

"Agreed. I enjoy it myself. Do you practice here at Remington's?"

"Often. If you're ever of a mind to practice together—"

"Absolutely," Michael interjected, relishing the possibility of championing Hester, even if he was the only one who knew his motivation. From the sight of Regmont's knuckles, the man preferred training sans mufflers, which suited Michael perfectly in this instance. "Name the time and date, and I will be there."

"I shall require the betting book," Lord Spencer called out, deliberately drawing attention.

Regmont grinned. "Spoiling for a fight, are you, Tarley? I've had such days. I would be happy to oblige you now."

Michael sized the earl up. Regmont was shorter than he and lean, with sinewy musculature that lent well to the prevalent fashion of snug tailoring in breeches and coats. Michael had the advantage in height and arm reach. Settling more comfortably into the butter-soft leather, he said, "I would prefer an early-afternoon bout. We'll enjoy ourselves more if we are both rested and free of drink."

The betting book was brought to the table, which lured an audience.

An unusual appearance of somberness possessed Regmont's features. "Excellent point. This day next week, then? Three o'clock?"

"Perfect." An anticipatory smile curved Michael's lips. He reached for the betting book and placed a wager on Alistair's behalf with odds on himself.

It was just the sort of bet his friend would appreciate.

8

Jessica awoke the next morning with what she likened to a megrim. The hard, insistent throbbing in her head and the horrid taste in her mouth made her ill. She fought nausea valiantly but lost. She was also highly aware of the tenderness between her legs. Memories from the day before made her blush, then cringe. How could she have been so undisciplined? And inflamed enough by Alistair's skillful hands and mouth to make a crude suggestion that led him to leave her bed in anger?

She knew the answer—Alistair Caulfield had always had a unique effect on her. She was not herself with him; she was a woman she did not recognize. And it was difficult to determine whether or not the woman she became with him was one she wanted to be. How could it be appropriate when she felt so conflicted, embarrassed, and guilty?

Beth, as always, was a godsend. The abigail arranged for a pitcher of warmed water for washing and secured a plate of hard biscuits, which eased Jess's stomach malaise considerably. By evening, she felt well enough to eat more substantial fare and to face Alistair. Too familiar with a man's anger to seek him out alone, she chose to take the evening meal in the great cabin along with the other gentlemen. As the meal progressed and Alistair studiously avoided looking at or speaking to her whenever it was possible to do so, she felt she'd made the best decision. However, the rift between them pained her.

But, perhaps, it was for the best. If she'd soured his interest, she would be spared the turmoil that had plagued her since their reacquaintance. What he had asked of her—to be her lover—was so far outside the scope of her own acceptance of herself that she could hardly credit it. Yet clearly he was more than capable of piercing her defenses. The restraint she desired would have to originate with him. And although she regretted achieving the aim by wounding him, abstaining from further interaction was better for them both.

Jess excused herself as soon as was seemly. As the men rose to their feet, Alistair said, "Would you grant me the honor of a walk around the deck, Lady Tarley? Perhaps the fresh air will revive you further?"

Nervous, she managed a small smile with her acceptance. They left the cabin along with the first mate, who vacated the passageway quickly, leaving them alone.

She paused beside her cabin door. "Let me fetch a shawl."

"Here." He unfastened the row of buttons securing his tailcoat.

She protested, averting her gaze from a direct view of his chest. "A gentleman is never seen in his shirtsleeves!"

His answer was delivered in a biting tone. "You are the only individual on board who will take offense, Jessica, and after what transpired yesterday, I find any attempt at modesty tiresome."

Her heart tripped over the austerity of his features. He had the glint of the devil in his blue eyes and a determined set to his square jaw that warned her he would not be easily deterred. How intimate she was with that look of barely restrained temper! It never portended well. "Perhaps we had best speak some other time."

"There are issues that need airing. The sooner, the better."

Despite her misgivings, Jess obliged him and set off toward the companionway. A warm weight settled on her shoulders as he dropped his jacket neatly over her. Immediately the smell of him teased her senses, stronger now, with an underlying unique masculine scent. Alistair was a virile male, and her body stirred with vivid memories of the evening before.

They took the stairs up to the deck. Caulfield paused in a space unshadowed by the masts and rigging. With an impatient and imperious gesture, he waved away the two sailors who worked nearby.

He loomed over her in a manner that made her both aroused and wary. He was flagrantly handsome. His classical bone structure took well to the moonlight that bathed him in silver. He could have been an ancient heroic statue come to life except for the vitality charging the air around him. Alistair Caulfield was alive in a way Jessica had never been.

"I don't know how to do this," he growled, raking a hand through his hair.

"Do what?"

"Dance around the truth, pretend things are not what they are, and use formality as a shield."

"Formality is indeed like dancing," she agreed softly. "It creates a known pattern of steps to follow that allow two disparate people to spend a length of time together with some purpose. It creates an avenue upon which strangers can travel together."

"I am not interested in dancing at the moment, or being strangers. Why did you stay?"

"Beg your pardon?"

"Don't be coy. Why did you linger in the woods that night?"

She clung to the lapels of his coat from the inside, holding the two halves tightly together. Not because it was cold, but because she felt too exposed. "You asked me to stay."

"Oh?" His mouth took on a cruel curve. "Will you obey all my commands?"

"Of course not."

"Why did you obey that one?"

"Why not?" she rejoined with lifted chin.

Alistair stalked closer. "You were innocent. You should have been horrified. You should have run."

"What is it you want me to say?"

He caught her by the elbows and lifted her up onto her tiptoes. "Have you thought about that night since then? Did you ever think of it when lying with Tarley? Has the memory haunted you?"

Jess was dismayed by how close to home he struck with his questions. "Why is it important?"

One of his hands lifted and cupped her nape, angling her lips to a position suiting him. His words puffed hot and damp over her mouth. "I remember every second you stood there. The rise and fall of your breasts as you panted. The feverish brightness of your eyes. The sight of your hand at your throat as if you forcibly held back begging little whimpers."

"There are witnesses around us," she whispered furiously, trembling with fear and excitement. She was astonished to be responding amorously to his rough handling. She, of all people, should not find such attentions thrilling. It horrified her to think some part of her mind might have been trained to seek such treatment.

"I don't care."

Torn by her confusion, she spoke harshly. "Your brutish lack of charm may be sufficient for some women, but I assure you, I am not amused."

His hands fell away so quickly she stumbled. "Sweetheart, it's more than sufficient for you. You look as hungry for me now as you did then."

She winced. Something dark and tormented passed over his features; then he turned away with a smothered curse.

He spoke over his shoulder. "I have attempted to forget that night, but it's impossible."

Jess looked away from his rigid back, allowing the crisp misty breeze to blow over her face. "Why does the memory trouble you so? You have had my discretion."

"For which I have long been grateful." In the periphery of her vision, she saw him shove his hands into the pockets of his satin breeches. "You have avoided me in the years since. Why, if what transpired was of no importance to you?"

"I know something of you I should not know. It made me uncomfortable."

"*I* made you uncomfortable," he corrected. "I still do."

Whether consciously or no, a part of Jess recognized the feeling of being hunted. She sensed the turbulence of his desire and was frightened by it. Perhaps not so much because of his appetite, but because of her own.

Alistair rounded her, so that he stood before her and took up the whole of her vision. "The more you hold yourself aloof, the more determined I become to draw you out. Yes, you know something of me that exists only between us. We should be more accessible to one another because of that, not more distant."

"As accessible as I am now, engaging is such candid conversation?"

"As accessible as you were last night, without the excessive drinking. Although it was not our intention to cross the threshold we did seven years ago, it has been crossed and there is no turning back. I asked you to stay and you did not run. We shared a moment uniquely separate from our lives before or since. You clutch social mores, propriety, and rules of conduct around you as you do the shawls you wear, but we are beyond such barriers. Fate has conspired to bring us together at this time, and I, for one, am weary of fighting against it."

The possibility that they were fated to be lovers was somehow comforting, as if taking the decision from her hands freed her from responsibility for the inevitable consequences. It was cowardly to view it that way, yet the thought also gave her courage.

She inhaled and spoke in a rush. "I am sorry for what I said to you last night before you left. I-I wanted you to stay—"

"I whored for money," he interrupted harshly. "I need you to know why."

Once the words were out, Alistair felt a profound relief, swiftly followed by a high tension. Baring himself was something he avoided at all costs.

Jessica's head tilted to the side, causing one thick pale curl to glide over her shoulder. She fisted the lapels of his coat, and fine lines bracketed her lush lips. She'd recently lost a husband she'd cared for deeply, yet Alistair had pushed her to ignore that for his own selfish need of her. Even now, her pale gray gown spoke of lingering mourning. He deeply resented the reminder of a man whose pristine conduct and fine morals were aspects of character he could never compete with.

"Tell me," she coaxed. "Explain so I may understand."

He spoke before he dissuaded himself from doing so. "At the urgings of my mother, Masterson granted me a parcel of land in Jamaica. The property was notable only for its insubstantial size and dearth of viable crop. It came with no slaves, no buildings, and no machinery. My mother also saw to it that his lordship provided a ship, and he was able to find the least seaworthy vessel I have ever had the misfortune of laying eyes on. I was faced with the possibility of being a man of means, but with no funds with which to purchase any of what was required to make a success of it."

She exhaled audibly. "I cannot imagine facing such a daunting endeavor while knowing your livelihood rested on the outcome."

"You will never face it, thank God. But perhaps you can see how I was motivated to sell what skills I had at my disposal to earn the coin necessary to prosper."

"That is how you came to be known as one who would accept any wager."

Alistair nodded. "Any race, any odds. Anything pitting my talents against another's for gain. I am also fortunate enough to be attractive to women."

"Impossibly handsome," she agreed. "But you were so young then . . ."

"Yet old enough to know I couldn't afford to have ideals," he finished tightly. It was not a decision he lingered over. If ruthlessness was required to survive, he had no qualms about doing whatever was necessary. "And in some respects, my youth was an advantage. I was randy, energetic, and far from discerning."

The last was said with more defiance than he would have chosen to share, but he was on edge, his stomach knotted with the concern that she might find his past insurmountable. "I enjoyed it in the beginning. All the sex I could manage, which was considerable, with women who were worldly and confident in their pleasures. The first time I was offered an expensive gift, it was a surprise. I realize now that for some it was a way to assuage their guilt over fucking a man less than half their age, but at the time I saw it as a game; what could I wheedle out of them in return for doing something I was enjoying immensely? I was also learning astonishing secrets about women's bodies—how to read them and listen to them, how to drive them wild. There is an art to bestowing pleasure, and I realized I could master it, similar to any other skill."

"You were clearly an adept pupil," she whispered.

"Women talk a lot," he pressed on grimly, unable to determine how she was responding to his brutally frank revelations. "Especially about things they enjoy. As with anything, the more demand there is for an object, the higher the price that can be set for it. I realized how I could profit and recognized that I'd be foolish to turn away any avenue of income, considering what my circumstances were. And after a while, it ceases to matter how you feel about the business. You learn to master your body regardless."

"Well." It took Jessica an interminably long time to say more. Finally, she said, "I'm an idiot. It never occurred to me that you might not . . . *appreciate* the act. After all, Lady Trent is quite lovely—"

"Some of them were; some weren't. Some were lovely only on the outside. Regardless, when you sell something, it no longer belongs to you. You lose any right to refuse or deny anything, and if you want referrals and repeat business you dare not be too difficult or unaccommodating. Once I understood that I'd become a commodity to be used as required, whatever enjoyment I'd found previously was lost to me. It became a chore like any other, albeit a lucrative one."

"What of your family? Couldn't they have—?"

"I took the blasted ship and land given to me. My pride

was not enough to impede my acceptance of those. Believe me, if I could have turned to anyone for assistance, I would have."

Alistair waited for her to ask why he was unable to turn to Masterson, and wondered how he could reply when she did. Already she knew more of his sordid past than he would ever wish to share with anyone. To share it with Jessica—the one person who appealed to him in a manner that was more than skin deep—was torturous. He wanted to be the man she desired above all others, yet he was so far below the heights to which she should aspire.

"Then, you did what had to be done," Jessica said with a conviction that surprised him. "I can appreciate the need to become whatever is required to survive untenable circumstances."

How easily she dismissed his disclosure. He could hardly credit it.

He stepped closer, unable to bear the slight distance between them. "Would you have me still? Can you look beyond it? As much as I wish it were otherwise, my touch will sully you. But it will also pleasure you. Worship you. I want nothing so much as I want you."

"I accept you, Alistair. I do." Jessica inhaled a shaky breath. "But the rest . . ."

"Go on," he ordered gruffly.

"I am no better than the others who've used you for their own pleasure." Her eyes were big and dark, her lovely features betraying an inner torment. "I wanted the right to command you, as Lady Trent did, not for reasons of safety but because it excites me to think of it."

The blood rushed to his cock so swiftly, it altered the way he stood. Her honesty aroused him, as did the image of her seizing her own gratification through use of his body. "Jessica."

She moved suddenly, skirting him and moving to the gunwale where one hand curled around the polished wood with white-knuckled force.

Alistair followed, crowding behind her and setting one hand on either side of her. Her spine was painfully straight, her body gripped by high tension. He lowered his head and pressed his lips to her right temple. Somehow, he had to make her see how her upset revealed deeper feelings for him. "Is my subjugation what you want? Does the thought of coercing me to service you stir your blood?"

"No!" He felt her swallow hard. "I want you willing, but you overwhelm me. I need control—"

"You think I have any? What there is between you and me has never been safe, nor will it ever be. You have to accept our attraction for what it is, with all its faults and detriments, trusting that it will be worth whatever the costs may be."

"I don't think I can."

"Try."

Turning in his arms, she looked up at him. "Forgive me for my thoughtlessness. I just wanted you to stay. So much so that I spoke without consideration."

He caught one glossy golden curl and rubbed it between his fingers. "Never apologize for your desire for me. But let me be clear—I come to you without affectation. You cannot have Lucius, not ever. That man no longer exists, and he never existed for you."

At the time, he'd told himself he used his second name to protect his identity. In truth, it was self-preservation and a way to distance himself from the degradation of accepting money to fuck women who wanted things from him they couldn't get elsewhere without risk of scandal and scorn. Though some had wanted him for his face and body, a great many had wanted something else entirely. They'd wanted a lover known to take any bet . . . any risk . . . a man willing to do anything for coin. They felt less depraved knowing they'd bought the right to be as debauched as they pleased.

She nodded. "I understand."

Alistair pressed his forehead to hers, miserable at the thought of her wanting a side of him he couldn't bear to share with her. "You've never had him, you know. That night, the moment I saw you, it was just you and me. Lucius serviced Lady Trent. I was with you."

She exhaled in a rush. "Good. I don't want him. I realize now that in offering to pay you, I was asking for him. After you had been the one to . . . touch me. I'm sorry."

Jessica's eyes were clear and open, filled with sadness and regret. Perhaps a tinge of pity, which was the last damned thing he wanted her to feel for him.

"I will give you whatever you want. Freely. You have only to ask." Slipping his hand beneath the lapels of his coat, he cupped her hip. "Tell me the details of your imaginings."

"No!" The horror in her prim voice made him smile. "It's indecent."

He bent farther and licked the shell of her ear. "Trust," he reminded as she shivered. "I trusted you with a truth that could only reflect negatively upon me—"

"I don't fault you."

"Which means a great deal to me. Let me repay you. Tell me what you desire."

"You shouldn't be so familiar." She glanced around him at someone visible on the deck. "There is no privacy here."

"Can I come to you tonight?"

Alistair waited forever for her reply, which didn't come. Instead she grew more and more restless, fidgeting with his coat and shifting on her slippered feet. Afraid to push her too far too soon yet again, he backed away from her.

99

"My cabin is two doors down from yours on the opposite side of the passageway," he offered instead. "You can come to me."

She faced him with widened eyes. "I could never."

He smiled. Perhaps not, but the anticipation would be its own reward.

9

As she had every morning for the past fortnight, Hester awoke with the overwhelming need to cast up her accounts.

Rolling from her bed, she stumbled to the chamber pot and proceeded to do precisely that. The next hour until dawn was marred by more of the same.

"Milady," her abigail murmured. "I've set out some weak tea and toast."

"Thank you."

"Maybe if you tell his lordship you're with child," Sarah ventured softly, "he'll mend his ways."

Hester looked at the maid with tear-blurred eyes, her chest heaving from her exertions. "Tell no one."

"Until you give me leave, milady, I won't tell a soul."

Pressing a damp cloth to her forehead, Hester allowed her tears to flow unchecked. During the early years of her marriage, there was nothing she'd desired more than a child to complete the joy she'd found with Edward. But God was kinder than she knew by withholding His blessings. When the darker aspects of Edward's character became apparent, she'd begun to use sponges soaked in brandy to prevent conception. She couldn't bring an innocent into her household the way it was now. After all that she and Jessica had endured as children, how could she possibly subject her own child to such a life?

But Regmont was not one to postpone his lusts until expected evening hours, and fate had its own designs.

"If only you were here, Jess," she whispered, selfishly longing for a sympathetic and knowing ear to listen to and advise her. She'd suspected she was *enceinte* before her sister departed, but could find no way to share the news. Jessica was deeply pained by her barrenness. It was impossible for Hester to lament a pregnancy that would have brought her sister endless joy.

When Hester struggled to her feet, Sarah assisted her back to bed. Regmont slept on in his room, blessedly oblivious.

"I pray you tell his lordship soon," the abigail whispered, arranging the pillows for Hester's comfort.

Closing her eyes, Hester heaved a sigh. "I believe part of his affliction is me, and I don't know how to address that. Why else would the men in my life battle such demons?"

But when she saw Edward at the dining table a few hours later, her husband looked far from afflicted. Indeed, he looked extremely fit. His smile was bright and his spirits high. He kissed her cheek when she moved to pass him en route to her chair.

"Kippers and eggs?" he queried before walking over to the row of covered platters on the buffet.

Her stomach roiled. "No, thank you."

"You don't eat enough, darling," he admonished.

"I took toast in my room."

"But you join me for breakfast anyway." His smile was glorious. "You are too wonderful. How was your evening?"

"Unexceptional, but enjoyable all the same."

She almost dreaded these moments of normalcy. The pretense that all was right in their world, that no malevolence lurked in the darkness, that he was a wonderful husband and she a contented wife. It was like staring at a box one knew would burst open at some point and not knowing if the surprise would be terrifying or not. There was agony in the waiting.

Her gaze strayed and moved around the room. Their home was lauded by friends for its bright cheery colors, such as the soft cream and bright blue vertical stripes she'd used on the walls of the dining room. They'd purchased the town house just before their wedding; it was to have been a fresh beginning for both of them, a place free of any taint of the past. But now she knew how futile that hope had been. The taint was on them . . . *in* them, and they carried it with them wherever they went.

"I shared a drink with Tarley last night," Regmont said between bites. "He was seeking refuge from the debutantes. The strain of being hunted is beginning to take its toll, I suspect."

Hester looked at him. The tempo of her heartbeat changed, increasing inexplicably. "Oh?"

"I remember those days well. You saved me in more ways than you know, my love. I'm providing assistance to Tarley via a release of tension. He learned of my interest in pugilism, and we've agreed to a match."

Dear God. She knew well how swiftly Regmont could move and how relentless he could become. He couldn't tolerate losing; it exacerbated his already overwhelming feelings of insecurity. Her stomach knotted further. "A match? Between the two of you?"

"Would you happen to know how skilled he is in the sport?"

She shook her head. "He sparred with Alistair Caulfield in our youth. That's all I know of his interest. He and I were close once, but I've seen little of him since you and I wed."

"A wager easily won, then."

"Perhaps you might suggest he consider a less learned opponent?"

He grinned. "You fear for him, do you?"

"Jessica thinks very highly of him," she prevaricated.

"Everyone does, so I gather. No need for concern, love. It's all in good fun, I assure you." Glancing at one of the two footmen standing at the ready, he said, "Lady Regmont will take buttered toast and jam."

She sighed, resigning herself to eating whether she wanted to or not.

"You look pale this morn," he noted. "Did you not sleep well?"

"Well enough." Hester reached for one of the day's papers that lay on the table by her elbow. She was thrown unaccountably out of sorts by the thought of Michael fighting Regmont, especially when his motivation might be aggravation over choosing a proper wife. In that respect, she could be of more assistance than her husband. There was very little she didn't know about the women of the *ton,* from the most established matrons to the newest debutantes. Perhaps he would accept her help.

It would do her heart much good to see him content with his lot. He certainly deserved happiness.

Regmont set his silverware atop his empty plate. "I should very much enjoy squiring you about the Park this afternoon. Tell me you don't have other plans."

If she had, she knew to cancel them. When Edward wanted her time, he expected to have it. She was his wife, after all. *His.* Irrevocably owned until death parted them.

Looking up from her paper, she managed a smile. "A lovely thought, my lord. Thank you."

There might come a moment this day when she could share the news that she was breeding. Outside in the sunshine, surrounded by the peers he so wished to impress, might be the perfect time and place to present the opportunity of a new beginning for them both.

She hoped so. Maybe there was a miracle in that as well—sometimes, she still had hope. She couldn't afford not to have it. There was no other way out.

Miller knocked on Jess's cabin door shortly after one o'clock with a request for her to join Alistair on the deck.

Trying to pay no mind to the nervousness brought on by uncertainty, she followed Miller up the companionway stairs and into the open air. Her last discussion with Alistair under moonlight had been fraught with tension. His invitation to visit his cabin had lingered in her mind for hours after they parted. It was not an offer she could act upon, and she believed he knew that, but it hung between them now like a gauntlet thrown at her feet. There was a part of her—the part he incited into mischief—urging her to indulge, but her greater nature overrode such abandon.

What did he wish to say to her? In a relatively short acquaintance, a multitude of searing intimacies had passed between them. She was now completely preoccupied by thoughts of him, in a way she'd never been with anything or anyone else. Jess had difficulty understanding how he could so thoroughly engage her physically and then capture her mental faculties as well, but he had. Alistair had left it to her to decide what to do about it, while making it clear he would not desist. She doubted there was anything Alistair Caulfield wanted that he didn't eventually attain.

As they turned toward the stern, the salt air hit her back in a rush, awakening all her senses. Invigorated and anticipatory, she slowed at the sight of a large blanket spread across the deck, anchored at each corner by crates of cannonballs. It was covered with several pillows and a shallow basket brimming with food.

A picnic. At sea.

Alistair stood on the other side of the counterpane, waiting. He was perfectly dressed in buff slacks tucked into polished Hessians, tan-striped waistcoat, and brown tailcoat. His hair had been styled by the wind in a fashion resembling the way he looked after she ran her fingers through it.

As many women did, Jess thought him the handsomest man she'd ever seen. Exotically so. Blatantly seductive. More than slightly dangerous.

Delicious. She wanted to strip him to the skin, to appreciate the full impact of his powerful form without the impediment of clothing. She couldn't resist such thoughts now, with their desire for one another bared so openly between them.

It was impressive to see him on the deck of such a fine ship, surrounded by men who worked for him. She could scarcely recall the scapegrace who'd accepted every wager and lived on the fine edge of a hazardous margin. But she knew he was there beneath the flawless surface. Tempting her with wicked promises she knew he'd keep.

"My lady," he greeted her, bowing.

"Mr. Caulfield." She looked around the deck, noting how the dozen or more men about them kept their gazes carefully averted.

He gestured for her to sit, and she sank to her knees. He joined her, then dug into the basket, withdrawing a loaf of bread he tore in half. That was followed by a hunk of dry cheese and a quartered pear. He collected her portion in a large napkin and passed it over.

She accepted with a smile. "An impressive offering for ship's fare."

"Soon enough, you will pine for variety."

"Some might consider a picnic on a ship's deck to be a form of courtship," she pointed out, deliberately using a teasing tone. "It could certainly be considered romantic."

"My aim is to please." He flashed his infamous smile, and a tingle moved through her. How easily he charmed women when he wanted to, while keeping his tone so light as to take any intensity from his words. She couldn't decide if the practiced, noncommittal discourse was meant to soothe her nerves, or make her long for his usual fervency.

He ripped off a bite of bread with his perfect white teeth and somehow made the act of chewing arousing, too. And he seemed not to do it on purpose, which was in keeping with her belief that sensuality was simply innate to him.

Taking a small bite of the cheese, she looked out at the endless expanse of ocean. The sun sparkled off the water, and although the day was a cool one, she thought it quite lovely. All the anxiousness she'd previously felt around Alistair had altered into a different sort of awareness, one she savored for how alive it made her feel.

She'd been raised to maintain a certain distance between herself and others. That space had been easily established through her speech and deportment, and most men were swiftly discouraged by lack of progress. Alistair, however, was challenged by her demeanor. He would not allow her to withdraw, which forced her to acknowledge that she didn't really wish to. She wanted to be right where she was—on an adventure with an infamously wicked man.

And then there were the memories of what he'd done to her body. She'd shared similar intimacies with Tarley, and had had no difficulty facing him over a breakfast table in the morning. With Alistair, she found herself flushing often and without warning, her body heating and softening in welcome just from his proximity. Somehow, his touch seemed more intimate to her than even her own husband's. How was that possible?

"Did you sleep well last night?" he asked, drawing her attention back to him.

She shook her head.

"That makes two of us." He stretched out along his side with his head propped in the palm of his hand. He watched her with those brilliant blue eyes that saw too much. Those windows to the soul aged him, revealing a darkness that shouldn't be there in one still young. "Tell me what happened the other day when you fled from the helm. What were you running from? Me?"

Jess shrugged awkwardly. "There was so much noise and activity. I felt . . . off balance."

"Does the lack of hearing in your left ear contribute to that sensation?"

She looked at him with raised brows. In hindsight, she realized he always whispered in her right ear. "You noticed."

"Michael told me." His eyes were kind.

It was a topic she would never discuss. She was so violently opposed to even the notion of such a discussion that she resorted to speaking about other topics she wouldn't have otherwise. "I was not running from you."

"No?"

"Tarley has been gone only a year."

The arch of his brow mocked her. "And you honor his memory with chastity? For how long?"

"Exactly twelve months, apparently," she said dryly.

"You are ashamed of your desire for me. That won't sway me."

Ashamed. Was that the right word? It wasn't shame she felt. Confusion was more apt. She had been raised to live in a particular world under particular rules. An affair with Alistair moved her into an entirely new realm. Remembering his dance analogy, she would say she didn't know the proper steps and so was stumbling around. She'd been rigorously trained against stumbles and missteps, and found it extraordinarily difficult to forsake those hard-taught lessons.

"An affair isn't necessary," she began, "to enjoy sex. It's

certainly possible and respectable—albeit unfashionable—to find pleasure in the marital bed."

"Are you suggesting we marry?" His tone was dangerously low and sharply edged.

"No!" She winced at the rushed manner with which she'd replied. "I shan't be marrying again. To anyone."

"Why not? You enjoyed your first marriage." Alistair reached for a pear.

"Tarley and I had a rare affinity. He knew what I needed, and I knew what he expected. We were able to blend the two into a harmonious arrangement. It's highly doubtful I'd be as fortunate again."

"Meeting expectations is important to you."

Jess met his gaze. As always, there was something in the way he looked at her that challenged her to be more than who she knew herself to be. Challenged her to speak aloud the thoughts she rarely contemplated even in private. "When expectations are met, there is harmony."

Alistair's head tilted, considering. "To value harmony, one has to know disharmony."

"Can we speak of something else?"

There was a long pause, then, "Whatever you like."

She nibbled at her bread for a few moments, gathering her thoughts. Why did it always seem as if he could see into her? It was unfair when he was a mystery. "Was it your choice to pursue the path of enterprise you follow?"

"Why wouldn't it be?"

"You said your father acquired the plantation and ship for you. I wondered if you requested those things, or if you simply made do with the avenue Masterson provided."

He looked down at his hand. "I wanted nothing from Masterson, but accepting his largesse meant a great deal to my mother. I suggested sugarcane because I knew it would be profitable and that the distance inherent in the cultivation would be appealing to Masterson. I've been a source of displeasure for many years."

Jess remembered saying something similar to Hester long ago, and felt remorse for the cruel thought. She'd prejudged him by assuming he had no ambition or mind for business. She had dismissed him because of the order of his birth. Also, because she'd bristled at Hester's admiration. She could admit that now. Although Hester's praise had been offhand and merely conversational, it had roused envy in Jess and territorial feelings.

"Some fathers mean well when they express affection in harsh ways," she offered. "Their methods may leave much to be desired, but the intent is laudable." She didn't credit such lofty ambitions to her own pater, but that did not signify.

"By what basis would you know?" he challenged softly. "You have always been perfect. I have always been far from it."

"Perfection, if that's what you choose to call it, isn't effortless."

"You make it seem so." He held up a hand when she would have demurred. "Masterson's affection is for my mother. She is the sole reason he showed any generosity. I am grateful for that and even for the least of what he did for me on her behalf. For all the ill will between us, his love for her earns my appreciation."

"Why is there ill will?"

"When you share your secrets, I will share mine." Alistair's smile was devastating and soothed the sting of his refusal. "You are a very mysterious woman, Jessica. I would be best served by keeping you equally intrigued with me."

Jess chewed thoughtfully. His belief in her extraordinariness made her wish she was as remarkable as he saw her to be. Her tutelage had been so strict, and any deviation so strenuously punished, that she'd been certain anything note-worthy about herself had withered and died.

But Alistair made her wonder if she was wrong. He made her wonder what it would be like to be the sort of woman who was equal to a man as fascinating as he was to her. A man who was so darkly sensual and flamboyantly hand-some that women paid for the privilege of possessing him, if only briefly.

Her imagination ran away with the idea, inventing a past interesting enough to make her notable.

"I suppose I could tell you about my time in captivity with the maharaja . . ." she began.

"Oh?" A very wicked gleam brightened his gaze. "Please do."

10

Alistair's fascination with Jessica deepened with every day that passed, and he feared this afternoon's picnic might seal his fate. What would her fictional tale reveal about her? The mere fact that she'd conceived of the idea to begin with told him a great deal—she could be imaginative, adventurous, playful . . .

But he'd known she had hidden facets. He had seen a glimpse of this other side. More than anything else, it was that affinity—that recognition of another soul who retreated behind an affected guise to survive—which drew him to her. He could hardly wait for the day when she knew herself better. What a formidable woman she would become when she accepted and exploited her many hidden charms.

Her head turned, shielding her face from his gaze. "I was traveling with a Bedouin tribe. We were transporting salt slabs on camelback when our party was raided by a rival tribe."

Such an exotic setting for a woman best known for being a proper English lady. And a damsel in distress? He loved the story already. "What were you doing in the Sahara to begin with?"

"Escaping the winter chill."

"Were you frightened?"

"At first. I had no notion of what they would do with a female in such a hostile place. I was taken to an oasis and the tent of the sheik."

A captive. The tale grew spicier by the moment. "Were you bound?"

"Yes." There was a betraying hitch in her voice. "My wrists were."

He relished an inner smile. As much as she professed a desire to command him in sexual matters, it appeared she might also carry a desire to be commanded. It was a highly provocative thought. "What was the sheik like?"

"He was younger than I expected. Attractive."

"What did he look like?"

Jessica glanced at him with a mysterious smile. "You."

"Delicious," he murmured, pleased to know he'd been included in her whimsical tale. It might also be telling that Tarley was not, but he would have to hear more to be certain. Perhaps her impeccable husband would be the hero, rescuing her from the clutches of the lascivious sheik. "What did he say when he saw you?"

"He was the one who abducted me. Tossed me over his horse and took me away from everything I knew."

The parallels to reality seemed quite prominent to him—stretches of sand or endless ocean. Alistair rolled to his back. He tucked a pillow behind his head and stared up at the clear blue sky.

"There was food and flasks of wine," she went on. "The ground was covered by rugs that were littered with pillows. He asked me to join him in sprawling there. Much like what you and I are doing now. He removed the bindings on my hands, but I was still very wary."

"Why? He sounds like an agreeable fellow."

"He stole me!" she protested with amusement in her voice.

"Can't blame him for running off with you. It isn't every day a man finds such treasure in a barren landscape." He could draw parallels as well.

"So a man should just take what he wants?"

"If no one is hurt by it, why not?"

Jessica laughed, and he loved the sound. "You, sir, are incorrigible."

"As often as possible," he agreed.

"The sheik was, too, I'm afraid. I found him quite charming, but obstinate. Despite the number of times I warned him that I occupied a more rigid world than he knew and it would eventually intrude, he remained unconcerned."

"I like him already."

"Yes, you would." Jessica took a moment to eat.

"So what did you do?"

"You are a horrible person to tell stories to," she complained. "You won't allow me to reveal the details in my own time. Fortunately for me, the sheik was better behaved than you in that regard."

"What details were you telling him?"

"You persist after I point out the error of your ways?"

Alistair looked at her and found her studying him. Not his face, but the rest of him, which he quite enjoyed. "Persistence is a virtue."

"I believe it's 'patience.' Regardless, I wasn't telling him details. I told him stories."

"To distract him from his amorous interests? Like Scheherazade?"

"In a fashion." She looked down at her fingers, which were presently picking at her bread. "What else would we discuss? Drawing room etiquette or the stratagems of chess? Such things would swiftly bore a man of adventure."

"I'm certain anything you said would have been of interest to him," he rejoined. "Whether or not you said anything at all, he still would have had a splendid time just looking at you."

Her mouth curved. "Flattery comes easily to you."

"Feel free to practice your flattery skills on me at any time. Although I can't vouch for my ability to remain decorous if you do."

"What sorts of things do you prefer to be admired for?"

"Anything, so long as the admiration is sincere." He took another bite of the pear and knew there was no place else he'd rather be, which brought him an unusual sort of calm. For as long as he could remember, Alistair had felt pulled in many directions simultaneously. Ever on the lookout for possibilities and new avenues of income. Failure to be successful had never been an option.

Jessica's lips pursed in thought. "I would like to be admired for something I'm actually responsible for. It has yet to happen, but I hope to change that."

"Explain."

"How can I take credit for my appearance? My parents are responsible for that. How can I take credit for my deportment, when I could not carry myself differently if I wanted to?"

"Couldn't you?"

"I had no choice as a child, and now it is so ingrained I cannot imagine acting otherwise."

"No choice," he repeated. "We always have a choice—to do what others want us to do or to do what we want to do."

Her gray eyes were somber when she looked at him. "That depends on the consequences."

Alistair weighed her change in mood, knowing the waters of this particular topic were far from shallow. He also knew she wasn't yet willing to let him swim in them. Still, he couldn't resist an attempt.

"I had a friend at Eaton," he began, "who was probably

the most intelligent fellow I've ever come across. Not so much with his studies, but he was observant and quick to think. However, whenever I complimented him on his rare ability to scan for advantages and make swift use of them, he hurried to dissuade me. He lacked confidence, yet I couldn't collect why. Later, when I met certain members of his family, it became clear that his sort of mental acuity wasn't appreciated, which undermined Barton's personal esteem. His parents wanted to see high marks for his school work; everything else was useless in their opinion."

"I can sympathize."

"I'm sure you can, as there are similarities between you. Like Barton, you also make great effort to dissuade me from my high opinion of you. But you do not lack confidence, as he did. You aren't undermined by your peers, as he was. In your case, you don't value the traits in yourself that inspire admiration in others. Now you suggest it's because you acquired those traits under some type of duress. From what quarter? Your mother? Competition with your sibling?"

The look Jessica shot him was full of exasperation. "Are you always so curious? If so, is this level of interest applicable to everyone? Or only to women you wish to bed?"

"You are as prickly as a porcupine, and equally hard to grasp. I love it."

"You love a challenge," she corrected. "If I were pursuing you, you would feel different."

"Try me," he said, meeting her gaze. "Let's put it to the test."

"Another challenge. Or a wager. Irresistible to you." She popped the last remaining bit of bread into her mouth, then set to work arranging pillows to her liking. When she leaned slightly against them, using her elbow as a prop, he found the view quite charming. Relaxed elegance and artless beauty.

Choosing not to argue about the root of his interest, Alistair returned to an earlier point in the conversation. "So how will you distinguish yourself in the future? What plan do you have?"

"Perhaps I will manage Calypso well." She bit carefully into a pear slice. "I hope to prove myself worthy of the task."

"There is nothing for you to do. Tarley has an excellent foreman and a competent steward, as well as a superior agreement for the transport of goods, if I say so myself. The wheels are well greased and they turn without need for you to exert any effort."

When a shadow passed over Jessica's features, he realized his error. The truth of it was, he was alarmed by the prospect of her having no need for him, which might be the case if she wasn't hunting for a buyer. But that wasn't reason to dash her hopes. She wanted to tackle and conquer a task of heretofore untried scale. Regardless of how that impacted his access to her, he should support such a brave endeavor. Lord knew he admired it.

"That isn't to say adjustments cannot be made," he corrected quickly. "There is always room for improvement."

The look she gave him was both grateful and knowing. Though new to the game of seduction and sexual conquest, she was yet aware that he was making concessions to woo her. "I hope so. At the very least, I should like to keep it running smoothly."

He grinned. "Nothing intriguing about you, you say."

Jessica looked down at her hand and the large sapphire gracing it. "Maybe a little something," she conceded. "At least in your view."

"No other view matters." He would have selected a ruby for her. Red would suit the inner fire she kept carefully banked.

"Can you . . . *will* you, help me?" She looked up, her eyes veiled beneath thick lashes. "You started with nothing. I would expect you know everything there is to know about growing and selling sugarcane."

The surge of relieved triumph he felt was accompanied by a softer, warmer emotion. "Absolutely. Once you gain your bearings and feel settled enough, I can expand your knowledge. I wouldn't want to intrude too soon, but if you ever have any questions or difficulties, I would be honored to assist you."

"Thank you."

They ate in companionable silence for a time. While Alistair was content just to share a meal and a lovely day with Jessica, he noted that the set of her shoulders relaxed the longer he held his tongue. Which led him to wonder just how deeply she allowed people to know her. She evaded more questions than she answered. Altogether, it was clear that her upbringing had known moments of harshness, with "consequences" grave enough to mold her into a skin she did not wear comfortably.

He looked again at the sapphire wedding ring on her slender hand and wondered how well Tarley had known her. Most peerage marriages were shallow associations based on the mutual understanding that disruptive discussions would not take place. It was not unusual for spouses to touch upon only brief highlights of their separate daily schedules and delve not at all beneath the surface to discover how each other felt about any particular event or acquaintance.

Was there anyone in Jessica's life who shared her confidence?

"You had a dog," he remembered. "It was always with you."

"Temperance," she said with a note of wistfulness. "She passed away a few years ago. I miss her terribly. There are times when my skirts will brush my ankles in a certain way, and for a moment I forget and think it might be her."

"I'm sorry."

"Have you ever had an animal you were attached to?"

"My brother Aaron had a beagle I liked well enough. Albert had a mastiff that drooled a lake every hour. And Andrew had a terrier named Lawrence who was indeed a terror, which made us fast friends. Alas, by the time Lawrence was done ruining the furniture and rugs, Masterson had decreed there would be no more animals in our household. My poor luck to be the youngest and last in line."

Her smile was soft. "I suspect you'd spoil a pet."

He wanted to spoil *her,* lavish her with gifts, drape her nude body in jewels . . .

Clearing his throat, he said, "Does Lady Regmont also have a fondness for animals?"

"Hester has always been too busy to dedicate time to a pet. It is the rare day when she does not have a full schedule."

Alistair recalled how vivacious Hester had been during his long-ago acquaintance with her. "Michael was quite enamored of that quality in her. He, too, enjoys the companionship of many people."

"Everyone loves Hester." A breeze pushed a thick blond curl across her cheek, and she brushed it back. "It's impossible not to."

"Michael had eyes for no one else when she was in the same room."

"She can be the brightest light in any company."

He caught the wistfulness in her words. "You miss her."

Jessica sighed. "In many ways. She's altered a great deal in the last year. I am ashamed to say I don't know if the change was gradual or sudden. After Tarley became ill, I had little time to visit with anyone."

"Altered in what way?"

She lifted one shoulder in a helpless shrug. "I fear she might be ill. She has become quite thin and is often pale. There are times when there is a pinching around her eyes and mouth, as if she might be in pain. But when I've begged her to call for the doctor, she insists nothing is amiss."

"If anything is wrong, I am certain Michael will see to it in your absence. You can rest easy."

"With everything demanding his attention, I doubt he has time to see to himself. Dear man. He needs a wife to ease some of his burdens."

"Your sister still has the ability to garner the whole of his attention, which is why, I believe, he hasn't wed."

Her eyes widened. "Are you saying Michael has a *tendre* for Hester?"

"Has for years," Alistair said dryly. He knew well how consuming such an obsession could be.

"No," she breathed. "I can't credit it. He's never shown any signs of affection greater than friendship."

"And you have paid strict attention to be certain?"

She stared at him for a long moment, then smiled sheepishly. "I had no idea."

"Neither does Lady Regmont, which was the bulk of his problem."

"She did mention him once, when listing desirable qualities to be found in her future spouse."

"Oh? What did she say? Perhaps it might offer him comfort to know she finds him appealing in some regard. Then again, perhaps it would be torturous since there's nothing to be done about it now."

"She appreciated his congeniality, I believe." Jessica's eyes sparkled. "However, you possess the appearance she most admired."

"Flattering. Did you agree?"

"I lied."

His brows rose.

"In a fashion," she qualified. "I told her you were too young for me to assess in that manner."

Alistair clapped a hand over his heart. "Ho! The fair lady cuts me to the quick."

"Stuff," she scoffed.

"Youth does have its advantages. Vigor, stamina—"

"Impetuousness."

"Which can be delicious," he retorted, "when done properly. Since you admit to lying, you are confessing that you found me physically appealing even then. Why didn't you say as much to your sister?" Did she share nothing personal with anyone?

"I couldn't encourage her interest! I don't believe you two would suit. You would quickly overshadow her, I think."

"I would not have been receptive in any case. It would be very unwise for a man to court one sister while secretly pining for the other."

Jessica flushed. "You have never pined for anything. It's not in your nature. Besides, like Mr. Sinclair, you never once gave any indication of knowing I even existed."

"The same can be said of you in regard to me. Both of us appear to have been aware of each other, but you were promised to Tarley and I *was* too young. I had no notion of what I wanted to do with you beyond unrestrained fornication, and I was confounded by how to achieve that end. You are such a perfect, pristinely glorious creature. Rutting atop you in a frenzy of adolescent lust seemed obscene and impossible."

It was a testament to her growing ease in his company that she wasn't completely scandalized by his bluntness, as she certainly would have been mere days ago. "You appeared to have more skill and control in such matters when I bore witness to them."

"It would have been different with you."

Her blush deepened. She looked down at the food between them. "Perhaps if Michael had been more obvious or forthcoming about his feelings for Hester—not that she isn't remarkably happy with Regmont . . ."

"I avoid speculating on past possibilities. Life is what it is. Making the best of it takes energy enough. Pointless to waste any effort regretting what cannot be changed."

Jessica nodded as if she agreed, but her gaze was slightly unfocused, betraying the inward turn of her thoughts. "You act with the intention of not regretting your decision to do so," she murmured, almost to herself. "While I have always chosen not to act, so there would be no possibility of regret."

"Who is to say which approach is better?"

"I should like to try your way. At least for a little while."

Alistair looked up at the sky to mitigate any pressure his next words might exert. "It would seem to be the perfect time. You can reinvent yourself while away from home, and no one will be the wiser."

"*You* will know."

"Ah, but I won't tell a soul."

She wagged a finger at him, a gesture he found enchanting for its playfulness. "You are influencing me. Whether that is for my betterment or detriment remains to be seen."

"I know precisely what you need."

"Do you?"

"Freedom without censure." He sat up. "It does exist, and I can show it to you."

"Freedom and consequences go hand in hand."

"Yes. But is censure a consequence or simply a nuisance? Does it really matter what others think of you, if you have the means to ignore them?"

Jessica exhaled audibly. "I am beginning to care about what you think of me."

"I'm mad for you." Alistair reached for the bottle of wine protruding from the basket. "And I have liked all the sides I have seen of you so far."

"Both of us cannot flaunt convention."

"We can't?"

"Someone has to be the voice of reason. I designate you."

He laughed. "Do you?"

"We shall reverse roles. I will proceed without concern for consequences, and you will act with an eye toward propriety. You certainly will need the practice, since you intend to rejoin Society when you return to England."

Alistair was beyond intrigued with her bold suggestion.

"Come now," she prompted. "We both know you are well versed in how to break rules. The question is: can you follow them? Can you withdraw from an endeavor, goal, or desire simply because it would be scandalous to continue? Can you pass opportunities in order to avoid censure?"

"Can you break rules?" he rejoined. "Can you continue, even if doing so is scandalous? Can you risk censure to seize opportunities?"

"I can certainly give it my best effort." Her smile was brighter than he'd ever seen it. "Shall we wager to make my proposal more appealing?"

"Oh, it's appealing enough." The reversal of their roles introduced a host of wickedly wonderful possibilities. "But, as you know, I never walk away from a challenge. Twenty guineas?"

Jessica extended her hand. "Done."

11

"It's a lovely chapeau!" Lady Bencott exclaimed.

Hester stared at the monstrosity on Lady Emily Sherman's head and tried to decide whether Lady Bencott was being facetious or simply the victim of horrendous taste. Because Lady Bencott was widely lauded for her fashionable attire, Hester had to assume it was the former.

"There is a bonnet in the window," Hester offered. "I think it would be exquisite on you, Em."

Moving toward the front of the shop, Hester was acutely aware of how much she missed Jessica. Her sister's presence always enhanced shopping excursions, such as the one Hester had arranged today. Jessica had a way of keeping women such as Lady Bencott in line with a carefully worded chastisement that made its point in the most genteel of ways while leaving no room for reproach. That thread of steel in Jessica was a source of envy for Hester. She did not possess the same strength as her sibling. She was the conciliatory sort, quick to ease tensions and avoid conflicts, no matter the cost to herself.

Hester reached for the aforementioned hat perched so prettily on a stand, but paused when her gaze was caught by a figure outside. Bond Street was congested with pedestrians, as usual, and yet one form caught her attention and held it.

The man was tall and fit, elegant, with a horseman's thighs and shoulders requiring no padding. His dark green coat and doeskin breeches were modestly adorned but clearly expensive. He had such a confident way of moving that others instinctively made way for him. The women watched him with feminine awareness; the men moved out of his path.

As if he felt the intensity of her regard, the man turned his head toward her. Beneath the brim of his hat, Hester saw a square jaw she would know anywhere.

Michael. Warmth spread through her veins, a feeling she hadn't experienced since the first time Regmont had struck her. Something inside her had numbed that day, but it stirred now, awakening.

Dear God. When had he become such a fine specimen of a man?

When had her childhood companion left boyhood behind? When he became Lord Tarley? Or prior to that? She so rarely saw him anymore that she couldn't pinpoint when he might have become so formidable.

He paused as she did, a lone stationary figure in the midst of a flurry of activity. He carried himself so beautifully, so easily. Comfortable with his height in a way her husband, who was a few inches shorter, had never been.

Hester's hand fell to her side. Before she quite knew what she was about, she found herself outside, waiting for Michael, who weaved through traffic en route to her with graceful impatience.

"Good afternoon, Lord Tarley," she said when he reached her. She was surprised her voice was so clear and steady, when she felt fuzzy headed and shaky.

He removed his hat, revealing rich chocolate-brown hair.

With a bow, he greeted her. "Lady Regmont. I am feeling most fortunate to have crossed paths with you this morning."

She was ridiculously pleased by the smoothly voiced platitude. "The feeling is mutual."

Michael looked over her shoulder into the milliner's shop. "An afternoon with friends?"

"Yes." Which meant she couldn't speak to him about the matter weighing heavily on her mind. "I must see you as soon as you can possibly spare the time. I have something I wish to discuss with you."

He tensed. "What is it? Is something amiss?"

"I've heard about your wager with Regmont."

With brows raised, he said, "I won't hurt him. Too much."

"It isn't Regmont I worry about." Michael had no notion of what sleeping beast he might awaken.

His lips twitched, then he lost the battle and smiled in truth. The gesture took her breath away, making her realize how rarely he ever smiled around her. His reserve had always been notable. He'd never been soothed by her charm as so many others were.

"I cannot decide," he said, "whether to be flattered by your concern or insulted by your lack of faith in my pugilistic abilities."

"I cannot bear to think of you injured."

"I will endeavor to protect my person on your behalf. In all fairness, however, you should know that my doing so could result in injury to your husband."

Had he always looked at her with such warmth in his dark eyes? "Regmont is physically capable of defending himself."

When Michael frowned at her tone, she realized she

might have revealed more than she should. She deflected his concern with distraction. "I very much enjoyed your visit the other day. I do wish you would call on me more often."

"I wish I could, Hester." His voice was low and intimate, his gaze shadowed. "I will try."

They parted ways. It was with great force of will that Hester refrained from looking back over her shoulder when she returned to the shop. It was one thing to take a moment to speak to her sister's brother-in-law. It would be quite another to be seen ogling after him.

When she returned to her companions, Lady Bencott said, "The title suits Tarley."

Hester nodded, knowing the grief and other burdens that came with his new station.

"With any luck, Emily," Lady Bencott went on, "a new bonnet will catch his attention and secure you a fine match."

"Would that I should be so fortunate." Em removed yet another unflattering hat from atop her lovely raven curls. "I have admired him for some time."

Hester felt a sharp pang in her chest at her friend's dreamy tone. She told herself it was a symptom of increasing, not something far more complicated and impossible . . . like jealousy.

"You wished to see me?"

Michael looked up from his desk as his mother entered his study. Despite the not-inconsiderable size of the room, the Countess of Pennington's slender frame seemed to dominate the space. It was the force of Elspeth Sinclair's will and the command of her bearing that made her so formidable. Her strength of character was complemented by her physical beauty and elegance.

"Yes." He set his quill aside and stood. Rounding the mahogany desk, he gestured to one of the settees and waited for her to be seated. Then he settled across from her with a slight smile. "I have a favor to ask of you."

His mother studied him with a keen gaze. The recent loss of a beloved son was reflected in the depths of her dark eyes, and sadness clung to her like a shroud. "You know you have only to ask. If it is within my power to see it done, it will be."

"Thank you." He collected his thoughts, pondering the best way to phrase his request.

"How are you?" Elspeth linked her fingers in her lap and lifted her chin. Strands of silver hair lined her temples, but her face showed few signs of aging. She remained beautiful and faultlessly composed. "I have tried to give you as much privacy as I am able, but I confess, I worry over you. You have not been yourself since Benedict passed on."

"None of us have been." He deflated into the seatback with a harsh exhalation.

This conversation had been a long time coming. His mother had shown remarkable restraint in waiting so long, considering her usual need to be kept apprised of every minute detail affecting the members of her immediate family. While Pennington grieved in the country, Elspeth had arrived weeks ago, hovering on the fringes of Michael's new life in the most unobtrusive way possible. She appeared to occupy herself with friends and social activities, but he knew the true reason why she had come—to be there as support for her remaining son as he tried, and failed, to fill the void left by his brother's death.

"In the most well-meaning and innocent of ways," Michael said wearily, "we took Benedict for granted. It never occurred to any of us that he might one day leave us floundering without him."

"You are not floundering," Elspeth argued. "You are more than capable of carrying your new responsibilities in your own fashion. It isn't required that you should proceed in the same manner Benedict did. You can forge your own path."

"I'm trying."

"You're expending great effort to squeeze yourself into the mold shaped by your brother. I pray you do not believe your father and I want you to do so."

Michael's mouth twisted. "There is no finer man to emulate."

Her hand lifted and gestured at him, flowing gracefully and encompassing his form from his boots to his cravat. "I hardly recognized you when I first arrived. The somber hues of your new wardrobe and the sparseness of embellishment . . . It isn't you."

"I am not simply a Sinclair any longer," he retorted, somewhat defensively. "I am Tarley and one day—God willing, a faraway day—I will be Pennington. A certain restraint and decorum is required."

"Stuff and nonsense. What is required is your sanity and happiness. Your unique abilities and viewpoints are more valuable to the title than slavish adoption of your brother's sensibilities."

"Sanity is a luxury I must earn. Presently, I am barely keeping pace. I have no notion how Benedict met all his obligations, but by God, the amount of work to be done seems overwhelming at times."

"You should rely on the estate stewards more. You don't have to do everything yourself."

"Yes, I do, until I know enough to allow someone else to manage. I cannot place the responsibility for our family's financial stability in the hands of hired employees simply because it simplifies my life and saves me the trouble of rectifying my ignorance." Michael looked around the room, feeling like a fraud in the space that was imbued with the very essence of his brother. The somber reds and browns were not what he would have chosen for himself, but he'd changed nothing since taking over the space. He felt as if he lacked the right to do so, as well as the will. "And unlike Benedict, I don't even have Calypso to worry over, yet I still feel as if I am hanging on by the tips of my fingers."

Elspeth shook her head. "I remain ambivalent about your brother's bequeathment of such a large obligation to Jessica."

"She will want for nothing for the rest of her life."

"Her per annum stipend alone is sufficient to make her a very wealthy widow. That plantation was the bulk of your brother's personal income for good reason—it consumed a great deal of his time and attention. The burden of maintaining the property will likely be too great for her to bear. The mere thought of facing such a challenge is daunting to me."

"He discussed it with me prior to finalizing his will, and I understood his mind."

"Then explain it to me."

"He loved her," he said simply. "He claimed there was something about the island that affected her; an alteration to her countenance and personality he wished to foster. He wanted her to feel the power of self-sufficient affluence, if she should ever have to go on without him. Something about her being restrained and needing absolute freedom, or some such."

"He meant well, I suppose, but she should be here with us. It pains me to think of her alone."

Michael seized the opportunity to segue into the reason he'd summoned her. "Her sister, Lady Regmont, feels similarly. And speaking of Hester, I am led to the point where I ask a favor of you."

"Yes?"

"I should like you to deepen your association with her. Draw her into your social circle. Spend more time with her, if you would."

Elspeth's brows rose. "She is charming, of course, but there are a notable number of years between us. I am not certain our interests are aligned."

"Try."

"Why?"

Leaning forward, he set his forearms on his knees. "I fear something is not right with her. I need your opinion. If I am correct, you would note it straightaway."

"I meant, why the interest in Lady Regmont in particular? Because of Jessica?"

"Certainly easing Jessica's mind would please me," he prevaricated. "The sisters care a great deal about one another."

"Which is expected and laudable. Yet I still fail to see why the welfare of Regmont's wife is your concern." Her tone was more warily curious than argumentative. "If there is anything requiring attention, Regmont will see to it. You, on the other hand, need a spouse of your own to occupy you."

Groaning, Michael's head fell back and his eyes closed. "Is marrying me off all anyone can think about these days? The gossip rags are rife with speculation over my intentions, and now I cannot even enjoy a respite in my own home!"

"Isn't there any woman who appeals to you?"

Absolutely. As you've so astutely surmised, I am mad for another man's wife. He straightened. "Enough of this. I am well. Our affairs are well. There is no need for concern in any respect. I am tired and feeling ill equipped, but I'm learning quickly, and soon all will be as second nature to me. Settle your mind, if you would, please."

His mother stood and moved over to the bell pull, her

peach-hued satin skirts rustling as she moved. "I feel the need for a strong cup of tea."

Michael felt the need for something much stronger.

"So." Elspeth's tone was resigned. "Tell me what rouses your concern over Lady Regmont."

He felt precious little satisfaction over gaining his mother's capitulation. What cause would Hester have to dread an amateur bout of pugilism between two civilized gentlemen? The recollection of the imploring, almost-fearful look on her face when they'd spoken earlier was still fresh. And troubling.

"She is gaunt and far too pale. She seems overly delicate, both physically and otherwise. It isn't like her. She was always vivacious . . . full of energy and life."

"Men rarely take note of such things about their own wives, let alone another man's."

Holding up his hand, he warded off further speculative admonishments. "I know my place and hers. Note that I am placing this matter in your hands. My mind will be eased by your assistance, allowing me to return my focus to affairs falling within my purview."

A white-capped maid appeared in the open doorway, and Elspeth ordered a tea service. Then she returned to her former seat, straightening her skirts as she sat. "Your widely gazetted boxing match against Regmont suddenly takes on new meaning. I thought it wasn't at all like the new man you've become to risk censure from the magistrates. I was actually hopeful it was a sign of the old Michael returning."

"You are seeing motives that aren't there. And it isn't a match, which—as you pointed out—would be frowned upon by the magistrates. We've simply agreed to practice the sport together."

She shot him a mother's exasperated look. "You cannot tell me I don't see how you fidget with the fob of your

132

pocket watch, or tap your right foot against the floor. Those are long-standing habits of yours, which you have managed to suppress in the last year. Yet thinking of and talking about Lady Regmont reawakens those dormant tendencies. She has a profound effect on you."

Michael scrubbed a hand over his face. "Why do women insist on ascribing deep meaning to random events?"

"Because we take note of life's details, which men fail to do. That is why women are cleverer than men." She bared her pristinely white teeth in an overly sweet smile.

He grew wary due to familiarity with that particular smile and the mischief it portended.

"I will see to Hester for you," she said in a honeyed tone. "For a price."

Right. He knew it. "What will it cost me?"

"You must allow me to introduce you to some suitable young ladies."

"Bloody hell," he snapped. "Can you not simply act out of the kindness of your heart?"

"Kindness for *you*. You are overworked, overtired, and underappreciated. Not surprisingly, you find yourself drawn to someone who is familiar and comfortable."

Realizing that arguing against her points would only work against him, Michael kept his mouth shut and pushed to his feet. Tea was most definitely not going to be sufficient for him. Benedict's cognac in the bookcase behind the desk was far more appealing. He approached the wall of books and bent to open one of the carved wooden cabinet doors lining the bottom row.

"Good that you aren't speaking," she went on, "because you should be listening. I married a Sinclair male and raised two more; I know precisely how you are built."

He'd stopped pouring at the halfway point, but decided to continue to the rim. "We are built differently from other men?"

"Some men choose their mates with their reason, weighing the benefits and detriments in a purely analytical manner. Others—like your friend Alistair Caulfield—respond to physical attractions. But Sinclair men choose from here"— she tapped her chest above her heart—"and once the choice is made, they are hard to dissuade."

Michael tossed back the contents of his glass in two gulps.

Elspeth made a chastising clucking noise with her tongue. "It was years before your grandmother truly accepted me. She thought I was too hardheaded and intractable for a woman, but your father would not be denied his choice."

"I wonder why she thought that."

"And Jessica . . . I love her as if she was my own child, but I had reservations about her in the beginning. She is the type of individual one can never truly know well, but Benedict would not be gainsaid."

"And he was very content."

"Was he? Why then was he still making such grand efforts, like the bequeathment, to reveal a deeper side of her? It is the nature of love to wish to possess the other person completely—body and soul. I think it likely that he would have eventually grown resentful of her inability to share herself. Regardless, their match is no longer a concern. You are the one who is attached to an inappropriate love interest. You are the one who requires a new object of affection. It is the best way to recover from unrequited love."

"I have larger issues to address."

"Perhaps you could have remained a bachelor previously, but no longer."

Michael stared down at the tumbler in his hand, tilting it to and fro to catch the light from the large window to his left. Of all the duties he'd acquired along with the Tarley title, it was the need to wed and bed a suitable spouse that most pained him. He would be tying himself into a fraud he would have to perpetuate for the rest of his life. Just the thought of it was disheartening and exhausting.

"See to Lady Regmont," he said grimly. "Give her whatever counsel or sympathetic ear she may need, for as long as she may need it. In return, I will make myself available to your matchmaking."

Elspeth's mouth curved. "Done."

12

Jess strolled along the deck with her arm linked with Beth's. The ocean breeze was strong, filling the sails and hurtling the ship toward its destination. Still, the pace was not swift enough for the abigail.

"I grow weary of the ocean and this vessel," Beth grumbled. "And we 'ave weeks yet to endure."

"Oh, it's not so odious as that."

The brunette looked at her with a mischievous smile. "You 'ave a 'andsom distraction to 'asten the journey."

Jess attempted to look innocent. "Not that I would ever admit to such."

Through her interactions with Alistair, she'd come to a new understanding of the pervasive infatuation most young women experienced in adolescence. Jess had never experienced it herself until now. She thought about Alistair with alarming regularity, both awake and while dreaming.

"Remind me of your fellow in Jamaica," Jess said, hoping for a respite from her fascination.

"Ah . . . my 'arry. A sweet and randy man. The best kind, I say."

Jess laughed. "How naughty you are!"

"At times," Beth agreed, unabashed.

"Sweet and randy, you say? No one told me to esteem such qualities."

"You were told well enough to catch yerself the comeliest gentlemen I've ever seen," the abigail shot back. "O'course the prettier they are, the 'arder it is for their women."

"Oh? Why is that?"

"They are treated differently. More is expected of them, yet less is expected of them. They are excused from some things and 'eld to a 'igher standard for others." Beth looked at her. "No disrespect intended, milady, but you should know."

Jess nodded. She did know.

"So what you 'ave," Beth explained, "are men who know greater freedom with fewer consequences. They are forgiven more often than not. And we women cannot seem to stop caring for them anyway, which 'urts. If I've a choice between men—one 'andsome and charming, one sweet and randy—I'd choose the sweet one. I know I'd be much 'appier."

"You are a wise woman, Beth."

Beth shrugged. "Lessons 'ard won. But I'm grateful for them all the same. Although, to tell the truth, I'd likely break that rule o' mine for Mr. Caulfield. There's 'andsome and then there's men who make yer toes curl. Something to be said for that."

"Yes, he does do that, does he not?" Which made it so deucedly hard to resist him and the consequences that would assuredly follow a liaison with him. She had yet to find suitable justification for such risk. A few hours of plea-sure seemed too flimsy.

"You needn't frown so, milady. Yer safe enough."

Feeling far from safe, Jess looked at the abigail curiously. "In what way?"

"It's too soon for you. Yer still grieving. When the 'eart is still 'ealing, we find someone who 'elps us forget it hurts. But one day we don't want to forget any longer and we let 'em go. When that time comes for you, you'll say farewell to Mr. Caulfield with gratitude and no regrets. It's the way we women survive the passing of our men."

"Truly?" Jess was taken with the notion of being immune to deep attachment to Alistair. The prospect was both astonishing . . . and a relief.

"Well . . . there's no pain for the one 'ealing, because in the process, the 'eart forms a shell like a clam. Until it's strong enough to love again." Squeezing Jess's arm, Beth said, "And I wouldn't worry too much on Mr. Caulfield's account, milady. There's a particular way about 'im. In my experience, men who 'ave that way 'ave been building their own shell for a long time. They like it in there, and they 'ave no intention o' coming out."

A child ran across the aftcastle. The unexpected sight so startled Jess, she lost track of what she'd been about to say. The lad looked to be no more than ten and one, with a mop of blond curls and cheeks that were still chubby. He was racing toward the helmsman when a booted foot was thrust into his way. The boy tripped, crashing into the deck with a pained cry.

Horrified by the cruelty of the act, Jess was further infuriated when the responsible seaman yanked the boy upright and cuffed his ears, then proceeded to scold the child with words coarse enough to burn her ears. As the child cowered in the face of such vitriolic rage, his small chin lifted with white-faced courage.

In that moment, Jess remembered vividly what it felt like to be standing in his place. She was taken back to that place where fear and rising panic assailed her along with the dreadful waiting for the next blow. Because there was always a next blow. The sick fury that gripped men such as her father and this man fed on itself, escalating until only sheer physical exhaustion prevented them from inflicting further abuse.

Unable to turn a blind eye, Jess unlinked her arm from Beth's and strode forward. "You, sir!"

The sailor was so involved in his tirade, he failed to hear her. She called out again, louder, attracting the notice of a crewmember next to him who shoved at his shoulder to gain his attention.

She drew to a halt in front of them. "Sir, I cannot abide such treatment of children. There are more effective ways to discipline."

The man eyed her with cold, dark eyes. "This isn't any business of yers."

"Mind yer manners with 'er ladyship," Beth scolded, which earned her a dark glower.

Jess knew that look well. His blood was hot with spite and the need to vent it. It was a sad fact that there were many men like her father, men who lacked the sense or willpower to purge what ailed them in noninjurious ways. They only knew how to spew their hatred on others and were so morally afflicted, they drew pleasure from doing so.

"You don't know 'ow to run a ship, *yer ladyship*," he said with a derisive curl to his mouth. "And until you do, you'd best leave the learnin' of how to survive on one to me."

Other men slowly closed in around them, exacerbating her growing anxiety.

"Teaching," she corrected, struggling against nervous tension so fierce her shoulders and neck ached with it, "—if that is what you presume to call it, is equally applicable to all trades. You are going about it poorly in any case."

He shoved his hands in his pockets and rocked back on his heels, smiling through a reddish bushy beard in a chilling manner. "When a sailor is told to fetch something, 'e best not forget what it was 'e was sent to fetch or that 'e was sent to fetch it!"

"He is a c-child!" she argued. The cracking of her voice

struck her like a whiplash. She took a step backward without volition.

Something within her broke at the realization that her prized and hard-won equanimity was so easily assailable. She'd convinced herself if she were ever faced with another abusive individual in her adulthood, she would be capable of controlling the interaction in a way she hadn't as a child. She had believed she would be stronger and could say all the cutting words she'd imagined in her youth. Yet here she stood with her stomach knotted and spine rigid, her entire frame riddled with vibrating tension.

"The boy is a seaman first." He reached out and caught the little one by the hair, yanking hard. The child stumbled into him with a low cry. "And 'e 'as to earn 'is keep and not get in the way."

She swallowed past her fear. "From what I witnessed, it was *your* foot that was misplaced in *his* way."

"*Lady Tarley.*"

At the sound of Alistair's voice, Jess turned.

The loitering sailors parted for him as he drew near, and silence spread in his wake. The mere manner of his bearing commanded attention and respect. Her clenched fists relaxed, then tightened again when frustration rose anew. She should not need another individual to feel settled, but it seemed she did and that made her feel very weak and helpless. "Yes, Mr. Caulfield?"

His gaze was intent on her face. "Is my assistance desired?"

Jess debated her answer for a moment, then said, "Could we speak privately?"

"Of course." He raked their audience with a sweeping glance. "Carry on."

The sailors quickly dispersed.

Alistair pointed at the man who'd so angered Jess. "You."

The man pulled off his worn cap. "Aye, Mr. Caulfield?"

The change that swept over Alistair was astonishing. The blue of his irises took on a marked chill, causing Jess to shiver. She remembered that cool detachment from their youth, the icy ruthlessness that had lured women and reckless gamblers alike.

"Consider your treatment of that young sailor carefully," he warned in a biting tone. "I do not tolerate the maltreatment of children on my ship."

A potent rush of admiration and pleasure flowed through Jess. Alistair must have seen enough during his approach to discern a problem, and his position on the subject meant a great deal to her.

She extended her hand toward the child. "Perhaps he could make his egress with us?"

The boy's eyes widened with more terror than he'd shown while suffering abuse. He shook his head violently and stepped closer to the other men.

She was briefly confused, having expected relief and gratitude. Then comprehension set in. One of the harder lessons she'd learned in her youth was that delaying the inevitable only led to greater penalty in the end.

Unshed tears stung her eyes. Pity for both the child in front of her and the child she herself had once been. In all likelihood, she'd only made things worse for the boy.

Without waiting for Alistair, Jess pivoted and hurried toward the companionway. When she felt his hand at the small of her back, her vision blurred. She allowed him to lead her, grateful when he ushered her below deck and behind the privacy of a closed door.

His cabin. Despite her distraction and tear-clouded eyes, she knew it immediately by scent. His unique virile fragrance permeated the air and raised her temperature.

The space was of similar size to her own cabin and furnished much the same, but she felt different in his domain, aware of a heightened awareness and an altogether sensual sense of anticipation.

She exhaled a shaky breath, her hands knotting together in a physical manifestation of her inner turmoil. She was not free of her father, as she'd previously supposed. And now she knew she would never be free.

"Jessica?" Alistair rounded her. His breath hissed out. "Damnation . . . Don't cry."

She attempted to move away. He caught her to him, crushing her into the hard length of his body. Her cheek was pressed into the superfine of his coat. Beneath her ear, his heart beat in a strong and steady rhythm.

"Talk to me," he urged.

"Th-that man is offensive to me in every way. He is vile and unrepentant about it. I know his kind. He is an animal. You would be wise to be rid of him."

There was a long pause when she finished, during which Alistair's breathing was too sharply regulated to be completely natural. She knew him well enough to know he was weighing the import and implications of her concern, and speculating on the root of it.

His hands stroked the curve of her spine. "I intend to speak to Captain Smith. The man will be dismissed at port."

Straightening, she put distance between them. He made her want to lean on him in ways beyond the physical. Dangerous ways.

"Jess . . ." The familiarity of his address roused even more conflicted feelings. "It might benefit you to talk about the reason you are so upset."

"With you?" she scoffed, redirecting her frustration at him in self-defense. She was too susceptible to him, too exposed. "I should bare myself to a stranger?"

He accepted her crossness with grace enough to shame her. "Perhaps I am the best choice," he said calmly. "I'm an impartial party, over whom you hold the knowledge of a tainted past. And even if I were inclined to divulge information indiscriminately—which you know I am not—I'm far removed from anyone who might wield it against you."

"I cannot conceive of anything I would rather discuss less." She moved toward the door.

Alistair blocked her way and crossed his arms.

The entrapment aggravated her already volatile mood. "You intend to detain me?"

The curve of his beautiful mouth was a silent challenge. But unlike the seaman's mocking derisiveness, Alistair's regard empowered her.

"You're vulnerable now," he said. "You will stay with me as long as you are."

The parallels to what Beth had said on the deck mere moments ago didn't escape her. His intended meaning was different, but the phrasing was applicable regardless. Thanks to Beth's greater experience, she now knew why she was so drawn to the temptation Alistair presented. But an understanding of what he would gain in return still eluded her. "What concern am I of yours?"

"You are my lover, Jess."

"Not yet."

"Sex is merely a formality at this point." His tone was low and intimate. "You and I have always been inevitable. And I am not a man to take pieces of a whole. I must have everything. The good as well as the bad."

"Just spew it all over you?" Her words were sharply clipped, a reaction to a sudden violent rush of longing. "Would that not make me of similar ilk to that sailor? Forcing another individual to bear the brunt of my personal disquiet?"

Alistair took a step closer. "Unlike the boy, I can take it. Better yet, I *want* it. There is no part of you I don't want."

"*Why?*"

"Because my hunger for you is unrestrained, so you must be also. In all ways."

Jess felt the urge to pace, but resisted due to long training. Ladies did not pace. They did not reveal anything other than serenity. They existed to ease a man's burdens, not add to them.

Yet Alistair—the most thoroughly masculine creature of her acquaintance—was the only individual with whom she felt comfortable sharing the shadowy aspects of her soul. She knew, with unaccountable near certainty, that he would not think less of her as others might. He would not alter his treatment of her. Darkness was known to him. He'd lived within it, embraced it, and seemed all the stronger for the experience. It still amazed her to think of how driven he was, how ruthlessly focused he could be, how far he was willing to fall from grace to avoid failure and be self-sufficient.

At too young an age, his innate sensuality and stunning countenance had exposed him to the lascivious interest of those who were jaded and immoral. Knowing it was his responsibility to see to his own future, he'd taken what advantage he could from an untenable circumstance. But at what cost to him?

"Jessica. What are you thinking about when you look at me in that manner?"

She was staring at him, enthralled by his dark beauty and the undeniable edge to him. She hadn't the knowledge to understand the "way about him" that Beth had referenced, but she was a woman nevertheless, with all the primitive instincts of her gender. He exuded a raw sensuality that was nothing less than addictive. When she wasn't with him, she wished to be. That depth of craving had frightened her for the last sennight, knowing as she did that nothing permanent could ever exist between them.

Her world was not his; his was not hers. They were trav-

144

eling the same road for a brief time, but their paths would diverge. She could not stay in the West Indies forever, and he would not long tolerate London Society, whatever he might say to the contrary. His hunger for her was not the only thing unrestrained about him. He was a bold and brazen man, vibrant and powerful. The ton—whose mores she'd been well trained to epitomize—would stifle and bore him.

No, she didn't have the knowledge Beth possessed . . . but Alistair did. He, too, had spoken of their liaison as fitting within a brief span of time. Quickly come and as swiftly gone. Room enough only for fondness and gratitude. She had to trust their greater counsel in this.

"I admire you," she said.

Although he appeared unmoved, she sensed the stillness that gripped him. "After all you know about me?"

"Yes."

There was a weighted pause. "You are almost certainly the only person aware of my past transgressions who would say that."

"Yet you did not hesitate to be honest with me. You must have had some faith in my ability to be open minded."

"I was not without apprehension," he confessed, his jaw taut. "But yes, I believed you would be more likely to overlook my sins than hold them against me."

The recent emptiness in her chest now filled with something warm and tender. "I would not have believed it of myself."

She lacked the words to explain what she was feeling. It was something akin to victorious, and it was so much the opposite of the defeat she'd felt when leaving the deck, it seemed impossible that one emotion could so swiftly follow the other.

Her mind was her own.

There was no denying that her body had been damaged and her emotions could so easily be overrun by fear. But her mind remained uncorrupted. She was capable of judging Alistair with criteria outside the narrow scope to which she had been taught to conform. For all his strenuous efforts, her father had failed, because she did not think as he did. There were pieces of her he hadn't been capable of reaching. The freedom inherent in that revelation was profound and deeply moving. And Alistair had made the discovery possible. Without him, she might never have faced a choice capable of enlightening her. She had never before been presented with the option of accepting something that was unacceptable. Her world did not have such decisions in it.

Alistair remained still as a statue as her world tilted on its axis, his handsome features hard set.

She saw through his exterior and understood; he hadn't yet accepted his choices. Not the way he so readily accepted her.

With great care, Jess untied the ribbons of her bonnet and removed it, setting it carefully atop the seat of a chair. En route to the door, she skirted Alistair, but though he turned to watch her, he didn't stop her. She knew he'd follow her if she left and thought herself lucky for that.

She engaged the oval-shaped brass latch and heard his sharp inhalation behind her.

Jess walked to the bed and sat carefully on the edge of the mattress.

The feral look that swept over his handsome face made her quiver with heated expectation. But it was quickly masked, leaving behind an unusually austere countenance.

"As per our wager," he said, clasping his hands at the small of his back, "I must remind you of the impropriety of your presence in my locked cabin."

A wide smile curved her mouth. Until now, there had not been an opportunity to play the reversed roles they'd agreed to adopt. "Do I look as if I care about propriety?"

"Have you considered the consequences?"

His hands on her. His mouth. All that raw expertise concentrated on ensuring her pleasure. She needed that heightened intimacy with him. She felt such a surfeit of affection for him and gratitude for the changes he was effecting in her life. "Oh, yes. I have considered them all."

His gaze heated at her breathy reply. "I should enumerate them, just to be certain."

"No." Jess set her hands on her bent knees. "No games or wagers, please. Not now."

"Tell me why you've suddenly conceded."

"Why not?"

"Why now? I extended an invitation to visit my cabin and you've ignored it for days. Only a moment ago, you attempted to leave. What brought about this swift change? Do you wish to forget? Will bedding me work as well as the claret? I must warn you, I am not nearly as fine a vintage."

"I've no wish to forget anything. In truth, I hope to remember every moment of this day."

Alistair showed no emotion, yet the air around him seemed strangely turbulent.

"I feel very close to you," she said. "But not nearly close enough. Undressing would help considerably."

"I don't want you overwrought or impaired in any way."

"I'm not. Not any longer." His caution said so much about his intentions. If he wanted only sex, he would not be so concerned about her reasons for offering it. "Isn't it enough that I want you? Must there be more?"

"I am not prepared to stop as I did before. It's midday. Hours will pass and you will be missed. At the very least your abigail and my valet will know what occupied you. Perhaps others, if we forget ourselves and are overheard."

Jess considered him carefully. "You are attempting to dissuade me. Perhaps it is you who has had a change of heart?"

She knew that was not the case, not with the indecent way he was looking at her, but his reasoning was a mystery.

"I have wanted you for so long now," he said roughly, "I've no memory of how it feels to be devoid of the craving. But you must know what you do. I need you to think of who you are and where you are and who I am. Think of how things will be once we've crossed this threshold. Think of how you will leave this cabin—disheveled and well fucked. Think of how you will sit across the table from me at supper, surrounded by men who will know the minute they look at you that I've had you long and hard this day."

His crudity jolted her physically, surprising her with a surge of arousal she could never have expected. Her face heated. This was no tender lover who stood before her. This was the man once known for his acidic wit, whose tongue could charm and shred with equal effectiveness. A man who would do anything to have what he wanted.

And he wanted her. Her shaken confidence drew strength from that.

Alistair crossed the distance between them. "Know what you do here, Jessica," he said again, his voice harsh and unyielding. "I can wait until you're ready."

"I don't want to wait any longer." She stood in a rush and pointed at the nearest chair. "Sit, Mr. Caulfield. It's time I had you."

13

Alistair's chest expanded with a sharply drawn breath, then deflated in a rush. He pivoted on his heel and moved to the chair, pausing to remove his coat and drape it over the back before sitting. "According to our agreement, I am supposed to be the voice of reason. A model of propriety."

Jess watched him, admiring the sleek sensuality inherent in his movements. She also admired his taut backside, eager to see it bared. "Be my guest, but I won't be swayed. I do understand, however, that you have a strong dislike for losing wagers."

Setting his hands on his knees, he waited. His tense expectancy was reflected in his heavy-lidded gaze. Between his legs, the outline of his thick arousal quickened her breathing. "Not in this instance. I would give up my fortune to bed you; losing our bet is a ridiculously small price to pay for the privilege."

Her chest tightened at his fervency, her corset becoming an unbearable restraint. Needing to be free of it, she went to him and presented her back. "Help me."

The touch of his fingers was light, too light to quench her thirst for him. As the halves of her gown parted, Jess began to feel warm and slightly intoxicated. The scent of his skin, the exotic blend that was uniquely his, filled her nostrils with every inhalation. She knew he had to be as heated as she was, and she longed to touch his bare flesh, to press her nose and lips against it.

Alistair pushed her sleeves off her shoulders, and she wriggled out of her dress, allowing the garment to pool on the floor. He caught her stays next, loosening them with a dexterity born of experience. She'd enjoyed that skill first-hand, remembered it vividly, dreamed of it.

He helped her push the corset down past her hips, and she stepped out of the boning, feeling a novel sense of freedom and lack of inhibition.

"Jess," he breathed, a moment before his arms came around her and he nuzzled against her back. His large hands cupped her breasts, kneading the aching flesh with a firm yet tender grip.

Her head fell back and her eyes closed, a sigh escaping her. The desire to give herself over to him was nearly irresistible, but she restrained herself. If she allowed him to, he would take over, and she didn't want that. He'd had more than his share of women who wanted him to work in bed. She did not want to resemble those women, especially after her rash words the other evening. She wanted to give pleasure, and she wanted him to take it.

Turning carefully in his embrace, Jess filled the space between his spread thighs. She caught his face in her hands and pressed her lips to his, wanting the kisses that made her feel seductive and desirable. His hands encircled her waist, pulling her closer.

"Allow me to enjoy you," she breathed into his mouth. "You refused me last time . . ."

"After seven years, you cannot be asking me for patience."

She pushed her splayed fingers into the thick silk of his hair. "After seven years, what are a few moments more?"

Alistair's head fell back on a low groan, his eyes staring up at her with a bold, heated passion. It amazed her that she could incite such a response in a voluptuary as beautiful and sensual as he was. She, a peeress known for her chilly deportment, while Alistair radiated a sexual heat that made her melt and soften.

Her fingertips stroked over his dark, winged brows. Their shape lent wickedness to his countenance, while framing his stunning eyes and thick lashes. Her thumbs caressed the sculpted line of his cheekbones, holding him still as she pressed her lips to the tip of his aristocratic nose.

"Christ, Jess," he said gruffly. "If your aim is to kill me, be mercifully quick about it. Don't torment me."

Pulling back, she began to work on the knot of his cravat. "I've yet to do anything."

"You drive me to madness." He tugged on her hips, drawing her close enough to capture a hard, peaked nipple in the heat of his mouth. He made a rough sound of desire, and Jess sagged into his grip.

Even through the thin lawn of her chemise, the contact was scorching. She arched and gasped, her womb clenching in greedy hunger. Catching his shoulders, she steadied herself as her knees weakened. His tongue flicked over her with ruthless skill, reminding her of the last time his mouth had been on her. When her breast grew heavy with need, her nipple swollen and red, he moved to lavish similar attention on the other side. Jess felt the hot trickle of her own arousal, the flesh between her legs growing moist in welcome.

She moaned. "I want you naked. I want to feel you inside me."

He released her with a low growl. "Oh, you will, love. You'll feel every inch. I have never been so hard. I am going to cram you full, and you'll come over and over and over again."

Tackling the ivory buttons of his waistcoat, Alistair quickly divested himself of the garment. When he pushed to his feet in a powerfully graceful movement, she stepped back on shaky legs, her entire body feeling alien to her. She was a mass of sensation and wanting, her emotions so riotous she might've run in fear if her limbs hadn't been weighted by longing.

Seven years. It felt as if her attraction to him had been simmering the whole of that time, waiting for his touch to free it. Now it spilled over her in heated waves, flushing her skin and making the ephemeral weight of her chemise and pantalettes a burden. But she dared not remove them. As it was, she was too vulnerable. Too bare. None of the shields she was used to erecting—her rigid deportment, biting rejoinders, and faultless manners—were available to her now. She didn't know who she was beneath all that protection, which left her feeling so open and unprotected.

Blissfully unaware of Jess's turmoil, Alistair finished unwinding his cravat and tossed it aside. The next moment his shirtsleeves were yanked over his head. He was reaching for the placket of his breeches when she stayed him.

"Stop," she said, swallowing hard at the sight of him. As elegant as he was while dressed, he was pure unadulterated male beneath his clothes. The evenness of his sun-kissed skin color betrayed how often he went about without a shirt, while the thickness of his biceps and the taut roping of abdominal muscles told her how often he worked alongside the men he employed.

Her hand lifted to touch him, her feet moving her forward without volition. She pressed her palm to his warm skin, and a shiver moved through her. She felt his heart racing. There was so much power and strength in him. His anticipation was tangible and visible; his muscles were hard and delicious. She was searingly aroused by his virility, quivering with eagerness at the thought of that pure masculine energy focused on pleasuring her body.

Alistair caught her wrist. "I am aching with lust for you."

"You are not alone," she whispered, tugging free of his easy grip to touch his shoulders. Both of her hands stroked over the broad curves, then slid down his biceps, her fingers squeezing and finding no give to her applied pressure. He was like warm marble. She wanted to touch him all over, take her time, nuzzle her nose against him and breathe him deep into her lungs. She wanted *him*. In that moment, she wanted him more than anything else in the world. She felt as if her repressed hunger had overtaken her completely. Her need and longing for him was all that was left of her after he'd stripped the entirety of her defenses away.

His fists clenched at his sides as her hands drifted over the rock-hardness of his rippled abdomen. "Are you wet for me? Do you feel empty without my cock in you?"

Jess nodded, feeling her sex clench tight with greed.

"Let me fill you," he purred, temptation incarnate. "Let me push inside you and make you come—"

"Not yet." Wrapping her arms around him, she drew closer still, delaying her surrender because she desired his first. With the flat of her tongue, she licked across the hard disk of his nipple.

He hissed and gripped her hips with bruising strength. "In a moment, I will pin you to the bulkhead and take the choice from you."

"Where is the laudable restraint you displayed the other night?"

"You were intoxicated; I knew before we began that I wouldn't be having you. Now . . . There is no turning back. I know I am only moments away from having you as I've needed you for far too long."

"*Alistair.*"

"Damnation, I am trying to be civilized." He pressed his lips to her forehead in a quick, hard kiss. "I am trying to keep from pushing you to the deck and rutting atop you like a maddened beast. But I am only a man—a vastly flawed one—and I know damn well how good it will be between us. I'll never want to stop; therefore I cannot wait to begin."

Jess stilled, her breath panting across his skin, her chest constricted by the weight of his expectation. Disappointing him would crush her. She couldn't allow it. He expected great pleasure, and she was determined that he should have it. She reached for the fastenings of his breeches, slipping the buttons from their holes.

Alistair reached for her coiffure, withdrawing the pins that secured her tresses. "I want to feel your hair brush all over my body. I want to fist it in my hands and hold you still while I ride you deep and long."

Her hands shook as she reached into his smalls and wrapped her hands around him. He groaned and jerked in her grip.

"You are so hot," she said, scorched by the heat of him. She shoved his clothing out of the way, releasing him. He made a low, animal sound as he fell heavily into her palms.

Jess sucked in a sharp breath, staring down at the magnificent penis thrusting so hungrily toward her. Perhaps she should have expected his body to be uniformly awe inspiring, but in this matter she was at a disadvantage. She had accustomed herself to one man and had never expected to become intimately familiar with any other.

Her fingers explored carefully, following her gaze. She traced the sinuous curving of the thick veins that coursed the rigid length. He was fully, ragingly aroused. His bollocks were drawn up tight, but they were no less impressive for their readiness. He was large there, too, giving proof of the virility promised by his confidence and arrogance. She wondered if her body could accommodate him. He was so thick and long, wide from the tip to the root.

"Say something," he said gruffly. "Tell me you want it."

"I shall show you instead." Licking her lips, she dropped to her knees.

"Jessica."

The serrated edge to his voice thrilled her, made her disregard the discomfort of the hardwood beneath her. Alistair stood still, his hands tangling in her hair. His chest heaved with labored breaths, and a slight sheen of perspiration glistened across his abdomen.

At least in this, she was assured of giving him pleasure. Her lips parted. Mouth watering, she engulfed the thick crest.

"Bloody hell," he groaned, shuddering violently.

A slow, heated spurt of pre-ejaculate flowed over her tongue. She moaned at the taste of him, her cheeks hollowing on a drawing pull, seeking more of the rich flavor.

"Yes . . . Jess. Yes." Alistair held her face in his hands, his thumbs stroking over her cheeks. "I have dreamed of this. Wanted you like this so fiercely I was certain I'd lose my mind."

His hips moved, stroking his cock in and out of her working mouth. His beautiful features were harsh with lust, the skin stretched taut over his sculpted cheekbones, his sensual mouth twisted in a grimace of pained pleasure. The ferocity of his need might have frightened her if not for the fierce tenderness in his eyes and touch.

Sweat bloomed across her flushed skin, her mind reliving his ministrations to her the other night, remembering the feel of his tongue and fingers on her. In her. Remembering the unbearable ecstasy. She wanted to give him that ecstasy in kind, wanted to leave a similarly indelible memory with him.

Gripping his lean hip in one hand, Jess cupped his scrotum with the other. His curse was bitten out, his body jerking as she tested the heavy weight, her fingertips massaging the tightened sac with luring caresses. Her tongue was equally adventurous, swirling around the plush head of his cock, flickering along the tender underside.

"Dear God," he gasped, the muscles of his stomach clenching and quivering. "Suck me, Jess . . . take me deeper . . . yes, like that . . ."

She gripped the thick base of his penis, fisting him just to feel him quake and hear him curse. He was riveting, so darkly erotic in his unrestrained abandonment. Her thighs clenched tightly together, her body's attempt to ease the unbearable aching and swelling of her needy flesh. She was searingly aware of the slickness of her sex, the way she trembled in longing. But she wanted this more, wanted no distractions from witnessing his release, wanted to absorb every nuance of his expression when he succumbed to the climax she knew he was swiftly approaching. She felt like a different woman, a fiercely feminine creature who knew no boundaries or restraint, no rules or law, a force of nature wild and untamed.

Alistair's callused thumbs rubbed along the edges of her straining lips. Her jaw stretched wide to accommodate him, the slight discomfort anchoring her to the moment. The act had never been this way with Benedict. Her husband had always been sweet and solicitous, their sexual relationship marked by tenderness and care. Alistair was raw and unguarded in his pleasure, creating a rich intimacy. She'd never felt as close to another person, never felt such a brilliant and binding sense of connection.

"I'm close," he said hoarsely. "Ah, Christ . . . your mouth is divine . . ."

Alistair held her head still and took what he needed, the thrust of his hips accelerating until she could only grip his thighs and tighten her suction, her tongue stroking his cock-head with fevered desperation. The sounds he made, the mindless groans and gruffly voiced praise, brought her to the brink of orgasm.

"Yes!" he growled, swelling farther a moment before the first hard burst of semen poured over her tongue.

He climaxed with the same unmitigated intensity with which he did everything. The cords of his neck stood out in harsh relief as he threw his head back and flooded her mouth with a guttural cry. She worked him with her hands, milking his release, wanting the entirety of his lust and hunger, claiming it as her due with savage exultation.

His rigid tension had just barely begun to ease when he caught her beneath the arms and hauled her to her feet.

"Jessica." He caught her up and carried her to the bed.

In the aftermath of an orgasm so powerful it weakened his knees, Alistair held Jessica tightly to his chest, consumed by the need to reduce her to the same base state she'd stripped him to. His skin felt too small and stretched too thin. Sweat soaked the roots of his hair and slid down his nape. His mouth was dry from hoarse mutterings.

He'd never imagined anything could feel so good. She'd sucked his aching cock as if starved for the taste of him, moaning and clutching him as if she would die if he denied her. As if he could. He doubted even the sinking of the ship could have pulled him away.

Jess's hands dug into his hair, her lush body writhing against his torso. Alistair seated her on the edge of the mattress and pulled her chemise up and over her head. He tossed it aside, his attention focused on the full breasts that heaved with her every ragged breath. He cupped their lush weight in his hands, his thumbs stroking over the hard, peaked nipples. She leaned back, her weight propped on her canted arms. Her lovely face was flushed, her gray eyes so dark they were nearly black. Her rich golden hair fell around her shoulders in total disarray. She looked glassy eyed and ravished, certainly the most beautiful thing he'd ever seen.

"Thank you," he murmured, pressing her backward to take a nipple into his mouth. Her selflessness meant more to him than he could express with words. He'd needed so much from her for so long, and she had given generously and with heartening enthusiasm.

His tongue stroked over the taut point of her breast, his lips pulling with deliberately soft suction. Teasing. Making her want more.

"Alistair . . ." Her breathy tone was ripe with surrender. There was no resistance left in her, no caution or wariness. He was uncertain of what had transpired to make her so free in his arms, but he would have time enough to discern the cause later. For now, all he wanted was to make her come apart in his arms, to hear her say his name as she climaxed.

Reaching between her legs, his questing fingers slid into the slit of her pantalettes and found her sex gratifyingly slick. He parted her, sliding through the silken skeins of her desire, then pushed two fingers into her. She was ready for him. More than ready. Wet and hot, ripe for the taking. He thrust gently in and out, his teeth gritting as he felt her clenching hungrily around him. He tugged on her breast with a hard suck, then released her.

Jess's arms gave out, and she sprawled across his dark brown counterpane, looking like a debauched angel. Straightening, he gripped her knees with both hands and spread her wide.

"So pretty," he praised, coveting the exposed glistening pink flesh between her thighs. He briefly debated removing the rest of their garments, then discarded the notion. They'd undress next time, after she was soaked with his seed and limp with satiation.

He gripped his cock with one hand, angling downward to glide the sensitive head through her petal-soft lips. The feeling was exquisite, engorging his penis as if he hadn't had a galvanizing orgasm only moments before.

"You're still hard," she breathed, pushing up onto her elbows.

"For you, always. I intend to ride you all day," he promised darkly. "All night."

"I await the proof of such stamina."

"A challenge, my lady?" He bared his teeth in a semblance of a smile. "You are aware of how I respond to those."

Notching the thick crest into her tiny slit, he pushed through the token resistance of tightness caused by her year of abstinence. She gasped as the crown breached the stretched opening. He bit back an animal sound of pleasure and fought the urge to fall upon her with a hard, deep thrust that pierced her to the womb. That would be too quickly done, robbing her of the full awareness of his possession. He wanted her to feel the stretch of every wide inch, wanted her to writhe as he sank deeper, wanted her to remember the sensation of that last leisurely stroke that seated him to the bollocks.

So he kept her spread and worked his way into her, his eyes riveted to the point where they were joined. His lungs burned as he gulped in air, every nerve in his body attuned to the feel of her satiny tissues quivering and clasping around him. A surfeit of sensation burned through him. Sweat coursed down his back and chest, a physical manifestation of the rigid control he exerted.

"So tight," he gritted out, his jaw clenched with strain. "Like a fist . . . so hot and tight . . ."

She moved restlessly beneath him, biting her lower lip as he slid in and out, pushing deeper and deeper with every leisurely thrust. "Please. Hurry."

Hunching over her, Alistair sank his teeth into her shoulder. Hard enough to leave a mark, but not enough to break the skin. She moaned and arched into his mouth. It was a primitive act, one goaded by the feel of her greedy cunt pulling and sucking at the head of his cock, luring him to sink home. Bare. Nothing between his most sensitive flesh and hers. In all his life, he'd never taken a woman without the protective sheath of a French letter. Only with her would he do so. Jessica—a woman he'd known was meant to be his from the moment he first saw her.

His hands moved from her thighs to the bed, supporting his weight as he pumped his hips in a timed, unhurried rhythm. She took advantage of her sudden freedom, wrapping her legs around him and tugging him deeper. Her breath left her in a gasped cry of his name as he slid in to the root, buried completely.

Alistair held still, struggling for control. He fought to make allowances for her straining body to grow accustomed to him throbbing hard and thick inside her. She stared up at him, her eyes wide and luminous, windows to her soul. There was no evidence of the chilly hauteur she was renowned for. She was burning hot beneath him, around him; all artifice and distance melting away. The look on her face was one he'd never seen on anyone, yet it mirrored how he felt—profoundly affected, split wide open, with nowhere to hide.

When she pushed upward and kissed his clenched jaw, something shifted inside him, shaking him to the core. His blood was raging for her, spurred by seven years of waiting to be right where he was, but she stayed his violent need with a single soft, sweet kiss. He was devastated by her tenderness in the face of his ferocious desire. Pressing his damp cheek to hers, he nuzzled against her, breathing in the smell of sex and lust and beloved woman. She fit him perfectly, if tightly, as he'd known she would. His beautiful, irreproachable Jess. A woman capable of reining in an entire roomful of exuberant people with a single quelling glance. Yet her body had been designed to hold him, a man built for plea-suring women in the most exuberant way possible.

Without conceit, he knew how generously he was en-dowed. His size had been a tool he'd used to his advantage once he had become aware of how pleasing it was to women.

But he had not been meant for those women. He had been fashioned for Jessica, just as she had been crafted for him. If it killed him, he would make her see it.

He traced the shell of her ear with his tongue, feeling her slick sex clasp him in response. "Perfection," he whispered, following her down as she sank back into the bed. "Two halves of a whole."

Jess gripped his upper arms and licked her lower lip, her hips moving in tight little circles, loosening the way for him. "Please," she pled again in that throaty murmur that undid him.

Bracing himself with palms flat to the bed, he withdrew slowly, relishing the feel of her clinging to his cock. He re-turned with effort, pushing through the tight resistance. Her head thrashed and her eyes closed, which he could not allow. He needed her to stay with him, to see him through the storm he knew was coming. The pressure of his impend-ing orgasm was fisted around his bollocks and pulsing through his cock, warning him that he would soon be wasted by the woman beneath him. Even knowing how she could destroy him, he couldn't pull away. She'd snared him completely that long-ago night, bewitched him beyond re-demption. There was no other choice for him. Somehow, he had to make himself the only choice for her.

Pushing his arms beneath her shoulders, he cupped her head in his hands, pinning her completely. His mouth came down over hers, his head tilting to deepen the contact. She caught his waist, arching into him. Their perspiration sealed their torsos together, adding another raw layer to their heated coupling. He moved. She moved. They found a rhythm. She clawed at his back; he kissed her as if he'd die if their lips were parted. His tongue plunged and retreated along with his cock, both seeking to drive her wild. He *needed* her wild, as crazed and desperate as he felt.

Alistair rolled his hips, probing with the iron-hard length of his penis, absorbing every nuance of her fevered response. He found a spot that made her shiver beneath him and exploited it, stroking over it again and again. He growled when she climaxed, the delicate muscles inside her rippling and gripping his plunging cock. He hung on to his control by the thinnest of threads, needing to see her through first before he took any more than she'd already given him.

He slowed, gliding in and out, lifting his head to watch the pleasure take her. The way was easier now, her body accepting his possession with rich creamy moisture. Her eyes were dazed, her lips swollen. She breathed his name . . . *Alistair*. He thickened.

"You didn't— You still . . ."

"All day," he reminded, lunging heavily, accelerating his tempo. "All night."

Her fingertips flexed into his back. Her legs tightened around his hips. "Yes. Please."

14

Jess awoke to the feel of firm fingertips gliding back and forth across her forearm. She lay on her stomach with one arm tossed over Alistair's torso. Her body felt achy and heavy, well used. For a long moment, she lay there, absorbing the odd reality of waking up to a man beside her. It was surprisingly pleasant, reaffirming the intimacy established through lovemaking.

It was growing dark outside. The sunlight that had shone through the porthole earlier was dimmed now. Hours had passed, as had several shattering orgasms. She hadn't known her body was capable of repeating a climax so soon, or that a man's body was capable of such sexual stamina. Although Benedict had sometimes taken her more than once in a night, it was always with hours between one encounter and the next. Alistair had required little time for recovery ... mere moments. He said that was because of her, because of his desire for her. Of course, he was younger than Benedict. Younger than she ... but she refused to think about that.

The bigger revelation was that his fervency no longer frightened her. How could it when she felt equally fervent toward him? The gratitude Beth had told her she'd feel was only one of a dozen emotions swirling through her. Her affection for the man beside her was powerful enough to constrict her chest.

Shifting, she slid one leg over his and pressed her lips to his biceps. He made a low sound of approval. "If I'd known," he said with glittering eyes, "that sex would make you so agreeable, I would have taken you to bed sooner."

"A sennight wasn't soon enough?" she asked, startled at the vocalization of how quickly he'd slipped under her guard.

"Several years preceded that sennight." He caught the hand she had splayed across his chest and kissed her knuckles. "What softened your resistance and sweetened your temper?"

"I didn't understand the many facets involved in our association. I could only see an entanglement between us as an unnecessary complication. I had no notion that a love affair was a natural progression for a widow, part of a process of healing that allows a woman to resume her life without her spouse."

His grip on her hand tightened marginally. "You discovered this today?"

Jess nodded and slid closer, draping half of her body over the side of his. She felt comfortable with him. Safe. Free. "I am now prepared to enjoy you fully, knowing that when the time comes to part we'll do so with fondness. And I will be stronger and more resilient for the experience."

"So, I am to be an experience for you." He sounded mildly contemplative. "When do you anticipate this time for amicable farewell will arrive?"

She shrugged. "I haven't the faintest idea. And, frankly, the end no longer concerns me."

She'd already changed profoundly because of him, in so many ways. He would not be merely an experience for her but an adventure, as fraught with possibilities as her voyage to the West Indies.

"What if it concerns me?" he murmured.

The casualness of his tone took the weight from his words. That pained her, but she endeavored not to show it. It was not his fault that she didn't know how to conduct a casual affair, and she did not want to give him cause to regret becoming involved with her. "Fustian. We both know you will tire of me first."

"To be clear, you'll keep me as your lover until one of us no longer desires the other?"

"You know the etiquette of such things better than I."

Alistair flipped her to her back in an economic, agile movement. He rose above her, kneeing her legs open and settling between them. The scent of his skin, now mingled with her fragrance, was as stimulating as always. "You do realize you've challenged me again," he purred. "This time, to keep you enthralled with me indefinitely."

She stared up at him, adoring the way his dark hair hung around his face, making him look wicked and sinful. Her fingers traced the arch of one of his brows. "You would swiftly grow bored with a fawning paramour, I'm certain."

With a practiced swivel of his hips, he positioned his cockhead at the entrance of her sex and pushed a scant inch inside her. She was slick with his seed, filled with him. Yet she wanted more; it frightened her how much. He reached between them, finding her clitoris and stroking over it with a feather-light touch. Her breath left her in a sighing moan. She was sore and swollen, but that was no deterrent. She needed to lose herself to his skill and his focused pursuit of her pleasure. She needed to forget this talk of endings while she was still so enamored with the beginning.

His mouth hovered above hers, his sensual lips curved in a smile that didn't soften his determined gaze. "I challenge you to prove it."

Bearing down, he drove into her, making her cry out at the suddenness of his invasion. Alistair had been so careful before, giving her time to process every sensation before moving on to the next. This time felt like a claiming, a bold and undeniable possession. She writhed beneath him, trying to accommodate the thick, deep impalement.

"Fawn over me," he coaxed darkly. "Lavish me with your attention. See what comes of it."

Jess would have told him she had no desire to hasten his leavetaking, but he began to thrust. As fluid as his movements were, they were rougher than they'd been previously. Harder. Every downstroke hit the end of her, the thick club of his magnificent penis stroking over nerve endings in a contact that curled her toes. She clawed at his back, pulling him closer.

He brushed his lips across her temple, then rubbed his cheek against hers, sharing the perspiration misting his skin. "This time," he whispered, "I'm going to fuck you, Jess. The way I've needed to fuck you all these years."

The coarseness of his hoarsely voiced threat was opposed to his tender kiss. Her hunger sharpened. He caught the back of her knee and pulled her leg upward, opening her wider. His next hard lunge wrung a cry from her, the sensation of his endless penetration bringing a fierce pleasure bordering on pain. She bit her lip to stifle further sound.

"Let me hear you." With his palms on the mattress, he supported his torso easily. His hips were held aloft by his knees, affording him impressive fluidity of movement. With her leg hooked around his biceps and her pelvis canted upward, she had no defense against him. His cock plunged and retreated with blurring speed, his hips lifting and falling, his heavy sac smacking against her in a swift erotic rhythm. "Tell me how much you like it," he purred. ". . . how good it feels . . ."

Soft sobs of pleasure escaped her, spilling from her mindlessly. His large body mantled hers, dominated her, left her with no awareness beyond him. Everything she clung to faded away, leaving her with only base desire and heated yearning, every cell in her body attuned to the man who rode her with marked possessiveness.

"Jess . . ." He groaned. Sweat dripped from his hair as his hips pistoned against hers. "I will never tire of this. Of you. My God . . . I don't think I can stop."

"Don't stop." Jess slung her free leg over his hips and possessed him in kind, flexing into his pounding tempo. "Don't. Stop."

Her womb clenched desperately, the rush of orgasm licking across her skin like fire, whiplashes of pleasure cutting through the outer shell she'd lived in her entire life. The violence of his lovemaking rocked her to the core, leaving her defenseless against his relentless siege on her emotions. She felt herself unraveling, her eyes burning with a sudden wash of tears.

Alistair watched her as she fell apart beneath him, his azure eyes feverishly bright in the semidarkness. She shook with the violence of her climax, moaning when he thrust deep and rolled his hips, applying the perfect pressure to her clitoris to keep her coming and coming and coming.

She wrapped her arms around his nape and lifted to him, taking the connection she needed in a lush, fervent kiss. The swollen tissues of her sex rippled along the length of his throbbing penis, luring him to begin thrusting again.

Releasing her leg, he caught her up, his arms sliding beneath her shoulders and embracing her tightly. His lips moved across her cheek, his breath gusting hot and fast across her ear.

"My turn," he growled, gripping her shoulders and lunging powerfully. "Hold me."

Jess pressed her face into his sweat-slick chest and held on, absorbing the feel of his body flexing and working against her. The sweet friction of his plunging strokes threatened to push her over the edge again, but she resisted, wanting to experience Alistair's race to orgasm. He'd spent the afternoon focused on her, restraining the sexual animal she knew was in him. Now, finally, he seemed to be losing his grip on his steely control, the ferocity of his passion betraying a depth of emotion that might rival hers.

She felt the tension grip him, heard his teeth grind as he fought it. "Come in me," she urged, accepting the pounding of his hips and cock. All her reserve was burned away by the heat of his lust, leaving behind a woman brave enough and wanton enough to say the libidinous words that would incite him to madness. "You feel so good . . . *so good . . .*"

"Damnation," he hissed, swelling inside her. The first hard, thick spurt made her gasp in delight. He jerked against her, shuddering with every wrenching pulse, his hands fisting in the bedclothes on either side of her head.

He came hard and long, groaning her name, rubbing his face and torso against her as if to mark her with his scent. Jess took it all, cradling him as he shattered like she had mere moments earlier, anchoring him in the midst of the storm.

Alistair's fingers rubbed restlessly across the wood grain of the table in the great cabin, his gaze on Jessica as she spoke to the captain over supper.

She wore a high-necked gown to hide the evidence of Alistair's bite, the soft grayish-purple hue of the silk a reminder of her widowhood. As he'd known she would, she looked well fucked, her color high and her lips swollen from his kisses. Her eyes were bright and her voice throaty, while the expressive movements of her hands and arms were marked by a more pronounced sensual grace. He'd never seen her appear so relaxed or look more beautiful, yet his pleasure in that accomplishment was marred by agitation.

He was mad for her, enamored as he'd never been of another woman. Yet she seemed far more composed than he was. His future had altered drastically this day; everything he'd considered inviolate—his bachelorhood, his freedom to come and go as he pleased, his ability to avoid Society whenever and however he wished—was gone. Jessica would now dictate the paths his life would traverse from this point forward, because he couldn't proceed without her. It was a revelation that shook him. He had long known he was meant to have her; he hadn't realized until this afternoon that he was meant to keep her.

Alistair heaved out his breath and ran a rough hand through his hair. Jess glanced at him over the rim of her wine-filled glass and frowned. He waved her concern away with an impatient flick of his wrist.

He had gotten more than he'd bargained for with her. Her generosity in bed extended far beyond the gift of her body. She held nothing back. Tears, smiles, provocative whispers . . . His back bore the marks of her nails, but it was the interior cuts that stung now. She'd allowed him to see every emotion filtering through her as he made love to her, and that knowledge flayed him open. Every time she'd held him tightly at the extremity of his climax, as if to hold him together, she sliced a little deeper.

How in hell could she sit there so serenely after what they'd gone through that afternoon? It seemed almost as if the ramifications of what had transpired escaped her, yet he knew that couldn't be true. Jessica wasn't the kind of woman who engaged in indiscriminate sex. The connection for her had to be twofold—one of mind and body. She *had* to be engaged more than she appeared, but her damned inviolate perfection of deportment shielded her too well. Meanwhile, he was coming apart at the seams and couldn't hide it.

The walls of the great cabin closed in on him. His breath

shortened and he grew overwarm. He slipped a finger between his cravat and his neck, attempting to alleviate the feeling of constriction.

Supper seemed to last an eternity. He refused the customary glass of port and excused himself as soon as he could politely do so. He offered a brief smile to Jessica, then fled. Reaching the main deck, Alistair sucked in a deep breath of crisp sea air and gripped the gunwale, waiting for the restoration of his equilibrium.

"Mr. Caulfield."

His eyes closed at the sound of Jess's voice. As vivid images from the afternoon raced through his mind, he realized his mistake. She was there in his head; there was no escape. "Yes, Jessica?"

"Are you— Is everything all right?"

He looked out across the sea and nodded.

She drew abreast of him. Together, they stared at the moon's elongated reflection on the water. "You were so quiet over supper."

"I apologize," he said automatically and absently.

"I would prefer to know what has you so thoroughly occupied."

"Thoughts of you."

"Oh?" She canted her body toward him. "Not quite so flattering when you look so grim."

"Contemplative," he corrected, although he conceded to himself that he felt grim. Which was extremely out of character. His livelihood—past and present—was often benefited by his ability to keep his face carefully schooled. "We did not finish our conversation about your altercation on the deck this morning."

Her chin lifted, and she sucked in a deep breath. "I am not refusing to answer," she began, "but I have to ask: Do you truly want to delve into the unsavory aspects of my past? I confess, I would rather you think of me as a romantic figure than one who is flawed and damaged."

"Is that all you want of me in return?" he asked tightly, inwardly raging against any distance between them. "To see only the surface and nothing of depth?"

"No." Her hand came to rest gently on his forearm.

Alistair swiftly caught her by covering her hand with his own.

She met his gaze. "There is a great deal I would like to know about you. Everything, actually."

"Why?"

A slight frown marred the space between her brows. She was lovely in moonlight, her gilded hair made silver, her skin as luminous as a pearl. There was a new softness to her he'd failed to notice before. He wondered if it had been there throughout supper or if it was making itself apparent only now because they were alone. The anxious part of him seized on the latter possibility, which soured his mood further. Damned if he would be needy.

"Because you fascinate me," she said softly. "Just when I assume I might know you, you show me another side of yourself that is completely unexpected."

"Such as . . . ?"

Her lids lowered. Her thick lashes shadowed her eyes. "Such as when you took the helm. And when you arranged the picnic on the deck. And when you left my cabin that night."

He nodded.

She caught her lower lip between her teeth, then swiftly released it, as if she'd noted her nervous gesture and rejected it. "I don't understand your mood. Have I displeased you in some way?"

"If I was any more pleased with you, I would lose what little remains of my sanity." He linked their fingers together.

Jessica inhaled a long, slow, deep breath before speaking. "My pater believed sparing the rod spoiled the child."

Alistair tensed. "Oh?"

"Suffice it to say I was not spared nor spoiled." Her grip on his hand tightened. "That is why I'm disturbed by bullies, especially those who grant no immunity to childhood."

Rage heated his blood. "That's the consequence you spoke of the other day? You were beaten if you were not well behaved? By Hadley?"

"In retrospect, I was an unruly child, I suppose."

"That's cause for patience, not abuse! You know this."

"What's done is done," she dismissed, although her voice was unsteady.

"But not forgotten." He stepped closer. "You were distraught today. The unpleasantness festers in your mind."

"In a fashion." Jessica offered him a sweet, tentative smile that served as another nail in his coffin. "But I realized today that I'm stronger than I gave myself credit for. For all of Hadley's strenuous efforts, I am still capable of admiring your novel approach to life and the problems presented to you. I'm still capable of enjoying you without reserve."

A tightening afflicted Alistair's chest. "You gave yourself to me in rebellion because Hadley would not have approved."

"No; I took you in celebration, because Hadley's thoughts on the matter are of no concern to me. Not any longer. I don't think you collect how profound the realization was, to learn that the control he exerted over me is not absolute after all. I managed to retain some of my individuality, and as an individual, I wanted you."

"Does this tie into your discovery that taking me as your lover will act as a balm for your grief over Tarley's passing?" He hated the bitterness that seeped into his tone, but the painful knotting of his gut wouldn't allow him to be nonchalant. Not about this. He seemed to suit her every purpose except the one most important to him—to be entrusted with her heart. He wished he could be content with being the means through which she overcame her sorrows, but helping her past Tarley and Hadley wasn't enough. Not when he was so fundamentally altered that the life he'd once known was forever lost to him.

"Alistair . . ." Jess turned away abruptly, her free hand gripping the gunwale. Her back was ramrod straight, her head held high. There was defiance inherent in her posture; it won his regard and roused his body. "I feel as if you want me to say something—*anything*—that will lower your esteem for me or give you cause to retreat."

Retreat? The very notion was absurd. He was addicted to the pure, innocent feeling of connection he'd found in bed with her. He could no more give that up than he could change the order of his birth. Reliance on anything was a circumstance he'd fought against his entire life, and now there was no escaping it. Leastwise, not for him. "What do you think you can reveal that will mitigate my captivation with you? Enlighten me, so I'll know what I must hide from you to prevent a loss of interest on your part. Of course, if my whoring didn't accomplish that, perhaps only proper behavior will make me unsuitable. Perhaps it's because I'm unsavory that I am useful to you."

"Stop it," she hissed, shooting him a narrow-eyed glare. "I don't care for your tone."

"My apologies. Did I venture too far toward unacceptability for your tastes? Do you want only moderately aberrant behavior from a lover?"

Yanking her hand free of his grip, she turned away. "I'll see you on the morrow, Alistair, and will pray that after a good night's rest you'll be in better spirits."

"Don't dismiss me," he snapped, fighting the urge to

forcibly stay her. He would never use physical force against her, especially not after learning what she'd suffered through in her youth.

Jessica rounded on him. "You are being impossible. Ugly. I don't know why."

"I've always believed I could have anything I wanted, if I worked hard enough. If I just sacrificed as necessary, made devil's bargains and concessions, paid outrageous sums . . . I thought everything was possible and within my grasp." He silenced the voice in his head that pressed for caution and self-preservation. "Now, I'm faced with one thing I want more than anything else on earth, and I know I can't buy you or cajole you or force you to accept me. The feeling of powerlessness is one I cannot abide. It shortens my temper and leaves me extremely frustrated."

Fine lines bracketed her lush mouth. "What are you saying?"

"I want you to start thinking of our arrangement as limitless, rather than finite. I want you try envisioning endless days like today. Mornings waking up in my arms. Nights passing with me inside you. Rides together in Hyde Park and waltzes in front of the ton."

Her slender hand lifted to her throat. "You would be miserable."

"Without you, yes." He crossed his arms. A stiff ocean breeze whipped through his hair. Now it was he who felt rebellious and defiant. "I'm sorry I didn't present these terms to you in the beginning. I know I spoke of our affair as fitting within a short duration of time. But my intentions—my *needs*—have changed."

"I'm not certain I fully collect what your intentions are," she said carefully. "What are you asking of me?"

"You said you're no longer concerned with the end, but you still think of it as inevitable. I would prefer you to think of it as avoidable."

"I thought we agreed that we would remain lovers until one of us lost interest in the other. What more can be done?"

"We can work at this"—he gestured impatiently between them—"*thing* between us, instead of allowing it to fade and wither. When problems arise, we can address them. If the attraction begins to wane, we can devise ways to reignite it."

She licked her lower lip. "What would you call such an arrangement?"

Alistair pushed aside the anxiety that threatened to steal his voice. "I believe," he said neutrally, "it's called a courtship."

15

Hester drank her tea slowly, making a valiant attempt to keep something in her stomach. Though she was ravenous in the evenings, the afternoons found her still suffering from nausea. "I suggest swapping the ribbons, Your Grace," she said to the Countess of Pennington. "Try the brown with the blue, and the green with the peach."

Elspeth looked over her shoulder to where Hester sat on a settee in the countess's boudoir. "Truly?"

The countess returned her attention to the material and ribbons laid out across her bed. She gestured for the modiste to do as advised, then nodded. "You're right."

Hester smiled. While she'd been slightly confused when Elspeth first began making persistent, yet friendly, overtures, she'd come to realize that the countess looked upon her in the capacity of a daughter. It was a role Jessica had filled, and Hester found herself enjoying the maternal companionship. She understood that Elspeth's need was temporary, part of her re-acclimation to Society after years spent in the country. Hester envied her that idyllic life on the stunning Pennington estate.

"You should try the lemon scones," Elspeth urged. "I vow you've never tasted the like. They melt in your mouth."

"Thank you. I should like to. Another time, perhaps."

The countess shook her head and came to her, settling on the settee opposite the one Hester occupied. "Have you tried ginger tea or broth, or both? Either will help to settle your stomach. And be moderate with greasy foods in the evening. Salted water crackers also help."

There was a pause, and then Hester said softly, "Is it so obvious?"

"Only to an observant woman who has spent nearly every day of this last week with you."

"Please, I must beg for your discretion."

Elspeth's dark eyes brightened at the hint of a secret. "You and Regmont are keeping the news to yourselves? Delightful."

Hester hesitated, reluctant to share a confidence she'd held so close to her breast. "Regmont doesn't yet know."

"Oh . . . ? Whyever not?"

"I feel very unwell. I cannot help fearing that something is wrong. Regmont wouldn't— He isn't—" Hester set her cup and saucer down on the low table between them. "It would be better to wait and be certain that all is progressing as it should be."

"My dear." The countess reached for the tongs and moved a scone from the serving tray to a small plate. "You are squandering one of the few opportunities in a woman's life when she can ask anything of her husband and receive it."

"Regmont gives me too much as it is." But not the one thing she most wished for—his peace of mind. "I also wanted to spare Jessica for a while longer."

"She would be overjoyed on your behalf."

"Yes." Hester smoothed her skirts. "But she might grieve for herself, and she has enough to feel sorrowful about at the moment."

"She will hurt more if you don't tell her."

"I wrote her shortly after she left. I think this is best. She won't feel the need to put a brave face on if I'm not there when she learns the news. She can react in whatever manner is most comfortable for her, and when we see each other again, it will be with pure joy in her heart."

Elspeth washed down a bite with a sip of tea. "You two are very close."

Hester rubbed at the ache in her breast. "Yes. She is a sister and mother to me, as well as my dearest friend."

"Jessica said your mother passed away when you were young."

"I was ten, but in many ways my mother was lost to me before then. Her melancholia was debilitating. I most often saw her only in passing. She was a ghost to me—frail and wan and lacking any vibrancy whatsoever."

"I'm sorry." Elspeth offered a gentle, commiserating smile. "Motherhood is a gift. It is truly a shame Lady Hadley was unable to see it that way."

"Jess would have made a wonderful mother. And Tarley, a wonderful father."

"The same can be said about you and Regmont, I'm sure."

Hester looked away from the countess, managing a shaky smile at the modiste's assistants as they exited to the gallery with Elspeth's selections.

"My dear," Elspeth said, quietly commanding Hester's attention. "Is it possible that you might be suffering from melancholia as well?"

"Oh, no. Truly, it's just that I feel so wretched most of the day. And I confess, I worry about the match between Regmont and Michael tomorrow. I wish there was some way to dissuade them. Regmont takes such things so seriously."

"You care about Michael."

Hester felt a blush sweep over her cheeks. Over the past week, she'd found herself paying undue attention to Michael.

She'd looked for him at events and around the city, hoping for a mere glimpse. The sharp prick of excitement she felt when she found him both exhilarated and saddened her. It was undeniable proof that her love for her husband had lost its ability to consume her. "He's a good man."

"Yes." Elspeth set her cup down with a sigh. "I must be honest with you. I have more than one reason for cultivating our friendship. Though I'm deeply grateful for assistance with my attire, I have a need for another of your skills more."

"If I can help in any way, I would be honored to."

"I should like your expert opinion on the debutantes who might best suit Michael. Since you care for him as I do, I know you want to see him content in his marriage."

"Of course." Hester met the countess's examining gaze directly, drawing upon years of Jessica's coaching to hide her dismay. It was unreasonable for her to wish for him to remain as he'd always been.

Elspeth smiled beautifully. "Thank you. I hope to see him settled before the year is out."

"That would be wonderful," Hester agreed softly. "If we cannot manage sooner."

A knock came at the door.

Jess smiled, knowing who it was just by the cadence. The door opened without any encouragement from her. Alistair swept into the limited confines of her cabin with absolute confidence of his welcome.

He was so comely, he took her breath away. He had changed since they'd been at sea, most especially over the past week in which they had been lovers. His beautiful blue eyes were brighter now, prone to amusement and warmth. There was a new softness to his features that, impossibly, made him even more handsome. And the way he moved . . . there was an underlying leisure to the sensuality that marked him. As if she soothed the beast within him. It was a fanciful thought, but one that pleased her immensely.

He came to where she sat at the table and bent to press his lips to her temple. She lifted her mouth to his with an admonishing hum, securing a real kiss from him.

"Good evening," she breathed, feeling her usual inordinate pleasure at the intimacy between them. It was similar to the ease with which she'd lived with Tarley, yet it was not the same. Her response to Alistair was far richer and deeper in tone. It pained her to realize her relationship with Benedict hadn't been all that it, perhaps, could have been. Yet she'd come to suspect that whatever was lacking in her marriage had been due to Alistair. Unbeknown to her, he'd been there in the shadows, occupying a space in her mind that he'd allowed no one to usurp.

"It is now." He straightened, revealing a leather-bound ledger tucked under his arm.

"What is that?"

"Work." He set it down on the table.

She smiled and set aside the quill with which she'd been writing a letter to Hester. "I'm happy you came to me even though you have more pressing matters to attend to."

"I would prefer to make love to you instead, but I suspect you'll soon be indisposed to such exertions."

Her brows rose. Her courses had begun just that morning. "How did you know?"

He shrugged out of his coat and draped it over the chair opposite her. "How could I not know? I touch your body more than I touch my own. Your breasts are swollen and tender, and your desire for sex has been at a fever pitch the last two days. Among other signs."

Jess's mouth curved with wry amusement. "Observant man."

"Can't be helped," he said, smiling back at her. "I cannot take my eyes off you."

"Flatterer," she teased. "And, sadly, I *am* indisposed. I could accommodate you in other ways, though . . ."

He sat. "A delicious thought, but I am content to simply be with you."

Jess inhaled a deep breath, an involuntary response to the sudden racing of her heart. He said the words so casually, but she was deeply affected by his openness and the vulnerability inherent in his lack of guile. Lord knew, she was vulnerable, too. "I feel the same," she said softly.

"I know." Alistair reached across the table for her hand. "I cannot tell you what it means to me that whether or not we have sex doesn't affect your desire to spend time with me."

She couldn't say why it surprised her to learn that a handsome man wanted to be appreciated for more than his exterior and desired for more than his sexual prowess. "Alistair . . ."

"Don't pity me," he said sharply in response to her softened tone of voice. "I will take any emotion from you but that one."

"I adore you."

The harsh line of his mouth smoothed. "That one will do nicely."

She shook her head. "I won't have you feeling ashamed of yourself because of me. I have not—nor will I ever—judge you harshly for your past choices, but if you cannot abide yourself when we're together, we are better off apart."

He scowled. "Now, see here—"

"No, *you* must see. You have to decide, right this very moment, that you are as worthy of my affections as any other man. If you cannot, I would like for you to leave."

Alistair cursed under his breath. "You cannot say such things to me."

"Damned if I can't," she shot back. "You may delude yourself into thinking I'm perfect, but I am only a woman and only partly a woman at that, since I'm barren. I must say, it's vastly unfair that I cannot have children; yet I bleed as if it was possible."

"So, you *are* menstruating?" he asked in a tone that was too light.

"If you were worried I wouldn't, you should not have been."

He held her gaze. "Are you certain? Perhaps the fault was Tarley's."

"No. He had a child with a mistress before we wed."

"Perhaps the child wasn't his?"

"If you saw the boy, you would have no doubt. Like your brothers, he is the very image of his father."

Alistair nodded and directed his attention to his ledger.

A chill moved through Jess. The end of their relationship was inevitable if he wanted children, which most men did. And he deserved that sort of happiness.

"I've watched you with the boy," she said, referring to the child she'd tried to rescue from abuse a week before. Alistair had taken an interest in the young sailor, working with him on knots and other useful skills, and she had enjoyed watching them together. "You will make a wonderful father someday."

He glanced up at her, then leaned back in his chair and crossed his arms. His hair had grown slightly longer, and she loved how the black strands framed his face. Her hand lifted to her throat and massaged the tightness there.

"Jessica." He exhaled harshly. "I've never given much thought to having children. Now, I won't give the matter any thought at all."

"Don't say that. You cannot deny yourself the joy arbitrarily."

"Procreation requires a partner, as you know. You are the first link in that chain. If you are also the last link, so be it. I cannot even begin to contemplate making the effort with anyone else."

Her vision blurred. Blinking through an embarrassing sting of tears, she pushed back from the table in a rush and hurried over to the crate of claret waiting in the corner.

"Jess . . ."

She heard the scrape of chair legs atop the sole behind her; then firm hands gripped her shoulders the second before she bent down to grab the neck of a bottle.

"Hearing how I feel about you drives you to drink?" he asked with his lips to her ear.

"No. Being selfish enough to feel glad about it does."

"I *want* you to feel selfish about me."

Jess shook her head violently. "Love is selfless. Or it is supposed to be."

"For some, perhaps. You and I have had so much taken from us. It is as it should be for us to take from each other."

Closing her eyes, she leaned her head back against his shoulder. His arms came around her, and she placed her hands over his. "You have many siblings. You must want a large family of your own?"

"If we are going to discuss my family, we'll need that claret."

He walked away. Jess grabbed a bottle and straightened. When she turned around he was pulling two goblets out of the small chest by the cabin door.

She put the wine on the table and sat. Alistair set the glasses down, then pulled the cork from the bottle. He left the claret to breathe and settled back in his chair, eyeing her in a manner that was both examining and contemplative.

She waited patiently.

"Have you never wondered why Masterson's paternal traits exerted themselves so strongly in my brothers, yet I am the mirror of my mother?"

"One doesn't question such blessings."

The compliment earned a small smile from him.

"So," she said. "I surmise Masterson isn't your father."

"And you do not care," he noted softly.

"Why would I?"

"Jess . . ." He gave a perfunctory laugh. "I feared telling you, you know. You are so renowned for your adherence to propriety; I thought you might think less of me."

"Impossible. But did your brothers think less of you? Do you not still feel close to Albert?"

"It was never an issue with my brothers, no. But Masterson . . . I cannot please him." The lack of inflection in his voice betrayed deeper emotions. "Personally, I no longer care, but my mother frets over the distance between us. If I could ease her mind, I would, but it isn't something I can change apparently."

"That's unfortunate for him." Finally, she understood why Masterson had been so reluctant to assist Alistair in making his own way in the world. "He is denying himself a fine son."

Alistair gave her a bemused shake of his head. "I'm still astonished at your nonchalance. I should warn you—every time you accept a dirty secret I share with you, I grow more and more determined to keep you. It seems nothing I say can turn you away from me."

Warmth unfurled in her chest. "Someone has to keep you out of mischief."

"Only you are up to the task."

"I should hope so, for your sake."

"Why, my lady, I could swear that was a warning of some sort."

Jess adopted a stern expression. "I value steadfastness and loyalty, Mr. Caulfield."

"As do I." His fingertips drummed atop the table. "I once believed Masterson truly loved my mother deeply, and that she felt similarly toward him. He allowed her to keep me and claimed me as one of his own, despite the way it eats at him, because he knew she would never forgive him if he forced her to give me up. But now . . ."

When he faltered, she prompted, "Now . . . ?"

Exhaling harshly, he said, "I appreciate the not-inconsiderable difference in their ages. I understand how that impacts Masterson's physical ability to maintain marital intimacy. But, by God, I could not turn a blind eye to your seeking the relief of your sexual needs elsewhere and call my disregard 'love.' I would see to you in other ways— my mouth, my hands, implements of pleasure . . . whatever was at my disposal. I keep what's mine, and I do not share."

"Perhaps neither of them know how to broach the subject. I wouldn't judge them too harshly."

"Promise me that you will feel free to discuss any topic with me."

It was a remarkably painless promise to commit to. He made it so easy for her to unveil herself just by the way he looked at her. Benedict had regarded her in the same manner, but he had asked no questions. His affection had been quietly given, with no liens or expectations. Alistair's demands were greater and far more comprehensive. But so, then, were the boundaries of his acceptance.

She nodded her acquiescence to his request.

He gestured at the parchment in front of her. "A letter?"

"To my sister. Telling her about my travels thus far."

"Have you mentioned me?"

"I have."

Pleasure brightened his eyes. "What did you say?"

"Oh, I'm not done yet."

"You have so much to relay?"

"That, and I must exercise care in how I relay it. After all, I did warn her away from you."

"Selfish girl."

185

Jess stood and rounded the table. His gaze followed her as she approached, watching her with open, heated appreciation. Setting one hand on his shoulder, she brushed his dark hair back from his forehead and pressed a kiss there.

"It pleases me to lay claim to you," she murmured, thinking of Masterson and how foolishly prideful the man was.

Alistair caught her by the waist. "I wonder if you'll feel that way in London," he murmured, "when surrounded by those who may judge you harshly for your choice."

"Do you think I'm so malleable? So easily influenced?"

"I don't know." He looked up and into her eyes. "I don't think you know either."

He was correct, in a fashion. She'd always done exactly what was proper and expected. "My father would disagree with you. He would tell you that it takes a great deal of effort to convince me to conform."

She was pulled and arranged gently on Alistair's lap. His arms tightened around her. "Thinking of him and how he treated you incites me to violence."

"He isn't worth the effort. Besides, in some ways, I am grateful to him. What was once difficult for me became second nature and made life easier for me." She pushed her fingers through his hair. "And look at how you've unraveled so much of that training in just a fortnight."

"I want to unravel *you*."

"You are succeeding." With every hour that passed, she felt a little freer. Much as she did when shedding her corset at the end of a long day. She was beginning to doubt her ability to accept her former constraints if faced with them again. "Does that frighten you? Or cool your interest? As I fall so easily into your arms, does the lack of a worthy challenge bore you?"

"You challenge me every moment, Jess. You frighten me just as often." He rested his head against her breast. "I don't know how to be dependent upon someone else for anything, yet I find myself dependent upon you."

Jess wrapped her arms around his broad shoulders and set her chin atop his crown. She might have guessed that a man like Alistair, who never did anything in half-measure, would give his affection with similar abandon. But she hadn't expected that he would want to commit himself to one woman when his choices were so vast. "I confess, I'm terrified. Everything has changed so swiftly."

"Is that so terrible? Were you so happy before?"

"I was not unhappy."

"And now?"

"I don't recognize myself. Who is this woman who sits on rakes' laps and offers sexual favors with the ease of offering a cup of tea?"

"She's mine, and I like her quite well."

"You would, naughty man." She nuzzled her cheek against his hair. "Did your mother love you well, Alistair? Is that why you are so adept at caring for me?"

"She did, despite all the grief my conception and birth caused her. I would do anything to ensure her happiness."

"Wouldn't she love to have grandchildren?"

Pulling back, he looked at her. "That is Baybury's responsibility as the heir. He will see to it."

"And what is your responsibility?" she queried, stroking her thumb tenderly across his cheek.

"To be the scapegrace of the family, corrupting fine young widows and luring them to sin."

She kissed him. With her lips against his, she said, "While I endeavor to see that you remain upon the straight and narrow path you've set for yourself these last years."

His strong hands slid up either side of her spine. "What a pair we shall make. The wicked widow and the reformed rake."

Jess quelled the quiver of unease in her stomach, telling herself there was time enough to address the brutal realities of their association. So much had happened in such a short time, and there was still a long road to travel before it could be said with certainty that they were meant to go on together. In the interim, she would follow his lead. If it was meant for their happiness to be temporary, so be it. It was too late for her to retreat now.

She pressed her lips to the tip of his nose. "Let's have that glass of claret now."

16

"Beg your pardon, Lord Tarley."
Michael paused with his foot on the first step of Remington's Gentlemen's Club and turned his head to find a coachman standing off to the side with his hat in his hands. "Yes?"

"My lady begs a moment of your time, if you would be so kind."

Looking past the coachman's shoulder, Michael noted the hackney waiting nearby with curtains drawn over the windows. His pulse quickened with hope and expectation. The occupant could be any overly bold debutante, he supposed, but he wanted it to be Hester.

With a nod, he acknowledged the summons and approached the equipage. He paused directly outside the door. "Can I be of service?"

"Michael. Get in, please."

He almost smiled, but refrained. Opening the door, he climbed in and took the squab across from Hester. Her perfume filled the enclosed space. While the sunlight was strong enough to filter through the curtains and offer enough illumination to see, the sense of illicit intimacy was overpowering.

And surely contained entirely within his own mind.

At least he thought so, until he saw the handkerchief she smoothed over her lap. She had given him a kerchief once before, as a sign of her maidenly esteem when he'd played at being a knight in shining armor. Ages ago. Another lifetime.

"Have you come to give me a token to carry into battle?" he asked, forcing levity into his tone.

She stared at him for a long moment, looking fragile and beautiful in a pelisse of soft green trimmed in a darker color he couldn't quite determine in the semidarkness. She sighed. "I cannot alter your mind about this, can I?"

Her sorrowful tone prompted him to lean forward. He was struck by the change in her; the weight of unhappiness suppressed the vibrant spirit she was best known for. "Why does a simple boxing match worry you so?"

Her gloved hands clenched and unclenched in her lap. "Regardless of who wins or loses, it will not end well."

"Hester—"

"Regmont will likely begin the match playfully," she said without inflection, "but as your skill becomes apparent, he will become more focused. If he cannot best you, he may succumb to his temper. Be careful should that happen. His technique will slip and he will fight to win, perhaps not cleanly."

A pistol's report could not have jolted him more violently.

"I would say none of this to anyone else." Her chin lifted, reinforcing her quiet dignity. "But I suspect you'll be more deliberate in the ring. Levelheaded. You will follow the rules of the sport, and that, I fear, will preclude you from anticipating the most injurious blows."

"Succumb to his temper with whom?" He had no right to ask, but he couldn't withhold the question any longer. "Are you mistreated, Hester?"

"Worry about you," she admonished, managing a smile that did little to alleviate his suspicions. "You're the one about to engage in fisticuffs."

And he was ferociously eager for that engagement to begin, more so now than just a few moments ago when he'd simply been looking forward to it.

She held out the kerchief to him, but yanked it back when he moved to accept. "You have to promise to call on me, if you want this."

"Extortion," he said hoarsely, seeing the answer to his question in her evasion. His blood was boiling. She thought he would be deliberate and levelheaded? He was far from it.

"Coercion," she corrected. "Just so that I may see for myself that you are not unduly damaged."

Michael's jaw clenched against undeniable helplessness. There was no way for him to intercede. What a man did with his wife was his own affair. The only recourse available to him was the one he'd set in motion a week ago—a few far-too-brief moments in a boxing ring, during which he could pummel Regmont to his heart's content. "I promise to visit."

"Before a week is out," she persisted, her green eyes narrowed in silent admonishment.

"Yes." He accepted the kerchief with fierce possessiveness. A beautifully rendered "H" in the corner made the token even more personal. "Thank you."

"Be careful. Please."

With a curt nod, he exited the hackney. It pulled away before he'd set foot on the bottom step of Remington's wide entrance staircase.

"Don't be fooled by his size."

Hopping from foot to foot to limber himself, Michael glanced in the direction of the voice speaking at him. He found the Earl of Westfield, an unmarried peer who suffered the same sort of matrimonial attentions he did. Lauded for his good looks and charm, the earl was liked by both men and women. "Nothing about the man fools me."

"Interesting," Westfield said thoughtfully. He stepped into the eight-foot-square boxing area, which was delineated by painted lines on the hardwood floor. "Makes me very glad I bet on you."

"Did you?" Michael's gaze drifted around the massive room, which was damn near packed with spectators.

"Yes, I am one of the few." The earl flashed the grin that stole many women's hearts. "Regmont's shorter stature makes him quick and nimble. And he has stamina such as I've never seen, which is how he wins so often—he can outlast damn near everyone. That's what the others are wagering on: that you will tire before he does."

"I should think that would be dependent upon how hard he is hit, and how often."

Westfield shook his dark head. "For some men, such as myself, losing is an inconvenience we'd rather avoid. For others, like Regmont, it unmans them. His pride will fuel him long after you've satisfied whatever grievance you may have against him."

"This is simple sport, Westfield."

"Not with the way you're looking at him. Clearly you nurse a personal score to settle. I don't care. I just want to win my wager."

Michael might have smiled at another time, but he was too furious now. Regardless, he knew when to take the advice given to him. He also knew from the broad grin with which Regmont started the fight that the other man believed he would win. Although physical pain was the least of what the earl deserved, Michael decided humiliation would be the longer lasting punishment. He feinted around a few exploratory punches from Regmont, then channeled all his fruitless love for Hester and his hatred for her unworthy husband into a single solid blow.

Regmont crashed, unconscious, onto the hardwood less than a minute into the match.

"It's very difficult to concentrate when you are staring at me." Jess looked across the deck to where Alistair sat with his back to a crate. He'd removed his coat and now rested with one leg stretched out before him and the other pulled up to support the papers he worked with. It was a pose she'd seen him adopt in bed while reading or working, and it never failed to rouse her admiration.

"Pay me no mind," he said.

An impossible request. Not with him looking so handsome and rakish in his shirtsleeves. Not with his long, powerful legs showcased so beautifully in expertly tailored breeches and polished Hessians. Not with the wind playing in his hair the way her fingers wished to.

It was a lovely day, slightly overcast. Cool enough that she needed a shawl, but warm enough to still be pleasurable. She'd come above deck for the fresh air and was joined an hour later by Alistair and one of his portfolios. He'd chosen to sit a few feet away from her, but he looked up at her often and with unexplained intensity.

Jess snorted, then returned her attention to her needlepoint.

"Did the exemplary Lady Tarley just snort at me?" he asked, glancing at her with a raised brow.

"Ladies do not snort." She thought it was sweet how often he went out of his way to be near her, even while occupied with affairs far removed from her.

He'd become a friend. Someone she shared most everything with. It was a miracle that she'd found two men who wanted her just the way she was. Not because of the exterior crafted by her rigid upbringing, but for the woman hidden inside, the one they made it safe for her to reveal.

"Perhaps not other ladies," he said in a voice pitched low enough to reach only her ears. "You, however, make all sorts of delightful noises."

Jess became aroused by the simple provocative statement. She'd gone a week without sex with him, and the craving she felt now that her courses had passed was nigh intolerable.

"Now, you are the one staring," he teased without glancing at her.

"Because you are too far away for me to do anything else."

His head snapped up.

Smiling, she stood. "Enjoy the rest of your afternoon, Mr. Caulfield. I think I'll retreat to the comforts of my bed for a spell before supper."

She returned to her cabin, where Beth was working industriously on freshening her gowns.

"Lord 'ave mercy on Mr. Caulfield," Beth said, pausing. "You 'ave a wicked look in yer eye."

"Do I?"

"You know you do." Beth smiled. "I 'aven't seen you this 'appy in years. I'm beginning to pity the man."

"You said he was well insulated from heartache."

"I am occasionally wrong, milady. Rarely, but it does 'appen at times."

The thought widened Jess's smile. It was a relief to hear Beth's opinion. The only thing tempering Jess's contentment was the fear that such happiness couldn't last and that she was incapable of holding a man like Alistair Caulfield's attention for long. Not because she was unworthy of him, but because there were women who were worthier. Women who could give him things she couldn't—experience, an adventuresome spirit to match his own, children . . .

As she removed her shawl, her smile faded. They were both young. For all that he'd accomplished so far in his life, Alistair still had years yet before he would feel the urge to wed and breed. He couldn't know now that such instinctual longings would assail him, but *she* knew. It was up to her to do the correct and responsible thing in regard to their relationship.

Alistair's easily identifiable brisk knock came at the door. Beth laughed softly and draped the gown she'd been working with over a trunk. She opened the door with a broad grin. "Good afternoon, Mr. Caulfield."

Jess kept her back to the door, her eyes closing with anticipation and pleasure at the sound of his smooth, cultured reply.

"Will you be needing me for anything else, milady?" Beth asked.

"No, thank you. Enjoy your afternoon."

The door had barely shut when she heard the thud of something hitting the sole. A heartbeat later she found herself pinned to the bulkhead by over six feet of wildly aroused male. Delighted by his unexpected fervency, she threw her arms around his lean waist and returned the passion of his kiss.

"Vixen," he accused, his mouth moving across her jaw. "You are deliberately trying to incite me to madness."

"I have no idea what you're talking about."

He nipped her ear with his teeth, and she arched away, laughing. Her gaze fell to the portfolio he'd dropped on the floor, and she stilled.

"When you are no longer indisposed," he growled softly, seething with sexual intent, "I intend to make you pay for teasing a man who's gone without you for a sennight."

"I am not indisposed," she said absently, riveted by the drawings she saw peeking out from the edges of his carelessly discarded portfolio. "I haven't been for two days now."

Alistair pulled back. "Beg your pardon?"

"What are these?" She slid out of his arms and bent down beside the scattered parchment.

"Two days," he repeated.

Lifting the black leather front cover, Jess's breath caught. "My God, Alistair . . . These are astonishing."

"What's astonishing is your lack of desire for me."

"Don't be absurd. A woman would have to be dead to escape desire for you." She stared at her image rendered in fine, precise pencil lines. The uppermost picture was of her on the deck mere moments ago, explaining his preoccupation with watching her. "Is this how you see me?"

"It's how you are. Bloody hell, Jess. I've been dying for you this last week. You had to have known this. You could not have missed the cockstand I've been sporting for the last several days."

Her fingertips floated gently over the rendering. He'd made her beautiful, with softened features and warm eyes. She had never seen herself look lovelier. "Yes," she breathed, distracted. "It would be impossible to ignore an appendage of that size when it's prodding you in the back as your cock is wont to do when you lie with me."

"Don't jest," he snapped. "Explain."

"Do I truly look like this?"

"You do when you're looking at me. If you don't answer me, Jess, I cannot be held responsible for my actions."

"Stuff and nonsense. I wanted you to know, with proof, that I desire your company for more than the multitude of orgasms you are so adept at eliciting." Standing with the portfolio in hand, her breath left her in an audible rush. She flipped through the other portraits he'd drawn of her, awed by his talent and skill. "There is no mystery to me at all, is there? I do not wear my heart on my sleeve; I wear it on my face for all to see."

"You needn't sound so put out about it," he muttered, coming to her. "I'm certain to regard you the same way."

Jess looked at him then. "No, you don't. You look at me like a feline about to pounce on its prey. While I yield and melt, you become sharp as a blade."

"I'm a sexual man," he said brashly. "That doesn't mean I'm not soft on you. I should hope you see how I feel in other ways, if not on my features."

"Yes, I do." She shuffled his drawings, stilling when she found a picture of herself from a distant time. She was clearly younger and the parchment was yellowed with age, but what truly arrested her was the pure lust radiating from the rendering. Her eyes were wide and dark, her pupils dilated, her lips parted as if panting. The picture was a raw, intimate glimpse into the very heart of her craving for the man who stood beside her. "Alistair . . ."

"The night in the garden."

"How can you possess an image of me like this, yet doubt my desire for you?"

He pulled the items from her hands and tossed them on the table. "I swear you will drive me insane. You deny me the means through which I feel the most connected to you in order to prove the depth of your affection?"

Her mouth curved wryly. "You are hot blooded. Sex is like eating and sleeping to you."

His insatiability had been established early in their affair, and it helped to explain how he'd been physically able to prostitute himself. Sex for her was an intimate act, always. For Alistair, it was as necessary to his health as polishing his teeth and was equally inconsequential to his emotional state. That wasn't to say she didn't feel cherished when she shared his bed, but she knew he used the sexual act to achieve ends she didn't fully understand.

He claimed the sale of his body had been born of necessity, and she believed him, but not for the reasons he presented. As young and randy as he'd been, as needful of funds as he had felt, those truths didn't explain how he'd come to monetize himself as a commodity. That, she suspected, came from something within him. Not without. Whether it was due to Masterson or his absent father or something else entirely, Alistair had come to find value in himself through the prices others paid to be with him. She'd wanted to counter that experience by showing how she valued him in other, nonphysical ways, but it seemed he wasn't yet ready for such demonstrations. Though he relentlessly and ruthlessly forced them both to reveal their most private and painful memories to each other, in the end, he still needed her touch and her lust to feel wanted.

He backed her into the bulkhead once again, thrusting his muscled thigh between her legs to pin her in place. With one hand pressed to the wood on either side of her head, he glared down at her. "You are severely trying my patience."

"That isn't my intent," she said honestly, her body heating in response to the aggressive proximity of his. "Personally, I am so touched by your drawings and amazed by the purity of your talent that my heart aches."

His firm lips brushed across her temple. "Do you ache elsewhere?" he asked gruffly, his stance altering so that his knee pressed against her sex.

For a moment, Jess closed her eyes and absorbed the feel of his hot, hard body and the beloved scent of his skin. His desire permeated through her pores, sinking into the very marrow of her bones, forging her into an uninhibited wanton capable of reaching between his legs and cupping the rigid, pulsing length of his penis.

Alistair jerked violently, his breath hissing between his teeth. "*Christ.*"

"I've wanted you from the moment I first saw you," she confessed, licking her dry lips. "Every hour I want you more."

His blue eyes were dark with need. "Have me every hour."

She stroked him through his breeches and smalls, her body softening and moistening in heated expectation. "Sex is innate to you; you exude it like a heady and addicting fragrance. But how can I distinguish myself from the other women who've desired you, unless I show you that I want more than your body?"

"What other women?"

That made her smile, but the severity of his features didn't change. "Touch me," she begged, feeling as if she'd inadvertently created a gulf between them.

"Not yet." Alistair's refusal to put his hands on her was an unexpected enticement. She was so accustomed to his command of their bedsport that his lack of participation made her want him even more.

"Why?"

"You should burn as I have, as I do, every minute I'm not inside you."

Tilting her head back, she kissed his tense jaw. Prickles of heat swept across her skin. "You want to punish me."

He caught her face in his hands. "No. You've wedged sex between us. We have to put it back into its proper place."

Jess tugged his shirttails free of his breeches and touched the scorching skin of his back. "You are forgetting I deliberately lured you here to ravish you."

"While you seem to think I'm exceptionally obtuse."

"I do not!" she protested. "In fact, I think you have an exceptionally fine mind."

"Oh?" The pad of his thumb stroked along the curve of her lower lip, the chaste touch igniting a raging hunger to feel his hands everywhere. "You've been teaching me how to make love for weeks, yet you do not believe I've learned the lesson."

Her fingers clenched into the rigid muscles bracketing his spine.

"The very first time I had you," Alistair whispered, leaning his forehead against hers, "I understood the difference between what I thought I knew about sex and what I had yet to grasp. Now, I cannot remember how I ever managed the act before you or how I could ever possibly attempt it without you."

Pushing onto her tiptoes, Jess surged into him, hugging him tightly in an effort to expend the surfeit of emotion rushing through her.

"I need you." Her face pressed into his throat. "You've made me need you."

"I cannot believe I ever thought of an orgasm as anything other than deeply personal." Alistair withdrew his thigh from between her legs.

She made a small sound of protest, the aching of her sex unrelieved without the pressure he'd exerted. "Please . . ."

He caught up fistfuls of her skirts until he bared her pantalettes. He gripped her buttocks firmly, squeezing hard enough to be almost painful. While there were times when he was playful or tender in bed, she was most violently aroused when he was ferociously lustful.

Her fingers fumbled with the hidden buttons securing the placket of his breeches. She eventually released his straining erection, her breath catching as he fell heavily into her palms. She stroked the thickly veined length with eager hands, her desire stoked to a fevered pitch by his words and his drawings and the haste with which he'd followed her from the deck. He had the ability to make her feel special and emminently desirable, as well as safe and secure. He enabled the freedom she needed to be whoever she wanted to be. As wild and unrestrained and overly bold as she chose.

Alistair watched her from beneath his lush, inky lashes. His hips rocked, thrusting his cock in and out of her greedy grip. Her sex grew slick and swollen, jealous of her hands.

As if he knew, he reached between her legs from behind, piercing the slit of her pantalettes to part her. "You're wet for me."

"I can't help it."

"Nor do I want you to." Without warning, he clutched

the backs of her thighs and lifted her. He was pulled from her hands, eliciting a soft cry of protest.

She felt the silky heat of his erection brush across her opened sex, and she whimpered in longing. Her arms encircled his broad shoulders, her mouth seeking the sensitive spot behind his ear to goad his passion.

"Pay attention," he ordered grimly as he began to push inside her.

Jess's head fell back against the bulkhead with a helpless moan. He lowered her onto his rigid penis with excruciating slowness, making certain she felt the stretch of every incredible inch.

"God," she gasped, writhing in his unyielding grip. She could barely accommodate him in this position. And still he impaled her relentlessly, stuffing her full until she fought for every breath. When he was finally in her to the root, she was sobbing with the need to pump and grind and take her pleasure. The fact that they were both fully dressed except for the place where they were joined was searingly erotic. Her façade was no impediment to Alistair. It never had been.

He kept her immobile and pinned to the bulkhead with his weight. Encircling her wrist, he pulled her hand up and pressed it over his heart. It thundered beneath her palm. His chest lifted and fell in a markedly elevated rhythm. "I have exerted myself not at all. You weigh little more than a feather. Tell me, Jess, why does my heart race? For the strenuous sex we've yet to begin? Or because it beats for you?"

The fingers of her free hand threaded into his hair; her hot cheek nuzzled against his. She wanted to say something, *anything,* but her throat was too tight.

"If I could," he went on, "I would remain like this indefinitely—clasped by you, held inside you, a part of you— without moving at all. When we make love, I fight climax with everything I have. I don't want to come; I do not want it to end. No matter how long I make it last, it isn't nearly long enough. I am furious when I cannot hold back any longer. Why, Jess? If all I seek is the physical relief of natural lust, just as I would seek sleep or food, why would I deny myself?"

She turned her head and caught his mouth with hers, kissing him desperately.

"Tell me you understand," he demanded, his lips moving beneath hers. "Tell me you feel it, too."

"I feel *you*," she breathed, as intoxicated by his ardency as she was by the finest claret. "You have become everything to me."

Clasping her tightly, he pivoted toward the bed.

17

Jess sank into the mattress with Alistair directly following on top of her. The descent jolted them both, his cock piercing deep as he pinned her to the bed. She moaned, perspiration blooming across her skin. He growled, fisting the counterpane on either side of her head and lunging again. The thrust was powerful, pushing her across the slippery velvet only to be stopped by his steely forearms at her shoulders.

"No," she gasped, on the verge of climax. If she let him, he'd hurtle her into her first of many orgasms within moments. He would ride her relentlessly, delaying his own release until she was witless with pleasure and trembling. He would undress her and himself while she was too satiated to move; then he would continue for hours, stripping her defenses with merciless determination.

He paused, staring down at her with a gaze so hot it flushed her skin. "No?"

She pushed up onto her elbows. "Let me have you."

Alistair straightened. He made swift work of removing his waistcoat, cravat, and shirtsleeves, all without leaving her body. He was forced to withdraw to remove his lower garments, his breath leaving him in a harsh rush as her tender tissues clung greedily to his length as he stepped back.

She took a long moment to admire the perfection of his naked body. It was a sight she would never tire of. He was long and lean, so fit that every sinewy length of tight, hard muscle was rendered in stark relief beneath his smooth skin. Her gaze traveled from his shoulders to his feet and back up again, lovingly caressing him—every virile inch. He moved not at all, unabashedly affording her the pleasure of looking at him. By the time their eyes aligned, she was breathless with infatuation and potent desire.

"You are exquisite," she whispered, sliding her feet to the hardwood sole. She approached him and wrapped her arms around his trim hips, her lips pressing a kiss over his heart. "And priceless."

His returning embrace was so fierce it nearly crushed the air from her. "And yours, Jess. Never doubt it."

"I'm glad, because I am madly besotted with you." She laid her cheek against his chest, breathing in the purely masculine scent that cloaked him. His heartbeat quickened at her words, proving what she'd begun to suspect—her fears were affecting him, making him anxious to cling to her as if she might drift away at any moment. An impossible notion to anyone who knew how anchored to him she was. But he didn't know.

"I wish you would say such things to me more often," he said gruffly, as ever so brutally, vulnerably honest that he shamed her for being so reticent.

"I don't know how." She leaned her head to the side as he began to unfasten the buttons securing the back of her gown.

"You cannot do it wrong." Alistair kissed the top of her shoulder, then bit her, his teeth sinking deep enough to border on painful. The feral act startled and aroused her. "Did you never discuss your affection for Tarley?"

"The subject wasn't one that came up in conversation. It was just there, between us, understood and comfortable."

He turned her away from him to loosen her stays. "That isn't enough for me."

"I am falling so far, so fast," she confessed in a low, shaken tone. "I cannot stop it or moderate it. I'm dizzy with it. My feelings for you frighten me, and so I expect their intensity will frighten you as well."

"Give voice to your fears, as I do."

Jess closed her eyes, knowing there was still so much to learn about him. It was her fault she knew so little about the events that had shaped him; she didn't question him as he questioned her. She'd been trained not to pry, but she would have to break that training if she hoped to make Alistair truly happy.

"I will try. You vocalize your affection without hesitation." Her gown puddled around her feet. "I envy you that ease."

He divested her of her corset, chemise, and pantalettes with now-familiar expertise.

"Have you—" Jess cleared her throat. "There must have been someone you cared for?"

"Must there have been?" He stepped back.

She looked at him over her shoulder. He waited, and she finally collected that he waited for her, anticipating the vocalization of why she'd stayed him earlier. "Lie on the bed."

He moved to do her bidding with sleek and graceful fluidity. He arranged himself in a half-reclined position against the pillows, his long legs stretched out before him, supremely comfortable in his nakedness. She reached the side of the bed and debated where to begin. His erection was an irresistible lure—thick and hard, curving up toward his navel— but she adored all of him.

"Who was she?" she asked, suddenly jealous of the phantom woman—or few—from his past who'd seen him thusly.

"You are so certain."

"You did not begin your sexual experience as Lucien, so I cannot be the only woman you've known carnally as Alistair."

He fisted his penis in his hand and stroked slowly, his heavy-lidded eyes unable to hide the look that said he was deliberately testing her.

"You're shameless," she said in a husky voice, climbing onto the bed.

"You're naked. My cock aches for you."

And she was hot and wet for him, no longer on the sharp precipice of orgasm, but it would take him only a moment to arouse her back to that edge.

When he reached for her, she shook her head. "I want you to lie still and take what I give you."

"Lie still? Are you mad?"

"I shall tie you up, if I must."

"Jess . . . Damnation." He glowered. "It has been seven days. Play your games later, when I'll be more receptive."

She wrapped her hand around him, her breath leaving her at the heat and hardness of him. The tendons of his neck stood out in harsh relief, his teeth grinding as she caressed him far more gently than he did himself. She licked her lips.

"No," he bit out. "I'm too close to coming to enjoy your mouth properly."

"Fine." She mounted him, tossing one leg over his hips to position her sex above his erection. She hummed a chastising sound when he grabbed her waist. "No touching."

"Bloody hell. How can I see to your pleasure if I can't touch you?"

She smiled. "That's the point."

He opened his mouth to protest, but the words were strangled when she sank onto the broad, flared head of his cock. An unbidden whimper escaped her. The muscles of her thighs weakened, and she lowered, her slick sex sliding down his full, throbbing length. The entry was slow and in-exorable, a fine tremor spreading across her limbs. Alistair bowed upward, grabbing her and burying his damp face be-tween her breasts.

His hips were already moving, circling, his arms holding her still as he screwed deep into her, seeking and finding the tender spot inside her that drove her insane.

"Lie back," she gasped, fighting her selfish desire to suc-cumb to his skill.

"Let me make you come," he whispered starkly. "Let me . . ."

"Not yet." She shivered as he rocked her pelvis against his, applying pressure to her clitoris. "Stop. You promised!"

He cursed and went still, his large body so hot it burned her skin. "Christ, Jess. What are you doing to me?"

"I want to make *you* come," she said, unwrapping his arms from around her. "I want to watch you when you do."

Alistair sank back into the pillows with a groan. With his eyes closed, he shoved his hands through his hair. He had beautiful arms. The bunching and flexing of his biceps made her sex flutter with appreciation around his rigid penis. He cursed, his abdominal muscles lacing tight with strain.

Jess bent over him and pressed her parted lips to his. As personal as he claimed his orgasms with her were, he didn't share them. Not truly. He ensured she was exhausted from pleasure and barely lucid first, then he climaxed with his face pressed into her neck and hair, clutching her tightly even as he hid from her. Even when she brought him plea-sure with her mouth, he tilted his face up and back, hinder-ing her view.

He caught her head in his hands and angled it, taking her mouth the way he needed to, breathing in her quick exhala-tions as he stroked his tongue across hers. Her toes curled. Her nipples tightened in a silent plea for similar attention. His kisses were indescribable, the emotion behind them enough to break her heart. He kissed her with such passion, his lips clinging to hers, his tongue licking erotically.

Deep inside her, she felt him lengthen and thicken. It made her stomach flutter to think he could climax just from kissing her. He broke away, panting, fighting the inevitable.

Catching his wrists, she pulled his hands away and straightened. She laced their fingers together and lifted, sliding her sex along his cock in a satiny-slick caress. She lowered her body slowly, using his upraised arms as leverage, keeping them occupied so that he couldn't shield his face behind them.

Alistair's breath hissed through his clenched teeth, his blue eyes so dark they looked like sapphires. He was flushed, his lips swollen from her kiss, his black hair tousled by her grasping fingers. She'd never seen anything as extravagantly beautiful in her life.

Her heart swelled and caused her chest to ache. Rolling her hips, she lifted again. Lowered. Listened to the soft liquid sounds that betrayed her own raging desire. She watched him from beneath her lashes, searching for clues to his pleasure. How fast to stroke over him, how deep to take him, which angle made sweat bead along his hairline.

"Jesus," he gasped when she thrust down hard, his body quaking at the jolting impact. He was deep, the broad crown of his penis touching the end of her. The tension, strung wire-tight through his powerful frame, was tangible.

Jess tightened her grip on his hands and began to ride him in earnest, pumping hard and swift, tightening on the up-strokes, releasing on the downstrokes. Taking him to that deep place inside her that made his head thrash and his legs kick restlessly beneath her.

"Wait—" He struggled to sit up. "Damnation . . . Slow down!"

"Let go," she coaxed breathlessly, reaching behind her

and between his legs to tease the taut heavy sac of his testicles. "I'll hold you."

"*Jess.*" Alistair yanked his hand free of her grip and grabbed her hips. Holding her immobile, he pounded upward, his hips pistoning with such speed she could only grip his forearms and let him have his way.

He gave a feral growl at the first wrenching spurt of semen and released her abruptly, his arms dropping to the bed so his hands could fist the counterpane. His back bowed up from the bed, his neck arching. The ferocity of his orgasm was magnificent, the way he bit out her name even more so.

"Yes," she urged, riding out his climax, holding off her own so that she could absorb every nuance of his release. She was riveted by his pleasure, awestruck that she could make him feel so strongly about an act he'd once disregarded completely. "God . . . you're beautiful."

And totally vulnerable. Undone. Emotions raced across his face—pained ecstasy, need, love . . . even anger.

Alistair rolled them both, taking her to the edge of the bed. He was thrusting before she could catch her bearings, grinding against her, the friction of his thick cock forcing the orgasm from her overstimulated body. She cried out as the spasms flowed through her, her fingers gripping his sides, her legs opened wide to accept everything he had to give her.

His mouth covered hers, muting the sounds they made as they climaxed violently.

I love you, she exhaled into his near-frantic kiss, no longer able or willing to contain the words or the sentiment behind them.

In answer, he caught her close and crushed the air from her lungs.

The dipping and swaying of the ship felt apropos to Alistair, whose existence was similarly rocked. His fingers tangled in and out of Jessica's luxurious hair, his thoughts focused on the three little words he was almost certain she'd said to him.

He knew from experience that women said such things in the throes of powerful orgasms and paid them no mind later. He knew she'd been flush with her own feminine power, finally understanding how easily she could unravel him and strip him bare. He couldn't fight it when he was with her; he had no idea how to.

And now she was so quiet curled up against him, their skin cooling and breaths slowing. For the moment, he was well and truly spent; the dearth of arousal left him with no distraction from his turmoil.

Why wasn't she saying anything? Why didn't she repeat the words aloud?

He began speaking only to save his sanity. "I began my sexual experiences as most randy adolescent boys do: with anyone who was pretty enough and willing."

"Dear God." Jessica laughed softly. "I expect girls were throwing themselves at you shamelessly."

Though it was true, Alistair said nothing to that, having no desire to rouse any misplaced jealousy. "My eldest brother, Aaron, took me carousing with him one evening. I was nearly fifteen, and I wanted so much to be as worldly as he seemed to me. We eventually found ourselves at a small gathering in the home of a demimondaine."

Her head lifted. She looked at him. "At fourteen years old?"

"Nearly fifteen," he reminded. "And not very innocent, if I ever was. Remember, my mother was forced to explain early on why Masterson couldn't bear to even look at me."

She folded her arms across his abdomen and rested her chin upon them. "He is the only one who could ever feel that way."

His fingertips drifted along her delicate jaw. "There was a

courtesan at the party. I caught her eye, and she caught mine."

"What did she look like?"

"She was slender. A blonde. Delicate looking, with pale blue eyes. Depending on her mood, they occasionally appeared almost gray."

"Oh . . ." Jess's eyes became stormy. "Fortunate for me that I fit into your preferences."

He held back the smile certain to get him into trouble. "Actually, it was *you* who'd recently set my preferences, a fortnight before, when I met you. She just happened to fit them."

Confusion marred her brow, then a dawning awareness moved across her expressive features.

"She was a poor substitute, I'm afraid," he went on, his gaze lifting to the wall beyond her shoulder. "Nowhere near as refined as you. She'd long ago lost the ability to care for anyone more than she cared about herself, which suited me fine. I didn't have to like her to want to fuck her."

Jess jolted softly at his crudity, but held her tongue.

"For a short time, our affair was ideal. She found relief from her boredom in instructing me how to bed a woman properly, and I was an eager pupil. She taught me how to focus on the mechanics of the act, most likely in an attempt to prevent me from becoming emotional over her."

"Did it work?"

"After a fashion." He shrugged. "Perhaps not enough, because one day I arrived and found she had an acquaintance with her. Another courtesan. She wanted me to service them both, which I did."

Her arms came around him, slipping through the small gap where his reclined back curved away from the affixed headboard.

"Soon one friend became two," he said. "Sometimes she didn't participate at all. She merely watched. There were other men as well, when she felt like having two or more cocks in her at once."

"My God," Jessica whispered, her eyes big and dark in her pale face. "Why did you go? Why didn't you leave her to her own debauchery?"

"Go where? Home? My presence caused tremendous strain between Masterson and my mother. She was made miserable when I was around. Regardless, I never acted against my will. It wasn't odious, Jessica. At that age, I had a cockstand damn near all the time, and her bedsport provided plenty of opportunities to alleviate it."

His voice was carefully light, but she must have recognized the underlying emotion. Her cheek rubbed back and forth across his stomach, her nose nuzzling through the thin strip of hair bisecting his abdomen.

"I should not have pushed you so hard today," she murmured. "I'm sorry."

Alistair snorted. "I cannot accept an apology for giving me the best orgasm of my life."

She pulled her arms out from beneath him and wriggled her way up his torso. "The best orgasm *so far*," she corrected, straddling his hips and embracing his shoulders. "Henceforth I will endeavor to bring you greater and greater pleasure every time we make love."

His cock twitched in its initial effort to rally. She'd wrung him dry in every respect.

"Not yet," she said, with her lips to his ear. "Let me hold you; I promised you I would. You don't always have to use sex to show me how you feel."

The rush of longing that assailed him was nearly too great. It stung his eyes and burned in his throat. He set his hands on the bed to hide their unsteadiness.

"Was she the only woman you cared for?" she asked, leaning fully against him.

"If that is what you want to call it."

"What would you call it? Lust?"

"I've no notion. I know it was never like this."

"But there are women who've loved you." It wasn't a question.

"Those who have, came to lament it. The detriments outweigh the benefits."

Her fingertips curled around the back of his neck, kneading the tense muscles. "There is no shame in what you did."

"You don't know what I did."

"I know *you*. I love you, and I will not regret it."

Alistair was horrified by the violent shudder that moved through him. She was deep under his skin now, able to see everything he was so adept at disguising on the surface.

God, he didn't want her to see . . .

"You don't know that, either," he said sharply.

"You'll have to trust me, Alistair, and take my word for it." Her embrace lightened, her body withdrawing as if giving him room and permission to flee.

In truth, he was tempted to. He'd done things in his life that made him unacceptable . . . the very nature of his birth made him unsuitable for her. She'd suffered so much to become the polished, elegant, irreproachable woman she was. And with his courtship, he would destroy the social esteem she had worked so hard to attain. If he could, he would keep her captive in his bed, the one place he knew he could make her forget everything but the pleasure he could give her.

Alistair caught her close, fighting for the strength to be gentle when he felt so violently. She needed tenderness and sheltering, and he was like a battering ram against her, constantly trying to crash his way through the defenses she'd been forced to build as an abused child. "I do trust you," he said gruffly. "Don't I tell you everything?"

"You tell me all the disreputable things about yourself."

Jessica pulled back to look at him. "And you say them with such defiance, as if you're daring me to turn away from you."

Better now than later. With every day that passed, she became more and more indispensable to him. Soon, he wouldn't be able to breathe without her. He already felt that way at times.

She kissed one corner of his mouth, then the other. "Remain constant, and I will remain with you."

"You are my every desire." He groaned as she moved sinuously against him.

"Prove it," she breathed.

As always, he accepted the challenge. He knew his strengths—he could disregard his conscience, he was adept at making money, he was attractive, and he was good at sex. It was precious little to offer to a woman such as Jessica, but he would offer it in spades and pray it would be enough to keep her.

18

Hester paused on the threshold of her bedroom and stared at her sleeping husband. He'd come to her often over the past sennight, seeking surcease from his torment in her bed. She tried to comfort him, tried to tell him that no one remembered a boxing match a week old, that he wasn't humiliated or diminished, but nothing she said or did soothed his inner turmoil. She was exhausted from the effort, disheartened, and sickened by his weakness and her own weakness for him. Despite everything dark and twisted that had passed between them, she still couldn't wish him ill.

It was her greatest failure that she couldn't save the man she'd once loved from himself. She could not even save their love, which had withered and was surely dying. As much as it pained her, she could no longer afford to waste her energies and affections on a man who couldn't accept and value her efforts. She had a child to consider now, a tiny being who would need all her time, attention, and adoration. The strength she hadn't been capable of finding for herself, she'd found for the babe growing within her.

Her shoulders went back and she moved toward the bed.

Regmont had the potential to be such a wonderful man.

He was handsome and emminently charming. He had a fine wit and was brilliantly adept at everything he set his hand to. Women coveted him and men respected him. Yet he saw none of those admirable qualities in himself. Sadly, his father's demeaning and belittling words were all he heard in his head; they drowned out the praise directed his way. He felt unworthy of love, and he reacted to those feelings in the manner his father had taught him by example—through violence.

But she couldn't make excuses for him any longer. His most prominent traits were the need for absolute control over her—from the clothes she wore to what she ate—and manipulation. He laid the blame for his rages on the spirits he drank to excess and, sometimes, on her. If he couldn't accept his own culpability, there was little possibility he would change. She had to take steps to protect her child.

As she neared, he stirred, one sleekly muscled arm reaching toward her side of the bed. His head lifted from the pillow when he felt her gone. When he found her, he gifted her with a slow and sleepy smile. A soft tremor flowed through her. Tousled and naked, his golden masculine beauty was undeniable. An angel's face hiding the demons that ruled him.

He rolled to his back and pushed up to recline against the carved wooden headboard. The sheet pooled around his hips, leaving the breathtaking expanse of his chest and stomach bared. "I can hear you thinking from here," he murmured. "What thoughts have you so occupied?"

"I have something to tell you."

He slid his legs off the side of the bed and stood, shamelessly and gloriously naked. "You shall have my undivided attention . . . in just a moment."

He kissed her cheek on his way to the chamber pot and screen in the corner.

When he appeared again, she spoke. "I'm increasing."

He came to a halt so abruptly, he stumbled. Wide eyed, he paled. "Hester. My God . . ."

She couldn't say what reaction she had been expecting, but his terrible stillness wasn't it. "I hope you're pleased."

He breathed roughly. "Of course I am. Forgive me, I'm a bit startled. I had come to think you might be barren, like your sister."

"Is that partly why you become so angry with me?" How much angrier would he become if he learned how she'd worked to prevent conception these past few years . . . ? The thought alone terrified her.

"Angry—?" He flushed. "Do not start a row. Not today."

"I never start rows," she said neutrally. "I abhor discord, as you know. I had quite enough of it in my childhood to last me a lifetime."

His blue eyes glittered dangerously. "If I didn't know your gentle nature so well, I would wonder if you were deliberately attempting to provoke me."

"By speaking the truth?" Fear made her heart race, but she refused to give in to it. "We are simply having a discussion, Edward."

"You don't seem happy to be breeding."

"I will be, once I know the baby is safe."

"What's wrong?" He jerked into motion then, striding to the chaise where he'd discarded his robe the night before. "Have you called for the doctor?"

"I have morning sickness, which is quite normal. I'm told that everything is progressing nicely so far." She fought against the urge to lift her chin, knowing the silent challenge would only aggravate Regmont further. "However, I must take care of myself and a-avoid injury."

A warning muscle in his jaw ticked. "Of course."

"And I need to eat more."

"I tell you so all the time."

"Yes, but it's difficult to eat when one is in pain." His lips whitened, a warning sign she forced herself to ignore. "With that in mind, I should like to retire to the country early. You can join me when the Season ends."

"You are my wife," he bit out, yanking the belt of his robe into a knot. "Your place is by my side."

"I understand. But we have to think of the babe."

"I dislike your tone, and your intimation that I am somehow a danger to my own child!"

"Not you." A necessary lie. "The spirits you drink."

"I won't be drinking." His arms crossed. "In case you hadn't taken note of it, I have not had a drink in nearly three weeks."

He'd abstained for longer stretches, but something always tipped him into his cups again. "Can any precaution be excessive when it concerns our child?"

"You'll stay here," he bit out, heading toward the connecting door to his rooms. "And I will not listen to any further nonsense about you leaving."

"Edward. Please—"

The slam of the door ended the conversation.

"How dashing you look!" Elspeth praised as she descended the stairs to the visitor's foyer. "Which fortunate debutante will be enjoying your call today?"

Michael ceased fiddling with his immaculate cravat and met his mother's gaze in the mirror's reflection before him. "Good afternoon, Mother."

Her brow arched when he collected his hat from the console and said nothing further. The afternoon sunlight slanted onto the marble floor through the arched window above the double front doors. The indirect illumination flattered his mother, whose floral gown made her appear far younger than she was.

Her mouth curved. "Lady Regmont helped me put the list of debutantes together. She's very perceptive, well connected, *and* most eager to see you wed."

He stiffened. The perfectly tailored fit of his blue coat was suddenly overly tight. "I'm pleased to hear you two are rubbing along well. I thought you might."

"Yes, we suit better than I expected. The poor dear has been without a mother for many years, and with Jessica gone, I can dote on Hester as I would a daughter."

He wished they could have been mother and daughter in truth, through marriage. But fate had other designs.

"And now that she's increasing," Elspeth went on in a breezy tone, "I can experience that joy as well. Preparation for your wife, whoever she may be."

Breath hissing between his teeth, Michael gripped the edge of the console and fought to collect himself. A poker through the chest could not have hurt worse.

He rounded on Elspeth. "Sheath your claws, Mother. You're drawing blood."

She recoiled, then paled. "Michael . . ."

"Why?" he asked bitterly. "We both know she's beyond my grasp. You've no need to wound me with it further."

"I'm sorry." Her shoulders fell, her lovely features aging before his eyes. "I . . ."

"You what?"

"I am afraid your love for her will hold you back."

"I know my responsibilities. I'll see to them."

"I want you to be happy." She stepped toward him. "I want that so badly. I thought if you knew . . ."

"That I would simply shrug off my troublesome affection and move forward unencumbered?" He laughed without humor. "If only it was that simple."

219

She sighed. "I want to help you. I wish I knew how."

"I told you how." He set his hat on his head. "See to Hester. Give her whatever support she may need."

"I'm afraid there's nothing to be done for the girl, Michael. Leastwise, nothing you and I can do."

He looked at her. "Regmont," he bit out, acid sliding through his veins.

"The way she reacts to his name . . . I have seen that look before, and it never bodes well. But what can be done?"

"We can extend our friendship." He moved toward the door, which was hastily opened by the butler. "And pray."

Hester's breathing quickened as she entered her parlor. Michael stood when she swept in, his dark eyes heating with masculine appreciation. She basked in that warmth, allowing it to thaw the frozen recesses of her heart.

"You waited the entirety of the sennight before keeping your promise to call on me," she accused.

A faint tinge of sadness marred the smile he gave her. "My mother suggested I wait."

"Ah." She sat on the settee across from him. "She is a wise woman."

"She likes you."

"The affection is mutual." Hester smoothed her skirts, feeling unaccountably nervous. "How are you?"

"I've been half-mad with the need to ask that question of you. You spoke of some things when I last saw you. I feared I might have aggravated . . . that I caused you unnecessary . . ." He scrubbed a hand over his face. "Christ."

"I'm well, Michael."

"Are you?" His hand fell to his lap, and his gaze sharpened. "I should have let him win. I was too arrogant—too angry—to do so. I should have been thinking of you."

Hester's heartbeat thudded in a strong, steady rhythm as

if revived. In truth she felt more alive in Michael's presence than she had in many years. "You *were* thinking of me, were you not?"

He tensed, then flushed.

"Whatever promise you made to my sister to look after me," she went on, "I doubt she expected you to take the responsibility to such lengths. But I'm touched that you did."

"Do you need a champion?" he asked softly, leaning forward.

"There is a princess out there waiting for you, gallant knight."

"By God." He pushed to his feet with graceful violence. Controlled, despite his frustration. "I hate talking in riddles."

She nodded at the maid who set a tea service on the low table in front of her. When the servant departed, Hester said, "You didn't answer my question about how you're faring."

He exhaled harshly and resumed his seat. "As well as can be expected, under the circumstances. I never realized how many tasks Benedict faced. He bore them all with quiet efficiency. I have yet to figure out how he managed. He must have found more hours in the day than have been allotted to me."

"He had a wife to support his efforts."

"By God, if one more individual posits that a spouse will alleviate all my burdens, I cannot be held responsible for my reply."

Hester laughed softly, secretly and horribly pleased to hear that finding a wife was not high on Michael's list of priorities. "You don't believe you would find a wife helpful?"

"I am barely keeping my own head above water. I haven't the faintest idea of how I would care for a spouse at this time."

"I want you to find a wife who will care about you. It shan't be hard. You are very easy to adore."

"If only you spoke from experience," he said quietly.

"I do, of course."

His beautiful mouth twisted wryly. "Of course."

"More than I realized," she confessed. "More fool I."

"Hester . . ." Surprise swept over his features, followed swiftly by stark despair.

How had she missed the signs that Michael carried a *tendre* for her? She had been blinded by Regmont's rakish charm and the sensual spell he wove so well. By the time they wed, she'd been desperate for the consummation of their union, aroused to a fever pitch by clandestine touches, ravenous kisses, and hotly whispered promises of boundless pleasure.

"We shall find you someone who loves you madly," she said hoarsely. "Someone whose primary concern is your happiness and pleasure."

"She would resent me after a time."

"No." Hester set about preparing the tea, spooning tea leaves into the steaming pot. "You will reciprocate her affections soon enough. You won't be able to help yourself. And then you shall live in contentment ever after, as you deserve."

"And what of you?"

Leaving the tea to steep, Hester straightened and set her hand over her stomach. "I have my own joy on the way."

His smile was genuine, if melancholy. "I could not be happier for you."

"Thank you. So let's narrow the list I assisted your mother with." She stood, and he stood with her. Moving to the escritoire by the window, she opened it and withdrew a sheet of foolscap. She settled onto the wooden seat and opened her inkwell. "You can list desirable attributes, and I will record them."

"I should rather go to the tooth drawer's."

She assumed her most formidable expression.

"Blast. Not that look, Hester, please. I thought you liked me."

"Hair color?"

"Not blond."

"Eye color?"

"Not green."

"Michael . . ."

He crossed his arms and arched a brow. "Have to give the gel a fighting chance. Wouldn't be sporting otherwise."

She laughed softly. Beside her, on the other side of the window, whips cracked against horseflesh and whinnies rent the afternoon. On most days, Hester sat by the window and watched the world go about its business. The thought of happier homes and lives just beyond the one she was trapped in offered her comfort. At the moment, however, she was content to focus her attention on her own life and the vibrant man who so briefly occupied it. "Tall or short?"

"I don't have a preference."

"Slender or voluptuous?"

"Proportional is all I ask."

"Any particular talents?" she queried, glancing at him as he approached. He moved with such economical grace and confidence that she couldn't stop herself from watching.

Michael drew to a halt beside her, resting his arm along the top of the escritoire. "Such as?"

"Singing? The pianoforte?"

"I truly don't care about such things. I will follow your discretion."

Hester looked at him, her gaze taking in his smartly

dressed form. "Blue flatters you, my lord. I can say in all honesty that no other gentleman wears the hue better."

His eyes sparkled. "Why, thank you, my lady."

The warm pleasure on his face arrested her, freezing her in a moment weighted with impossible possibilities. She struggled to find the will to break the sudden tension and ended up with irrelevant discourse spoken in a throaty voice. "I am a terrible hostess. The tea is getting cold."

But she didn't move. He was close enough that she could smell the verbena from his toiletries. It mixed wonderfully with his personal scent, creating an invigorating and enticing fragrance.

"I don't care," he murmured. "I will enjoy the company regardless."

"I danced my first waltz with you," she said, remembering.

"My feet are still recovering, I fear."

Her mouth fell open in exaggerated affront. "I followed your lead flawlessly!"

He grinned.

"Don't you remember?" she pressed. She'd wanted him to be her first public partner because she trusted him and felt safe with him. She had known he might tease her, but only good-naturedly, and he would make the whole torturous first experience fun. He'd led her so well and kept her too engaged to fret, so that she left the dance floor with a feeling of triumph. She hadn't felt so good about herself in years.

"As if I could ever forget any moment when you'd been in my arms," he said softly.

Clinging to those phantom feelings, she pushed to her feet so quickly, she upended the chair. She caught him by the lapels and pressed her lips to his. The kiss was swift and chaste, a show of gratitude for reminding her of the bold and vivacious girl she used to be.

She pulled away, blushing. "I'm sorry."

Michael stood rooted, his dark eyes hot and avid. "I'm not."

Smoothing her hair back with shaking fingers, Hester moved to the tea service. She focused on breathing deep and evenly, attempting to regulate her racing heart. She heard him right the chair behind her just as she caught sight of Regmont filling the doorway.

Her heart stopped beating altogether.

"My lord," Hester breathed.

Michael froze, hearing the fear in her voice as if she'd screamed in terror. Pivoting, he faced whatever threatened her and found himself staring into the face of a man who festered with fury and ill will. Michael sized up his opponent, noting the earl's fisted hands and clenched jaw. Though he'd never known Regmont well, he was certain the man had changed over the past few years. Michael remembered a cocky fellow, whose saving grace had been the warmth and affection in his eyes when he looked upon his wife. There was none of that tenderness now. Only cold calculation and sharp suspicion.

"Regmont." Michael was amazed his tone was so nonchalant when he felt like lunging across the room and pummeling the man responsible for Hester's unhappiness.

"Tarley. What are you doing here?"

Michael gave a deliberately casual shrug, uncertain of what Regmont had seen and knowing he would have to tread carefully if he was to spare Hester any further undue suffering. "My mother sent me. It was either come here and assist with her matchmaking efforts or find myself paired with a spouse I can't tolerate."

Regmont looked to his wife. "Oh? I've been told Lady Pennington has begun visiting often."

Hester looked pale, her eyes haunted. She swallowed and

said, "She would turn to Jessica, if my sister were here. Since she is not, I've been helping the countess become acquainted with the debutantes this Season."

"That's very kind of you, darling."

"Dear God," Michael said, returning to his former seat. "Please don't encourage them."

The earl joined them, taking the seat beside Hester. She took a deep breath and began serving tea.

Regmont received his cup and saucer first, then took a sip. He set the china down on the table. "This is barely warm."

Hester winced.

"My apologies," Michael said. "I burned the tip of my tongue with coffee this morning and it still stings. Lady Regmont was kind enough to oblige me."

Regmont pivoted on the seat, angling his knees toward his wife. "And what occupied you while you waited for the tea to cool?"

Straightening her shoulders, Hester looked at her husband with a smile as cool as the beverage he complained about. "I was transcribing Tarley's spousal wish list."

The earl's gaze shot over to the escritoire. He stood in a fluid rush and crossed the room with short, swift strides. He lifted the length of foolscap, his icy gaze raking over the few notations. Then he glanced up at Michael with a smoothed brow. "Brunettes and redheads only?"

In answer, Michael waved one hand carelessly.

Regmont laughed, his tension broken and agitation eased. "Redheads are handfuls, you know, Tarley. Ask Grayson, or Merrick."

"I like spirited women." *The way your wife used to be before you bullied her . . .*

"Lady Regmont will steer you in the right direction."

Michael turned his back to the earl, hiding the hatred, disgust, and sick helplessness he was certain he couldn't disguise on his face. If Benedict had still been with them, Michael could have stolen Hester away from this misery. They could have fled to the West Indies or the Continent or America. Anywhere in the world she wanted to go. But he was chained to England now.

They were both trapped in lives they did not want.

And there was no way out for either of them.

19

"*Lady Tarley!*"

Jessica altered the angle of her parasol and caught sight of the short, portly gentleman waving madly at her from the end of the gangplank.

"Your steward," Alistair explained as he steadied her with a hand at her elbow. "Mr. Reginald Smythe."

"What is your impression of him?" She lifted one gloved hand in a slight wave that acknowledged the man's vigorous efforts to attract her attention amid the noise and activity of the quayside. The smells of tar and coffee blended, teasing her nostrils, and raucous cries of seagulls competed with the calls and shouts of able-bodied sailors loading crates and barrels onto fat-bellied ships.

"A decent fellow. Certainly competent. Calypso has nearly two hundred slaves and they are content enough to be highly productive. However, he could stand to be less antiquated in his views of women in trade."

"You are more progressive than most gentlemen, I suspect."

"In my experience, women can be shrewd and ruthless in financial matters. It pays to do business with them."

"And I would wager they make concessions to you that they would for few other men."

He looked at her, his blue eyes brilliant even when shadowed by the brim of his hat. "Perhaps."

She smiled. Alistair's presence only added to her swelling happiness at returning to the lush, verdant island she remembered so fondly. Her memories had painted the landscape in jeweled tones, and she was delighted to see she hadn't embroidered her recollections. Behind her, the ocean was the pale blue of an aquamarine. In front of her, the emerald hills and mountains rolled across the landscape. Benedict had once told her that at no point on the island was the ocean more than a score of miles away.

Paradise, she'd called it. *A lucrative one,* he'd agreed.

"Mr. Caulfield." Mr. Smythe touched the brim of his brown hat in greeting.

"Mr. Smythe."

The steward looked at Jess. "I trust you had a safe and enjoyable journey, my lady."

"It could not have been more pleasurable," she said, thinking of Alistair and how different she felt now from when she'd boarded his ship. She'd started the journey as a widow, certain she would be alone for the rest of her life. She ended with a lover, a man to whom she'd bared her body and soul, revealing memories of a past she had previously shared only with Hester.

Alistair's fingers stoked the bend of her elbow.

Mr. Smythe nodded, then turned to gesture at the landau waiting nearby. "We'll have your trunks brought along after you, Lady Tarley. Good day, Mr. Caulfield. I shall be making an appointment to meet with you later this week."

She looked at Alistair. After six weeks at sea, during which their relationship had sprouted and blossomed, they were finally faced with separation. This was the point where they parted ways, she to her residence and he to his.

He met her gaze; his own sharply focused as he waited.

Jess could see the question in his eyes—how would she react now that they were once again faced with the rules of Society?

Her reaction was fiercer than she could reasonably share. She wanted him beside her, always. In public and in private. Across their personal dining table for the morning meal and next to one another in a box at the theater. She wanted that, and she would have it if he agreed.

She spoke with feeling. "I know you must have a great deal to attend to, Mr. Caulfield, but would you be able to join us for supper? It would save you from making an appointment, Mr. Smythe, and having to report to me after the fact."

Smythe blinked, clearly startled.

Alistair grinned at her first salvo in the battle for control of the plantation. He tilted his head in a regal acknowledgment. "It would be my pleasure, my lady."

Raising her skirts, Jess climbed up the side of the hill. Her boots slipped occasionally in the rain-soaked soil, but Alistair was behind her and she knew he would grab hold of her if she fell. He was always catching her, always urging her to take great leaps with the security of knowing he waited with arms outstretched.

"There," he said, drawing her attention to a gazebo set in a clearing to the left of where they ascended. The structure was immediately recognizable—it was a miniature replica of the one on the Pennington estate, with the addition of netting around the back and sides. In the center, a low dais supported a wealth of blankets and pillows.

She turned, facing Alistair as he joined her. From this

vantage, they had impressive views of the sugarcane fields below and the ocean in the distance.

He drew abreast of her. "Have you seen the cane fields burning?"

"No."

"We'll remedy that when the time comes. I will take you to a vantage downwind of the smoke and stench. For all the danger and destruction, it is a sight not to be missed."

"I can't wait to see it with you." She looked at him, admiring his proud profile. "I want to see everything with you."

His returning look was fierce and heated.

She moved toward the gazebo. "This is what has been occupying you during the day?"

He'd started coming to her at night with small cuts on his hands and the occasional darkening of a faint bruise on his forearms. No matter how she tried to wheedle the cause out of him, he resisted—although he did encourage her to use every means at her disposal to convince him to be forthcoming . . .

"Do you like it?" he asked, studying her reaction.

"I'm flattered to have such effort expended to seduce me." Her mouth curved on one side. "I also see that whenever my courses run, you burn with restless energy. I do believe you require sex more than food and water."

"Only with you." He moved under the roof and set down the basket he'd carried up with them. "And you know why. When I'm inside you I know you won't be getting away. I know you don't want to."

She turned her back to the view and faced him, the most wonderful view of all. "What if you could claim the outside of me as well? With your name as my own and your ring on my finger. Would that calm you?"

Alistair grew painfully still. He did not even blink. "Beg your pardon?"

"Are you frightened now?" she asked softly.

"Afraid I'm dreaming." He broke his stillness to move toward her.

"I've already told you I love you. Many, many times. Every day, actually." She exhaled in a rush, fighting for courage. She couldn't restrain her affection; it was too big to contain, swelling her chest and making it hard to catch her breath. "I love you enough to walk away if there is any possibility you might desire to be a father someday."

His throat worked on a hard swallow. "There are a great many foundlings, if we want children to spoil."

Her heartbeat quickened with hope.

He held out his hand. She placed hers within his and allowed him to lead her to the dais. He urged her to sit and she did. Then, he sank to one knee in front of her.

Understanding dawned. *"Alistair."*

"You weren't supposed to beat me to it, Jess," he said with tender gruffness, reaching into the tiny pocket of his waistcoat. He wore no coat, no cravat. Scandalous and completely unacceptable, but who would see them up here? That had been the most difficult part of the past week—acting as if they were no more than acquaintances in public when they were searingly intimate in private.

It was the worst sort of torture watching the local debutantes, widows, and even some of the married women paying him elaborate, fawning attention. She'd had to suffer through watching those who claimed him as a dance partner or an escort into dining rooms. She had watched pretty young girls flirt with him, girls capable of giving him the family he'd never truly had and that she could never give him.

Alistair encouraged none of them, his gaze finding her in quiet moments and revealing his ferocious hunger. She tried not to seek him out, knowing her face would betray how smitten and besotted she was. How desperately in love she'd fallen. How bleak and lifeless her existence would be without him.

The truth of it was that he managed the public side of their relationship much better than she did. As proprietary as he felt about her private self, he wasn't possessive of her public face. Instead, he seemed to relish watching her swim the social waters, admiring the ease with which she managed the necessary interactions—the discourse, the dancing, and all the rest. He was *proud* of her, content to watch her shine in her element, which made all the pain and sorrow she'd experienced to become so consummate seem worthwhile.

He withdrew a ring. A thick gold circlet topped with an ostentatious ruby as big as her knuckle. The brilliant blood-red stone was a pillowed square surrounded by diamonds, boldly proclaiming the worth of the man who'd purchased it. The gem was almost vulgar in its size and purity of clarity, which made her smile. If her marriage to Alistair wasn't enough to show the world she'd changed, the ring would certainly manage the task.

"Yes," he murmured, sliding the ruby onto her finger. "I will marry you. As soon as possible. By the end of the week if we can manage it."

"No." She cupped his face in her hands, her fingers brushing his inky hair back from his forehead. "We'll do this properly. In England. With the banns read and endless celebrations and our families in attendance. I want the world—and most especially you—to know that I do this after a great deal of thought and careful consideration. I know what I do, Alistair. I know what I want."

"I would prefer to be wed before we return."

"I won't leave you," she vowed, knowing his concern.

"You can't. I won't let you." He caught her wrists with a

gentle, yet unyielding grip. "But there will be women who . . . at routs and luncheons . . . they'll know—"

"—Lucius," she interjected. "They do not know *you*, not as I do. And they never will."

Leaning forward, she pressed a kiss to his furrowed brow. "My darling. You haven't faith that anyone can love you unconditionally, because no one ever has. But I do. How could I help myself? And over time, you'll see that the changes you wrought in me are not reversible. I am who I am at this moment because of you, and without you I would cease to exist. I have no notion how I'll survive the next few months until you can join me in—"

"Join you?" he asked sharply. "Where?"

"A letter from Hester arrived this afternoon. She must have sent it directly after we left, perhaps even the same day, which tells me she knew she was increasing before I departed and didn't want the news to stay me."

"Your sister is with child?"

"I cannot believe she could ever think I wouldn't return to her posthaste. As I told you, she hasn't been well for some time. She will need looking after. I must be with her now."

"I'll return with you, of course. With luck, I can arrange for us to sail within a fortnight."

"I cannot ask that of you. You came to the island for a reason."

"Yes. *You*. The same reason I returned to England. I traveled with you because there was no reason to stay there while you were here, and the same is true in reverse."

Jess's thoughts froze with surprise, remembering the night they'd spoken on the deck of the *Acheron* and she had wondered if he was going home for a woman. To learn *she* was that woman was slightly overwhelming. And deeply moving.

He must have seen the realization on her face. His jaw tensed. "My lust was fierce, you know that. I won't say it

234

was love, but it was deeper than flesh. My desire for you gave me hope that I could find joy in sex again, that I could approach the act with something beyond detachment and a need for base physical release. I had to have you, Jess, whatever the cost or effort."

She stared at him, wondering why he wouldn't say he loved her. Perhaps he didn't. Perhaps he couldn't. Perhaps what they had was all she would ever claim from him.

After a moment's contemplation, she decided that whatever he could give of himself was enough. She loved him enough for the two of them.

Releasing him, she pulled away and reclined. She stretched out on the pillows, reaching her arms above her head and arching her back in blatant invitation. If his need was the only part of himself he had to give her, she would take it all.

Alistair crawled onto the dais. He straddled her, his hands pressing into the pillows on either side of her shoulders. Lowering his head, he took her mouth, his lips sealing to hers.

A warm, humid breeze blew over them. In the distance, she heard the shouts of men and the distant screeching of gulls. They were outside, where anyone could see, and that increased her excitement. She wrapped her arms around his neck and hummed her pleasure into his kiss.

"I thought," he murmured against her parted lips, "that I might have to convince you to wed me. That it might take some time. Weeks. Months. Maybe years. I built this place to make it hard for you to run while I presented my arguments."

She smiled. "A captive audience. How would you have stopped me from leaving?"

"Perhaps hiding your clothes and keeping you pinned with my cock. I also brought a few bottles of your favorite claret with me. I remember your being much more agreeable after a glass or two."

"Wicked man." Her gaze lowered to his throat and the

strong pulse beating there. "Do your worst. I rescind my acceptance."

"Ah, but you didn't accept. You asked; *I* accepted." He nuzzled the tip of his nose against hers. "And I cannot tell you what it means to me that you did."

"You can show me." Her fingers stroked his nape in just the way he loved.

Alistair slid to the side of her. "Roll over."

She did as he bade, her spine tingling as she faced away from him. He released the tie at the small of her back, then deftly unfastened the buttons that secured her pale lavender gown. As the pressure of his fingers worked downward, her anticipation grew. For all her teasing about his sexual appetite, hers for him was equally fierce. After a week without him while her courses ran, her hunger for his touch and attention was ravenous.

"I want you to buy a trousseau," he said. "Spare no expense. I do not begrudge your mourning for Tarley—I know he was good to you—but I don't want to see you dressed in tribute to your grief whilst wed to me."

Looking over her shoulder, she nodded, loving him all the more.

He stroked his tongue between her shoulder blades. "I should like to see you in red. And gold. Also a vivid blue."

"To match your eyes. I would like that. Perhaps you should come with me to the modiste's."

"Yes." His strong hands reached into the parted halves of her gown and gripped her waist. "You'll be half-dressed while they measure you. I would enjoy the view."

"At the moment, I would enjoy being *un*dressed."

He squeezed her gently, then rolled to his back. "As you desire."

Jess slid off the end of the dais and stood.

Tucking a pillow behind his head, Alistair settled more comfortably. He bent one knee and set one wrist atop it, presenting a relaxed and somewhat insolent pose. The multitude of colorful pillows and the netting between the posts reminded Jess of the story she'd told about a desert adventure and a lusty sheik.

She lowered her head deliberately, affecting a meek and submissive posture. Lifting her hand, she caught the neckline of her gown and tugged it over her shoulder. First one side, then the other. The bodice caught on her breasts and she stilled.

"You could ransom me, Your Highness," she whispered. "The price you could fetch for me, in addition to the spoils from the caravan, would certainly outweigh whatever pleasure you might have from me in your bed."

The surprise Alistair felt was tangible. For a moment, he held his silence, his chest lifting and falling with studiously steady breaths. Then, "But *you* are the reason I raided that caravan, my lady. Why expend the effort if I only intended to give you back?"

"For the fortune you will gain upon my return."

"The only treasure that interests me is between your thighs."

A rush of heat swept over her skin.

He jerked his chin imperiously. "Take it off. Let me see you."

Jess licked her dry lips and took a heartbeat longer to obey. Catching her skirts in her hands, she tugged downward gently, as if she was shy about revealing the body he knew better than she did. The dress slipped from her arms and torso, and pooled on the planked floor.

"Now," he said gruffly, "the rest."

"Please . . ."

"Don't be frightened. In a few moments, I will give you pleasure such as you've never known." His gaze narrowed slightly. "Nor will you again after me."

Jess shifted from foot to foot, glancing at him furtively.

He reached between his legs, brazenly stroking the thick length of his erection. A voluptuary to his bones. Skilled . . . far more experienced than she would ever be. Unless he remedied that lack of knowledge, which she doubted he would unless she pushed him. She suspected he feared corrupting her any more than he believed he already had, while she feared his boredom in her bed.

"I cannot say the same," she said softly.

Alistair rose gracefully to his feet, moving with a sleek and predatory fluidity. "Yes, you can."

He rounded her, as if examining her charms. Then he drew to a halt at her back, sliding his arms under hers and embracing her from behind. In a swift possessive grasp, he filled his hands with her breasts, startling a gasp from her.

Her head fell back onto his shoulder. "But you've had so many concubines who are more adventurous than I know how to be. What will become of me once the novelty wears thin?"

"You underestimate my desire for you." His lips moved against the shell of her ear. He pulled her against him, making her feel the undeniable evidence of his arousal. "Feel how hard I am for you? I've wanted you too badly, for too long. I'll never have enough of you."

"Before the raid, did you imagine having me? Did you dream of *how* you would have me?"

"Every night," he growled, his fingers clasping around her taut nipples.

Turning her head, she pressed her cheek to his. "Show me how you dreamed of me. Teach me all the ways I can please you. I want to learn."

One hand slid down her stomach, then between her legs. "You no longer wish to be ransomed?"

Jess gasped as his fingers slipped into the slit of her pantalettes and parted her. With fingertips roughened by the woodworking required to build her this place of seduction, he stroked over her clitoris, knowing just how to touch her to make her writhe. "If you do, who will quench this fire in my blood?"

"No one else." Alistair's teeth nipped at her earlobe. "I'd castrate any man who tried."

Maddened by the rolling of her nipple and the sudden slide of a long finger into her grasping sex, Jess rolled her hips and whimpered. A second finger joined the first, thrusting slow and easy. She sucked in a deep breath, intoxicated by his sun-warmed scent. "Please . . ."

"Bend over." He punctuated the order by pushing her down.

Jess tumbled forward, stemming her fall by extending her arms. Alistair straightened, allowing the breeze to blow over her back. He pushed down the stockinette of her pantalettes. Perspiration misted her skin.

"So pretty," he praised, running his hands over her derriere. Cupping her sex, he massaged her with his palm. "So swollen and slick. Do you need a cock to fill you, my lovely captive? Do you ache with emptiness?"

She was so vulnerable like this, unable to watch his face or movements. "Always."

There was a faint rustle of displaced clothing, then the wide head of his cock notched against her. It was the only warning she had. Gripping her hips, he yanked her back as he thrust, piercing deep with a single lunge of his hips.

Crying out, she fought to keep her arms steady and extended.

"*Christ.*" He rolled his hips, nudging against the end of her. "I'm so deep in you, Jess. Do you feel how deep I am?"

Her eyes closed on a shaky exhalation. She felt the doeskin of his breeches against the backs of her thighs and the cuffs of his shirtsleeves against her hips. When she looked down, she saw his muddy boots. He was fully dressed, shielded from exposure, whereas she was mostly nude and mounted. The lascivious image in her mind of how they would look to a bystander spurred her desire. Aroused beyond bearing, she rippled along his length. Alistair's answering groan carried on the breeze, but she didn't care if anyone heard them. Her focus had narrowed to the point where they joined and the tender flesh that quivered around his thick penetration.

He began to move. Not with the rough, pounding tempo she'd expected in such a primitive position, but at a leisurely pace. Deliberate. Taking her with long, sinuous glides of his thick penis into her clenching depths. He devastated her when he took her like this. He was unhurried. Rhythmic and graceful. Wickedly practiced. He worked her hips in time to his thrusting, circling, rubbing, and stroking over every tender spot.

Her legs gave out. She fell to her knees on the dais, and he slipped out to the tip, then rammed deep as he followed her down. She cried out . . . conquered. He kneed her legs wider, quickening his rhythm. His heavy sac smacked against her wet flesh again and again, the cadenced erotic slapping against her clitoris adding an entirely new level of sensation. Her arms lost their strength and her shoulders sank into the pillows, angling her hips even higher. Nothing impeded Alistair's possession of her now, but still he kept that controlled and steady pace that had her clawing at the silk around her.

"God, you're tight like this," he said hoarsely. "And so wet. I want to come in you now . . ."

"Yes!"

"Not yet. I'm going to fuck you until I can no longer stand."

His crudity surged through her in a violent shiver. She climaxed in a heated rush, her body vibrating with the force of it. He cursed as she milked him with ecstatic pulses. He held still and ground against her, staving off his own pleasure. His fingers dug into her thighs with bruising force. And she loved it. Loved that she could break his steely control just by taking whatever he needed her to take.

Jess surrendered, letting the orgasm flow through her unchallenged. Alistair's grip lightened as she relaxed, his hands soothing her with gentle caresses and soft murmurs. She was so lost in the languid afterglow of her climax, it took her long moments before she realized he was too still. Opening her eyes, she turned her head and found him looking down at her with a clenched jaw having nothing to do with desire.

"What is it?" Her pleasured haze receded in the face of the darkness sweeping over his features.

His voice came clipped and furious. "What are these marks on your skin?"

Jess winced, hating that he'd seen the thin silvery scars marring her derriere and upper thighs. If they hadn't been outside in the unforgiving sunlight, he might never have seen them. Although she detested the truth, she gave it to him. "Surely you recognize the marks of a switch?"

"Bloody hell." He curled over her, mantling her body with his own, his grip around her torso like iron bands. Fiercely protective and obstinately comforting. "Do you bear other scars?"

"Not on the outside. But, regardless, they no longer signify."

"The hell they don't. Where else?"

She hesitated, wanting nothing more than to leave their painful pasts behind them.

"*Where*, Jessica?"

"I cannot hear in my left ear," she said softly, "as you know."

"Hadley is responsible for that?" He pressed his hot face into her back. "Jesus . . ."

"I don't want to think about it now," she complained. "Not here. Not while you're inside me."

Alistair's open mouth rubbed against her spine, his breathing rough. "I'll make you forget."

She moaned her relief as he cupped her breasts, her thoughts scattering with the ocean breeze.

"But I won't," he growled. "I'll never forget."

20

Alistair assisted Jessica down from his town carriage and took comfort in the sight of the lump beneath her white glove that betrayed the presence of his ring on her finger. Behind him, the Regmont town house waited. The redbrick home was innocuous to passersby, but it contained something undeniably hazardous to him.

He had no notion of what Jessica would do if her sister protested their nuptials. He had no notion of what *he* would do, since letting her go would kill him.

"She only wants my happiness," Jessica murmured, offering him a reassuring smile from beneath the brim of her straw bonnet. "It may surprise her to learn how wicked my inclinations are, but she won't object."

He snorted. Clearly he'd lost all ability to keep his emotions hidden when they related to Jessica.

Offering his arm, he escorted her up the short steps. He offered his card to the butler when the door opened and swiftly found himself in a cheery yellow parlor. He remained standing while Jessica sat. He was too restless to settle in any one spot and had no intention of lingering once Lady Regmont presented herself. They'd been in port only a few hours, and he had much to attend to. His London staff had been given no warning of his return, and so his home was not yet prepared for his residency. He had a note to pen to his mother, requesting a visit so he could tell her about Jessica. And another to send to Baybury.

Impatience spurred him. There was too much to be done between now and when he and Jessica could officially announce their engagement.

"Jess!"

He looked toward the door as Hester rushed in and found himself speechless. It had been years since he'd seen her, and even then she'd inevitably been with Jessica, who always stole his attention. Still, he was certain Lady Regmont had never been so delicate. He calculated the weeks. She should be five months along by now, or thereabouts, yet her condition wasn't apparent. She was far too thin and pale, making the rouge staining her cheeks seem unnaturally bright.

A chill moved through him. Had she lost the baby?

The sisters embraced. The differences between the two were made more apparent by their similarities. Jessica glowed with vitality—her eyes were bright, her lips plumped and reddened by his kisses, her skin flushed a healthy pink by the frequency and vigorousness of his ardor. Hester looked almost ghostly in comparison.

"My God," Hester said breathlessly. "You look so well! I've never seen you so fit and happy."

Jessica smiled. "I have Mr. Caulfield to thank for that."

Hester's verdant gaze moved to Alistair and remained warm. She approached with her hands outstretched. He caught them and lifted the backs to his lips, noting the prominence of blue veins beneath her parchment-like skin. The visible capillaries around her eyes and temples were also concerning.

"I owe you a huge debt of gratitude," she said. "As busy

as you must be, it was exceedingly generous of you to look after my sister."

"It was my pleasure," he murmured, managing a smile. What the devil was wrong with Regmont that he allowed his wife to waste away in such a manner? Especially while carrying his child? If Jessica ever looked so thin and ill, he'd keep her abed and hand-feed her relentlessly, never leaving her side until he was certain she would recover.

"How are you faring?" Jessica asked, her gaze meeting Alistair's over her sister's shoulder. She looked as worried as he felt.

"Famously." Hester pivoted carefully and moved to the settee. "You must have turned about directly after you arrived."

"What did you expect me to do after I received your letter?"

"Wish me happy and enjoy yourself."

Jessica began to tug off her gloves. "I've done both, and now I am here."

"I am absolutely fine," Hester said. "The dratted morning sickness has passed, thank God. I am exhausted much of the time, but the doctor says that is to be expected. Come have a seat, Mr. Caulfield. It's been ages."

"Thank you, but I cannot stay. I've been out of the country for some time and there is much to be done."

"Of course there is." Her smile faded. "Shame on me for detaining you. I'm grateful you brought my sister to me. Will you be seeing Lord Tarley soon?"

"Without a doubt."

"Good. Please send him my best wishes, and know that you already have them."

Jessica set her gloves on the floral-covered seat beside her. "I should like to stay with you a while. I've missed you."

"You're worried about me," Hester argued. "And you needn't be."

"My reasons are entirely selfish," Jessica said smoothly. "Who will help me plan my wedding if not for you?"

Hester blinked. "Beg your pardon? Did you say 'wedding'?"

"I did." Jessica's mouth curved and she turned to him.

Alistair couldn't look away, not when she regarded him in that manner. Her face was so expressive, her love given so fully and freely. His throat clenched tight.

"To *Alistair Caulfield!?*" Hester cried.

He winced inwardly at the pervasive shock in her tone. Then she stood in a rush and hugged him.

I told you, Jessica mouthed from across the room, her eyes glinting with moisture.

His tension deflated by relief, he hugged Hester back. And felt nothing but bones.

After departing the Regmont town house, Alistair headed directly to Remington's Gentlemen's Club. He needed a drink, maybe a few.

Leaving Jessica behind was damned difficult. Everything would work against them here in London, with multiple forces attempting to drive a wedge between them. When they were together, he felt as if they could manage anything. When they were apart, his driving need made him fear the worst.

Striding through the double-door entrance, he crossed the gaming area and entered the great room beyond it, his gaze skimming over faces before spotting an empty seating area in a distant corner. His brother Albert was, unfortunately, not in attendance. The sooner Alistair apprised his family of his betrothal, the sooner he could take the steps required to shut the rest of the world out of his romantic concerns. Once Jessica was his wife, Society and its meddlesome mores and opinions could go to hell. Some institutions were still sacred; what a man did with his wife was no one's business but his own.

As he crossed the room, he became aware of the numerous gazes following him. He gave curt nods to those he did business with and ignored the rest. When he reached the bar, he ordered scotch and asked for quill, ink, and parchment. His membership credentials were verified first, reminding him how long it had been since he last socialized in London. He moved to the quiet seat he'd found earlier and settled into the leather wingback.

"Damnation," he muttered, lifting the tumbler to his lips. He felt the multitude of eyes on him, but couldn't fathom the interest. He even checked his attire, looking for anything out of place that might attract undue attention.

Finding no discernible reason for the curiosity he'd roused, Alistair raked the room with a challenging glance, daring someone to approach him instead of furtively assessing him. To his surprise, some of the gentlemen smiled and waved, as if they were old friends. His sharp-edged wariness fled, replaced by mounting confusion. When a familiar tall, dark figure entered the room, Alistair stood with relief.

Michael's gaze found him. With eyes widened by surprise, he crossed the distance between them with long strides and caught Alistair in a fierce embrace.

"Has the world gone mad?" Alistair barked, holding his arm out to prevent spilling scotch down his friend's back.

"How are you?" Michael searched Alistair's face, then shot a telling glance at the fellow tending the bar.

"Alive and kicking."

"Yes, well, there is something to be said for that, is there not?"

"Absolutely."

They sat. A moment later a tumbler was set before Michael. "I wasn't expecting you for another few months, at the earliest," he said.

"That would have been ideal. However, once Lady Tarley learned her sister was in the family way, she desired to come home at once."

Michael inhaled sharply, but said nothing.

Alistair took another drink, knowing how it felt to covet another man's wife. "Lady Regmont sends her regards. In fact, she seemed most concerned that I find you in order to do so."

"Most likely she was thinking that you and I have a great deal in common at this point."

"Because we both love Sheffield women? What are we to do, exchange notes?"

Michael stilled. "What did you say?"

"Come now. I've known how you feel about Jessica's sibling for many years. Like Jess, your face reveals everything."

"'Jess' you say? What in bloody hell?" Michael's glass hit the wood tabletop with a decisive thud. "I pray you haven't been wool headed enough to play your games with my brother's widow."

"Never."

Michael exhaled his relief.

"However," Alistair went on, "the games I play with my betrothed are no one's concern but my own."

"By God, Alistair . . ." Michael stared for a long moment, then tossed back the contents of his glass in one swallow. He signaled for another. "What do you think you're doing? Jessica is not the type of woman a man takes lightly. Your station and means, even with marriage, won't be enough to keep her happy. You will have to be cautious and discreet—"

"Or simply steadfast."

"Don't jest!"

"This is no joke to me, Tarley." Twisting his tumbler back and forth, Alistair surveyed the room again, aware that others would think as Michael did—that Jessica would be better served by another man. "I have loved her since you and I were boys. At the time, I thought she was flawless; the one finely wrought thing in this world that might have a hope of saving my blackened soul."

"Spare me the poetry. Byron, you're not."

Alistair smiled, his mood softened by thoughts of Jessica. He was about to marry a diamond of the first water, a woman so heartbreakingly perfect for him that he ached just thinking about her. There wasn't a man in this room who didn't know her worth, and she was his. "But I've since learned it is our defects that make us perfect for one another. I expect to live in monogamous marital bliss for the rest of my days."

"And what does Masterson say about this?"

"As if I care what he thinks."

"What of your mother, then?" Michael challenged. "She might view this as an opportunity for you and His Grace to find common ground. Jessica is barren, Alistair. For a certainty."

"I know. I care not."

"You cannot be so vindictive. I know you and your father have never gotten along well, but this is a matter far greater than either of you."

A fresh beverage was set before Michael. Alistair grabbed it for his own and drained it. "Your brain has been addled by overwork," he said, wiping his mouth.

"You must be accountable now for decisions that will impact generations—"

"Bloody hell. Let us be clear . . . Your objection to my marrying Jessica comes not from unsuitability or incompatibility, but from your belief that I have an obligation to spawn?"

"Responsibility is a nuisance, is it not?" Michael said with surprising bitterness.

"Obviously the stress of your brother's passing has driven

you mad. Damned if I'll give up the one thing in this world I cannot live without simply to whelp offspring in a pitiful attempt to gain acceptance."

"Whether or not you mend the rift with your father is secondary to honoring your duty to the title."

Alistair was of the mind that walking away might be wise. Otherwise, he was certain he was only seconds away from strangling his oldest friend. While Michael had no knowledge of the circumstances surrounding Alistair's parentage, he was spouting nonsense nonetheless. "Ensuring the longevity of Masterson's lineage has never been, nor will it ever be, my duty."

Michael's head tilted, his gaze narrowing. Suddenly, something akin to horror swept over his features. "My God . . . You don't know, do you?"

"Alistair Caulfield," Hester repeated, shaking her head. "I would never have guessed. You two were always so cool and reserved toward one another. I always believed you didn't much care for him."

Jessica lifted one shoulder in an offhand, slightly sheepish shrug. "He's changed, but more than that, there are depths to him one cannot see unless he reveals them. And I confess, I always found him physically attractive."

"What woman doesn't?" Hester leaned forward, as if imparting a great secret. "There is something deliciously wicked about him. Something sinful and decadent. And dear God, he is a man now, so large and strong. More handsome than ever, and he was stunning in his youth! It is difficult not to stare at him."

"I know. I'm horribly besotted. Truly, I have to wed him or I will embarrass myself by making calf-eyes at him."

Her sister straightened and poured more tea. "The way he looks at you is indecent. Have you shagged him yet?"

"Hester!"

"You have!" Hester threw her head back and laughed, reminding Jess of the energetic girl of long ago. "Well? I must know if he is as good in bed as he looks."

Just thinking about Alistair made her toes curl. "How can you leap to the conclusion that we've been intimate? Perhaps he was a perfect gentleman."

"Alistair Caulfield? On a ship for endless days?" Hester laughed her sweet, tinkling laugh. "Any other man, perhaps. But not a scoundrel like he. So . . . ?"

"So . . . He is as delectable as he looks."

"I knew it!" Hester smiled over the rim of her cup. "I am so happy for you, Jess."

Jess wanted to feel equally happy for her sister, but the circumstances didn't warrant it. Hester was far too frail, especially for a woman who was midway through a pregnancy. "How are things between you and Regmont?"

"He's equally consummate in bed," Hester said with the faintest note of bitterness in her tone. "Far too skilled, actually. No man should be so knowledgeable about a woman's body."

"Is he unfaithful?"

Hester's cup lowered and she looked contemplative. "I have no notion. If so, his appetite for me hasn't decreased at all."

A long stretch of silence ensued as Jess tried to understand what was causing her sister so much pain. "Hester . . ." she said finally. "Please tell me what's wrong. You've lost far too much weight. What of the baby and the nourishment required for it to grow plump and healthy?"

"I'll eat more now that you're here."

"And when I'm not?" Jess pushed to her feet. Restless, she paced, a bad habit her father had beaten out of her in her youth.

"You have changed," Hester noted.

"So have you." Pointing to the lemon cream scones sitting untouched on the tea service tray, she said, "You adore those scones. They are your favorite. You always eat too many of them, with heaping scoops of clotted cream that fall off your fingers when you take a bite. Yet you haven't touched a one. You won't even look at them."

"I'm not hungry."

"I am certain your child is."

Hester winced and Jess felt horrid, but something had to be done.

Returning to her sister, Jess sank to her knees and caught up Hester's hands, noting the skeletal thinness with growing despair. "Tell me. Are you ill? Have you seen a doctor? Or is it something else? Is it Regmont? Are you afraid to tell me because I suggested the pairing? Tell me, Hester. *Please.*"

Hester's pent-up breath left her in a rush. "My marriage is no longer a happy one."

"Oh, Hester." Jess's heart broke. "What happened? Did you fight? Can it be salvaged?"

"I once hoped so. Maybe it would be possible if I was stronger, like you. My weakness angers him."

"You are *not* weak."

"Yes, I am. When Father turned his wrath to me and you interceded, I *let* you. I was *grateful* you were taking the switch and not me." Her mouth turned down at the corners. "So damned grateful."

"You were a c-child." Jess's voice cracked with unshed tears. "You were wise to allow me to intercede. It would have been foolish to do otherwise."

"Perhaps, but courageous, too." Hester's eyes were giant verdant pools in her pale face. The rouge she wore to feign a healthy glow was incongruous against her bloodless skin, making her appear like a caricature of a bewigged and pow-dered peeress from times gone by. "I need that courage now, and I don't know where to find it."

"I will help," Jess vowed, squeezing her sister's fingers

gently. "We shall find it together. As for Regmont, I'm certain he must be worried sick about you, as I am. Once he sees you regaining your strength, your relationship will improve. It's natural for a woman to experience moodiness and melancholia while increasing, but that might be difficult for a man to grasp. We will just have to educate him."

Hester smiled and cupped Jess's cheek. "I'm so sorry you cannot have children, Jess. You would be so good with them. Far better than I."

"Nonsense. You will be a doting mother, and I shall be a very proud aunt."

"Your betrothed loves you very much."

"I think he does," Jess agreed, laying her cheek against Hester's knee. "He cannot seem to bring himself to say it aloud, but I feel it when he touches me. I hear it in his voice when he speaks to me."

"Of course he adores you, and his desire is unquestionable." Hester's cool fingers stroked Jess's brow. "You will be the envy of every woman in England. Alistair Caulfield is rich, breathtakingly handsome, and mad for you. Toss in the dukedom and there isn't a woman alive who would not kill to trade places with you."

Jess lifted her head, laughing. "Your dreams are too lofty. He'll never inherit the title."

Hester blinked. Then, her eyes widened with something akin to horror. "Dear God . . . You don't know, do you?"

21

Alistair paced before the grate in the family parlor of the Masterson residence in Town, his sleekly polished Hessians treading silently across the oriental rug. His fingers were laced at the small of his back, his hands tingling from the strain of his white-knuckled clasp. "Smallpox."

"Yes." His mother's voice was soft with anguish.

Louisa, the Duchess of Masterson, sat on a carved wooden chair with her back painfully straight. Her hair remained as dark as Alistair's, the glossy tresses unmarred by any gray, but her lovely face betrayed both her age and the agony of outliving three of her four sons. The portrait of her above the mantel was taller and wider than Alistair's height, and it served as the focal point of the room. Her younger self smiled down at anyone occupying the expansive space, her blue eyes naively clear of the many tragedies yet to come.

Alistair had no notion of what to say. All three of his brothers were dead, and grief weighted his heart like a heavy, oppressive stone. Of equal burden was the title he now bore, a distinction he'd never coveted. "I don't want this," he said hoarsely. "Tell me how to get out."

"There is no way out."

He looked at her. Masterson was at home, but she dealt

with this impossible situation alone because her beloved husband couldn't face the bastard who would now bear his exalted title.

"He could denounce me," Alistair suggested, "which would open an avenue for a relative to inherit."

"Alistair . . ." She lifted a handkerchief to her mouth and sobbed, the wretched sound tearing through his innards like claws.

"He cannot even face me. He must want a way out as well."

"If there was an alternative he could live with, yes. But he will not be a cuckold or shame me, and the next in line to inherit is a distant cousin whose worth is questionable."

"I do not want this," he said again, stomach churning. Alistair wanted a life of travel and adventure with Jessica. He wanted to bring her joy and challenges, and the freedom to erase the oppression of her youth with an adulthood that was boundless.

"You will be one of the wealthiest men in England now—"

"By God, I won't touch a shilling of Masterson's precious coin," he bit out, his blood boiling at the mere suggestion. "You have no notion of the things I've done to be solvent. He gave me scant assistance when I most needed it. I damned well won't take anything from him now!"

Louisa rose, her hands twisting in her kerchief. Tears coursed unchecked down her hollowed cheeks. "What would you have me do? I cannot regret your birth. I would not go back and give you up. To have you in my life I had to risk this, and Masterson took that risk for me. With me. We made the decision together, and we will abide by it."

"Yet here you stand, alone."

Her chin lifted. "My choice. My consequence."

Abandoning the fireplace, he approached her. The ceiling hung thirty feet above them; the nearest wall was a score of feet away. Every Masterson holding boasted similar cavernous spaces containing furnishings and artwork accumulated over centuries.

The distant walls closed in, squeezing Alistair's chest like a vise.

He'd never felt connected to any of it, had never felt a sense of familial pride or a sense of belonging. Bearing the title would be akin to wearing a mask. He'd donned a role once before to survive, but now he was comfortable with who he was. Comfortable being the man Jessica loved unconditionally.

"Your choice," he said softly, feeling very much like the impostor he was being told to be. "But I must pay the price."

Staying as a guest in Regmont's house, Jess slept not a wink all night. Her thoughts sped too swiftly through her mind, her heart breaking at every turn.

Alistair was now the Marquess of Baybury. Someday in the future, he would become the Duke of Masterson. Immense power and prestige came with those stations, but so, too, did grave responsibilities.

He could not take a barren woman to wife.

On both the *Acheron* and the island, they'd slept until noon. On their second morning in London, however, Alistair came calling at the ungodly hour of eight o'clock. She was dressed and ready for him, knowing he would come to her as soon as it was acceptable to do so. Knowing she had to be strong enough for both of them.

She descended the stairs with as much decorum as she could manage while feeling as if she was headed toward the gallows. When she rounded the bend in the stairs leading to the foyer, she found Alistair waiting with one hand atop the newel post and one foot propped on the bottom stair. He retained his hat and wore black from head to toe. His features appeared as stark as she felt.

He opened his arms to her, and she raced to fill them, dashing down the remaining stairs and launching herself against him. He caught her easily, squeezing tight.

"I am so sorry for your loss," she breathed, her fingers kneading restlessly into his tense nape.

"I am sorry for my gain." His voice was flat and cold, but his embrace was not. He pressed his temple to hers and held her as if he would never let go.

After a long moment, he allowed her to lead him into the parlor. They both remained standing, facing each other. He looked tired and older than his years.

Running a hand through his hair, he groaned his frustration. "It seems we are to be trapped."

She nodded, then stumbled toward the nearest chair. Her heartbeat was too quick and erratic, making her dizzy. *We,* he said, as she had known he would. She sank into a yellow damask-covered wingback and sucked in a deep breath. "You'll be busy."

"Yes, damn it all. It has already started. The moment Masterson learned I'd returned, he began filling a schedule for me. I haven't a free quarter hour to myself over the next three days. God knows if I'll even be allowed to relieve myself."

Her heart ached for him. He resented the road set before him, but he was more than competent. He had a brilliant head for business matters and an air of command that earned the respect of great men. "In no time at all, you will have everything running so smoothly others will stand back in awe."

"I don't give a damn what he thinks."

"I wasn't referring to Masterson, but regardless, you care what your mother thinks and she cares about what he thinks. She loves you and fought for you—"

"Not enough."

"What is enough?"

The look he shot her was combative. She held his gaze.

He growled. "God, I miss you. I detest this game of waiting for certain hours to see you and lying in bed at night without you beside me. I miss having your ear and being the grateful recipient of your counsel."

Jess's eyes stung. He looked so hard faced, discouraged, and alone. He'd retained his hat, and he worried the brim with restless hands, twisting the chapeau around and around. "I will always be available to you."

"I know what you wanted," he said gruffly, "but I can't wait for it. It may take months to work through the morass my life has become, and I cannot focus on that while starving for you. I've come to ask you to elope with me."

Her hands linked in her lap. The pain in her chest was agonizing, nearly debilitating. "That wouldn't be wise."

He stilled, his fevered gaze narrowing. "Don't do this to me."

"You knew I would. That is why you're so agitated and why you came to me with the sun barely in the sky." She blew out a deep breath. "You need me to do this so you can move forward."

"Do what, Jess?" he asked with dangerous softness. "Say it."

"Afford you the time and space to become accustomed to who you will have to be from this point in your life onward."

"I know what I want."

"You know what you wanted," she corrected, "but now you have so much more to consider. Where do all the pieces fit? Do some overlap? Are others obsolete? You won't know until you immerse yourself in this role you've assumed."

"Don't," he snapped, his voice vibrating with fury. "Don't you dare sit there so primly and speak about the dissolution of our relationship in that toneless voice as if you are asking me if I want more tea instead of ripping out my heart!"

"Alistair . . ." Her lower lip quivered and she bit it, tasting blood.

"You're afraid," he accused.

"Aren't you? It is the worst state of mind in which to make life-altering decisions."

His nostrils flared. "You cannot live without me, either, Jess."

She couldn't; she knew that. She hoped she wouldn't have to. But they both had to be certain. "Hester needs me now. I can't leave her."

"But you can leave me."

"You are much stronger than she is."

"I still need you!" he bit out, enunciating every word. "She has Regmont and Michael and you. I only have you. You are the only one who takes care of me; the only one who thinks of my happiness first and last and always. If you leave me, Jess, you leave me with nothing."

"I'll never leave you," she whispered. "But that doesn't mean I should be with you."

Jess knew he could see on her face how she felt about him, how she breathed for him. But love was supposed to be selfless, despite his protestations to the contrary. Their marriage could irrevocably damage his relationship with his mother, the only person aside from Jess who loved him truly. If he was willing to take that risk, she would take it with him, but he wasn't acknowledging it now. He was rushing forward without thought, defiant in the face of a future he didn't want.

"Jess." His gaze was as hard as gemstone. "I knew you were mine the moment I saw you. Young as I was, I still had no doubt. I never married, never even considered for a moment all the merchant and landowner daughters who were set in my path, bearing sizable dowries and advantageous alliances. I spurned them all, certain you would one day belong to me. It was unfathomable to me that you wouldn't be. I would have waited two score years for you. Double that. You cannot ask me now to proceed with my life without any possibility of having you. I might as well be dead."

"Don't misunderstand me." Her voice gained the strength of her conviction. "I am not going anywhere. I won't be seeking anyone. I will be here with Hester."

"Waiting?"

"No. I cannot. That will hold you back." She tugged at the ruby on her finger, feeling as if she were cutting out her own heart with a dull blade.

"Enough." Dropping his hat, Alistair lunged for her, staying her before the gold band slipped free of her fingertip. He pushed the ring back on, his forehead touching hers. His breath came quick and shallow, gusting over the tip of her nose. "Make me understand."

"First, you must know that *I* understand." She clutched his hand, willing him to absorb all the strength and love she had. "I thought of how I would feel if I were forced to give you up to spare someone I loved, and how much more unfair it would be if Hadley benefited in any way from that sacrifice."

"I am *not* giving you up, Jess. I won't. I can't."

"Shh . . . I've inferred what you have left unsaid about your mother and Masterson. I collect how it must have been—the illusion of acceptance and understanding broken by carefully rendered cuts and barbs. He has never allowed your mother to forget her transgression or how much it's cost him, has he? And she has been burdened with guilt and remorse for all of your life. She's allowed him to wound her in countless tiny ways as penance. And you have watched it all transpire, and suffered your own feelings of blame and regret."

"You inferred all that, did you?" He cupped her tense jaw with heartrending tenderness.

"You are very protective of her, to your own detriment. One doesn't seek to protect something that isn't in danger of being broken."

Alistair brushed his thumb across her cheekbone. "My mother is so strong willed and assertive, except when it comes to this. To me."

She leaned into his touch. "It isn't you, my love. You are not at fault. Consider it carefully . . . There are ways to prevent conception for both men and women. If she was simply addressing her physical needs, wouldn't she be prepared? And her lover also?"

"What are you saying?"

"Perhaps your mother had a grand passion. A whirlwind affair. A sexual craving that drowned out all thought and reason. Perhaps that is why she feels such shame."

"She loves Masterson. God knows why."

"And I love you, with abandon, to a degree I have never felt with anyone else. And yet there were times when I lost my head with Tarley; times when I felt as if I would go mad if he didn't touch me."

He covered her lips with his fingers. "Say no more," he said gruffly, but his gaze was soft.

"You, too, know that fierce sexual pleasure can come without love. If I am correct, it would help to explain your mother's need to be penitent." She grasped the wrist of the hand he stroked her with, squeezing gently in a silent offer of support. "It's also possible that she secretly desired to conceive again. If she'd tried to arouse Masterson for a length of time prior to his decision to ignore her indiscretions, she might have felt less of a woman. Perhaps she wondered if Masterson's inability to become aroused was in some way her fault. There are many possibilities for the tension you've witnessed. None of them have anything to do with you."

He stared into her, seeing how and why she commiserated with his mother. She'd suffered through her own feelings of despair and inadequacy.

"It isn't you," she said again. "But you feel responsible and you have worked the whole of your life to stay out of sight and be as little a burden as possible. Now, you will be the most prominent face of a family you don't feel a part of, and you will be expected to carry that family forward. I am useless to you in that regard."

"Don't." Alistair pressed his lips to her forehead. "Don't ever talk about yourself in that manner."

"My barrenness pained me before. But Tarley and I had Michael and the children he would father. There is no one to carry that burden for you, or you wouldn't be here."

"I am not a damned martyr, Jess. I have sacrificed all I am willing to for this farce. I will never give you up. Not for this. Not for anything."

"And I won't lose you to remorse and blame. I would rather lose you now, with love between us, than years down the road with your mother's unhappiness and your feelings of responsibility for it wedged between us."

"What would you have me do?" His gaze darkened to a deep sapphire. "If I cannot have you, I won't have anyone. No one gets what they want then."

"Settle your affairs, then settle yourself. Live this life you've assumed. Accustom yourself to it. Gain your bearings. If you still want me after you've done that and your mother can give her blessing without reserve, you know where to find me."

He kissed her sweetly, his lips clinging to hers. When he pulled back, he looked at her with shadowed and sultry eyes, his face a stunning mask of masculine beauty and aching torment. "I will see to this; you see to your sister. Be quick about it. It won't be long before I come for you, and you'd best be ready, Jess, with my ring still gracing your hand. You won't stay me then. I'll drag you to Scotland in irons if I have to."

He left her in a rush. As always, taking her heart with him.

Jess was still in the parlor when Hester joined her, three hours and three glasses of claret later.

"I was told Baybury called this morning," her sister murmured.

Wincing inwardly at the sound of Alistair's title, she nodded and took another drink.

Hester paused by the table and frowned down at Jess. "Claret for breakfast?"

Jess shrugged. She'd begun imbibing as a young girl, after the cook took to slipping brandy into her tea when her body ached too much to allow sleep. It swiftly became apparent to her that liquor dulled emotional pain as well. In the early years of her marriage, she'd had no need to drink. But once the consumption had dug its greedy talons into Benedict's lungs, she'd turned to the comfort found in a bottle and hadn't yet turned away.

Hester took a seat on the settee beside her. "I have never seen you look more melancholy, and there is no good reason to drink spirits first thing in the morning."

"Don't fret over me."

"Did he throw you over, Jess?" Hester asked softly.

Of course Hester would leap to the obvious and most sensible course of action. She had been raised by the same parents as Jess, after all. Women of the peerage served one vital purpose—to bear heirs, as many as possible.

Reaching over, Jess squeezed her sister's thin hand. "No. And he won't. He loves me too much."

"Then why do you look as you did when Temperance died? Does he wish to delay the wedding?"

"On the contrary, he hoped I would elope with him."

"You refused? Why?" Her eyes glistened. "Dear God . . . Please, don't say you stayed for me! I couldn't bear it. You have already given up too much on my behalf."

"I did it for him, because it's best for him. He needs time, even if he refuses to acknowledge that need. The man I intended to wed no longer exists. The man he will have to be now has different needs, and goals to which I am an impediment. It is the former who clings to me so stubbornly. And so I've asked him to spend some time living the life of the latter. If that man wants me and if he can love me wholeheartedly, with no regrets or recrimination, then we can be happy and I will gladly marry him. But he can't know that yet. He still believes he can be Alistair Caulfield."

"He will come back for you, won't he?"

Jess's heart ached. "For a certainty. He's wanted me a long time. Since before I wed Benedict."

"Truly?" Hester brushed at the wetness on her long lashes. "I find that wonderfully romantic."

"He is the world to me. I cannot tell you what he's done for me . . . how he's changed me. He knows me as well as you do. All my secrets and fears and hopes. There is nothing to hide from him and no reason to try if there was. He accepts my faults and shortcomings as a means to bind us closer together."

"And what of the errors of his ways?"

Jess found her sister's question very telling. "There are plenty of those, as everyone knows, and he goes to great pains to tell me about them."

"He does? Why?"

"He wanted anything that might later turn me away from him to be disclosed from the outset, before our attachment to one another grew and the possibility of separation became too painful." All his best intentions, for naught.

Hester's face took on a wistful cast. "I would never have guessed Alistair Caulfield would be so . . ."

"Mature?" Jess smiled sadly. "His circumstances have been more difficult than anyone would expect. His maturity comes from cynicism and a jaded outlook. His is far older than his years."

"What will you do now?"

"Focus on seeing you hale and hearty. Rejoin Society in truth." Restless, she stood. "I need new gowns."

"Your mourning is over."

Was it? Perhaps she would be in mourning still, but not for her former husband. "Yes. It's time."

"It is," Hester agreed.

Jess looked at the wine on the table, her fingers clenching against the need to reach for it. That dependency would have to be addressed, as well. She had no right to ask Alistair to conquer his demons while still clinging to her own.

"We'll need to eat a hearty breakfast to sustain us through the volume of shopping I intend to accomplish today."

Hester rose to her feet like a graceful wraith. "I would love to see you in a berry-hued gown."

"Red. Also gold."

"Astonishing," Hester said. "Father would have an apoplectic fit."

Jess almost laughed at the image that came to mind, but Hester gasped, then slumped against her. Jess barely caught her unconscious sister before she hit the floor.

22

"She is starving to death," Dr. Lyons said, his pale blue eyes grim behind his spectacles. "She's too thin for any woman, but dangerously so for a woman in her delicate condition."

"She's been eating more since I arrived, but that was only a couple of days ago." Jess's stomach twisted with concern and fear. Where in hell was Regmont? She had yet to see him. Either he kept odd hours, or he'd yet to come home . . . for nearly three days.

"Not nearly long enough." He set his hands on his lean hips. For all the doctor's concern over Hester's weight, he appeared unusually slender, too. "She should begin her lying-in immediately with bed rest for the duration and many small meals throughout the day, every day. And no excitement in her delicate condition—her heart is weakened by her emaciation."

"I don't understand. What ails her? She has grown progressively more ill for many months now."

"I've rarely been afforded the opportunity to examine Lady Regmont thoroughly. She is very reticent; I'm inclined to say excessively so. Regardless, I can say that she seems prone to melancholia. Mood affects the body more than we fully understand."

Jess's lower lip quivered, but she stemmed the rush of tears that threatened and nodded.

Life. Too fragile. Too precious. Far too short.

The doctor collected his fee, then made his egress.

Moving into her sister's bedroom, Jess sat on the edge of her sister's bed and took in the sickly pallor of Hester's once luminous skin.

Hester smiled weakly. "You look so serious. It isn't that dire. I am just weary and my morning sickness was severe, but it's over now."

"Listen to me." Jess's voice was low and angry. "I have had my fill of bedside death vigils."

"You have had one," Hester retorted dryly.

"One too many. If you think I will do it again, you are sorely mistaken." Jess caught her sister's hand to soften the sting of her words. "My nephew or niece is making a valiant effort to grow within you, and you are going to help, damn you."

"Jess . . ." Hester's eyes watered. "I am not as strong as you are."

"Strong? I'm not strong. I drink too much, because it's a way to hide. I sent the man I love away because I am terrified that if I don't *he* will eventually send *me* away, and I couldn't bear it. There was a man on Alistair's ship abusing a child, and when I confronted him, I thought I might faint or vomit or soil myself. I am weak and flawed and absolutely incapable of watching you waste away. So I will not be listening to any further excuses. You will eat what I bring you to eat and drink what I bring you to drink, and in a few short swift months you will reward us both with a healthy child to love and spoil."

There was a flare of irritation in Hester's green eyes. "As you command," she said crossly.

Jess took the show of temper as a good sign. She also took the lesson of the day to heart: life and happiness are both too dear to throw away. She would give Alistair the time he needed to regain his bearings, but she wouldn't allow him to slip away from her without a fight. If she had to lock him, his mother, and Masterson in a room to clear the air between them, so be it.

She pressed a kiss to Hester's forehead and went to speak to the cook.

Michael entered Alistair's study and found his friend poring over architectural renderings of a prospective new irrigation system. He took a moment to absorb the sight of his friend, taking in the changes the time away from home had wrought in the young man with whom he'd spent so much of his youth.

"You look horrendous," Michael said, noting the day's worth of stubble shadowing Alistair's jawline and the crumpled state of his shirtsleeves. "And why are you here instead of at Masterson Place?"

Alistair looked up. "Nothing on earth could entice me into residing under the same roof as Masterson."

"I knew that's how you would answer."

"So why ask?"

"To aggravate you."

With a low groan that sounded suspiciously like a growl, Alistair straightened and ran a hand through his hair. Michael knew all too well how overwhelming the first few months would be for his friend. A year and a half after Benedict's death, and he was only just beginning to feel as if he wore his own skin. "I have enough aggravation without your assistance."

"What are friends for?" Michael held up a hand before a

retort could be made. "You will have bigger troubles once you come out of hiding and appear in public. The scandal sheets say you have replaced me as the bachelor most hunted, for which I will be eternally grateful."

Alistair sank into the leather chair behind the desk. A nautical feel embellished the space, not overt, but present nevertheless. It was there in the color palette of blue and white, the shape and fluidity of the designs carved into the walnut furnishings, and the touches of brass spread all around the room. The study suited the gentleman who used it, a man best known as an adventurer and wanderer, which made Alistair's next statement seem even more out of place.

"I am not a bachelor."

"You're unmarried," Michael pointed out dryly. "That makes you a bachelor."

"Not to my mind."

"You are still determined to have Jessica?"

"She's mine already." Alistair lifted one shoulder in an insolent shrug. "Everything else is merely a formality."

"I pray you aren't implying that you've taken liberties." It was a thought that didn't sit well. Jessica was his brother's widow. She was a member of his family and a friend. She'd loved his brother and brought him great happiness, and when Benedict had fallen ill with consumption, she had stayed by his side to the very end. She had shunned Society and social events in favor of tending to Benedict and entertaining him on the days he felt up to it. For her care and consideration, Michael would protect her safety and interests for the rest of her days.

Drumming his fingers on the armrests, Alistair studied him with a narrow-eyed stare. "My relationship with Jess is none of your concern."

"If your intentions are honorable, why not announce your engagement?"

"If the decision were mine alone, we'd be wed and under

one roof now. Jessica is the source of the delay, for reasons I don't fully comprehend. She acts as if there might be something capable of diminishing my affection for her."

"Such as?"

"Such as Masterson's need for an heir combined with a young debutante capable of producing one. Or my mother's unhappiness over my choice. Or some future urge to procreate that might strike me."

"All reasonable arguments."

"I have been unreasonably in love with her as long as I can remember. That has trumped everything so far, and I don't foresee it changing."

"Everything except more women than I can count," Michael said dryly.

"You should hire a tutor for yourself, then, to help you with basic math."

"I didn't have to see them. There was rarely an evening when you didn't smell of sex and a woman's perfume."

To Michael's surprise, his libertine friend's cheekbones were flagged with a dull red flush.

"And the ones you did see," Alistair said gruffly. "What do you remember about them?"

"Sorry, chap. Your ladybirds didn't interest me as much as they interested you. And I rarely saw one more than once, as I recall."

"Hmm . . . It wasn't notable that all were blondes? Pale-skinned and light-eyed, too. I never found one with gray irises, like a brewing storm, but that was just as well. I have never been one who is satisfied by replicas of priceless things. There is nothing quite like the genuine article," Alistair murmured, his thoughts clearly elsewhere. "And once a man is fortunate enough to acquire a treasure, it is to his pleasure to protect her and coddle her and make her the most prominent feature of his life and home."

Michael frowned, thinking back. He exhaled in a rush,

understanding how deep and far reaching Alistair's captivation with Jessica went. Perhaps as deep and far reaching as his affection for Hester. "Damnation."

A knock came at the door.

Alistair's head turned, and one brow rose in silent query.

The butler's voice drifted over Alistair's shoulder. "Forgive me, my lords," the servant said. "Her Grace, the Duchess of Masterson, has come to call."

With a long-suffering sigh, Alistair nodded. "Show her in."

Gripping the arms of his chair, Michael moved to stand.

"Stay," Alistair said.

"Beg your pardon?" Both of Michael's brows rose.

"Please."

Michael settled back into his seat, only to rise a moment later when Alistair's mother entered. He smiled, pleased as all men were by the sight of a beautiful woman. Unlike his brothers, Alistair took after his mother to a marked degree. Both had inky black hair and piercing blue eyes. Both were elegant and innately sensual in build and carriage, with a rapier wit that charmed and sliced with equal measure.

"My Lord Tarley," she greeted in a breathless, lilting voice. She held out her hand to him. "You look well and far too handsome for a woman's well-being."

He kissed the back of her ungloved hand. "Your Grace, always the most sublime of pleasures."

"Will you be attending the Treadmore's masquerade?"

"I wouldn't miss it."

"Excellent. Would you be so kind as to assist my son in finding his way there?"

Michael glanced aside at his friend, smiling when he found Alistair scowling with both palms flat on his littered desk.

"I do not have room in my schedule for such nonsense," Alistair said.

"Make room," she retorted smoothly. "People are beginning to talk."

"Let them talk."

"You have been absent for years. People want to see you."

"Well, then," he drawled, "a masquerade is the last place I should go."

"Alistair Lucius Caulfield—"

"Dear God. When is this damned event?"

"Wednesday, which gives you five days to clear your schedule for one evening."

"The first of many," he muttered, "if you have your way."

"I am proud of you. Is it a crime to want to show you off?"

Michael crossed his arms, grinning. It was a rare pleasure to see Alistair bending his will for another.

"I will go"—Alistair held up one hand when she smiled triumphantly—"only if my betrothed attends. She will make it bearable."

"Your betrothed . . ." The duchess sank slowly into the chair beside Michael's. A look of wonder spread over her lovely features. "Oh, Alistair. Who is she?"

"Jessica Sinclair, Lady Tarley."

"Tarley," she repeated, glancing at Michael.

Michael's hands curled around the end of his armrests. Anger began to simmer. "My sister-in-law."

"Yes, of course." She cleared her throat. "Isn't she . . . older than you?"

"By the barest degree. Two years is hardly worth mentioning."

"She was wed to Tarley for some time, was she not?"

"Several years. A pleasant union by all accounts."

She nodded, but appeared dazed. And Michael's fury grew. The duchess could not care less how pleasant or not the marriage had been, and Alistair damn well knew it.

"She's a lovely girl."

"The most beautiful woman in the world," Alistair said, watching his mother with the predatory sharpness of a hawk. "I am eager for you two to become better acquainted, but Jessica holds back. She fears you will judge her on criteria having nothing to do with how happy she makes me. I assured her that was a misplaced concern."

The duchess swallowed hard. "Of course."

"Perhaps you could send a reassuring note to her? I am certain that would ease her mind considerably."

Nodding, she stood. "I will endeavor to find something appropriate to say."

Michael and Alistair stood. Michael helped himself to a glass of brandy as Alistair showed Her Grace out. That Michael was goaded to drink this early in the day aggravated him further. Alistair had always been dragging him into one crazed adventure after another in their youth, and it appeared his influence was still questionable.

When his friend returned, Michael rounded on him. "By God, you're a heel, Baybury. A complete and total ass."

"You must be spitting mad. You're wielding my title like the weapon it is." Alistair's stride was leisurely and arrogant. "If you are surprised by the way I handled the situation, you've been blind to my faults for too many years."

"There was no good reason to ask me to stay for that! It was awkward in the extreme, for both me and Her Grace."

"There was a damned good reason." Alistair went to the console and poured his own drink. "Your presence forced her to restrain any emotional reaction she might have had. Now, she will have the opportunity to think over the information before she says something we'll both regret. One can pray that once she absorbs it all, she will indeed put my happiness before other considerations."

"You have always been reckless, but this . . . *this* affects other people."

Alistair tossed back his drink and leaned his hip against

the console. "Are you telling me there is something you would *not* do to have Lady Regmont for your own?"

Michael froze, his hand clenching around his glass. Considering the murderous rage he felt toward Regmont, he couldn't answer that question.

Mouth curving, Alistair set his glass down. "Right. I have some errands to see to. Would you like to join me?"

"Why not?" Michael groused, finishing his drink. "We could end the day in Bedlam or clapped in irons. There is never a dull moment with you, Baybury."

"Ah . . . the title again. You must be ferociously angry."

"And you had best become accustomed to that title you so despise. At the masquerade alone you'll hear it a hundred times."

Alistair tossed an arm over Michael's shoulders and prodded him toward the door. "When I hear it paired with Jessica's name, I shall love it. Until then, I will simply have to keep you in good humor."

"God, I need another drink."

"That shade of red is astonishing," Hester said from where she sat up in her bed. Surrounded by mountains of pillows she looked small and very youthful, although the décor of her rooms was undeniably adult. In fact, Jess found her sister's private space far more shocking than the bolt of material Hester was considering. Unlike the relentless cheeriness that distinguished the rest of the house, Hester's bedroom and boudoir were decorated in shades of grayish blue, charcoal, and off white. The overall effect was dramatic, but also quite somber. Not what Jess would have expected at all.

"Quite daring," Lady Pennington agreed over the lip of her teacup.

Jess returned her attention to the blood-red silk, helplessly drawn to what it would signify to Alistair—that he had changed her, made her bolder, helped her find an inner peace she'd never dreamed was possible. "I have no notion of when I would have an occasion to wear a dress made of this material."

"Wear it in private," Hester suggested.

Glancing at Elspeth, Jess bit her lower lip and wondered how this conversation was impacting the woman who'd been like a mother to her for the past several years. Would she resent Jess's efforts to move forward with her life?

"My dear girl," Elspeth said, meeting her gaze. "Don't fret on my account. Benedict loved you. He would have wanted you to be as happy as possible. I want that for you, as well."

Jess's eyes stung and she looked away quickly. "Thank you."

"It is I who must thank you," the countess said. "As short as Benedict's life was, you filled his last years with tremendous joy. I will forever be indebted to you for that."

Movement from the bed caught Jess's eye. Hester had leaned forward to run her hands over the luxurious material. The modiste extolled its virtues in a hushed but rapturous tone, which perfectly suited the thoughts that would accompany the sight of a woman draped in such decadence.

"Perhaps you can use it just on the bodice?" Hester suggested. "Paired with a cream satin or even a heavier damask? Or just on the sleeves? Or as trim?"

"No," Jess murmured, crossing her arms. "The whole gown must be made of it, with a draped bodice and a low back."

"*C'est magnifique!*" the modiste exclaimed, beaming and snapping her fingers at her two assistants to begin taking measurements.

A white-capped maid entered and curtsied. "Lady Tarley. Something has arrived for you. Would you like me to bring it to you here?"

Jess frowned. "Is there a reason I must see it now? Can you put it in my room?"

"It came with instructions to deliver it to you immediately."

"Intriguing. Yes, bring it here."

"Whatever could it be?" Hester asked. "Have you any clue, Jess?"

"None at all." Although she prayed it would be from Alistair, whatever it was. Their separation of only a few days was fraying her equanimity. If not for Hester's precarious health and need of near-constant prodding to eat, Jess would have gone to him by now.

A few moments later, the maid reappeared carrying a handled basket. She set it down on the floor, and it rocked to and fro. A soft whine from the interior lured Jess closer.

"What is that?" Lady Pennington asked, setting her cup and saucer aside.

Jess bent down and lifted the basket's lid, gasping at the sight of the tiny pug puppy stumbling around the lined interior.

"Look at you," she breathed, instantly in love. She reached in carefully to pick up the tiny creature and laughed in delight at the feel of its soft, warm, and wriggling body.

"Dear God," Hester cried. "It's a dog."

That only made Jess laugh harder. Sitting back on her heels, she set the energetic pug in her lap and looked at the metal tag hanging from its red leather collar.

Acheron, it said on one side, causing a pang in her chest. The other side said simply, *All my love, ALC.*

"Who sent that creature?" the countess asked.

"Baybury, I would guess," Hester said, sounding wistful.

Jess retrieved the sealed missive that hung from the basket's handle by a black ribbon. The crest in the wax was a sharp reminder of who Alistair was now, but she pushed it aside and clung to her determination to fight for him.

My dearest, obstinate Jess,

May the enclosed little friend bring you joy. I pray he endlessly reminds you of the one who gifts him to you. I have tasked him with watching over you and protecting you, for I know he will love you to distraction as I do.

Her Grace requests that I attend the Treadmore masquerade five days hence. I told her I would go only if my betrothed did. I would brave any and all such hells to see you.

Please give my best regards to your sister for her speedy return to health. I can well understand her decline in your absence. I, too, am suffering the ill effects of it.

Yours always,
Alistair

There was a drawing with the missive, a rendering of her lying on the dais in the gazebo he'd built on the island. Her eyes were unfocused, dreamy and wistful, her lips plumped by fierce kisses and her hair in tumbling disarray around her bare shoulders. Her head was propped in one hand, her torso draped in the nearly translucent lawn of her chemise. Alistair hadn't brought his supplies with him that day, which meant this intimate image of her in an unguarded moment had been stored in his mind and savored later.

"Don't cry, Jess!" Hester said, alarmed when tears fell from Jess's lashes.

"Is everything all right, dear?" the countess asked, rising gracefully to her feet and approaching. "Are you mourning your Temperance?"

Jess hugged Acheron and the letter that accompanied him to her heart. "No. Although thinking of her reminds me again of how quicksilver life is. Benedict was the healthiest and hardiest man I knew. Alistair has lost three siblings. Hester and I lost our mother. We cannot afford to throw away happiness. We have to fight for it and claim it."

Elspeth crouched beside Jess and held out her hands for Acheron. "How adorable you are," she cooed when Jess passed him over.

Jess stood and eyed the red silk again. "I now have an occasion to wear the red."

"God help the man," Hester said, but with a sparkle in her green eyes.

"It is too late for that now." Jess lifted her arms to be measured. "He is well and truly caught."

23

It was an irrefutable fact that wearing a mask freed inhibitions.

Alistair was reminded of this over and over again as he stood by a Doric column in the Treadmore ballroom and dealt with the pressing crush of guests who greeted him. He was tempted often to place his hand over the letter he'd tucked into his pocket, but he refrained. Jessica's words contained therein gave him the strength and patience to deal with the overly accommodating and facetious guests eager to make a good impression on the future Duke of Masterson. They apparently weren't aware of how sharp a memory Alistair possessed. He remembered those who'd thought nothing of him when he was merely a fourth son. He remembered those who'd paid him to fuck them and made him feel unclean in the process. He remembered those who had inflicted pain and wounded his pride.

My beloved, determined Alistair,
Your gift and the words accompanying him both broke my heart and filled it with joy. When I see you next, I will show you the depth of my gratitude.
As for the masquerade, nothing could keep me

from you. Then or at any time or event in the future.
You have been duly warned.

Irrevocably yours,
Jessica

To his left, Masterson stood, so stoic and austere. To his right, his mother worked her charm on all who approached them. She hadn't, however, written to Jessica. Not that he had truly expected her to.

"Haymore's daughter is lovely," Louisa murmured now, using her fan to gesture at the young woman walking away from them.

"I do not recall."

"You met her scarcely a moment ago. She deliberately lowered her mask so you would see her."

He lifted one shoulder in a careless shrug. "I will take your word for it."

The orchestra in the balcony above signaled the onset of dancing with a few opening notes. The crush of guests somehow cleared the dance area by converging on the perimeters of the room.

"Beginning with a quadrille," his mother said dryly. "I wish you had asked at least one of the young ladies you met to dance. It would have been polite."

"I was exceptionally polite to every one of them."

"You are a beautiful dancer. I enjoy watching you. So would everyone else here tonight."

"Mother." He faced her as the orchestra began to play. "I will not have every gazette and scandal rag speculating over the significance of my selection of dance partners. I am not on the market, and I refuse to give any impression that I am."

"You haven't even perused the wares!" she protested in a low whisper that was hidden beneath the enthusiastic surge of music. "You are infatuated with a beautiful, older, worldly woman. I appreciate the appeal, especially under the circumstances. Certainly her expertise at maneuvering through Society seems exceptionally valuable to you now. But, please, consider the long-term ramifications of your decisions. She is a widow, Alistair. She has far greater license than a debutante and can be useful to you outside the bonds of matrimony."

Alistair inhaled a sharp, deep breath. Then another, fighting for control of the fury threatening to make an appearance in such a public place. "For both our sakes, I am going to forget what you just said."

Glancing at Masterson, his jaw clenched when the duke appeared unaware of the conversation taking place right beneath his nose. "How far must this hypocrisy go before you absolve my mother of her sins? Hasn't she paid penance enough?"

The duke continued to look straight ahead. Only a muscle tic in his jaw gave any hint that he'd listened at all.

Alistair looked at his mother and removed his mask. "I've damn well paid enough. I have wished for your happiness all of my life, Mother. I have tried to facilitate it in every way I can, but in this matter, I will not be swayed."

Louisa's eyes glistened with unshed tears. They cut him, but there was no help for her distress. Leastwise none that he could give her.

A swell of murmurs surrounded them at the same moment a ripple of awareness coursed down his spine. Anticipation slid through his veins, potently fierce and delicious. He looked at his mother's face and saw the wide-eyed astonishment with which she stared over his shoulder. He pushed his mask into her lax fingers and began to turn about. Slowly. Savoring the fine tension he felt only when Jessica was near.

The sight of her struck him like a blow, purging all the air from his lungs. Red. She was draped in it. Wrapped in silk like a gift. Her shoulders bared, exposing creamy skin and the lush upper swell of her breasts. Her luxurious hair was styled into a mixture of upswept curls and long, glorious strands. There was something slightly disheveled about the whole, reinforcing the overall impression of sin and seduction and sex. The pristine white gloves that stretched midway up her arms did nothing to mitigate the overwhelming carnality of her appearance.

Although he knew from the dancing in progress that the music continued, Alistair couldn't hear a single note over the roaring of blood in his ears. Nearly every eye was riveted to Jessica, who walked along the edge of the dance floor unimpeded, her stride slow and sensual. Erotic. Beckoning.

He sucked in a deep breath when his lungs burned. His chest was constricted with yearning, his gaze devouring every detail in a vain effort to appease the hunger that had grown ravenous over the many days without her.

A simple red satin mask was tied around her eyes and as she approached, she reached up and untied it. Letting it dangle from her fingers by the ribbons. Letting everyone get a good, long look at her while she looked at him. Letting them—the peers whose censure he'd feared she could not bear—see the deeply intimate manner in which she regarded him. Her gray eyes were luminous, lit from within by the surfeit of emotion she made no effort to hide. There wasn't a person who saw her who could doubt what he meant to her.

By God, she was brave. She'd been beaten to deafness and disfigured into conforming to the dictates of the people milling around them, yet she came to him without any hesitation or reservation. Without fear.

There was no one else in the room. Not for him. Not with her looking at him in that way of hers that spoke more clearly than words—she loved him with all that she was. Completely, unequivocally, unconditionally.

"Do you see, Mother?" he asked softly, riveted. "Amid all of these lies, there is no finer truth than what is bared before you now."

He was moving toward Jessica before he realized it, drawn inexorably. When he drew close enough to scent her, he stopped. There were mere inches between them, and the urge to reach for her, to pull her close, was a writhing thing inside him.

"Jess." His fingers clenched and released against the need to touch her soft, smooth skin.

Dancers cleared the floor around them, gawking, but he paid them no mind.

Her dress was a statement, and he would never fully be capable of putting his gratitude for it into words. She was not the same woman who had stepped aboard his ship. She no longer saw him as being "too much" for her, or herself as inadequate for him. And he loved her more now than he had then. He would certainly love her more tomorrow than he did today, and the day after that would find him only loving her all the more.

"My lord," she breathed, her gaze sweeping over his face as if she had been as starved for the sight of him as he'd been for even a glimpse of her. "The way you're looking at me . . ."

He nodded curtly, knowing he was wearing his heart on his face. It had to be obvious to all and sundry that he was mad for her. "I miss you abominably," he said gruffly. "The greatest torment ever devised is the withholding of you from me."

A few opening notes of a waltz played. He seized the moment, catching Jessica by the waist and carrying her onto the dance floor.

Alistair was the most lavish creature in the packed room.

Jess was left breathless by the sight of him, awed by his masculine beauty in formal attire. He wore black trousers and coat, the severity of his appearance only emphasizing his perfection of form and feature. His was a glittering, riveting presence with his glossy coal-black hair and brilliant aquamarine eyes. He needed no adornments to enhance him. His piercing gaze and slight smile were enough to lure women closer. Even men drifted near, drawn to the air of confidence and command Alistair carried so well.

The knowledge that this stunning, undeniably sexual creature was hers made her breathless. And the way he looked at her, with such aching tenderness and heated longing . . .

Dear God. She'd been mad to entertain—for even one instant—the possibility of letting him go.

"Are you asking me to dance?" she purred as he set her down in the middle of the dance floor.

"You are the only partner I will have; you must indulge me."

His hand gripped her waist, the other lifted her arm. He stepped closer. Too close. Scandalously close. She loved it. They'd yet to dance together, but she had imagined it many times. There was a graceful elegance to the way he moved. Paired with the innate sensuality of his nature, it made him mesmerizing to *watch* in motion, and she knew how he *felt* when his body was moving against hers. It would be the sweetest form of torture to be held so close to his powerful flexing body while restrained by decorum and too many layers of clothes.

"I love you," she said, tilting her head back to look at him. "I won't let you go. I'm too selfish, and I need you too much."

"I am going to remove that dress from your body with my teeth."

"And here I had hopes you would like it."

His eyes gleamed wickedly. "If I liked it any more, it would be hiked around your waist."

Her grip tightened on his. He smelled delicious. Of virile male and sandalwood, with the faintest hint of citrus. She hated the gloves between them and the hundreds of people around them. She could live alone with him for the rest of her days. Working in companionable silence, listening to him coax haunting notes from the violin, talking with him about her thoughts and feelings until nothing separated them . . .

The music began in earnest. His mouth curved in a lazy smile, then he spun her about in a vigorous turn. She laughed breathlessly, awed by how she fit in his arms as if they'd been made to hold her. He danced the way he made love—intimately, powerfully, with exquisite control and aggressive moves. His thighs brushed against hers with every step, his hold tightening until there was scarcely any space between them. He flowed with the music, embraced it, claimed it as his own. Just as he claimed her with his gaze, his look fraught with such intensity and focus, his eyes so soft and warm.

She hadn't realized how deeply she'd craved that look of love from him until now. "They can see how you feel about me."

"I don't care, as long as you see."

"I do."

They weaved around the other dancers at a slightly faster pace, her crimson skirts swirling around his trouser-clad legs. She became aroused, flushed. She ached for the feel of his mouth on her skin, whispering heated erotic threats and promises that made her hot and wet and very, very willing.

"How is your sister?" he asked, the rasp in his voice betraying his returning desire for her.

"Improving every day. Confinement and bed rest is just what she needed."

"It's just what I need, too. With you."

"But we do not rest when we're abed, my lord."

"Will she be well enough to make do without you four weeks from now?"

She smiled. "By the time the banns have been read, she should be strong enough to need me only occasionally."

"Good. I need you, too."

Jess did not inquire after his mother or Masterson. She'd seen the look on the duchess's face and watched as Alistair said something to her. Whatever it was, his gaze hadn't wavered, but Jess had seen the strength of his conviction. It was a mien he was infamous for—recklessly determined and boldly challenging; the countenance of a man who fearlessly accepted any challenge. When he wore it, all knew he would not be swayed. However his mother reacted to his choice, he was committed and his mind would not be altered.

"I cannot stay much later tonight," she said. "I've no notion of what occupies Regmont so completely, but he comes home long after we've all retired and leaves before we make an appearance at breakfast. If I didn't know better, I would think he was avoiding me. Regardless, someone needs to be with Hester at night, and Acheron needs me, too."

His head lowered farther, until their lips were too close. "This was enough for now. I needed to see you, to hold you. If you have no further objections, I will begin courting you publicly."

"Please do." She felt giddy, intoxicated by his nearness and affection in a way no claret could ever match. She hadn't had a drink in days, and though the ill effects of her abstinence had been heinous at the onset, she was beginning to feel better. Stronger. "I will be ruined otherwise. Labeled a brazen hussy. You must make me respectable, my lord."

"After I went to such lengths to lure you to sin?"

"I will always be sinful for you."

He slowed as the music stopped, but her heart still raced. He stepped back and lifted her gloved hand to his lips.

"Come. Let me introduce you to my mother and Masterson before you go."

She nodded and, as always, followed his lead.

Alistair collected his hat, great coat, and cane from a footman, then headed toward the door to wait for his carriage. When Jessica had departed a half-hour before, all the light had left the room with her, giving him no reason to linger.

"*Lucius.*"

His stride faltered. His back went up, every muscle tightening. He turned around. "Lady Trent."

She approached, her hips swaying gently, her tongue darting out to lick her bottom lip. "Wilhelmina," she corrected. "We are much too intimate to stand on formality."

He knew the lascivious look in her eyes. She remained lovely and lushly curved. Wasted on a man far older than she was.

His stomach knotted with shame. He no longer possessed the walls he'd once shielded himself behind. Jessica had torn them down, one by one, opening him to a precious understanding of his own worth. The choices he had made . . . the things he'd done with women like Lady Trent . . . They sickened him now.

"We were never intimate," he said. "Good evening, Lady Trent."

Alistair left the Treadmore manse in a rush, striding out the door and feeling relief at the sight of his carriage waiting for him. He vaulted into the softly lamp-lit interior and settled against the leather squab. The whip cracked and the equipage lurched into motion, rounding the circular drive. They slowed when they reached the open wrought-iron gate, their way blocked by the clogged lane. It would be this way the entire route home, he knew, as the streets filled with

Society carriages conveying their passengers from one event to another.

He exhaled and relaxed, his mind returning to the moment he'd introduced Jessica to his mother and Masterson. All three were so consummate and adept in the social graces that he had no notion of what any of them thought of one another. They'd been smoothly polite, exchanging platitudes and worthless observations, and parting ways at precisely the right moment to avoid even an instant of awkward silence. It had all been far too easy.

The carriage drew to a halt beside one of the brick gateposts bearing a sculpted lion on the top. A dark form emerged from beside it and opened his carriage door. The figure was met with the tip of the rapier hidden within his cane.

A gloved hand moved aside the shield of a cloak's hood and revealed Jessica's wry smile. "I was hoping you'd impale me with something more pleasurable."

The unsheathed weapon hit the floorboards, and he pulled her inside. The door was shut behind them, earning the footman responsible a raise in pay.

"What in hell are you doing, Jess?"

She tumbled into him, pushing him back into the squab. "The dance may have been enough for you, but it wasn't for me. Not nearly."

Pushing off his chest, she stooped and tugged the curtains closed. She hunched over him, yanking up her blood-red skirts with frantic impatience. He caught a glimpse of the lacy hem of her pantalettes, and then she was climbing over him, straddling him.

"*Jess.*" He breathed her name. His skin felt too hot, his chest too constricted to allow him sufficient air. The feelings he had for her were too volatile to contain. She overwhelmed him. Surprised him. Seduced him with ridiculous ease.

"I have to tell you . . . you have to know . . . I am s-sorry." The cracking of her voice broke him as well. "I'm sorry I was afraid. I am sorry I caused you even an instant of pain or doubt. I love you. You deserve better."

"I have the best in you," he said gruffly. "There is no one better."

Her gloved fingers fumbled with the placket of his trousers. He laughed softly, delighted with her eagerness. Staying her hands by covering them with his own, he said, "Slow down."

"I'm dying for you. The way you dance . . ." Her eyes were fever bright in the muted glow of the carriage lamps. "I thought it would ease when I parted from you, but it only worsens by the moment."

"What worsens?" he asked, wanting to hear her say it.

"My hunger for you."

His blood thickened along with his cock. "Then I must take you home with me."

"I can't. I can't leave Hester that long, and I can't *wait* that long."

The thought of Jessica planning his ravishment in a carriage almost stole every shred of his reason. Alistair was tempted to shove her beneath him and give her the hard, pounding ride she was desperate for, but the circumstances were not ideal. Just outside the curtains, coachmen shouted to one another. Pedestrians laughed and conversed on the street. He and the passengers in the equipages passing them were close enough that their fingers could touch if they reached out to one another simultaneously.

"Shh," he soothed, his hands stroking the length of her spine. "I'll make you come, but you must be quiet."

She shook her head violently. "I need you inside me—"

"Christ." Alistair's grip flexed into her waist. "We are moving at a snail's pace, Jess. Too slowly to disguise any rocking of the carriage. And we are surrounded on all sides."

Jessica arched into him, her graceful arms encircling his shoulders. "You can think of something. Be inventive." She brought her mouth to his ear, her tongue tracing the curve. "I am wet and hot and aching for you, my love, and you made me this way. You cannot leave me in this condition."

A hard shudder shook his frame. She could not have displayed her trust in him more clearly than this, yet her haste and frenzy told him more was at stake than her physical pleasure. Perhaps this was the ramification of meeting his mother and Masterson, who couldn't accept him, let alone the woman he loved. His familial situation was far different, he knew, from what she'd had with Tarley. Michael's protectiveness was ample proof of that.

Alistair was infuriated by her disquiet and the possible root of it. She was a brilliant social diamond, her facets perfect in every respect aside from the one she couldn't control. After all she'd suffered to become a faultless wife for any peer, she did not deserve to be diminished by anyone.

Alistair caught her face in his hands, urging her to lean back and meet his gaze directly. "Jess."

She stilled, registering the somberness in his tone.

Angling his head, he pressed his lips lightly to hers and breathed the words "I love you."

24

Jess didn't move for a long moment following Alistair's fervent pronouncement, then the tension left her in a rush, the driving need to connect with him receding to a softer, sweeter craving. *"Alistair."*

"I was afraid, too. So, you see, you and I are even."

Her eyes stung. Her throat clenched too tight to allow speech.

"Surely you knew," he murmured, bringing one hand to his mouth. His even white teeth caught the tip of the middle finger of his glove and tugged.

"Yes, I knew," she whispered. "But it still means a great deal to hear the words aloud."

"Then I will say them often." The glove slipped off his hand, and he released it from his teeth. It dropped to his lap between them.

To her surprise, she found the uncovering of his hand impossibly erotic. He switched his attention to his other glove, tugging on the fingertips one by one until it slid free, his gaze heavy lidded and filled with sensual intent. The sight of his bite gripping the short white glove roused some primitive instinct inside her. There was something primal about disrobing with one's teeth, which brought to mind the promise he'd made to utilize a similar method on her dress.

The second glove fell to his lap. The carriage made a slow turn.

Lifting her hand, she extended it to him. His bared fingers went to the buttons at her wrist, deftly releasing each one. When her skin was bared, he lifted it to his mouth. The flutter of his tongue over her pulse made her gasp. Her sex rippled with appreciation.

The glove caressed the length of her arm as Alistair drew it off. By the time he'd removed the other one, Jess was breathless with anticipation. He pressed a kiss to her knuckle above his ruby ring, then licked between her fingers. If that stroke of his tongue had been between her legs, it could not have aroused her more.

Boldly, she reached between his legs and stroked the rigid length of his erection. He made a rumbling sound very much like a purr. She loved the way he lounged without affectation, every inch the voluptuary and perfectly willing to let her have her way with him.

"It will take more than a lifetime," she said, "to have my fill of you."

His hands slid under her gown and gripped her thighs. She loved that, too. Alistair always began each touch with a firm, possessive squeeze, as if he needed that brief moment of fierceness to attain the control that followed. He watched her as he reached around to cup her buttocks in his hands, then pushed through the slit in her pantalettes to find her slick and scorching.

"You are indeed wet and hot," he murmured, parting her and stroking a fingertip over her clitoris. "And you make me so damned hard."

She felt how hard he was. It gave her a wild thrill to be responsible for arousing such a magnificent sexual animal to the highest degree. No longer hindered by her gloves, she freed him with a deftness born of practice. He fell heavily into her waiting palms, so broad and long. His penis was a brutal instrument of pleasure. The wide head stretched her to her limits, while the thick veins coursing the weighty length rubbed every tender nerve inside her.

Jess fisted him with both hands and pumped, priming him to proceed to the point where he lost all restraint and bared himself to the soul.

He groaned, his head falling back into the high back of the squab. Two long fingers pushed inside her and began to thrust, preparing her for the deep slide of his cock.

She was ready. Had been from the moment he'd turned around in the ballroom and looked at her as if she were an oasis in the desert and he'd been lost in the dunes for days. She had been just as parched for the sight of him, withering with every day that passed without his presence.

Rising onto her knees, she pulled free of his working fingers and angled his cock. The moment the flared crown notched against the clenching entrance of her sex, she began to tremble. He caught her hips in his hands, steadying her, but allowing her to set the pace with which she took him into her.

Wanting to feel every inch of him, Jess lowered herself slowly, a soft keening cry accompanying the deliberate, relentless impalement.

She reached up and gripped the narrow lip where the upholstered back gave way to lacquered wood, sinking down on him with a leisurely measured pace. He bruised her with his grip.

"Jess. Wait!" His thighs were rigid between hers. "Give me a moment. You're squeezing me like a fist. No. For God's sake, *don't move* . . . Ah, Christ!"

He climaxed with a primal groan, his teeth grinding audibly, his cock jerking inside her as his semen spurted in thick, creamy pulses. He was only halfway in her, but the sudden flood of lubrication gave her no traction to delay further. She sank onto him to the root.

Her toes curled; her nails dug into the leather and wood. He came hard and long, trembling beneath her. She watched him, awed by the ferocity of his pleasure and how erotic she found it. He was a man who knew sex in all its extremes, and she'd brought him to a raging orgasm with just her love and enthusiasm.

"Jesus." Alistair wrapped his arms around her, bent her backward, and buried his damp face in her cleavage. His laugh was sharp and humorless, derisive. "You went to all this trouble . . . for this."

She pushed her fingers into the silk of his hair, understanding that he'd learned to place literal value on the pleasure he could give; it would be a hard lesson to unlearn. "I would circle the world, barefoot, for this."

He looked at her, his face flushed and eyes gleaming. The carriage swayed as it moved at a crawl over cobblestones, the sounds of the city filtering into the hushed and humid interior. His jaw clenched as he rocked deeper into her.

"Your pleasure is mine, Alistair, my love. I would have none without yours. I would be empty without you to fill me." She kissed the tip of his nose and smiled. "And you're still hard inside me, with stamina to spare. You've never left me wanting."

He moved in a burst of graceful physical agility, lifting her and carrying her to the opposite squab. Everything shifted as she found herself beneath him, pinned to the seat by the relentlessly hard, thick length of his penis. Her back was cushioned by her lined velvet cape; her front was mantled by his large, powerful body. He braced himself with one palm against the backrest and the other above the armrest near the door. He held her open by planting one knee on the squab and pinning her leg to the back. Her other leg dangled off the edge, her foot flat to the floorboard next to Alistair's.

She was completely vulnerable, her shoulders curved in the corner in a manner that gave all the leverage to Alistair, who used it to his advantage. With a practiced roll of his hips, he massaged her with his cock. Heated pleasure spread outward from her sex, making her moan.

"You must be quiet," he whispered, then made that impossible with another devastating stroke.

Jess gripped his hips, achingly aware that they were both fully clothed except for where they were joined. His pelvis lifted, dragging the furled underside of his cockhead across quivering tissues. He paused with only the tip of him inside her, watching her as she writhed, his gaze darkening as her nails dug into his flesh. Then he sank into her in a long, deep plunge. She bit her lip but couldn't contain a plaintive whimper.

"Shh," he admonished, his eyes gleaming wickedly. He knew damned well what he was doing to her by setting this torturously slow pace. His hips lifted, then fell again. Shallower this time, a short fierce dig.

"Alistair . . ." She clenched tight around him, the tiny muscles rippling greedily.

"My God, you feel good," he breathed. He ground against her, teasing her clitoris with fleeting pressure, his cock so deep in her that she was utterly possessed. "I can feel my semen in you. You're soaked with it. But I have more to give you."

She was panting now, maddened, misted with perspiration. She needed hard, driving strokes, a deep relentless pounding that would give her the friction she craved. What he gave her was painstakingly slow withdrawals and leisurely surges. Like a liberally oiled apparatus, tireless, his hips smoothly pistoned, shafting her tender sex with his iron-hard cock. In and out, the rhythm so fluid and precise it rivaled Maelzel's metronome.

Arching, she fought to quicken his pace, her body strung

tight as a bow. He covered her mouth with his hand, muffling the sobs of pleasure she couldn't contain.

With his lips to her right ear, he murmured, "We are surrounded by dozens of people, and I'm fucking you."

She shivered, her passions raging beyond all reason. In a distant part of her mind, she heard the voices of pedestrians just outside the carriage. She heard the rolling of passing carriage wheels and the laughter of the passengers within. The very real threat of discovery was akin to throwing kerosene on an already raging fire. She was insensate with lust, reduced to a primitive state in which only the quest for orgasm mattered.

"If only they could see you as I do," he purred, "sprawled across a carriage squab with your skirts around your waist and your sweet, slick cunt drenched in my ejaculate and crammed full of my cock."

She met his gaze over the hand covering her lips, seeing a fierce love and aching tenderness in the aqua depths that belied the coarseness of his speech. There were so many sides to the man she loved—some smooth as river rock and others rough as gravel; some innocently vulnerable and others wickedly depraved. She couldn't imagine living without any of them. Together they made up the whole that completed her.

He rocked his hips, touching the end of her. "Your wantonness is a gift to me, Jess. *You* are a gift, and I know it. I know the breadth of trust and love required for you to give of yourself in this manner."

A lush, expert stroke took her to the edge. She hung there, arched and rigid, breathless.

"And I love you for it," he growled, taking advantage of a rut in the road to deliver a hard, ramming thrust that hurled her into orgasm. "I love you too much. More than I can bear."

Jess quaked violently beneath him, her sex clutching and

sucking at his throbbing erection. He climaxed with a serrated groan that he muffled in the sweat-slick curve of her neck. They clung to each other, grasping and writhing, straining for the closeness they required but couldn't attain while dressed.

Lost in each other while surrounded by the teeming city.

My sympathies to the debutantes hoping to snare the magnificent marquess. The previously icy Lady T, now widowed and ablaze in red, drew the mesmerized Lord B to her like a moth to a flame. Dear Readers, the heat was palpable.

So scandalous. Now infamous. Decidedly delicious . . .

Michael finished reading aloud and lowered the paper, staring at Alistair with brows raised.

"What?" Alistair asked, before enjoying a long drought of ale.

"Don't be coy. I saw Jessica last night. That dress . . . What have you done to my sister-in-law?"

"Why don't you ask what she has done to me? That answer is far more profound, I assure you."

Alistair's gaze swept over the great room of Remington's Gentlemen's Club. His casual perusal was met with many nods and smiles. He now understood the interest that had baffled him the week before. Everyone had known of his change in circumstance before he did. He was still catching up. Still reeling.

He'd called on Albert's widow earlier in the day, attempting to ascertain her circumstances and offering whatever assistance she required. She had been left with a large bequeathment, but she'd loved his brother and she would need more than coin and property to see her through the immediate future. She would need a strong shoulder to lean upon, and he offered his to her, knowing how vital a loved one could be to the simple acts of rising in the morn and breathing. In return, she had given him something that could change so many things. He held her gift close to his heart, debating what to do with it.

"Your name, paired with Jessica's, is all I have heard all day," Michael groused.

"The announcement of our engagement will appear in tomorrow's gazettes, smothering all prurient interest with the blanket of propriety and respectability. The notices would have appeared today, but I was ... detained last night." Alistair had decided he was going to keep that carriage for the rest of his life. He and Jess would christen others with their passion, but that one would remain in his carriage house forever, waiting for him to ravish Jessica in it long after the equipage lost its usefulness in serving its original purpose.

"What of your parents?" Michael asked. "They looked less than ecstatic."

Alistair shrugged, feeling a sharp pang of regret but no responsibility for it. "They will manage."

The crumpling of the newspaper drew Alistair's attention to Michael's clenching fists. He wondered what he'd said to elicit such a response. Then he noted that his friend was looking beyond him. Following the line of Michael's gaze, Alistair glanced over his shoulder and saw the Earl of Regmont enter the room with a boisterous pack of cronies following swiftly on his heels.

"Should we invite him over for a drink?" Alistair asked, turning his back to the man.

"Are you mad?" Michael's dark eyes narrowed in a dangerous fashion. "I can barely tolerate knowing the man breathes."

Alistair's brows rose. There was really nothing he could say to that. Despite the similarities in their circumstances, he certainly couldn't concur, not considering that in his situation it had been Michael's brother who'd laid claim to the woman Alistair coveted.

"What the devil is the matter with him?" Michael bit out. "His wife is home ill and increasing with his child, and he's carousing as if he was a bachelor."

"Most peers do."

"Most peers aren't married to Hester."

"I would suggest leaving the country as a solution, but you cannot."

Michael looked at him. "Is that why you were absent from England for so long? Because Jessica was married to Benedict?"

"Mostly, yes."

"I had no idea. You concealed it well."

Waving one hand carelessly, Alistair said, "I was adept at hiding it from myself as well. I convinced myself that my interest was base and easily resolved by indulgence. In hindsight, that self-deception was probably wise. If I'd known then that she would turn me so completely around and inside out, I might have run in terror."

"You do seem different," Michael mused, studying him. "Less agitated. Calmer. Tamed perhaps?"

"Bloody hell, lower your voice when you say such things."

Raucous laughter drew Michael's attention back over Alistair's shoulder. "Excuse me a moment."

Alistair sighed and shook his head, taking another drink. In truth, he didn't understand Regmont, either. The only reason Alistair was sitting in Remington's was because he didn't have Jessica to go home to.

"Lord Baybury."

He looked up at Lucien Remington and smiled. "Remington. How are you?"

"Too well. May I join you a moment?"

"Absolutely."

"I won't monopolize much of your time. If I'm not home

within the hour, my wife will come fetch me herself." The proprietor smiled and took an empty seat next to Michael's vacated one. "Forgive me in advance for my boldness. As you might be aware, I know a great many things about every gentleman granted membership here."

"You would have to."

"Yes." Remington's eyes, renowned for their rare amethyst color, lit with humor. "For example, I know you and I are alike in ways others wouldn't suspect, and I can guess from that affinity how difficult your present situation must be for you."

Alistair stilled. Remington was the bastard son of a duke. Although he was His Grace's oldest child, it was his younger legitimate brother who would inherit the title and entailed properties.

"Damnation," Alistair muttered, understanding that Remington knew of his bastardy—a secret only his mother, Masterson, and Jessica were privy to. He'd heard the rumors about the depth and breadth of information on file for each member of Remington's, but he could not have imagined this level of knowledge. Which led him to wondering if Remington knew who his father was . . .

"If you ever require assistance or just a sympathetic ear," Remington said smoothly, as if he hadn't just shaken Alistair to the core, "I would be honored to assist you."

"We bastards must stick together?" Alistair queried, refraining from asking questions he wasn't sure he wished to know the answers to.

"Something of that nature."

"Thank you." There were some men worth keeping in one's corner; Lucien Remington was one of them.

Shouts came from the bar. Remington pushed agilely to his feet. "If you will excuse, my lord. I must see to a problem that has become overly troublesome."

Alistair looked over his shoulder at Regmont's boisterous associates. "A moment, please, Remington. Regarding your problem . . . In light of the fact that his wife is soon to be my sister-in-law, should I assume he might be problematic for me as well?"

"Yes." Remington gave a regal bow of his head and departed.

Standing, Alistair looked for Michael and found him lounging insouciantly against the bar—near to Regmont's group, but not a part of it. He went to him. "Let's go."

"Not yet." Michael reached into the inner pocket of his coat for the silver case that held his cheroots. Nearby, Regmont laughed and began to protest Remington's admonition that he quiet down or quit the room.

"This isn't wise." Alistair could feel the ill will building in the air around them like a brewing tempest. Regmont was inebriated to the point of bravado and stupidity, and Michael was clearly spoiling for a fight.

Lord Taylor, one of Regmont's friends, stumbled backward. He bumped Michael, whose cheroot case and kerchief were dislodged from his hand. They fell to the floor, expensive cheroots rolling free of the opened case.

"Mind yourself!" Michael snapped, bending to retrieve his belongings.

Regmont made a cutting comment to Taylor, then crouched unsteadily to assist Michael. He picked up a cheroot, then the kerchief. He stilled, sobering as he examined the folded linen.

Michael held out his hand for it. "Thank you."

The earl's thumb stroked over the letters embroidered into the corner. "Interesting monogram."

Alistair looked closer, cursing silently at the unmistakable "H" stitched in red thread.

"If you would, please, Regmont," Michael demanded.

"I don't think I will." Regmont met Michael's gaze, then Alistair's, before tucking the kerchief in his own pocket. "I believe this belongs to me."

The tension that gripped Michael was palpable. Alistair set his hand on his friend's shoulder and squeezed a warning. The liquor on the earl's breath was strong enough to be pervasive, and Alistair recognized the look of mayhem in his bloodshot eyes—the devil was riding Regmont hard, spurring him into a dangerous place.

Michael stood. "I want that back, Regmont."

"Come and get it."

Michael's hands fisted. Remington stepped between the two men. The proprietor was tall and fit, perfectly capable of interceding physically, but he was also flanked by three liveried members of his staff. "You can take this downstairs, gentlemen," he warned, diverting them to the pugilist rings below, "or you can take it elsewhere, but there will be no violence in here."

"Or we can take it to the field," Michael challenged. "Name your seconds, Regmont."

"Bloody hell," Alistair muttered.

"Taylor and Blackthorne."

Michael nodded. "Baybury and Merrick will discuss the particulars with them tomorrow."

"I look forward to it," Regmont said, baring his teeth in a semblance of a smile.

"Not nearly as much as I."

25

My dearest,
  I confess, I have thought of you all day, in ways I
am certain you would enjoy. I pray that you are
looking after yourself.

Acheron growled from his pillow by Jess's feet. She paused with the quill suspended above the parchment, then she leaned over to frown down at the tiny pug.

"What troubles you?"

He repeated the small sound of disapproval, then bounded to the door leading to the gallery. There, he jumped and spun in circles. As Jess fetched her shawl to take him outside to relieve himself, his ears lay back against his head and he growled again. Then he whimpered pitifully and piddled on the hardwood before she reached him.

"Acheron." Her tone was soft with resignation. The pug whined in response.

Jess collected a towel from the washstand in the corner and moved to the door. As she neared, she heard a masculine voice raised in anger. She dropped the towel on the tiny puddle and turned the knob. The sound of shouting became clearer without the solid wood barrier, and its source became recognizable—Hester's rooms.

"No wonder you're upset," she murmured to Acheron, tossing her shawl on a nearby chair. "Stay here."

She strode swiftly down the hallway. Regmont's voice grew louder with every step. Her stomach knotted and her palms grew damp. As familiar fear set in, she fought to breathe in an even cadence.

"You've humiliated me! All these weeks . . . the match with Tarley . . . I will not be cuckolded!"

Hester's low replies were indecipherable, but the rapid delivery suggested anger . . . or panic. When a crash resounded, Jess lunged for the door and threw it open.

Dear God . . .

Her sister stood in her night rail, her face blanched and lips white. Her eyes were huge in her face and filled with a terror Jess knew all too well. A new bruise was already darkening her temple.

Regmont's back was to the door, his hands fisted at his sides. He was dressed for a night on the town, and he stank of liquor and tobacco. A side table had been overturned, and the decorative urn that graced it lay shattered on the floor. He began to advance. Jess shouted his name.

He stilled, his back stiffening. "Get out, Lady Tarley. This is none of your concern."

"I think you should be the one to depart, my lord," she retorted, trembling. "Your wife is breeding and has orders from the doctor to abstain from any excitement."

"Is it even mine?" he barked at Hester. "How many men have there been?"

"Go, Jess," Hester pleaded. "Run."

Jess shook her head. "No."

"You can't always be the one who saves me!"

"Regmont." Jess's voice cracked like a whip. "Please leave."

He rounded on her then, and her heart stopped. His eyes were bloodshot and filled with the single-minded malevolence Hadley always displayed when determined to use his fists on someone who couldn't fight back.

"This is my house!" he bellowed. "And *you* . . . you have come here with your harlot ways and attached scandal to my good name. Now your sister seeks to do the same. I won't have it!"

Jess's ears filled with the sound of roaring blood, muffling his vitriol, but she understood his threat to teach her proper behavior. The room spun. She'd lived through this moment before. Heard those same words. So many times . . .

The fear receded as swiftly as it had come, leaving an odd calm in its wake. She was not a frightened, lonely girl anymore. Alistair had shown her that she was stronger than she'd given herself credit for. And when he came for her, which he would do as soon as she could send for him, Regmont would pay for his actions this night.

"Hitting me," she said, "would be the biggest mistake you will ever make in your life."

He laughed and drew his arm back.

Michael vaulted onto the back of his horse, then watched Alistair do the same. A raging feeling of helplessness goaded his agitation. He wanted his handkerchief back, damn it. He wanted Hester. And he wanted Regmont dead with a fervor that scared him.

"Say something!" he snapped at Alistair, who hadn't spoken since he'd challenged Regmont.

"You're an idiot."

"Christ."

"So you kill him in a duel. Then what?" Alistair spurred his mount away from Remington's. "You avoid persecution by fleeing the country. Your family suffers without you. Hester hates you for taking her husband from her. Jessica becomes furious with me for being even remotely attached to this mess. Will you feel better then?"

"You've no notion of what this is like! How it feels to know she needs looking after and I cannot be the one to do it!"

"Don't I?" Alistair asked softly, glancing aside at him.

"No. You do not. Whatever envy you may have harbored for my brother's good fortune, you at least knew he cared for Jessica and saw to her comfort. He made her happy. You did not have to wonder at every minute of every day if he was raising his hand to her. If she was terrified or hurt or—"

Alistair yanked so hard on his reins that his horse reared up with a whinny of protest. The clap of hooves to cobblestone was like a thundercrack in the darkness. The gelding pranced in agitation, turning completely around. "What did you say?"

"He beats her. I know he does. From things I've observed, and things my mother has observed as well."

"Damn you." The fury in Alistair's tone was unmistakable. "And you allowed him to leave? What if he's at home now?"

Michael's own wrath boiled over. "What can I do? She is his wife. I have no recourse."

"Jessica is there! And her greatest terror is a man's rage."

"What the devil—?"

"Hadley was abusive," Alistair bit out, pulling his horse around. "He punished the girls as liberally and as painfully as possible."

Michael's gut twisted. "Jesus."

Alistair kicked his mount into a gallop, bending low over the horse's arched neck and weaving recklessly through the busy streets. Michael followed close behind him.

Jess watched Regmont's arm draw back and steeled herself for the blow, refusing to cower.

But before it came, a sickening thud reverberated through the room. She watched, astonished and confused, as Regmont's eyes rolled back into his head. He crumpled to the floor in a boneless heap.

Startled, she stumbled back. Blood seeped through his blond hair and glistened in the candlelight. A harsh clattering drew Jess's gaze to the fireplace poker rattling on the floor . . . dropped from Hester's lax hand.

"Jess . . ."

Her gaze lifted. Her sister doubled over with a sharp cry of pain. There was blood at Hester's feet, coursing down her legs, rapidly forming a spreading pool. *No . . .*

Pounding footsteps approached. "Jessica!"

She called out to him as she leaped over Regmont toward Hester.

Alistair appeared, followed directly by Michael. Both men skid to a halt at Regmont's body. Jessica caught Hester just as her sister's knees gave out. Together, they sank to the floor.

"Is he dead?" Jess asked as she paced the length of the downstairs parlor. Acheron sprawled beneath the table between the settees, whining softly.

"No." Alistair came to her, bearing a glass of brandy. "Here. Drink this."

She looked at the amber liquid longingly, wanting the soothing oblivion of liquor with a ferocity that was nearly undeniable. Her throat was dry and her hands unsteady, symptoms she knew would be alleviated by one small drink, but she found the will to shake her head. She wasn't going backward. The past was behind her. After tonight, she was newly determined to leave it there.

Her gaze roamed the room. The cheery yellow décor seemed absurd considering the state of the couple who laid claim to it.

"She brained him with the poker," she murmured, still trying to grasp the enormity of what had transpired and how blind she'd been to the signs of abuse

"Good," Michael said with vehemence.

Alistair set the brandy down and came up behind her. He caught her shoulders with his large hands, massaging the painfully tight muscles. "The doctor is seeing to your sister first, but he says Regmont will need stitches."

Jess's heart broke. "She was despondent before. Now that she's lost the baby . . ."

Michael snatched the brandy from the table and tossed it back in one swallow. His hair was a mess from the relentless raking of his fingers, and his dark eyes were haunted.

Finally, Jess saw the love he harbored for her sister. Guilt ate at her like acid. She had steered Hester toward Regmont all the while a man worthy of her was right beneath their noses.

She looked over her shoulder at Alistair. "After we are wed, I would like Hester to stay with us for whatever time she needs. I don't think she should remain in this house any longer than necessary."

"Of course." His beautiful eyes were soft and filled with sympathy and love.

She breathed him in, absorbing the soothing scent of sandalwood and musk with that invigorating hint of verbena. She set her hands over his, grateful for him in so many ways. He anchored her in the midst of chaos, giving her the strength she needed to do the same for Hester.

"In the interim," Michael said, "you should both reside with me. You have lived in the house longer than I have, Jessica, and the servants are well versed in your needs. It will be familiar to Hester. And my mother is there for now. She can be a great help, too."

The report of a pistol broke the silence, followed by a bloodcurdling scream. Jess's stomach lurched. She was running toward the stairs before she knew what she was about. Michael passed her on the first landing, but Alistair stayed with her, catching her arm just before they reached Hester's room.

Dr. Lyon stood in the gallery, grim faced. He pointed at Hester's door in front of him. "His lordship went in and threw the latch."

On the other side of the door, Hester was still screaming.

Panic stole the strength from Jess's knees, but Alistair held her up. Michael gripped the doorknob and rammed into the paneled wood with his shoulder. The frame creaked in protest, but the lock held fast.

The doctor spoke in a rush, his volume rising with every word. "He was unconscious in his bedchamber when I began the stitching. Then he woke . . . became enraged . . . asked after Lady Regmont. I told him to lower his voice, to calm himself. I explained his wife was resting after losing the babe. He went mad . . . ran from the room . . . I tried to follow, but—"

Michael rammed into the door again. The doorjamb cracked, but did not give way. Alistair joined him. Together they kicked the portal in unison, and it flew open with a thunderous crack. They rushed inside, followed by the doctor. Jess was swift on their heels, but Alistair pivoted agilely and caught her by the waist, carrying her back out to the gallery.

"Don't go in there," he ordered.

"Hester!" she shouted, struggling to look over his shoulder.

He clutched her trembling body close and held tight. "It was Regmont."

As the possibilities sank in, Jess felt all the warmth leave her limbs. "Dear God. *Hester.*"

Hester curled against Jessica's side and held on tightly. Cocooned in the counterpane of Jess's bed in the guest room, she was still so cold.

Jess's hand stroked over her head while whispering soft words of comfort. It seemed almost as if they were children again and Jess was providing the sense of safety and love Hester had only ever felt with her.

She ached everywhere. A bone-deep ache that stripped all the strength from her limbs. Her child was gone. Her husband as well. And she couldn't feel anything but dead inside. It amazed her to sense her breath blowing past her lips. She would have thought such signs of life were beyond her.

"It was Edward at the last," she whispered.

Her sister fell silent.

"He came into my room as the man I'd come to hate and fear. Wild eyed and brandishing that pistol. I felt such relief to see him. I thought, 'Finally, the pain and sorrow will end.' I thought he would be merciful and free me from it."

Jess's arms tightened around her. "You mustn't think of it anymore."

Hester tried to swallow, but her mouth and throat were too dry. "I begged him. *Please. Take my life. The babe is gone from me . . . Please. Let me go.*' And then it was Edward standing there. I could see it in his eyes. They were so bleak. He saw what he'd done when he wasn't himself."

"Hester. Shh . . . You need your r-rest."

The telltale break in her Jess's voice echoed through her. "But he didn't spare me this agony. To the end he was selfish and thought only of himself. And yet I miss him. The man he used to be. The man I married. You do remember him, don't you, Jess?" Her head tilted back to look up at her sister's face. "You do recall the way he was long ago?"

Jess nodded, her eyes and nose red from tears.

"What does it mean?" Hester asked, lowering her chin. "That I am happy he's gone, yet I am so sad . . . equally?"

A long stretch of silence ensued, then, "I suppose, perhaps, you miss the promise of what could have been, while at the same time you are grateful that what it was instead is over."

"Perhaps." Hester burrowed closer, seeking more of her sister's warmth. "What do I d-do now? How do I g-go on?"

"One day at a time. You rise, you eat, you bathe, and you talk to the few people you can tolerate while feeling so wretched. Over time, it hurts a little less. Then a little less. And so on." Jess ran her fingers through Hester's unbound hair. "Until one morning, you will awake and realize the pain is only a memory. It will always be with you, but it will eventually lack the power to cripple you."

Tears burned Hester's eyes, then wet the bodice of Jess's gown. Jess had climbed into bed with Hester fully dressed, offering the connection Hester needed before she even comprehended that she needed it.

"I suppose I should be happy," Hester whispered, "that I am no longer increasing with my dead husband's child, but I can't be happy about it. It hurts too much."

A sob broke the hush in the room, a raw sound of pain too fresh to manage. It clawed through Hester's numbness and ripped into her vitals, tearing her apart. "I wanted that baby, Jess. I wanted my baby . . ."

Jess began to rock her back and forth, words spilling out in a frantic attempt to soothe. "There will be others. Someday, you will have the happiness you deserve. Someday, you will have it all, and everything that transpired to get you to that place of contentment will make sense to you."

"Don't say such things!" She couldn't even contemplate another pregnancy. It seemed like such a betrayal of the child she'd lost. As if babes were replaceable. Interchangeable.

"No matter what happens, I will be with you." Jess's lips pressed to her forehead. "We will make it through together. I love you."

Hester closed her eyes, certain Jess was the only one who could say such a thing. Even the Lord Himself had abandoned her.

Alistair entered his home, weary to his soul. Jessica's pain was his own, and his heart was heavy with the sadness and horror that presently shadowed her life.

He handed his hat and gloves to the waiting butler.

"Her Grace awaits you in your study, my lord," Clemmons announced.

Glancing at the long case clock, Alistair noted the lateness of the hour. It was nearly one in the morning. "How long has she been waiting?"

"Nearly four hours now, my lord."

Clearly the news she carried was not good. Steeling himself for the worst, Alistair went to the study and found his mother reading on the settee. Her feet were tucked up beside her, and her lap was covered with a thin blanket. A fire roared in the hearth. A candelabrum on the table at her shoulder illuminated the pages in front of her and gilded her dark beauty.

She looked up. "Alistair."

"Mother." He rounded his desk and shrugged out of his coat. "What's wrong?"

Her gaze raked over him. "Perhaps I should ask the same of you."

"The day has been endless, and the evening even longer." He sank into his chair with a tired exhalation. "What do you require of me?"

"Must I always want something from you?"

He stared at her, noting the hints of strain around her eyes and mouth, signs he'd most recently cataloged on Lady Regmont—the signs of a woman in a troubled marriage. Signs he would never see on Jessica's face because he would die before he caused her such sorrow.

When he didn't answer, Louisa pushed the blanket aside and swung her legs over the edge of the settee. She clasped her hands in her lap and rolled her shoulders back. "I likely deserve your wariness and suspicion. I was so focused on what *I* was feeling that I did not pay enough attention to what *you* were feeling. I am so tremendously sorry for that. I've wronged you for many years."

Alistair's heartbeat sped up, confusion warring with disbelief. As a boy, he'd wanted to hear such words from her more than he had wanted anything else.

"I came to tell you," she went on, "I wish you happy. It does my heart good to see you well loved and admired. I did see it. I also felt it. She esteems the ground you walk upon."

"As I do for her." He rubbed the spot over his chest that ached for Jessica. "And her regard will never alter or diminish. She knows the worst there is to know about me, yet she loves me in spite of my mistakes. No . . . I would say perhaps she loves me because of them; because of how they've shaped me."

"It's a wondrous gift to be loved unconditionally. It is my failing that I didn't do the same, my son." She stood. "I want you to know that I will support you and your choice to the last. I'll hold her in my heart as you do."

His fingertips stroked over the smooth lacquered top of his desk. By God, he was exhausted. He wanted Jess beside him, close to his heart. He needed to hold her and comfort her and find his own peace with her. "It means a great deal that you came to me, Mother. That you waited for my return. That you give me your blessing. Thank you."

Louisa nodded. "I love you, Alistair. I will endeavor to show you how much, and pray that one day there will no longer be any reticence or mistrust between us."

"I should like that."

His mother rounded the desk. She bent and pressed her lips to his cheek.

He caught her wrist before she straightened, holding her close to gauge her reaction. Had she truly come, repentant and guileless, with warm sentiment? Or had she already been given the news he was about to share with her, freeing her to give her blessing with mitigated risk?

"You will be a grandmother," he said quietly.

She froze and her breath caught, then her eyes widened and filled with startled joy. "Alistair—"

So, she hadn't known. The warmth of her acceptance and blessing spread through him. "Not mine. As you likely surmised, Jessica is barren. But Emmaline . . . Albert saw to his duty after all. Perhaps not a boy I could name as my heir, but regardless of gender, you will at least have the joy of a grandchild."

A tremulous smile banished the melancholy reflected in Louisa's blue eyes—irises that were so like his.

Alistair smiled back.

Epilogue

"Your sister looks well," commented Her Grace, the Duchess of Masterson.

Jess looked across the veranda table at Alistair's mother. "Yes, she is healthy and strong. And every day, she remembers a little more about laughter and finding joy."

Just beyond the carved stone balusters that divided the veranda from the immaculate Masterson gardens, many of the dozen guests attending Jess's house party strolled through the neatly trimmed yew hedges. Even Masterson was out enjoying the beautiful day, holding hands with the infant Master Albert who was toddling along the gravel paths.

"Lord Tarley seems quite taken with her," Louisa noted.

Jess's gaze moved back to Hester and Michael, following as they walked together; Hester with her parasol, and Michael with his hands clasped behind his back. They made a lovely couple, his dark comeliness so beautifully complementing her sister's golden beauty.

"He's been a dear friend for a long time," Jess said. "But these last two years have proven him to be invaluable in so many ways. He's made her feel safe, and from that position of safety, Hester has found the peace of mind to heal. Much as your son did for me."

"It is no less than what you have done for him." The duchess lifted her teacup to her lips, her porcelain skin shielded beneath the brim of her wide straw hat. "Where is my son, by the way?"

"He's looking into an irrigation problem of some sort."

"I hope he knows that Masterson is impressed with him."

There was no way for Alistair to know since the two men rarely spoke, but such unfortunate rifts were topics best left for another day. "There isn't anything he fails to excel in. Truly, I find it remarkable that such a romantic and creative soul should also be so well versed in numbers, engineering, and countless other analytical pursuits."

There was also his physical prowess, but that was for Jess alone to know and enjoy.

"*Milady.*"

Her attention moved to the maid who approached with a missive in hand. Jess smiled and accepted it, immediately recognizing her husband's penmanship on the exterior. She broke the seal with a smile.

Find me.

"If you will please excuse me, Your Grace," she said, pushing back from the table and standing.

"Is everything all right?"

"Yes. Always." Jess moved through the open French doors into the house. The interior was quiet and peaceful, the large sprawling estate somehow retaining a feeling of intimacy and welcome. She and Alistair occupied one wing of the manse during the summer months, while the duke and duchess occupied the other most of the year. This was their second year summering with his family and, so far, it was progressing better than the first. Alistair's naming of Albert's son as his heir had been a great relief to all.

Jess had used the excuse of requiring assistance with a house party to bring Hester closer to rejoining Society with the start of the next Season. The past two years had been difficult, with the scandal surrounding Regmont's death and all the speculation that sprang from it. Jess's marriage to Alistair Caulfield, a future duke, had helped to divert attention, but nothing could hasten the healing process for Hester. Still, her sister's recovery was progressing slowly but surely, with Michael always nearby if she needed him, a solid and unobtrusive friend. Perhaps he would become something more to her one day, when Hester was ready. Alistair believed his friend would wait patiently, just as Alistair had done for Jess.

Heading to Alistair's study first, she found the space empty. She moved to the parlor, then the billiards room, but still didn't find him. It was only when she began ascending the right side of the split staircase that she heard the faint strains of a violin. Her heart swelled with joy. Listening to Alistair play was one of her favorite pastimes. Sometimes, after they'd made love, he would rise from their bed and engage the stringed instrument. She would lie there and listen, hearing in the notes all the emotion he couldn't convey with words. It was the same with his drawings. The finely wrought pencil lines captured moments and expressions only a lover would grasp and treasure. They told her more eloquently than speech how precious she was to him, how often he thought of her, and how deeply he felt about her.

Jess followed the haunting strains of a plaintive melody to their rooms. Two of the upstairs maids lingered in the hall, as awed as Jess, until they saw her approach and scrambled away. She opened the sitting room door, then shut and locked it behind her. Contentment swept over her along with the increased volume of music. She located her spouse in their bedroom, standing before the open window, his clothing removed except for his buff-colored trousers.

Acheron lay at his feet, staring raptly up at him, as entranced as everyone became when he played.

As Alistair slid the bow to and fro across the strings, the muscles of his arms and back flexed and clenched with the fluid movements, creating a view she would never tire of. She sat on the bench at the foot of the bed, watching and listening, her blood already beginning to heat and thicken with anticipation.

It was the middle of the day. Numerous guests surrounded and awaited them. Yet he'd lured her to their bedroom to seduce her with the refinement of his talent and the primitive lust of his virility—appealing to the disparate needs she hadn't been aware of until he'd shown them to her.

The music faded into the warm summer breeze, and she applauded softly. He placed the instrument carefully within its case.

"I love to hear you play," she said softly.

"I know."

She smiled. "And I love the sight of your bare back and provocative backside, as well."

"I know that, too."

He faced her and her breath caught. He was partially aroused and wholly beautiful.

Jess licked her lower lip. "I feel overdressed."

"You are." His approach was both predatory and graceful, his rippled abdomen and confident stride engaging all of her feminine instincts.

"What lascivious agenda do you pursue?"

"We've been wed just over a year, yet I have not been granted my husbandly right to a honeymoon."

A shiver of heated pleasure rippled through her. "Oh? My poor darling. Have you been denied any other husbandly rights?"

"You wouldn't deny yourself." Alistair caught her by the

elbows and tugged her to her feet. There was a roughness and urgency to his touch that belied the softness of the melody with which he'd mesmerized her. Her nipples beaded tight beneath her bodice in response.

He knew, of course. His hands cupped her swelling breasts and kneaded with slightly more pressure than necessary. The edge to him made her hot and wet, eager. She loved all the ways he made love to her, but the times he sought her out while at the end of his control were special. She no longer had to drive him to the precipice. He stood on the cliff and called for her, deliberately bringing her close at the times when he was capable of being most vulnerable. Then, they would make the fall together, as they did everything together.

She set her hands on his hips, tugging herself closer. "I'm too self-indulgent when it comes to you," she agreed.

"Indulge yourself with me on a honeymoon," he coaxed in that dark voice of sin. "Weeks on a ship. Months in Jamaica. We have unfinished business there, you and I. Hester is strong enough now to bear the loss of you for a time, and Michael will look after her with as much care as he would look after his own heart."

"Can you go now? Can you afford the time away?"

"I've spoken with Masterson. Now is the time to go, while he is fit and able." His hands slid up to her face, cupping her cheeks. Tilting his head, he brought his lips to hers, kissing her softly. "I want to swim with you naked. I want to show you the fields burning. I want to—"

"—fuck in the rain," she whispered, just to feel the tension grip him. "There is no need to seduce me to elicit my acquiescence. I would go with you anywhere, for any reason."

"But this way is much more enjoyable." Bending his knees, he matched his thick erection to the juncture of her thighs and rolled his hips against her. "With the windows open and our guests outside, you will have to be quiet in your pleasures."

"While you do your worst to make me scream?"

"My best."

Her mouth curved against his lips. "Perhaps *you* will be the noisy one. Perhaps *I* will make you groan and curse and beg for mercy."

"Is that a challenge, Lady Baybury?" he purred. "You know I cannot resist a challenge."

Jess reached behind him and gripped his taut, delicious buttocks. "I know. In fact, I am counting on that."

Acheron, well versed in the proclivities of his lord and mistress, padded out of the room and found his mat beside the chaise in the adjoining sitting room. Flopping to his side, he fell into a blissful canine slumber, lulled by the sweet sounds of laughter and love that spilled from the bedroom behind him.

Acknowledgements

My love goes out to my dear friends Karin Tabke and Maya Banks, who sat across a dining table from me in a Catalina Island vacation rental and offered support while I cried tears of frustration. My life is a brighter place because of your friendship.

Thanks to my editor, Alicia Condon, who let me write this story just exactly the way I wanted to. That's a gift, and I'm grateful for it.

Hugs go to Bonnie H. and Gina D., the best chat loop moderators ever! Thank you for all you do for www.TheWicked Writers.com

And to all the wonderful chatters on the Wicked loop. Thank you for all the fierce and fabulous things you bring to the loop every day. xoxo

SYLVIA DAY

BARED TO YOU

Our journey began in fire . . .

Gideon Cross came into my life like lightning in the darkness – beautiful and brilliant, jagged and white hot. I was drawn to him as I'd never been to anything or anyone in my life. I craved his touch like a drug, even knowing it would weaken me. I was flawed and damaged, and he opened those cracks in me so easily . . .

Gideon *knew*. He had demons of his own. And we would become the mirrors that reflected each other's most private wounds . . . and desires.

The bonds of his love transformed me, even as I prayed that the torment of our pasts didn't tear us apart . . .

'This is a sophisticated, provocative, titillating, highly erotic, sexually driven read and extremely well done. I enjoyed *Fifty Shades of Grey*, but I loved *Bared to You*' *Swept Away by Romance*

'*Bared to You* has an emotional feel similar to *Fifty Shades of Grey* . . . It is full of emotional angst, scorching love scenes and a compelling storyline' *Dear Author*

'A well written and sexually charged romance with characters who have real depth . . . I would highly recommend *Bared to You*, because it's what *Fifty Shades of Grey* could have been' *The Book Pushers*

'This is an erotic romance that should not be missed. It will make readers fall in love' *Romance Novel News*

SYLVIA DAY

REFLECTED IN YOU

Gideon Cross. As beautiful and flawless on the outside as he was damaged and tormented on the inside. He was a bright, scorching flame that singed me with the darkest of pleasures. I couldn't stay away. I didn't want to. He was my addiction . . . my every desire . . . mine.

My past was as violent as his, and I was just as broken. We'd never work. It was too hard, too painful . . . except when it was perfect. Those moments when the driving hunger and desperate love were the most exquisite insanity.

We were bound by our need. And our passion would take us beyond our limits to the sweetest, sharpest edge of obsession . . .

Intensely romantic, darkly sensual and completely addictive, *Reflected in You* will take you to the very limits of obsession - and beyond.

'It is full of emotional angst, scorching love scenes, and a compelling story line' *Dear Author*

'Far sexier than *Fifty Shades of Grey* . . . this is an erotic romance that should not be missed' *Romance Novel News*

'I became so attached to Eva and Gideon that I actually hurt for them. I shared their pain and their joy as they fought to keep each other' *Joyfully Reviewed*

Available from Penguin in October 2012

Sylvia Day

THE STRANGER I MARRIED

A tale of love and awakened desire in Victorian England.

They are London's most scandalous couple. Isabel, Lady Pelham, and Gerard
Faulkner, Marquess of Grayson, are well matched in all things – lusty appetites,
constant paramours, provocative reputations, and their absolute refusal to ruin a
marriage of convenience by falling in love. It is a most agreeable sham – until a
shocking event sends Gerard from her side. When, four years later, Gerard returns,
the boyish rogue is now a powerful, irresistible man determined to seduce Isabel.
He is not the man she married – but is he the one to finally steal her heart?

SYLVIA DAY

ASK FOR IT

England, 1770.

As an agent to the Crown, Marcus Ashford has fought numerous sword fights and dodged bullets and cannon fire. Yet nothing arouses him more than his hunger for former fiancée, Elizabeth.

Years ago, she'd abandoned him for the boyishly charming Lord Hawthorne. But now Marcus has been ordered to defend Elizabeth from her husband's killers and he has sworn to do so while tending to her other, more carnal needs. He will be at her service, in every sense.

SYLVIA DAY

PRIDE AND PLEASURE

A tale of ambition, love and lust.

Pursued by fortune hunters, heiress Eliza Martin is the victim of diabolical scheming to get her to the altar. She won't be bullied, however, and she will get to the bottom of this plot. She needs a man to infiltrate her suitors and find the villain.

Thief-taker Jasper Bond is entirely too devilish and too dangerous – who'd believe Eliza would be seduced by a man like him? But client satisfaction is a point of pride with Jasper and it's his pleasure to prove he's just the man – for all her needs.

Sylvia Day

DON'T TEMPT ME

Don't Tempt Me, part of the Georgian series, is a tale of mistaken identity, lusty liaisons and dangerous deceptions in eighteenth-century France.

Lynette Baillon's twin, Lysette, died in an accident. Or so Lynette believed until, at a seductive masked ball in Paris, sexy stranger Simon Quinn mistakes her for her sister Lysette. And Simon, who planned to hand notorious assassin Lysette Rousseau over to the French, finds his plans confounded.

However, on learning that her sister still lives – for now – Lynette vows to be reunited with her twin. Now she must enter an alluring but ensnaring underworld of dark and twisted desires, where Quinn rules.

SYLVIA DAY

A PASSION FOR HIM

A Passion for Him, part of the Georgian series, is a tale of heartbreak, forbidden love and true desire in Georgian England.

Miss Amelia Benbridge and the Earl of Ware are the most anticipated match of the Season. But Amelia's love will always belong to her childhood sweetheart, the gypsy Colin – who died tragically. She knows she'll never feel such passion again.

But when a brooding stranger at a masquerade offers a single, sensual kiss passions rise and she is determined to unmask her phantom admirer. And though deception lies in this stranger's heart, her body cannot hold her back.

SYLVIA DAY

PASSION FOR THE GAME

Passion for the Game, part of the Georgian series, is a tale of deception, lust and deadly desire in Georgian England.

Maria, Lady Winter, is coerced into using her searing beauty and siren body to find out why dangerous pirate Christopher St. John has been let out of jail. But pirate St. John's only chance of avoiding the hangman is to use his renowned seduction skills to melt Lady Winter's icy heart – to discover her secrets.

Entangled in a twisted game of deception and desire, Maria and Christopher are each determined to be the one to win this lusty battle of wits . . .

He just wanted a decent book to read ...

Not too much to ask, is it? It was in 1935 when Allen Lane, Managing Director of Bodley Head Publishers, stood on a platform at Exeter railway station looking for something good to read on his journey back to London. His choice was limited to popular magazines and poor-quality paperbacks – the same choice faced every day by the vast majority of readers, few of whom could afford hardbacks. Lane's disappointment and subsequent anger at the range of books generally available led him to found a company – and change the world.

'We believed in the existence in this country of a vast reading public for intelligent books at a low price, and staked everything on it'
Sir Allen Lane, 1902–1970, founder of Penguin Books

The quality paperback had arrived – and not just in bookshops. Lane was adamant that his Penguins should appear in chain stores and tobacconists, and should cost no more than a packet of cigarettes.

Reading habits (and cigarette prices) have changed since 1935, but Penguin still believes in publishing the best books for everybody to enjoy. We still believe that good design costs no more than bad design, and we still believe that quality books published passionately and responsibly make the world a better place.

So wherever you see the little bird – whether it's on a piece of prize-winning literary fiction or a celebrity autobiography, political tour de force or historical masterpiece, a serial-killer thriller, reference book, world classic or a piece of pure escapism – you can bet that it represents the very best that the genre has to offer.

Whatever you like to read – trust Penguin.